**Schaumburg Township
District Library**

schaumburglibrary.org

Renewals: (847) 923-3158

OUR
DARKEST
NIGHT

OUR DARKEST NIGHT

A novel of

ITALY

and the

SECOND

WORLD WAR

JENNIFER ROBSON

WILLIAM MORROW

WM *An Imprint of* HarperCollins*Publishers*

P.S.™ is a trademark of HarperCollins Publishers.

HarperCollins books may be purchased for educational, business, or sales promotional use. For information, please email the Special Markets Department at SPsales@harpercollins.com.

FIRST EDITION

Designed by Diahann Sturge

Library of Congress Cataloging-in-Publication Data has been applied for.

ISBN 978-0-06-267497-5
ISBN 978-0-06-305940-5 (library edition)
ISBN 978-0-06-306043-2 (international edition)

21 22 23 24 25   LSC   10 9 8 7 6 5 4 3 2

per il mio Claudio
il mio amato

OUR
DARKEST
NIGHT

Chapter 1

28 October 1942

*I*t was long past time to be heading home. With the help of Sandro, the nicest of the porters at the Casa di Riposo, Antonina had managed to get her mother into a chair, the one by the window, the comfortable one they'd brought from home, and she'd passed the time by brushing Mamma's hair and describing what she could see in the piazza below. She knew her mother could hear and understand, for didn't she turn to the sound of Antonina's voice when she arrived for a visit? Didn't she hold tight with her good hand, and squeeze her fingers when her daughter whispered that she loved her? Papà was the best doctor in Venice, besides, and he was sure that Mamma could understand them. All the more important, then, to spend as many hours as she could at her bedside.

But the campanile at San Geremia had just chimed five, and

Papà would be waiting at home, and it wasn't safe to be out alone after dark, not anymore.

"I have to go home and help Marta with supper, and if I'm not there to remind him to eat, you know that Papà will keep on reading until he falls asleep at his desk. Shall I help you back to bed? Or would you like to stay here until they bring your supper?"

Mamma nodded, the movement so fleeting anyone else would have missed it, and when Antonina bent to kiss her cheek, she closed her eyes and lifted her face—still unlined, still so pretty—to the last of the sun.

"I'll be back in the morning. Try to eat up your supper when they bring it, will you?"

Her journey home took her across the still-busy piazza, through the gloom of the Sottoportego de Gheto Novo, and up and down the steps of the bridge. Then a quick turn into a narrow and darkening *calle,* then another, and finally, perched at the edge of the murky waters of the Rio del Gheto, the slender afterthought of their house, its facade a patchwork of crumbling ocher stucco and rosy brick. The number had faded away long ago, but they'd never felt the need to repaint it. Everyone knew to knock on the green door for Dr. Mazin and he would come, no matter the hour.

Up the stairs she ran, her shoes squeaking on the freshly mopped landing, and along the hall to her father's study, but the sound of voices within stopped her short. He might be speaking with a patient, or writing down something important, and since she was old enough to walk, she'd known never to barge in.

She knocked twice and waited for the voices to still. "Papà?"

"Come in," came the reply, and she opened the door to discover her father was not at his desk but at the table by the window, and next to him was one of his oldest friends.

"Father Bernardi! Papà didn't tell me you were visiting—it has been months and months."

He stood, a little creakily, and shook her hand. "I know, my dear, and I am sorry for it. Your father was telling me that you were visiting your mother. How is she?"

"The same as ever, I suppose, but happy. At least I hope she is. And you?"

"I am well enough. Weary of travel, and longing for my own bed, but that's the worst of it."

"I'm glad to hear it. Hasn't Marta brought you anything?" she asked dutifully, though she doubted they had anything worth sharing with guests.

"I only arrived a few minutes ago, and you know how your father and I are when we get talking. But wait a moment—I have something for you."

He reached for the overcoat he'd slung over the back of his chair, pulling it across his lap until he could rummage in its pockets, and after a few moments held up a small packet wrapped in newspaper. An impossibly delicious scent filled the air. "From friends who live abroad," he explained.

"*Coffee*. Oh, Father Bernardi. You are so kind. Let me dig out our *caffettiera*. I won't be long."

She was standing on a chair, searching through the top shelves of the pantry cupboard, when Marta reappeared.

"What are you doing up there?"

"Looking for the coffeemaker. Father Bernardi is visiting. We haven't had coffee since his last visit, and that was months ago."

Marta sighed. Typical of her sighs, it was drawn out, mournful, and vibrating with resentment. "It will get people talking. A Catholic priest, of all people, coming to visit. How your father even *knows* the man . . ."

"He's been a patient of Papà's for years and years, and his friend, too. And Papà always has people coming and going. I doubt anyone will care."

Her protest was a formality, for Father Bernardi's visit would certainly be noted and remarked upon by everyone they knew. Had they lived anywhere else, no one would have cared; but the *gheto* was a close-knit place, the sort of neighborhood where people loved nothing better than burrowing into each other's business, and so her father's agnostic leanings, as well as his avowed determination to be guided by science rather than faith, had long been a focus of local gossip.

Her fingers closed around the worn aluminum of the *caffettiera*, dusty from disuse, and she pulled it from its hiding place. "Where's the grinder?"

"In the next cupboard over."

"Do we have any sugar for the coffee?"

"A little. You know, if your father had bothered to tell me he was expecting someone, I'd have made my *zaeti*. He really only has himself to blame," Marta grumbled.

Delicious as the *zaeti* were, Marta couldn't possibly have made the cookies. There was hardly any flour in the pantry, no raisins, barely enough sugar to sweeten the coffee, and they hadn't seen a fresh egg in months. But pointing it out would only lead to more sighs.

Instead, Antonina washed out the pot and set about grinding the barest handful of beans, so precious and rare they might as well have been gilded. There was just enough in the little drawer of the grinder, once she'd chased out every clinging speck, to make two small cups of coffee, hardly more than a mouthful each. She'd reuse the grounds for herself and Marta, for even watered-down coffee tasted better than the *caffè d'orzo* made of roasted barley that some told themselves was as good as the real thing.

It was enough, for now, to smell the coffee as it brewed, as she divided it between the prettily decorated porcelain cups her parents had bought in Florence on their honeymoon, as she set them and the sugar bowl on a tray and hurried back to her father's study. The smell was the best thing about coffee, after all. And it was only so tantalizing because she was hungry. Once she'd had her supper she wouldn't notice it as much.

The men were so intent on their conversation they didn't look up when she entered, and it would never do to interrupt. So she went about sugaring the coffee, setting the cups at their elbows, and taking her seat at a twin of her mother's chair at the *casa*.

Her father spared her a smile, and he drank down his coffee appreciatively, but his attention remained fixed on his friend.

"This city, these few islands, are the nearest thing we Jews have to a promised land in Europe. We have lived here unmolested for centuries, yet you suggest that we abandon it. And for what?" her father asked, his voice rising. "The dubious welcome the Spanish might offer us? A panicked trek through the mountains before the Swiss turn us back?"

"If you had listened to me when they first barred you from your work, from your profession—"

"I belong nowhere else. I am as Italian as you. I was born here. I have no other home. What would become of me—of my family? Of my patients? And the fascists have made no move against us beyond the racial laws."

"You speak of those laws as if they are something one might expect within the bounds of normal civil society, but they stripped you and every Jew I know of his profession. No—don't frown at me like that. Look at what they did to dear Dr. Jona. The man is well into his seventies, had retired years ago, yet still they removed his name from the register of physicians. His professorship at the university—gone, too. All he has left is his presidency of your Jewish community here, and that's hardly more than a formality."

"The laws are noxious. On that, my dear Giulio, we agree. But I have found a way to exist, just as we have always done." Her father leaned forward, his hands clasped so tightly his fingertips had gone white, and his voice faded to a whisper. "I've heard that defeat at El Alamein is all but certain. Surely the tide must be turning."

"That may well be, but it's turning far too slowly for my liking. And in the meantime, Il Duce grows more desperate, the Germans grow ever bolder, and we wait for the ax to fall. And it *will* fall, for it's only a matter of time before they seize power here. Just as they did with Austria. With the rest of Europe, for that matter. And what then?" Father Bernardi asked, his affable voice sharpening into solemnity. "Only think: What if they were in power here? What would prevent them from rounding you up, just as they're doing with the Jews of Germany, of Poland, of France—"

"And if I were to leave with Antonina, make the journey to Switzerland, what would become of my Devora? She cannot travel. You know that. And you know I will not leave her. Not as long as there is breath in my body. Bad enough that she must live in the rest home."

Her father wrenched off his spectacles and set about polishing them with a crumpled handkerchief, and from the way he pressed his lips together and pinched at the bridge of his nose, Antonina could tell he was fighting off tears. Just as he always did when he spoke of her mother, the stroke that had left her so weakened, and the agonizing decision to move her to the rest home earlier that year.

It was a good thing, she decided, that she hadn't allowed herself any of the coffee, for even the idea of abandoning her mother was enough to tighten her throat and turn her empty stomach upside down.

Her father was quick to notice her distress. "Don't look so alarmed. We are safe enough here. Aren't we?" he asked Father Bernardi, and it seemed to Antonina that his eyes, as he looked to his friend, held a warning of some kind. But was it to be truthful? Or to be kind?

The priest nodded, but his gentle smile didn't convince her. "For the moment, yes," the priest said. "But do not forget what we—"

"I won't," her father interrupted. "I promise I won't forget."

"Well, then. I ought to be on my way. I had only meant to stop by for a minute or two." Father Bernardi stood, took a moment to find his balance, and then shook hands with her father. "Thank you for your hospitality." Turning to Antonina, he grasped her outstretched hand in both of his. "I shall pray for your mother, my dear."

"Thank you, Father Bernardi. I wish you safe travels."

While her father said goodbye to his friend, she busied herself with collecting the coffee cups and tray and returning them to the kitchen. Rather than leave the cups to Marta, who had broken all but three of the set over the years, she painstakingly washed and dried and put them away. Only after the other woman, still grumbling about the annoyance and inconvenience of the priest's visit, had begun to prepare their supper did Antonina return to the study.

Her father was sitting in the chair he had occupied earlier, and he now beckoned her forward. "Come and sit with me. Were you happy to see Father Bernardi again?"

"Of course."

"I was happy to see him, but . . . well. Things are difficult, as you know. He risks a great deal in coming here."

"You were upset earlier. When I came in with the coffee."

"I was, but not with him. You know we've always relished a lively discussion. But I do regret . . ."

"What is it?" she pressed, and it was impossible to keep the fear from her voice.

He reached out to grasp her hand. As if he needed the reassurance of her presence. "I meant what I said, earlier, about belonging nowhere else. And I can bear it, you know—these slights and these difficulties. So long as I may call myself a Venetian. An Italian. But I do regret that your life has become so confined. I had hoped, once, that you might go to university."

"You—" she began, but the words caught in her throat, choking her. She swallowed hard, waited a moment, and tried again. "You never said. I never knew that you had wanted such a thing for me."

She'd been working her way through his textbooks for years, careful never to let him know, and not because she thought he'd disapprove. He'd always been so proud of her, and once he'd loved nothing more than to discuss her lessons and help with her schoolwork. But the racial laws of 1938 had expelled her and every other Jewish student in Italy from school, and when her father had told her of it, he had broken down and wept, and it was the first time Antonina had ever seen him cry. So she had decided that it would be far kinder to simply borrow his books and memorize as much as she could, and then, one day, when she was allowed to go to school again, she would be ready.

"Of course I did. I still do. A bright girl like you belongs in university, not spending your days in the rest home, or queuing up for bread or oil, or—"

"The war won't last forever. I might still go to school once it ends."

"You might," he admitted. "Or perhaps . . . perhaps I might teach you some of what I know. As if you were one of my students in Padua. I don't miss those long hours on the train on my teaching days, but I do miss my students. And I think you would make a very good doctor. Do you think . . . ?"

"I would love nothing more," she promised, blinking hard. It was silly to cry over something that was good.

"We'll be constrained by our circumstances. It will be far from a comprehensive education, but I can give you an idea, if nothing more, of what medicine is like. If it's something that suits you."

"When can we start?"

"You've been reading through my library for years, so I suspect you're well on your way."

"You knew?" she asked, though she ought not to have been surprised. She ought to have known he would notice.

"Of course I did. And perhaps I ought to have said something. Encouraged you in your studies. Still . . . books can only teach you so much. You'll learn more by coming with me on some of my visits. I'll ask permission, of course, but I think most of my patients will be content to have you present. And it will be helpful to have an extra pair of hands."

"So I will watch you as you work?"

"Yes. You will watch, and in time you will learn how to see. You will listen, and then you will learn how to hear. And that, my darling girl, is how a doctor is made."

Chapter 2

11 January 1943

*S*he'd gone to bed early, but even so it felt like she'd just fallen asleep when the knock at her door woke her.

"Antonina? Signora Mele needs us."

"Yes, Papà."

One of the first things she'd learned, once her father had begun taking her on his visits to patients, was to get out of bed straightaway. No lingering beneath the warm covers—that made it a hundred times harder to rise, especially in the winter. She was dressed and at the door before five minutes had passed.

Her father held out his stethoscope and thermometer; these she buried in the deepest pockets of her coat. The rest of his supplies went in the bottom of her knitting bag. "Who came for you?"

"Her neighbor's son. Poor child was frozen through."

Before 1938, they'd had a telephone. It had sat on a table on the landing, with a pencil and pad of paper next to it. When she'd turned ten, her father had declared her old enough to use the telephone, and after she'd practiced taking down messages and answering properly and promptly, it had become her special job to answer. But the telephone had been taken out years ago, after her father had been barred from practicing medicine, and now the table held only an empty vase.

It was raining, but only enough to dampen the air and make the paving stones slippery beneath her feet. The moon was bright above the clouds, and there was no shortage of light peeking through the shuttered windows of the houses they passed, for no one bothered to obey the blackout. Of all the horrors that war had brought to Venice, bombs from the sky were the least of them.

They kept to the narrower *calli*, pausing at every turn to ensure the path was clear, and if they did come across a patrolling policeman, she knew—at least she hoped she remembered—what to do. They had been visiting family, her father would say, and she would nod, and Papà would explain they had been waiting for the rain to subside, for it always seemed to be raining that winter. And they would hold their breath and pray the man who had stopped them was in a mood to be generous.

They never spoke of what might happen if the authorities found out her father was still practicing medicine.

Signora Mele's home was in the Gheto Vecchio, at the end of a dead-end passage off the Calle del Forno. Five stories high, it was one of the oldest buildings in the *gheto*, and over the centuries it had settled awkwardly on its sandy foundations. Even the famed tower in Pisa did not have such uneven floors.

The neighbor's boy had left the door on the latch, and an oil lamp, its flame turned low, waited on a high windowsill. Her father collected it in one hand, gathered his cloak in the other, and together they began the slow trudge to the top floor. They paused at each half landing, waiting for the pain in her father's arthritic feet to subside. It was the price he had to pay, he often said, for living in the most beautiful city in the world.

"I fear I am even slower than usual. A tortoise would surely take less time."

"I don't mind. And it's better than arriving even more short of breath than Signora Mele. I cannot imagine how she manages all these steps."

"I suspect she doesn't. I know she relies on Signora Spagnolo downstairs to do her shopping."

"And the housework?" Antonina asked.

"We shall see. But if her home is less than pristine we mustn't take any notice," he cautioned. "It would only shame her, and in turn make her less likely to ask for me when she's poorly."

They knocked at her door, paused to listen for footsteps, and when none came her father entered the apartment. "Signora Mele? It is Dr. Mazin. May we come in?"

A muffled response came from the far end of the apartment— the bedroom, Antonina remembered from their last visit. Following their ears, they found Signora Mele sitting in an upright chair next to her bed, a shawl around her shoulders. Her feet, just peeping out from the hem of her nightgown, were bare. She was clutching at the wooden arms of the chair, her fingers tinged with blue, and Antonina could easily hear the shallow rasp of her breathing from across the room.

"My dear Signora Mele," her father began, his tone a practiced mixture of warmth and concern. "It was very brave of you to get out of bed to greet us, but I would be happier to see you settled and comfortable. Will you allow Antonina to assist you? I shall wash my hands in the meantime."

Once his patient was sitting up in bed, the pillows arranged carefully at her back, Dr. Mazin examined her with meticulous care. When he was finished, he tucked the covers around her. "We don't want you to catch cold. There. Now I am going to give you a tincture—it will help with your breathing tonight. Antonina, will you bring over the bottle I set out?"

Signora Mele swallowed the medicine without protest, but even that small effort seemed to exhaust her. "What is wrong? Why am I so tired?"

"Your heart is tired," he explained, "and having to work harder than usual to keep you going, and that is why you feel light-headed at times." He looked in her eyes as he spoke, and when she began to clutch at the bedclothes, pulling and twisting, he calmed her hands with his.

He gave her a moment to take it all in, and when she began to cry he offered a clean handkerchief from his pocket. "I know you hate the idea of it, but I do think you must consider a move to the Casa di Riposo. There you will have help. You won't have to waste your energy on housework and the like. And the food is excellent."

"But I have lived here for almost fifty years," Signora Mele protested. "Ever since Daniele and I were married." Tears were streaming down her cheeks, but she didn't attempt to wipe them away. "All my memories are here."

"Where are your daughters?" Antonina's father asked.

"Giulia is in Austria with her husband. They moved long before the war. I haven't heard from her in months and months. And my Mara is in Bologna, but she is busy with the children, and her husband has been out of work for so long . . ."

"Of course. I understand. Well, let me see what I can do. Try to eat as much as your appetite allows, but not too much soup. Not too much water either."

"Thank you, doctor. I have a few lire—"

"No, no. None of that. Is there anything else we may bring you before we go? No? In that case we will let ourselves out, and Antonina will come in the morning to give you another dose of the tincture."

The walk home took an eternity. Her father was exhausted, and leaned ever more heavily on her arm as they moved from shadow to shadow, and by the time they were safely inside their own house, Antonina wanted nothing more than to retreat to her bedroom and bury herself under her eiderdown and blankets.

But her father always found it difficult to sleep after such calls, and without her mother at home Antonina was the only person who might offer him comfort. So she helped him out of his coat and crouched to unlace his boots, and once he was settled in his favorite chair in the study, she went to the kitchen to fix a hot water bottle for his arthritis and a dose of grappa for the rest of him.

He sighed happily when she set the earthenware bottle under

his feet and the glass of spirits in his hands. "Thank you. For this, and for your help tonight." He sipped at the grappa, his gaze intent upon her. "What do you think? What diagnosis would you offer?"

"Congestive heart failure?"

"Yes. Hence my insistence that she move to the rest home."

"Only if her daughter won't take her in."

"The one in Bologna? I doubt it. My guess is that she will plead distance, or poverty, or some such combination, and Signora Mele will have to move. If she were truly interested in helping she'd have fetched her mother away years ago."

"I'll visit her there when I go to see Mamma," Antonina offered. "That will help."

"It certainly will, and she'll be far safer there than alone in her apartment. All the same, I doubt she'll be alive in six months. Not with her heart failing as it is."

The way he said it, so baldly, and with such certainty, tore at Antonina's heart. "Can't it be treated with a diuretic?"

"Not when the heart is failing so rapidly. And it would only serve to make her miserable."

"What was in the tincture?"

"A mild dose of digitalis. As I said, you'll need to return tomorrow morning and again at supper to give her more. That will help a little."

"But not enough to keep her at home?"

"No. And that small bottle is all I have. I doubt I'll be able to procure more."

"So we do nothing?" she asked, her voice rising. It was unsettling to see her father so resigned to a patient's fate.

"No. Never nothing. We visit her, show her compassion, offer her help. That is very much more than nothing. And we will see her safely moved to the rest home."

"I wish there was more we could do," she fretted.

"Is that not the refrain of every decent doctor, every day of his—or her—working life?"

"I suppose. It's only that . . ."

He waited for her to finish, though she was certain he already knew what she was going to say.

"You shouldn't have to practice medicine like this. As if you're some sort of criminal. Creeping through the dark. Having nothing to offer your patients beyond your attention and your sympathy."

"I agree, but to do more is to risk arrest. And I can do nothing if I am confined to a prison camp."

He was right, of course he was right, but the knowledge rankled. To stay, to wait, to let themselves drown as the waters rose around them?

"Why can't we leave? Find our way to Spain? Or across the border to Switzerland?"

"I think of little else," he said, regret shadowing his eyes. "But I cannot imagine how we might take your mother safely. The Swiss would certainly never let us through at one of the official crossings. Not with her so clearly unwell."

"Then Spain—"

"No. They would be equally unwelcoming, and the journey across the sea is far too dangerous."

"Then we sneak across the border. We'll hire someone to help us—to help carry her. Mamma weighs hardly anything now."

"No. It's too great a risk. I know you've heard the stories. People pay for safe passage and then are delivered into the hands of the fascists."

"You have friends everywhere," she pleaded. "You can ask them to help us."

"Only to put their lives at risk. And that is something I cannot ask of anyone."

Her father had been staring at something over her shoulder, his gaze unfocused, and she didn't have to turn to know what was drawing his attention. It was a photograph of the three of them, taken on her eighteenth birthday, not long before Mamma had fallen ill. It had been the spring of 1938, before the racial laws had stripped away nearly everything that mattered. Only a few scant years, but it might as well have been a century.

"Papà?"

"Yes?" he answered, his eyes upon her again, and for a heartbeat she saw it—the absence of hope. It was there, and then he blinked it away, and even tried to smile, but she had seen it and he knew.

She ought not to have questioned him like that, needling away, ignoring how tired he was, for of course he had considered everything. Of course he had lain awake, night after night, slowly smothering under the crushing weight of their plight.

"I'm sorry. You're right—of course you are. We'll be safe here. We only need to keep on as we've done. I was wrong to panic just now." Useless, weak, impotent words, but what else did she have to give?

She crouched next to his chair and set her head upon his knees. And she waited, her breath catching in her throat, for the moment when he would smooth her hair from her brow, his hand so cool and comforting, and tell her that all would be well.

She waited, and after a while he did brush his fingers across her temple, and he bent his head close to hers, and she thought he might say something. She waited, but he had no words of comfort, and so she got to her feet, moved the now-cool hot-water bottle out of the way, and helped him stand on his poor, aching feet.

"Good night, Papà."

"Good night, my darling girl. I—"

"What is it?"

"Nothing. Only that I hope you sleep well."

Chapter 3

21 September 1943

"Are you all done?" Antonina asked, waiting—hoping—for a spark of acknowledgment in her mother's eyes.

It was nearly seven o'clock, and she'd spent the last hour helping her mother eat her supper, one scant spoonful after another, just as she did every day. Every morning and midday, too, for the attendants at the *casa* were hard-pressed to spare the time for the task, and she never found it a chore to spend time with her mother.

Yet for all the hours Antonina spent at her mother's side, the moments of connection they shared were growing ever more elusive, and there had been one awful day, not so long ago, when her mother had not recognized her at all.

Today, however, had been a good day, or something close to good, and her mother had allowed Antonina to feed her nearly the entire bowl of soup. "Let me wipe your face and hands with this cloth—isn't the water nice and warm? There. That must feel good. And what if I were to read to you for a while? We can pick up at—"

"Hello, Devora. Hello, my Nina."

"Papà! Look, Mamma—it's Papà. We weren't expecting you."

"I know, I know," he said, crossing the room so he might press a kiss to his wife's temple. Then he turned his head a fraction, just so he might look Antonina in the eye. "Will you come into the hall with me?" he asked, and the tone of his voice, so careful, so measured, alarmed her more than if he had screamed in her face. "We'll let your mother rest for a moment."

There was nothing for it but to follow, her hands clammy with apprehension, and wait for him to share the terrible news with her. And she knew it was terrible, for it was hardly likely to be good news. Not with the newborn Republic of Salò so desperate to please its allies in Germany.

"I am sorry for the haste. For frightening you. It's only that something has happened, and I . . . I hardly know how to begin."

"Say it," she implored. "Imagine I'm one of your patients and you're giving me bad news. You have to say it, no matter what, otherwise how can the cure begin? Go on, Papà."

He nodded, hesitated for a further heart-tearing moment, and then, finally, whispered in her ear. "Arrests are imminent. Any day now. Any *hour*."

Since the moment German troops had first occupied Italy, only weeks before, she had known this moment would come.

She'd been as sure of it as her next breath. And yet she still could not bring herself to believe. "How can you be certain? People have been worrying for weeks—why now? Why today?"

"They came to Dr. Jona. The Gestapo. Because of his presidency of the Jewish community. And they demanded he provide them with the names and addresses of every Jew in Venice."

"Has he given them the lists?" Dr. Jona was her father's friend. He was a good man. It was inconceivable that he should do such a thing.

"No. No, he told them it would take a day or two. For him to gather the information they needed. At least I believe that's what he said."

"Then we have—"

"Let me finish. He sent them away, and then he destroyed the records, all of them. And when he was done he killed himself."

The horror of it swept over Antonina, engulfed her for a moment, and rushed away like the ebbing tide. She was left shaken, and grieving, and utterly certain of what they must do next.

"We have to go now. It won't take long to pack, and if we leave things behind it doesn't matter. They're just things, you see, and not nearly as impor—"

"*Antonina.*" Her father took hold of her shoulders and pressed his forehead to hers. "Listen to me. I cannot leave. Too many people depend on me here. And I will not leave without your mother."

"But we could—"

"No," he insisted. "She is not well enough to travel. You

know that as well as I do." Now he enfolded her in his arms. "But you . . . you can leave."

"I could *never,*" she protested. "How could you even ask me?"

"I have made all the arrangements. I had hoped this day would never come, but now it is here—*no.* No, my Nina. Stop shaking your head and simply listen to me," he begged her.

He was crying, she realized suddenly, and that was far more frightening than anything he had yet told her.

"What do you want me to do?" she asked, defeated.

He looked over his shoulder, back down the corridor, but it was empty. "Father Bernardi has sent a man he trusts, a good man, and with his help you will go into hiding until this is over."

"You would send me away with a *stranger*?"

"No. Not a stranger. A friend of a friend. To the village where Father Bernardi lives."

She wanted to scream, to shout, to beg him to consider something else, anything else, but then he pulled away, just enough that she could see his ashen face and the fear carved upon his beloved features, and her protests withered to nothing.

"I understand," she said, and it was true. At last she understood. "Is there time to say goodbye to Mamma?"

"Of course. Don't say anything, though. Just your usual farewell. But first . . ."

He took out his handkerchief and wiped away her tears, and then she returned to her mother's bedside for the last time.

"I have to go, Mamma, but Papà will return later."

Antonina bent low to embrace her mother, and for an instant the desire to gather her up, as if she were the comforting parent and her mother the child, overwhelmed her. She would steal Mamma away, bear her weight for any distance, carry her over any mountain they were forced to climb. For her mother she would do it, and they would drag Papà along, too, and they would be together once more, and happy at last—

"We must be going," her father said, and sanity of a sort descended again.

"I love you, Mamma," she whispered, kissing her mother's face, her hands, her soft and shining hair. "I love you so much."

Then she stepped away. One step, another, another, and with her father's help she turned and walked along the quiet corridor, down the echoing stairs, and into the fading warmth of the setting sun.

She walked home calmly, arm in arm with her father, as if it were an ordinary evening and not the end of the life she'd always known. And since silence was painful and honesty even worse, she filled the journey with forced chatter that likely felt as awkward to his ears as it did to hers.

"When you arrived I was about to read to Mamma. I left the book on the table next to her bed—*I Promessi Sposi*. We're about halfway through. There's a page marker, one of those little ribbons that are glued to the spine, so you won't have any trouble finding where we left off. I think it was at the bottom of the left-hand page. You will read to her when you visit, won't you?"

"Of course, Antonina. Of course I'll read to her. Every day."

"And you mustn't rush her when she's eating. Sometimes she won't open her mouth, but it isn't always because she's done, or because she isn't hungry. I think she simply needs a few minutes, just the way anyone else would if they were having a meal and wanted a sip of wine or a moment to let the food sit. So don't give up right away, otherwise she'll never eat anything, and you know she can't afford to lose any more weight."

"I promise I will take my time," her father said. "I promise."

On and on she went, her father dutifully nodding and acknowledging her requests, and it dawned upon her that in no time at all she would have to say goodbye to him, too, and her mouth went dry with the knowledge and weight of it.

All too soon they were standing at the green door, so shabby and so dear, and her father's steps were even slower than usual as they climbed the stairs. He was clutching at the banister, his knuckles white against his skin, as if it were his only lifeline in stormy seas.

The house was cold and silent. "Marta?" she asked fearfully.

"I sent her home. Her husband is a Gentile. She doesn't have to worry. At least, not yet."

"But I wanted to say goodbye."

"It isn't wise to tell anyone where you're going, or indeed that you're going at all. So niceties like farewells will have to wait for another day." Her father glanced at his wristwatch and frowned. "Signor Gerardi should be here soon. Go and pack, but take as little as you can. You should use my rucksack, the one I used to take on our holidays in the mountains. I'll see if I can unearth it."

She was tempted, once alone in her room, to climb into bed, burrow under the covers, and shut out the world beyond. She would close her eyes, hold her breath, and pretend she was still a child, still ignorant of the world and its ugliness, still greeting each new day with a heart that brimmed with hope and gladness.

Instead she went to her wardrobe and began the straight-forward work of selecting the garments she would pack. She'd imagined this moment before; had even memorized a list of things she would take if they were forced to flee. How many sleepless hours had she whiled away in such a fashion? Yet not once, in all of those anxious moments, hemmed in by the dark and quiet of deepest night, had she ever truly believed this moment would come.

She had three dresses, the same number again of skirts and blouses, and two cardigans. To the growing pile on her bed she added the least shabby of her underclothes, her warm flannel nightgown, her walking boots, and her winter coat. None of the garments were anything close to new; all had been mended time and again. It was the one domestic skill she possessed, and even Marta had to admit that no one could darn a sock or turn a collar as well as Antonina.

She stepped back, assessing the collection of garments. Would they fit in her father's pack? Would there be room for anything else?

"A list," she muttered to herself. "I should make a list."

"No need for that," came an unfamiliar voice from the cor-ridor. A man stepped out of the shadows, but hesitated at the threshold to her room. "I'm sorry. I didn't mean to startle you."

"Are you Signor Gerardi?" He took another step toward her, and now she could really see him, and he was young, far younger than she'd imagined.

"Call me Niccolò, please. Or Nico, as my family do."

"My father said I should only pack what I can carry."

He held out her father's rucksack. "He asked me to bring this to you. But don't worry too much about everything fitting. I can help you. I can carry another bag if you need."

It was kind of him, and unexpected, and she had to swallow back the dam of emotion that threatened to clog her throat. "Thank you."

"I'll return to your father now. Will you join us when you're done? Then we can talk some more."

"Yes. I won't be long."

She turned, waiting until his footsteps had faded, and then forced herself to survey her room. Photographs first. She removed them from their frames, a half-dozen family portraits that chronicled her life, along with her parents' wedding photograph, and tucked them into the worn copy of *Anatomia del Gray* that she'd been slowly memorizing. To it she added her precious *Medicina Interna di Goldman-Cecil* and a dictionary of infectious diseases that had lost its cover years ago.

Her jewelry, what little there was, she emptied out of its papier-mâché box and into a handkerchief, its corners tightly knotted to hold her treasures. And then she took the empty pack that Signor Gerardi—Niccolò—had brought to her, pushed the books into the bottom, and methodically filled it with the clothing she'd already set aside.

She hefted the pack, testing it, and nearly buckled under the weight of all her books. And still she couldn't resist adding one more indulgence: the mohair-and-velvet rabbit, missing one of its pink glass eyes, that had been her companion since before her memories began. It was childish to bring it, and

Niccolò would think her silly if he noticed, but she could not, in that moment, bring herself to leave Pietro behind.

She was tempted to hide in her room, but she had so little time left with her father. Better to share those precious moments with him, even with a stranger as witness, than to forgo them altogether. She left the pack on her bed, switched off the light, and went in search of her father and the man who had come to take her away. Predictably enough, they were in her father's study, standing side by side in front of the desk. She paused at the door, glad of the chance to study Niccolò Gerardi, for neither man had noticed her approach.

He was fair, with a day-old beard the color of dark honey and a tracing of freckles across his nose and cheekbones. He stood at least a head taller than her father, with shoulders that strained at the faded seams of a much-mended coat, but his voice, from the little he'd said to her, was that of an educated man, and there was a reassuring gentleness to his manner.

As she waited, half-hidden in the darkened hall, her father opened his hand, his gaze fixed on a small object in his palm. From the way it glinted in the lamplight, she thought it might be a coin. Then he shook his head, blinking hard, and swiped at his eyes.

She must have moved, or made some slight sound. Her father turned, his reddened eyes the only sign of his earlier distress, and beckoned her forward.

"There you are. Are you packed?"

"What is that in your hand?"

He held it out to her: a circle of gold, now gleaming dully

in his palm. "Your mother's wedding ring. It's too big for her now, but see?" He took her right hand and pushed it onto her ring finger. "As I thought. It fits you well."

The ring was warm against her skin. He took her hand in both of his, lifted it to kiss her palm, and then, his head bowed low, pressed her hand against his cheek.

"I don't understand. Why are you giving me Mamma's ring?"

"You will need it." He did not let go of her hand. "You and Signor Gerardi will be traveling as man and wife."

She turned to the stranger who hovered an arm's length away, not bothering to hide her surprise and discomfort. He flushed, a flare of color beneath his boyish freckles.

"It is a fiction to keep you safe," he promised. "No more than that."

"This is all so sudden. An hour ago I was sitting with Mamma, and now . . ." Now she was the one who had to blink back her tears.

"I know. I know, and I am sorry. But you will be safe with Signor Gerardi and his family. I would not send you with him if I thought otherwise."

"If it helps, Antonina, we aren't leaving until the morning," Niccolò said. "You don't have to say goodbye just yet." She nodded, and managed to twist her mouth into a smile, but then she had to blink hard to keep back her tears. If she remained in the study any longer, she would break down, and that would only make things harder for her father.

"I think I'll go to bed now," she said, and was surprised by the steadiness of her voice. "Good night, Papà." She came forward to kiss her father's cheek, and only just managed not to throw her arms around him and beg that he reconsider. That he keep her close, no matter what lay ahead.

Instead she stepped back and, after nodding politely to Niccolò, retreated to the bathroom, where she washed her face and brushed her teeth and spent far too long examining her wan face in the mirror. As she tiptoed along the corridor to her room she could hear the sound of her father talking; and though his words were too faint to make out, the underlying timbre of his voice didn't seem at all distressed.

That slight comfort carried her through the minutes it took to close the shutters, to undress and change into her nightgown, which she had to retrieve from the bottom of the rucksack, and to crawl into bed.

Antonina lay motionless under the covers, under the hand-stitched coverlet that had been her mother's when she was a girl, and listened to the soft sounds of her father showing Niccolò to the spare room. The house grew quiet, and the last of the evening light faded away behind her shuttered window, and still her mind would not rest. Hours passed, her silent tears dampening her pillow, and still she could not sleep.

She ought to have convinced her father that they needed to leave. She ought to have persisted. She ought to have been more imaginative.

Why had she never suggested they go into hiding, all three of them, somewhere else in Italy? They might have found sanctuary with Father Bernardi, or another of her father's many friends, and done so years earlier.

She ought to have known. She ought to have convinced her father to try.

At the first glimmering of dawn she put on her robe and crept down the hall to the kitchen. They hadn't any coffee, nor even any *caffè d'orzo,* but after some rummaging she unearthed a tiny packet of dried chamomile blossoms. A simple tisane, then; it would warm her through, if nothing else.

She sat at the kitchen table, warming her hands around her cup, and watched the blossoms unfold, petal by wizened petal, in the steaming water. Footsteps, soft and measured, sounded in the corridor.

"Papà?"

But it was Niccolò who came to stand at the threshold. "I believe he's still sleeping. Do you mind if I sit with you?"

"Not at all," she said, though she'd have preferred to remain alone awhile longer. "Would you like some of this? It's a chamomile tisane. We don't have any coffee."

He smiled a little shyly. "Yes, please. My mother used to make it for us when we were poorly."

They sat together in silence, waiting for the tisane to cool. "I couldn't sleep," she admitted after a few minutes.

"I'm sure I would feel the same way in your shoes."

"What about you? It's not even six o'clock."

Another tentative smile. "I keep farmer's hours. I can't remember the last time I slept past dawn." He lifted his cup, but set it down without drinking. "We should probably leave soon. And you should eat something if you can. We've a long day ahead."

"I suppose I should make something for my father. He

isn't . . . he's a very good doctor but he has no notion of how to take care of himself. What will he do without me here? And he's sent Marta away, too."

"He and I spoke about that last night. He told me they've found a room for him at the *casa*. That way he'll be close to your mother, and can even care for the other residents if they fall ill."

She nodded, a little embarrassed not to have thought of it before. "That makes sense. I had better go and wake him."

"You do that," he agreed, "and in the meantime I'll make us some breakfast. Do you have any bread?"

"A little, yes. It's in the box on the shelf. And there's a jar of apricot jam in the cupboard."

Antonina hesitated outside her father's door, listening, before tapping on it lightly. "Papà? Are you awake?"

"Come in."

He was awake, and dressed, and had just slipped his feet into his shoes. Rather than stand and watch as he struggled to lace them, she went to kneel at his feet and helped him, one last time, with the troublesome task.

"Thank you," he said, ever courteous, but he made no move to rise, nor did she stand. Instead they simply looked in each other's eyes, memorizing beloved features, letting the silence speak for them.

"Will you promise me something?" he asked at last.

"Anything, Papà."

"You must try your best to fit in. I know it will be unfamiliar, but you must try. Eat the food they give you. Do the work that is expected of you. Never complain."

"Do you think it will be awful there?"

"Not at all. Life in such places is simple, of course, and without most of the modern conveniences we take for granted here. But you'll be safe, and that's what truly matters to me and your mother."

"I'll be so lonely."

"That I doubt. Signor Gerardi is an intelligent and educated man, and he feels certain his family will like and accept you. Don't forget that Father Bernardi will be nearby, too."

"But I won't be with you and Mamma," she protested, still unable to accept his assurances.

"Only if you chart the distance on a map." He took her hands in his, kissed them, and pressed both to his heart. "Since the day you were born, my Nina, you have been *here*. And here you shall remain."

"Oh, Papà," she whispered, blinking back fresh tears. "Please don't—"

"Signor Gerardi will be wondering what has become of us," he interrupted, ever so gently. "Will you help me up?"

She nodded, swallowing back the plea that still trembled on her lips, and helped him rise. Then she followed him back along the corridor to the kitchen, her steps marked by the echoing lament of her heart. *Too late, too late, too late.*

Niccolò had cut the bread into slices and spread them with the jam. "Good morning, Dr. Mazin." He waited until her father was seated and had helped himself to a slice of bread and jam before taking the smallest slice for himself.

She found it an effort to eat even a single bite of the food, for the bread was dry and the jam was watery, and her throat closed in with her every reluctant swallow. Yet she managed to finish the entire slice of bread, and drink the rest of her cooled tisane, while her father and Niccolò talked of inanities such as the weather and the coming harvest.

She collected her empty plate and cup and set them in the sink, and then she turned to face Niccolò. "Must we . . . ?"

He nodded. "Yes. I don't wish to hurry you, but—"

"But you must be on your way," her father finished. "Why don't you fetch your things, Antonina, while Signor Gerardi and I tidy up in here?"

Moving as dully as an automaton, Antonina went to her bedroom and collected the rucksack. The room was dim, for she hadn't seen the point in opening the shutters; yet still she knew where everything belonged. Her little room was a treasure trove of memories, its contents so familiar and precious, and now she was leaving them all behind.

Too late. Too late.

Her father and Niccolò were waiting for her on the landing.

"Are you sure there isn't time for me to see Mamma again?"

"No, my dear," her father said, shaking his head regretfully. "It's best that you go now."

"But she will worry so. She will wonder where I've gone."

"I know, but I will be there to comfort her. And no matter what happens, I will remain at her side. You must remember that."

"Yes, Papà."

"Then let me hold you tight for a moment, and when I see your lovely face again this madness will be over." He embraced her, his arms crushing her tight against his chest, but then, far too soon, he pulled away. "Now go, while the sun is shining and you have the entire day before you."

He set a final kiss on her brow, and then Niccolò's hand was heavy upon her shoulder, turning her gently, and her body obeyed even as her head was insisting that she plant her feet and remain rooted in place.

"Go, now, my darling child, my dearest Nina. Do this for me," her father begged, and as she had always been a dutiful girl, the most devoted of daughters, she knew she had to obey.

So she followed Niccolò down the stairs, out the door, and away from her home, her family, and the only life she had ever known or thought to lead. Away, away, and into the unknown.

Chapter 4

*W*hen they were only a few steps into their journey, Niccolò took her pack and slung it over his shoulder. Then he hurried them along, his hand at the small of her back, guiding her as they crossed the small bridge at the end of the *calle* and turned onto the Fondamenta dei Ormesini.

"Antonina?" he asked after five minutes or so.

"Yes?"

"I think it would be safer to change your name, or rather to alter it."

So she was to lose every part of herself—her home, her family, and now, it seemed, her name. "What do you suggest? Maria? That's a good Gentile name." She was being rude, but she couldn't bring herself to care, not in that moment.

"Your father suggested Nina."

The name Papà alone liked to call her. "I suppose that will do." She could remember to be Nina. "What will my surname be? My maiden name, that is." Simply talking about such a thing made her face grow hot.

"How about Marzoli? Not so different from your real name, hmm? We will tell people that you grew up in an orphanage in Padua. St. Anthony's is the biggest."

"St. Anthony's," she repeated.

"You only came to Venice a year or so ago. To train as a nurse—that makes sense, doesn't it? Since you've been learning medicine from your father."

"I suppose I could pass as a nursing student. All right. I was Nina Marzoli, an orphan from Padua, and I'd come to do my nurse's training in Venice."

"Yes. That should be easy to remember."

"Where are we going now?"

"To Fondamente Nove."

"It takes half as long to walk north to Sant'Alvise and take the *vaporetto* from there to the ferries."

"I know, but I've only enough money for the direct fare to Murano. Do you mind?"

"Not really," she admitted, for she was in no hurry to leave the city she loved. "Why Murano?"

"My cousin is meeting us there. He'll take us to the mainland, to Campalto, where he and his wife have a farm. From there, it's a two-day walk. About sixty kilometers."

"To *where*?" she asked tartly. "Or is that meant to be a secret, too?"

"Not at all. We're going to my father's farm. It's on the outskirts of a village called Mezzo Ciel." He was smiling now. "Hardly more than a dot on the map."

"I haven't heard of it."

"I'd be surprised if you had."

"Can't we take the train? It seems very far."

"We could, but it's best to do what's expected. People in Mezzo Ciel would never dream of wasting money on a train ticket if they could walk. Even having the mule and cart with us is a luxury."

"A mule?"

"Yes. An old fellow, and he doesn't like to be rushed. But he'll make the journey easier."

After that she had no more questions. Instead she concentrated on walking, breathing, and swallowing back her tears before they blinded her. She longed to break free and run home, but her father would only insist that she leave again. What else could she do but follow obediently and ignore the protesting drumbeat of her heart?

They turned onto the broad expanse of the Fondamente Nove, where long queues stretched for the ferries to the islands, and approached the ticket booth. The line there was shorter, and in only a few minutes they were standing in front of the ticket agent.

"Good afternoon, sir. Two tickets, please, for me and my wife. Only the one-way."

"To where, signor?" The agent didn't even look up from his newspaper.

"Oh, sorry. To Murano. Two one-way tickets to Murano. If you please."

Nina glanced at Niccolò, surprised by his hesitant manner. Earlier, talking to her father, he'd been at ease, one educated man speaking to another, but now he seemed another man entirely. He'd grown smaller, somehow, as if he had shrunk in upon himself, and his manner was diffident and unthreatening. Even his voice, halting and uncertain, was that of a man who rarely spoke Italian in place of his local dialect.

It was startling to witness, but she wasn't so silly as to remark upon it in front of the ticket agent. Niccolò collected their tickets and a few coins in change; she followed meekly in his wake, and only once they were on the *vaporetto,* and their voices were muted by the grumbling of the engine and the shouts of the crew, did she speak again.

"What *was* that?"

They'd been lucky enough to get two seats inside, hers against the window, but the woman next to Niccolò had enough bags and baskets to set up her own market stall, and he had been forced to sidle so close to Nina that the only place for his near arm was across her shoulders. His mouth now hovered a few centimeters from her ear.

"It was nothing, really," he admitted. "I was giving him as little as possible to remember. If anyone comes asking questions, he won't have any memory of me. I'll have been only one among dozens of anonymous men who bought tickets today."

"Do you think it likely?"

"That they look for you? Not anytime soon—Dr. Jona saw to that. But they won't stop, and they will find what they need elsewhere. Likely they'll begin with the census of Jews they took five years ago. If they don't have access to those records already, they will before long."

"My identity card," she remembered. In the rush to pack,

she'd left it and her little change purse behind. "I don't have—"

"Not to worry. I have papers for you. Breathe, Nina. You're safe with me."

She nodded, though she wasn't sure she believed him, not yet, and turned her head away so she might look out the window. But she had waited too long, for they had passed San Michele already, and the city, her home, was already hidden.

"You'll see it again," he whispered. "When we're sailing to Campalto. You can say farewell then."

Who was this stranger who spoke so kindly and seemed to understand, or at least wish to understand, how she suffered? Who *was* he, and why had he decided to care?

They alighted at the ferry's first stop, stepping carefully over their neighbor's baskets, and rather than follow the crowds to the center of the island, Niccolò led them along the Fondamente Serenella, with the salt-laden air of the lagoon to their left and the sulfurous stench of the glassblowers' kilns to their right. They'd only been walking for a few minutes when Niccolò pointed to a jetty about fifty meters away. "There he is. My cousin Mario."

A man was crouched on the jetty, his attention on his *sanpierota*'s mooring lines, and as they approached he stood, his arms outstretched in greeting, his smile wide and startling in his sun-bronzed face.

"So this is your bride?" he asked, embracing Niccolò and offering his hand for Nina to shake.

"Yes. Mario, this is my wife, Nina. Nina, this is my cousin Mario."

"Congratulations, and welcome to the family. Is this all you're bringing?"

"For now," Niccolò said easily. "And leave her alone. No more questions."

Mario shrugged, his smile unaltered. "Rosa will want to know a far sight more."

"She can ask as many questions as she likes. Doesn't mean I'll answer them. Can we get moving?"

"All right, all right. First we need to get your bride settled."

Mario helped Nina step into the *sanpierota,* and without any prompting she knew, like any Venetian native, that the best place for her was just forward of the mast. There wasn't any sort of seat, but the bottom was dry, and she was low enough that her head was safe from the boom if the wind changed suddenly.

She was content to sit unnoticed as the men busied themselves with casting off and getting under way. Mario stood at the stern, sculling out to clear water, and then he and Niccolò raised the sails without so much as a word between them.

"The wind is with us," Mario announced, and then, for her benefit, "we'll keep you dry the entire way. The lagoon is as smooth as glass."

"Look back now," Niccolò said, and she pivoted in her seat, peering under the foresail, glad for this one last chance to see her home. The city was no more than a smudge on the horizon, a wavering line that might have been penciled between the inky blue of the lagoon and the shimmering veil of the arching sky. She had only traveled a few kilometers, and been absent for the space of an hour, but her home now felt a world, and a lifetime, away.

Papà would go to the *casa* soon to help Mamma with her breakfast, and when she finished eating he would leave her to rest and return home. But their house would be cold and empty, for he had sent Marta away, too, and even after he'd moved over to the *casa* he would be lonely. The staff were so busy already; who among them would make sure he didn't forget to eat, or stay up all night reading? Who would sit with him when he worried about his patients, his neighbors, and the broken world that no longer had any use for him?

What would become of him now? Who would care for him, and Mamma, now that she was gone?

Niccolò had been crouching at the bow of the boat, but now he came back to sit by her, again seeming to know, without a single word or gesture on her part, that she was struggling.

"He isn't alone. He's at the *casa* with your mother, and the staff there will take good care of them both. He was very certain that he would be safe and comfortable there. Try to remember that if you can."

She nodded, not trusting herself to speak. Niccolò was kind to try to comfort her, but she knew just how cold and lonely her father's life had become the moment she had left him. And no amount of reassuring words could ever save her from that knowledge.

"Do you remember that summer you and Marco came to stay?" Mario asked. "And we took this old girl out every day and said we were fishing, but all we did was lower the sails and drop the anchor and sleep for hours?"

"Nonna was always so disappointed when we came home

without a single fish to show for it," Niccolò said, smiling as he remembered.

The wind was with them as they came about and began to sail along the inlet, but then, in a heartbeat, it faded to a scudding breeze. "How many newlyweds have their own *gondoliere*?" Mario asked as he stood at the stern and began to scull. "No need to thank me. Just consider it my gift to the bride and groom."

She knew that Mario needed to believe she was a newlywed, giddy with happiness and oblivious to the world's ills, so she tilted her face into the fading wind, let it dry her tears, and turned her attention to the mainland.

She'd lived her entire life only five or six kilometers away, but she'd never set foot in any of the coastal towns; when she and her parents had gone on holiday, they'd always taken the train from Santa Lucia to the mainland. Here, on the outskirts of Campalto, the farms came right down to the water's edge, with jetty after jetty occupied by variations of Mario's *sanpierota* and smaller craft.

As Mario directed the boat toward the only empty jetty, Niccolò took down the foresail and furled it neatly, then did the same for the mainsail.

"See? I haven't forgotten a thing," he told his cousin.

"It'll do. Take the bowline for me?"

It was a short walk from the shore to the closest of the farmhouses. A woman stood at its door, a baby in her arms, a toddler clutching at her skirts, and as soon as they drew near she smiled widely and waved in greeting.

"Niccolò! Welcome!"

"Good morning, Sofia. I'm sorry for taking up so much of Mario's time today."

"No need to apologize," she said, her smile directed at Nina. "You had to fetch your bride, after all."

"Nina, this is my cousin's wife, Sofia. In her arms is Chiara, and the little one is Emma. Sofia, this is my wife, Nina."

It was startling to be introduced in such a fashion, but she remembered to smile and admire the children, and then Niccolò papered over any remaining awkwardness by making funny faces at little Emma until she began to giggle.

"Are you hungry?" Sofia asked. "You've a long way to go before you get to Zia Elisa's."

"We're all right, for now," Niccolò hastened to answer. "We had breakfast not so long ago."

"You're sure to be hungry later. I've packed up a basket for you. There's bread I baked yesterday, some cheese, and some apples."

Mario had vanished into the stables, but he must have been close enough to hear them. "There's fresh water, too," he called back. "I put a cask in the cart. Should be enough to see you to Zia's."

"What about Bello?" Niccolò asked.

"He's here." Mario now emerged from the stables with a bridled and noisily protesting mule. "I'll leave you to hitch him to the cart," he grumbled. "Foul-tempered beast tried to take a bite out of me just now."

"He never gives me any trouble," Niccolò protested as he took hold of the bridle.

Only then did Nina look beyond the men to the mule, and

for an instant she forgot to be sad. How could she do anything but smile at the sight of such a ridiculous creature? He was almost as big as a horse, but a horse made of sinew and bone and flapping ears and enormous yellow teeth. She laughed, not unkindly, but the animal took offense all the same, stamping his feet in outrage, rolling his eyes, and hawing away like the worst sort of out-of-tune violin. Only when Niccolò produced an apology in the form of a carrot and a hard scratch between the ears did the mule grow calm, though no less wary of the stranger who had thought to laugh at him.

"Nina, this is Bello."

"Truly? Bello the beautiful?"

"My father's idea of a joke. Anyone else would have turned him into stew meat years ago, but I'm fond of him. All he needs is a bit of kindness to keep him moving."

"Isn't that true of most creatures?"

"It is indeed."

As soon as Bello had been hitched to the cart, they said farewell to Mario and Sofia and headed inland at a pace that was only fractionally faster than if they'd been walking.

"Bello may be slow, but he'll get us there in the end," Niccolò commented. "And we're only going as far as my aunt's farm tonight."

"Oh," Nina said, and then she couldn't think of any way to continue the conversation. She did want to know more about Mezzo Ciel, and Niccolò's family, and the woman named Rosa who, according to Mario, would insist on knowing everything, but not just yet. Not when she was so tired from her sleepless night that she could barely sit upright.

Again Niccolò seemed to understand, and apart from offering the occasional observation about the places they passed, he was happy to let them travel in silence. It would have been a pleasant journey but for the rutted and stony road, which made the cart bounce so endlessly that her entire body felt like one large bruise before the first hour was done. The morning sunshine was relentless, too, and by the time they stopped at midday to water the mule and eat some lunch she had a headache so strong that her skull was in danger of cracking open.

They sat under the silvery boughs of an olive tree and ate the bread and cheese and apples that Sofia had given them, and Niccolò filled a tin cup with water from the cask and handed it to her.

"Go on—drink it all. It will help with your headache. Is it really bad?"

"You noticed?"

"You've been rubbing at your temples for more than an hour. If it gets any worse, let me know."

The afternoon was more of the same, kilometer after kilometer under the baking sun, with the mule's gait slowing and slowing until they might as well have been moving backward. Niccolò got down to walk by the cart and led Bello by his bridle, which increased their speed the tiniest bit, but all the same it felt like the hours were stretching into days.

Just as she thought she could bear it no longer, Niccolò turned Bello and the cart through an archway built into the low stone wall flanking the road. "Here we are."

He had stopped the cart in the courtyard of a small farmhouse, its exterior walls neatly whitewashed, its front door open to catch the last of the afternoon sun. An old dog lay under a bench by the door, but after opening a single eye to inspect them, and thumping his tail in approval, he went back to sleep.

"Nico? Is that you?" came a voice from inside.

"Yes, Zia Elisa—we're here!" he called back.

Niccolò's aunt came rushing from the house, her arms open wide, and no sooner had Nina stepped down from the cart than she was kissed soundly on each cheek and enfolded in the other woman's capacious embrace.

"Such a happy day—a blessed day! Felicitations to you both! And never you mind what others may say, for I always thought you were meant to marry, my dear Nico, and have a family of your own. I did, I always did, and if your dear mother were still alive, she would agree, would she not?"

Rather than wait for an answer, Zia Elisa propelled Nina inside and insisted she sit at the head of the table for an early supper.

"You'll both be famished, I'm sure of that, and a bowl of my best soup is exactly what you need, and there's bread to go with it, baked fresh this morning, and I've wine, too. Is the soup too hot? No? Then eat, eat. Go on, now—eat!"

Nina hadn't realized how hungry she'd been until her first spoonful of soup. It and the bread were delicious, and the wine softened the edges of her worry, and rather than try to take part in the conversation she simply listened as Niccolò deftly avoided answering his aunt's questions about how he had met and courted her.

"Another day, Zia Elisa. Better for Nina to tell you the story herself when she isn't so tired."

She had begun to feel quite comfortable, and nearly at home in Zia Elisa's unfamiliar kitchen, when Niccolò pushed back his chair and announced that he and Nina were very tired and would be heading up to bed.

He held out his hand to her and she took it and followed him first to the outhouse—an outhouse, not a toilet, and there were squares of newspaper instead of proper paper, and she had to wait while he used it after her—and then back inside, where they washed their hands at the sink and he gathered up her rucksack and she tried not to drop dead of embarrassment right there on his aunt's pristine kitchen floor.

He led them to a small room under the eaves. The shutters were closed against the last of the early evening sun, and the lantern Niccolò carried left most of the room in shadows, but she could see it was spotlessly clean, if rather austere. A low bed swallowed up much of the space, its frame homemade and its mattress, if sight alone were a decent judge, lumpier than the farm's cobbled courtyard. Its sheets were clean and white, however, and its coverlet was embroidered with yellow daisies.

One bed. There was only one bed in the room.

There was a dreadful moment of silence before Niccolò cleared his throat and set the lamp on the table. "May I have one of the pillows?"

She handed it over without a word. He turned away, stretched out on the wooden floor, and settled his head on the pillow.

"You can't sleep there," she protested. "You might as well be lying on bare stones."

"I've slept on stone, and this is far more comfortable. I'll be fine. Now you get ready, and when you're done just turn down the lamp."

After half a minute or more, when she hadn't so much as blinked, he cleared his throat again. "Nina. We have to be up before dawn. Go ahead and change, and as the Lord is my witness I will not turn around."

He kept his promise. She changed in a rush, making a mess of her carefully packed bag, and once she was safely in her nightgown, she turned down the wick on the oil lamp until the flame guttered out. Of course the mattress had to make the loudest and most mortifying sort of rustling noises as she pulled aside the sheets and lay down, and she just knew that Zia Elisa was hearing everything and smiling to herself about the newlyweds.

Soon enough she was still, and the room was quiet, and she was alone in the dark, and then it was impossible not to cry, and with no way of finding her handkerchief in the pitch-dark room she could only sniff and blink and sniff again.

"I'm sorry"—*sniff*—"for keeping you awake," she whispered.

"You don't have to apologize. But your father will sleep better than he has in many months. He will miss you, of course, but his heart is lighter tonight. Can you remember that?"

"I think so."

"Then let's try to sleep, and if you need to cry just go ahead. But maybe you could try to be quiet? I truly don't mind, but if Zia Elisa hears, and she decides I've upset you, she'll whip off one of her *zoccoli* and start hitting me with it. A shoe is bad enough—that's what my mother used to hit us with—but a clog? She might as well use a hammer on me."

The thought of Niccolò dodging blows from his aunt, whose head came up to his armpit, shouldn't have made her smile—nothing should have seemed funny at the end of such a day. But she did smile, and it did make her feel as if she might be able to close her eyes, and when she opened them again it was dawn.

Chapter 5

You're awake. Come downstairs when you're ready."

Nina was lying on an uncomfortable bed in a strange room, and the light coming in from the window was all wrong. It took her a moment to recall where she was, and who belonged to the lovely, low voice, and when she did remember she was tempted to bury her face in the pillow and have a good, long cry. Instead she got dressed and packed her bag and went downstairs to join the stranger who was pretending to be her husband.

Zia Elisa gave them polenta with warm milk for breakfast, and for Nina there was a soft-boiled egg as well—a true sign of his aunt's affection, Niccolò whispered. "I could be lying on my deathbed and she still wouldn't give me an egg for breakfast."

Zia Elisa had prepared a basket of food to see them home, and only after listening to her itemize the contents, and accepting embraces and farewells and felicitations and blessings, were they able to clamber onto the wooden seat of Bello's cart and continue on their journey to Mezzo Ciel.

Their second day of travel was even worse than the first, for Nina was sore from the endless jostling of the cart, and still weary, though she had slept well enough on the lumpy mattress, and before long she was hungry and thirsty and headachy and ready to scream from the misery of it all. She would have, except Niccolò was so unfailingly pleasant, and he insisted on giving her most of the food, and he didn't seem to mind that she was too sad and wretched to do anything more than sit in Bello's horrible cart and try not to faint from the heat and dust and awful stench of the mule's very unclean and far too proximate backside.

Nor could she forget that he was doing this for *her*. The why of it mystified her, but he had said he was friends with Father Bernardi, and the priest was her father's friend, so it did make some kind of sense. And if he could endure the long hours of travel so serenely, then she could at least try to get through the day without collapsing in floods of tears.

The sun was edging close to the horizon when Niccolò finally stopped the cart by a low and sprawling hedgerow that bordered a grassy field.

"We're not all that far from Mezzo Ciel, but it's safer to stop before the sun has gone down."

"Even though we're close?"

"We won't make it there until long after sundown, and I don't want to risk being caught on the road after curfew. We'll rise at dawn, though, and be home by late morning."

"All right."

"Will you hop down and hold Bello's bridle for a moment while I open this gate?"

"But he'll—"

"He's just as tired as you, and he wants nothing more than to rest and eat his supper and go to sleep. He won't move a muscle."

"Are you sure we'll be all right here?"

"We'll be fine. My cousin Sandro owns this field. We won't get in trouble for staying here. Is that what you're worried about?"

"It's only . . . what if it rains?"

"No chance of that after such a fine day. It won't be as comfortable as my aunt's house, but we'll be warm enough, and there's enough food in the basket for supper. What more do we need?"

He took Bello's bridle and led the animal into the field, and without asking or receiving any help from her, he unhitched the mule and left him to graze, filled a wooden bucket from the cask—they'd passed a fountain not long after they'd stopped for lunch—and took it to Bello. Then he made up a bed for her from a stack of folded blankets that had been stowed in the cart, and set out the last of their food on a clean napkin.

"Not quite a feast, but we'll survive. There's bread and cheese, and we still have most of the wine that Zia gave us."

They ate in silence, and even though the bread had gone hard and stale, she ate every crumb of it. He poured some of the wine into the tin cup, and she drank just enough to wash down the bread and no more.

"I'll check on Bello, so if you need some privacy to attend to, ah . . . there are some shrubs in the far corner. No one can see you from the road."

She scurried across to the shelter he'd indicated, and though he kept his back turned he must have been listening for her, since he turned around as soon as she returned.

"We might as well go to sleep now. The sun is almost gone, and I'd rather not light the lantern. Best to let our eyes grow used to the dark."

She took off her boots and stretched out on the makeshift bed he'd made. Niccolò lay down about a meter away, once again wrapped in a single blanket.

The sun sank into the western sky, the moon began to rise, and the countryside fell silent. She felt perfectly safe with Niccolò so close by, but sleep did not come, no matter how earnestly she tried to empty her mind and banish her fears.

"Are you awake?" she whispered at last.

"Yes."

"What are you doing?"

"Watching the stars."

Nina rolled onto her back and looked up, and her breath caught in her throat. The dome of the sky was ablaze with stars, far more than there were people on earth, and set against the sweep of the heavens she could see, all too clearly, that she and her worries were only the merest specks of stardust.

"There's so much I don't know," she whispered. "I'm not even sure what I'm meant to say to people when they ask how we met."

"Why don't we figure that out now? If you aren't too tired."

"You don't have a story ready?"

"Not really. I do have some ideas. We could say we met at the hospital—remember that you were a student nurse. I'd come in with a complaint of some sort. A broken wrist, or a cut that needed stitching, and you helped to care for me." He paused, and then he sighed, a low, grumbling sort of noise that might have been drawn from Bello's lexicon.

"What is it?"

"If we tell her that, my sister will worry about me even more than she usually does."

She decided to ignore the question of why his sister was given to worrying about him. "What if we tell them a romantic story? That's how people meet in books, and in films, too. They bump into one another, or the heroine drops something, and the hero rescues it for her. People will forget about the other parts if they have that one story to remember."

"Very well. How did the hero and heroine meet in our story?"

She closed her eyes, shutting out the wondrous starlight, and made herself imagine a different life, a different *her*, in which she was the heroine and life was a series of charming romantic vignettes, and the hero was a man who looked and behaved exactly like Niccolò. She'd never been terribly interested in romantic stories, but this one might end up holding her interest.

"I was getting on a *vaporetto* at Rialto," she began, "and the strings were frayed on my bag of shopping, and the onion I'd bought fell out and was rolling around the deck. It was about to go into the canal, and you stopped it with your foot and picked it up and wiped it off with your handkerchief. And you gave it back and said something funny . . ."

"How about, 'Here's an onion you don't have to cry over'?"

"Yes! Oh, that's *perfect*. We started talking, and when I got off you alighted, too, and we kept talking as we walked, and then we were at the front door of . . . where would I have been living?"

"Not at the hospital, since it isn't anywhere near Rialto. Hmm. What about one of the university residences in San Tomà? Or maybe those are just for men. A boardinghouse for female students?"

"Yes. Yes, that would work."

Now Niccolò took up the thread of the story. "I asked if you might agree to meet for a walk the next day, and even though you didn't know the least thing about me, you agreed."

"We went for a walk every day until you had to leave."

"But I wrote to you—"

"And you came to see me every time you were in the city—"

"And I asked you to marry me in the summer, the last time I was there, and even though it meant giving up your studies you agreed. We were married the day before yesterday."

"And now you're bringing me home to your family," she finished.

"Yes."

"I think they'll remember the onion. Good night, Nico—sorry. I meant to say Niccolò."

"Nico will do. You're family now."

THEY WERE AWAKE at dawn.

"I'm sorry we don't have anything for breakfast, but we'll be home in a few hours. Do you mind walking for a while? Bello is feeling the damp this morning."

"I don't mind, no." Walking had to be better than another day spent on that horrible cart, and if she was walking she wouldn't have to dwell on how tired and anxious and sad she was.

They walked and walked, the sun climbing ever higher in the brightening sky. The road rose slowly, steadily, the flat plains giving way to soft, low hills and the distant, stony spine of the mountains beyond.

She'd forced herself not to ask the question before, but now she gave in. "How far do we have to go?"

"Not far at all. We're just outside San Zenone now. My mother was born here. She died when Carlo was born." And then, as if anticipating her next question, "I have six siblings still living. The eldest of us was Marco, but he was killed in Tobruk two and a half years ago. Then there's me, then Rosa, then two babies who died. Then Matteo—he's seventeen now— and after him there's Paolo, Agnese, Angela, and little Carlo. He's nine."

So Rosa was his sister. The one who worried and would expect to be told everything. "Who took care of them after your mother died?"

"Rosa did, with some help from my aunts. I wasn't living at home then—I went away to school when I was fourteen. I only returned after Marco was killed. Papà couldn't manage the farm on his own, and Matteo and Paolo were still too young to take on the heavy work."

"I'm sorry. About your mother, and Marco, and the babies, too. That must have been very hard."

"It was. Still is. And I should also tell you—"

"What is it?" she asked, instantly apprehensive.

"I was in the seminary. I was training to become a priest. When I came home to help my family, that's what I left behind." His expression, already solemn, grew graver still.

She nodded, taking it all in, and then she remembered: Catholic priests weren't allowed to marry. "And now you can't ever go back. Because of me."

"That may be how people see it, but you and I know the truth. As does Father Bernardi."

"Your family will be upset. Your father—"

"He knows I've been questioning it. My vocation, I mean. He'll understand."

"What about your sister? Mario said she'll have questions for you."

"Rosa has a good heart. She wants the best for us, for all of us, and she's never been happy that I left the seminary. So my having married may . . . upset her."

"Upset her how?" Nina pressed. "Will she be sad? Or angry?"

"I'm not sure," he admitted, and his accompanying smile was rueful. "I think a little of both? But she'll come around. I know she will."

"All right. Well, thank you for telling me."

She was grateful for his honesty, but his admission made her anxious. The journey a man took to become a Catholic priest wasn't something Nina had ever thought about, but she did know it was a position of some status. And now she had become the impediment that prevented him from attaining that position, and never mind that he hadn't truly married her or broken any sort of vow he might have made in the past. To his family, she would be the woman who had made him abandon, forever, his dream of becoming a priest. She wouldn't be surprised if they all turned their backs on her.

They were walking through a village, the first since they'd left Campalto; Niccolò had taken care until now to keep them to the quieter side roads. It wasn't much more than a cluster of buildings at a crossroads, with a public fountain and a church that loomed over the other buildings, and as they passed by one of the outlying farms a woman waved at them and greeted Niccolò by name.

"Good day, Zia Nora. Your garden is looking fine," he answered, but he kept walking, and the woman, still smiling, returned to the basket of beans she'd been shelling.

"A cousin of my father," he explained.

"You have cousins everywhere."

"I do. My father is one of twelve and my mother was one of seven. I have cousins upon cousins upon cousins."

"It was only ever me and my parents. They married late, and my grandparents died before I was born. My mother had a sister, but she was much older than Mamma. I was still a little girl when she died."

"You'll be surrounded by family in Mezzo Ciel. Everyone will want to know your business. Everyone will have an opinion."

"It was like that in the *gh*—"

"Shh," he warned, shaking his head.

"Yes, sorry. I meant to say that my neighborhood was very close-knit."

"I know it will be hard to not speak of your family or your friends, but it's far safer. You can tell me about them when we're alone."

They were approaching a crest in the road, and now he stopped and pointed to a cluster of buildings in the middle distance. "Can you see the church and campanile? The sun makes them look very white. That is Mezzo Ciel."

"But it's halfway up the mountain!"

"I swear it only looks that way. We'll be there in another hour. Maybe a little more."

They walked on, and the sun grew hotter and hotter, and before long her hair was plastered to her nape and temples. She'd lost her handkerchief at some point, so she mopped at her face with her sleeve and kept moving.

"Are you all right?" Niccolò asked.

"Yes. The sun is warm, that's all."

She concentrated on walking, just walking, for there was nothing she could do about her hair or sunburned face until they arrived. All she could do was walk.

"Here." He handed her a folded cloth, damp and blessedly cool. "Take this. It's clean—Zia Elisa used it to wrap the bread."

Never had anything felt so good as that cloth against her face and neck. "How far?" she managed.

"Not even a half hour. If you look up you'll see—one more hill and we're there."

She was too tired to look up. She was too tired to think of how stiff she was after sleeping on the ground, how hungry and hot and wretched she felt. She wouldn't think of the blister on her left heel or her sunburned face. She wouldn't let herself think of how sad and lonely and adrift she felt with her parents so far away. She wouldn't think of all she had lost. She wouldn't—

"We're here, Nina. This is Mezzo Ciel."

Chapter 6

They stood at the edge of a small, sloping piazza, its far corner dominated by the church and campanile that Niccolò had pointed out earlier. Its few modest shops—a cobbler, a general store, and a bakery—were shuttered for lunch, and outside the square's lone osteria, a trio of white-haired men sat dozing in the midday sun. The buildings were old, though not old enough to be interesting, and their stucco was cracked and faded, but every window was clean and every stoop was freshly scrubbed.

"There isn't much more to it than this. The two main streets meet here at the piazza—via Mezzo Ciel and via Santa Lucia."

"How far are we from the farm?" she asked, hoping it wouldn't be more than a few kilometers.

"It's just past the church," he answered, and then, in response to her disbelieving look, "I swear it isn't far."

They crossed the piazza, taking the road that led past the churchyard's flanking walls, and almost immediately found themselves in the countryside again, the stone giving way to shambling hedgerows, the cobbles of the piazza vanishing into a dusty roadbed, and Bello was straining at his bridle and grumbling at Niccolò to hurry, hurry—and suddenly they were there.

The farmhouse was set back from the road, with a tidy courtyard of old cobbles interspersed with patches of gravel, and stables that met the main building at right angles, their stalls and pens just visible beyond the open doors. The house stretched to three stories, the bottom of fieldstone and the upper two of a mellow, rosy brick, though the top floor was only two-thirds the height of those below. The windows that faced the courtyard, four to each story, were shuttered against the midday sun. The entrance was set into the center of the bottom floor, its threshold shaded by the silvery boughs of an ancient olive tree, and next to it a pair of low stools sat waiting for occupants.

A rangy, rough-coated dog came barking toward them, then two girls and a boy emerged from the house, their cheers of "Nico! Nico!" rising in counterpoint to the dog's delighted yelps, the hawing of an agitated Bello, and the laughter of their brother as he lifted them high and swung them round and round.

Two teenage boys came striding out from the stables, followed more sedately by an older man who so resembled Nico that he had to be his father. He smiled readily enough, coming forward to greet them, but faltered when a woman came out of the house. She, too, had the family face—she might even have been Nico's twin, with the same dark, solemn eyes and honey-colored hair.

"We weren't expecting you back until next week at the earliest," the older man said.

"I know. I'm sorry." Nico steered Nina forward, his arm a bracing weight around her shoulders. "Nina, this is my father, Aldo, and my sister Rosa. I'll introduce you to the others in a moment. Everyone, this is Nina. My wife."

"Your *wife*?" Rosa clutched a hand to her heart, just as people did when they received news of a tragedy. Whirling around, she rushed back inside.

Nico's arm tightened a fraction, but he made no move to hurry after his sister. It would be up to Nina, then, to smooth things over. "It is a pleasure to meet you, Signor Gerardi."

"And I am delighted to meet you—but please, no *signor* here. You are my daughter now. Papà will do." He took her hands, kissed her cheeks, and offered a tremulous smile. "Welcome to our family." And then, calling to the older boys, "See to the mule and cart."

He ushered her into the kitchen, the low door set deeply into the stone walls, and gestured for them both to sit at the long table. The room was dominated by an enormous hearth that took up most of the far wall; opposite the table was an iron range and a wall-hung enamel sink with a single faucet. So there was running water, and electricity, too, judging by the overhead light fitting and the walnut-cased tabletop radio that sat on a shelf next to the door.

Rosa was there, washing dishes in the sink, her back straight, her demeanor as forbidding as a tomb. She did not turn around to greet them.

Aldo did his best to paper over the awkwardness, directing

the younger girls to fetch a fresh tablecloth, and then bowls and spoons and glasses.

"There's still some soup, I think, and Rosa baked the bread yesterday—didn't you, Rosa? Ah, well . . . she's busy. I'll see what there is, and I'll fetch you some wine, and while I'm doing that the children can tell Nina who they are, although don't worry about keeping them straight just yet, my dear."

The children had been hovering at the door, but with this invitation they hurried inside and gathered around Nico, and the youngest boy—he had to be Carlo—sat on his brother's knee with the ease of a child who knew he was loved.

"*I'll* tell you who everyone is. I'm Carlo, and these are my sisters Agnese and Angela, and even though they look almost the same, Agnese is the older one by a year. Then there's Paolo and Matteo—he's the one who's trying to grow a mustache, even though *I* think it looks like a feather got caught under his nose. And Rosa is the grumpy one who is mad at Nico. She's nearly always mad at one of us, so you shouldn't be too worried."

"*Carlo,*" Nico warned.

"Perhaps you might tell us a little about Nina?" Aldo asked, his tone uncertain but hopeful.

"I will tell you, Papà, I promise. But we're both tired, Nina especially. I hope you don't mind if we rest for a while. It was a long walk from Venice."

"From Venice, then? I—yes. Of course. We can wait."

They ate in silence, and though Nico seemed perfectly at ease with his brother hanging off him, the dog curled up at his feet, and his sister washing the dishes with such vigor it was a miracle she hadn't smashed the lot, Nina could barely swallow her soup.

She'd expected his family to be surprised, certainly, and even disappointed over his decision, but his sister was reacting as if Nina had made Nico the accessory to a crime, her hostility so palpable that the air in the room was buzzing. And if Carlo was right, his eldest sister was a woman who took more comfort in anger than she did in happiness.

"She's very pretty," Carlo whispered into his brother's ear just then, and naturally he waited for a moment when the silence around them was absolute. "I like her hair. It looks like it's made out of springs."

"They're called ringlets, and yes, she is very pretty, but you mustn't talk about Nina as if she isn't here. It's not polite."

"What should I say?"

"You might ask her about Venice."

"What is Venice like, Nina?" Carlo asked readily.

"Haven't you been? No? Well, it's very beautiful, and instead of streets there are canals—"

"I know that. Everyone knows that."

"Of course. Well, did you know that instead of having mules like Bello, people move their things around on handcarts? And some very grand people have houses with a space for boats at the bottom, right where the cellar would be in an ordinary house."

"Was your house like that?"

"No. Mine was, ah"—and then, remembering just in time—"I lived in a house with other students. It was too small for that."

"When did you and my brother get married?"

"Carlo, that's enough. Didn't you hear me tell Papà that we were tired? We're going to have a rest now, and then I'll tell you the whole story at supper. Now off you go, all of you, and get started on your chores."

Nico stood, shooing the children away, and then gathered up their empty bowls. These he took to Rosa at the sink, and though it felt wrong to watch, Nina couldn't look away. He kissed his sister's temple, and whispered something in her ear, and whatever he said must have eased her spirits, or helped to temper her anger, for she bowed her head, and wiped at her eyes with the back of her hand, and even gave him a fleeting smile. But she did not look around to acknowledge Nina.

After collecting their bags, Nico guided her through a door at the far corner of the kitchen. A few steps beyond was a dark and quiet room—"The parlor, but we never go in there," he told her. Now he took her hand and led her up a short flight of stairs to a landing, then up a second, narrower run of steps to a corridor with two doors on either side.

"This is Papà's room, and opposite it is the girls' room, then next to it the boys' room, and this is my room. Our room, now."

It wasn't so different from the bedroom they'd occupied at his aunt's house. It had the same wooden floor, plain furniture, and whitewashed walls. The bed was covered by an immaculate white counterpane, a crucifix hanging on the wall above, a faded rag rug ready to warm chilly feet; next to the bed, in lieu of a nightstand, was a simple stool. On the far wall was a wooden peg rack hung with Nico's shirts and trousers, and there was a dresser, too, its top covered by a stack of books and a leather case left open to reveal a man's shaving things.

In front of the window was a wooden chair, angled to allow its occupant a view of the bottle-green slopes of the mountains.

Nico set down their bags and crossed the room to open the window and close the shutters. "There. Now it's dark enough to sleep."

He hung up his coat, shrugged off his braces, and sat on the bed to unlace his boots. Pulling back the counterpane, he folded it neatly at the end of the bed, and did the same again for the blankets and top sheet. Then he lay down and patted the narrow space next to him.

"Take off your coat and shoes and lie down. You're safe next to me—you know that. Although"—and here he grinned—"your ears may protest. My brothers tell me I snore."

It was silly to protest, and she certainly didn't want to see him sleeping on the floor again. So she did as he suggested and lay down on her side, but the bed was so narrow it was impossible to maintain any distance, and his body was so distractingly warm against her back that she wasn't certain she'd be able to sleep. Yet the rhythm of his steady breaths was comforting, and the room was pleasantly dim and quiet, and she resolved to simply close her eyes for a moment. Only for a minute or two, and then she'd sit by the window and let herself think of home and her parents.

When she woke, the room had grown so dark she could scarcely see, and she was cold despite the blanket that Nico, rising, must have draped over her. She listened, tuning her ears to the unfamiliar sounds of her new home: children's voices, the far-off lowing of oxen, the tinny sound of a radio, the clang of pots and pans.

Sitting up, she put on her shoes and, as there was no mirror, she smoothed down her hair, straightened her clothes, and ventured back to the kitchen.

Rosa was at the range, stirring away at something in a huge iron pot. She must have heard Nina come down the stairs, but she didn't turn, didn't speak, didn't acknowledge her in any way. Nico and his father were just outside—their voices seemed close enough to touch—and rather than test her courage with a confrontation, Nina walked past Rosa to the courtyard, her feet following the seam between two rows of tiles as if it were a tightrope.

As she'd hoped, Aldo and Nico were there, sitting on the stools under the olive tree, the dog at their feet.

"I'm sorry I slept for so long."

"You were tired," Aldo replied. He stood, offering her his stool, and the dog, who had been fast asleep a second before, jumped to her feet and looked up at both men adoringly.

"What is her name?" Nina asked.

"Selva," Nico answered. "She's my father's dog but she prefers me."

"True enough," Aldo said. "She pays me no mind when he's around."

"I was just telling my father the story of how we met," Nico said easily.

She nodded, suddenly nervous. If only they'd agreed upon a story that wasn't quite so romantic.

"Your family didn't object to your leaving?"

"I told you, Papà—Nina has no family. That's why I was so certain she had to come with me. With the way things are? In my place you'd have done the same."

No family. *No family.* She'd agreed upon the fiction, but to hear it said so baldly, as if it were the truth . . .

"I expect so," Aldo admitted, "but your sister. Well. The shock has upset her."

"I know. And I will speak to her. I will explain."

"You know she had hoped you'd return to the seminary one day. You know she'd have preferred you never left at all—"

"Yes," Nico interrupted, his voice rising, "but after Marco was killed there was no choice. I had to come home. And I was happy to do it. You know I was."

"I do. And Rosa's sure to come around before long. You know she's never loved surprises. Remember how she reacted when Marco and Luca enlisted?"

"She's still angry about that. Never mind that they got themselves killed not a month later."

"Nico. *Enough.* Why don't you visit Father Bernardi? There's still time before supper."

"Very well. What do you think, Nina? You aren't too tired?"

"No, not at all," she said, and let him pull her to her feet. "It will be nice to see him again."

"You know him?" Aldo asked. "But I thought—"

Only then did she realize her mistake. "I'm sorry. I meant to say that I was looking forward to meeting him."

"Of course. Well, off you go now, and don't let Nico and Father get so caught up in talking that they forget the time. Supper will be your first proper meal in your new home—you don't want to be late."

Chapter 7

ico took her arm as they walked away, and even after they turned onto the road he didn't let go. Perhaps he, too, needed a bit of comfort after their awkward homecoming and her mortifying mistake in admitting a prior acquaintance with Father Bernardi.

"I can't believe I was so stupid just now."

But Nico was unconcerned. "My father barely noticed. Don't trouble yourself over it."

The rectory where Father Bernardi lived, only a few meters distant from the church, was a modest stuccoed building, its window baskets brimming with leggy geraniums. The priest opened the door himself when they knocked, beckoning them into a cozy entranceway that smelled of furniture polish, incense, and the faintest whiff of strong coffee.

He led them into his study, past his desk stacked high with papers and books, to a sitting area at the far end of the room. With Nico's help he cleared yet more books off the furniture and, after some ineffectual plumping of the upholstery, directed them to sit on the settee.

"I have a little coffee left. I'll just ask dear Signora Vendramin to prepare it for us."

"That's all right, Father," Nico said. "We can't stay for long—supper is almost ready. Maybe another day."

"Very well," the priest said, and made himself comfortable in his chair. "How are you both? How was the journey?"

"Long," Nina said, and though she was glad to see her father's friend again, she didn't have the energy, or the spirit, to indulge in conversational niceties. "When I saw you in Venice last year, did you know?"

"Of your father's wish that I hide you? Not then. Not until last month, when he wrote to me and asked if I would find a safe place for you to see out the war."

"Why only me? Why not him and my mother, too?"

"I asked him—more than once I asked—but he was worried that a move of any kind would be too disruptive for your mother. Too upsetting."

"He didn't seem very concerned about upsetting *me*," Nina grumbled.

"Only because he knew you were strong enough to bear it," Father Bernardi countered, his tone reassuring rather than reproving. "And you can. You're among friends here."

"I don't know anything about living on a farm. I don't know how to cook, or clean, or do anything useful."

"You'll learn. Niccolò will help you."

At this Nico nodded. "I know my sister wasn't very friendly when we arrived earlier. I'm sorry about that."

"It feels wrong to deceive her and your father."

"Father Bernardi and I did consider telling them. We did. But it's imperative that we keep your true identity a secret."

"Don't you trust them?" she asked, suddenly nervous.

"We do," Father Bernardi answered. "Neither of them would ever betray you. The greater problem is the difficulty of keeping such a secret when there are young children about. They listen to everything, you know, and Carlo is still in school, and as you've seen he is a talkative little fellow. It would only take one slip, one careless word overheard at supper, to doom us all. It also doesn't help that his teacher is the worst sort of fascist mouthpiece."

"I agree," Nico said. "Far better that only the three of us know the truth."

He and Father Bernardi were so matter-of-fact about it. As if it was an everyday thing to offer her shelter. As if it wasn't something that could lead to their imprisonment or worse.

"Why are you doing this?" she asked, turning to Nico. "My father is friends with Father Bernardi—not you. Yet you're risking so much for me. For a stranger."

"What kind of man would I be if I didn't offer to help you? And you were only a stranger before I met you."

"Most men would look away."

"I can't account for their decisions. I can only do what I know to be right. And I do believe we'll be successful. Mezzo Ciel is a quiet place. No one will come looking for you here."

"You are safe here," Father Bernardi insisted. "But I do have something to ask of you, something rather difficult. I'm afraid you will have to attend Mass while you're here."

Of course. She should have known to expect such a thing. Even the kindest Gentiles believed they were doing Jews a favor when they impelled them to embrace Christianity. "Are you saying I have to convert?" she asked, her throat tight with horror.

His shocked expression was encouragingly genuine. "Goodness, no. No—I would *never* ask such a thing of you. You need only attend and make a show of following along. Your thoughts and beliefs are yours to own. As the Lord is my witness, I swear this to you."

She believed him. She did. So why did she have to fight off tears?

"We ought to be getting back," Nico said, and if he'd noticed that she was struggling, he didn't embarrass her by mentioning it. "We won't win over my sister by being late for supper."

"Of course, of course. I'll see you both on Sunday."

Only then did Nina think to ask Father Bernardi one last question. "If you hear anything of my parents?"

"I shall let you know straightaway. That I promise."

They were back at the farm a few minutes later, but rather than beckon them inside for dinner, Aldo—still sitting under the olive tree—told them that supper wasn't quite ready.

"You might as well show Nina around," he suggested.

"I would like that," she said, and it wasn't only because she wanted to put off returning to the kitchen and Rosa's arctic company as long as possible. She genuinely was curious to see more of the place where she'd be staying until she returned home to her parents.

"Has your family always lived here?" she asked as they walked away.

"As far as I know. My grandfather's grandfather built the house. The one it replaced was much smaller."

"More like your zia Elisa's?"

"Yes. I've always thought my ancestor must have come into some money. That's why this house is so large, and why some of the details are so fine."

"What's on the top floor? More bedrooms?"

He shook his head. "That's the granary. The stairs to it go up the outside of the house—you'll see in a minute. And here are the stables. We've the pair of milk cows over there, and the oxen next to them. We've a few dozen chickens, too. Forever underfoot during the day, but they go back to their coop at dusk."

They stopped by another pen, this one empty, and she looked at him questioningly.

"My father took the pig over to my uncle's farm last week. We'll fatten it up alongside the other pigs, and when it's time to butcher them my father and brothers will go."

"But not you?"

"No. I'm too softhearted. I can't even wring the chickens' necks for Rosa, and the sight of blood makes me dizzy."

She giggled at the thought of it. "A grown man like you?"

"I know, I know. Laugh all you like. I pay for it, though—when they're off dealing with the pig I have to run the farm on my own." He turned to her, frowning, as if something had just occurred to him. "Nearly everything is cooked in lard. Will you be all right?"

She nodded uneasily, remembering her father's insistence that she do her best to fit in. That she eat whatever was put in front of her. If lard was so important to their diet, there was no way she could refuse it. Not without ensuring that Rosa's initial dislike would transform into outright antipathy. "I'll survive," she promised. "Although I'm not sure I could eat a pork chop."

"No fear of that. Most of the meat you'll see comes from the chickens, and even then it will only be a mouthful or two."

They walked past a sleeping Bello in his stall, his ears twitching with every snore, and Nico stooped to scratch the head of a passing cat.

"This fellow is tame enough, but keep your distance from the others. They're all more than half-wild."

They walked under the hayloft, which was so low that Niccolò had to duck his head, and then out the back of the stables and around to the rear of the house. There the granary stairs he'd mentioned ran steeply up to the top floor; a meter or so beyond them was a back door and, angled into the ground next to it, a pair of cellar doors.

"The entrance to the *cantina*," Nico said, following her gaze. "The only time we use the back door is when we need something that's stored down there. And—oh, I should have told you before. The outhouse is just over there. But don't worry that you'll need to go outside at night. There's a chamber pot in our bedroom."

She nodded, her face burning, but Nico didn't seem to notice. Instead he led them on until they'd come around the end of the house and were facing the fields. "You can see nearly all the farm from here," he explained. "At the top, where it's really steep, we have the olive trees, and some fruit trees as well. Apples, peaches, apricots. On the hill below we grow hay for the animals. Then we have the big fields—over there where it's nearly flat. We harvested the early wheat in June, then we put in the corn. That came out the week before last. Once the stalks have dried down some more we'll bring them in, too, and then we'll sow the winter wheat. There are grapevines as well, just over there, and beyond them is the vegetable garden."

"And you manage all this on your own—you and your father and the others?"

"For the most part. Our uncles and cousins help when we bring in the corn and wheat, and when it's time to pick the grapes, and we help them in turn. It's a lot of work, but it's a good life. It can be a good life, if you don't mind doing without some things that others might never dream of giving up."

"Like what? Hot running water and soft mattresses?"

"Yes. And a life that doesn't involve rising before dawn every day of the year to milk the cows and feed the other animals and work straight through until nightfall."

"You don't regret having to come home when your brother died?"

"Not at all. Not ever. It was awful at first, because we just wanted him back and alive and safe with us. But I don't imagine I'll ever leave here again."

"Before, when you and your father were talking about Marco, you mentioned another man."

"Luca. My brother's best friend, and Rosa's sweetheart. They were killed on the same day at the start of 1941. At the siege of

Tobruk. I wasn't here when we got the news. Papà hadn't even told me that Marco had enlisted, I think because he knew I would have come home. And then, when the news came that they'd been killed, everyone reacted as you'd imagine. Everyone except for Rosa. She didn't cry. Just kept on with her chores as if nothing had happened. And she hasn't said Luca's name since. It's as if he never existed."

How could such a thing be possible? To love someone, to mourn them, to wake up each morning with the fresh realization of their absence, and yet never again speak their name? How could his sister simply erase the man she'd loved from her life?

"Nico! Nina! Nico-Nina! Nico-nico-nina!! Time for supper!"

Carlo came roaring up, his arms outstretched like an airplane's wings, and squealed when Nico swept him into the air.

"Do you hear that, Nina? Supper is ready, and what will happen if we don't hurry? Carlo?"

"Matteo and Paolo will be greedy and eat up all the food!"

"They will indeed. Let's fly back, just like you're one of the Pippo bombers, and see if Nina can catch us. Ready—now go!"

Not wishing to be left behind, Nina ran as fast as she could, faster than she'd run for years, but it wasn't quite enough; and Nico, noticing, reached back to catch her hand in his, and so pulled them both along; and when she stumbled, as she'd feared she would, he simply gathered her in his arms and ran on until they were at the kitchen door and the race was done.

Chapter 8

25 *September 1943*

She woke at dawn, roused by the empty space at her back. "Nico?"

"I'm here." He sat on the end of the bed and set about lacing up his boots. "Did you sleep well?"

"I did."

They'd gone to bed not long after the children the night before, and as he'd done on their two previous nights together, or rather the single night they'd slept in an actual bedroom, Niccolò had turned his back and waited for her to slip into bed and pull the covers up to her chin before he so much as unlaced his boots. But he'd gone on to undress more—she couldn't be sure how much, nor if he'd put on pajamas, and as her back was turned and her eyes were shut tight she couldn't even have guessed. Certainly she wouldn't have dreamed of asking him what he was wearing as he stretched out next to her and, moving carefully so as not to tip her out of the narrow bed, arranged his big body at the very edge of the mattress.

He had risen and dressed silently, and if he'd been wearing pajamas he had put them away. Perhaps she would find out what he had worn when it was time to do the laundry. And it was silly, besides, to obsess over such a—

"I know that for you it's the Sabbath, but to my family it's just an ordinary Saturday, and that's the day for housecleaning. I'm sorry about that."

"I don't mind. My father never made a fuss about keeping the Sabbath. He couldn't, not with his patients needing him all the time. Babies especially—he swore they only ever came in the middle of the night."

"I think that's true of animal babies as well. I'll see you at breakfast. But don't hurry down, not yet. You've earned a rest."

She listened to his careful footsteps in the hall and on the stairs, and for a while she let herself indulge in the lovely feeling of being not quite asleep, but not fully awake either, until her stomach was growling and the children were up and she worried that she'd annoy Rosa if she were to lounge abed even a minute longer. Dressing in the same garments she'd worn for the past few days, she brushed her hair, twisted back the sides and fixed them with a pair of hair grips, and joined everyone except Niccolò and Aldo at the table. Likely they were still busy with the animals.

"Good morning, Nina," Carlo said. "I'm glad you sat next to me."

"I'm glad, too. What are you eating? It smells delicious."

He sighed dramatically. "Polenta and milk. I hate it."

"You're lucky to have it," Rosa said, her eyes fixed on whatever she was stirring on the range. "So stop whining, or I'll tell Father Bernardi and he'll set you an entire novena."

Nina had no idea what being set a novena entailed, but from the look on Carlo's face it didn't seem like something she ever wished to experience herself.

Rosa now ladled a scoop of steaming polenta into Nina's bowl and topped it with a splash of warm milk. It was warm, she realized, because it had just come out of the cow, with flecks of yellow butterfat clearly visible in the puddle of ivory milk, and yet nothing would have induced her to complain. At a muttered command from Rosa, Carlo fetched a mug and set it at Nina's elbow. "Coffee," he whispered shyly, but only after swallowing a great gulp of the stuff did Nina realize it was *caffè d'orzo*, the awful imposter made of roasted barley that she'd always vowed she would never be desperate enough to drink. She drank it now.

The men came in as she was finishing, and were also served polenta and milk and ersatz coffee, along with a thick slice of fried ham that Rosa dropped into their bowls once most of the polenta was gone.

It would have been nice to sit and talk for a while, but a stern glance from Rosa had Agnese and Angela fetching brooms and rags and an ancient wooden bucket from the corner.

"You girls get started, and I'll finish up with the kitchen," Rosa said, and Nina wasn't sure if that included her, too, or if she was meant to do something else entirely.

Nico noticed, of course. "What do you think if Nina helps the girls today? Rosa?"

"Fine."

"Remember, girls, that Nina has been busy studying how to become a nurse. She knows a lot about helping sick people, but it's been a while since she's had time for housecleaning."

"You'll probably have to remind me how to do everything," Nina admitted, and when she looked to Nico with a grateful smile he just nodded and winked at her.

They began by stripping the sheets from the bed in Nina's room, revealing a mattress that was nothing more than a thick felted pad on top of an enormous fabric bag, its contents flattened almost to nothing. Following Agnese's directions, Nina and the girls shook out the bag, rather as one might fluff a giant's pillow, and laid it back upon the interlaced ropes of the bed frame.

"What is inside?" Nina asked, since she'd never known a feather bed to crackle and crunch so noisily.

"Corn husks," Angela said. "With a nice soft pad on top to stop the pokey bits from coming through."

They remade the bed with much-mended but crisply ironed sheets, dusted every stick of furniture with dampened rags, and Angela carried the simple rag rugs outside to be beaten and aired.

Then it was time for the floors. They swept each one, with the girls patiently showing Nina how to angle the broom so as not to set the dirt flying, and even though she made more work for them all they were generous with their praise.

She helped to carry the buckets of hot, soapy water upstairs, and then, after learning how to fold the extra dust rags so they cushioned her knees, the girls taught Nina how to scrub a floor.

"Start in the corner so you don't go over the parts that are clean," Angela advised.

"Give the scrubbing brush a good shake so you don't get the floor too wet," Agnese added. "And use the clean cloths to dry as you go. Will you be all right in here? Angela and I can get a second bucket and start on Papà's room."

"That's a sensible idea. I'll call if I need help."

By the time she was finished with her bedroom floor the girls had scrubbed the other bedrooms, all three of them, but she helped them with the corridor and stairs, and by the time they had finished drying the bottom step it was time for lunch.

She ate the food that was placed in front of her without looking up or joining the conversation, and despite her fatigue she did enjoy her meal. For a first course they had *pastina* in *brodo*, and then for the *secondo* there was a chicken stew that had little in the way of chicken but a great deal of greens and potatoes, all of it delicious. She ate every bit of her food, and drank the entire glass of wine Aldo poured for her, and even finished the cup of *caffè d'orzo* she was given at the end.

All the while, she wondered how she would get through to the end of the day. How was it that she was so tired? Not even the long nights helping her father on his visits to patients had left her so exhausted, and she'd never been an idle sort of person. Yet one morning of chores had left her flatter than a week-old cornhusk mattress.

"Agnese, Angela, you finished ages ago. Time for you to get started on the henhouse," Rosa ordered.

"Would you like me to help?" Nina asked. It would make a nice change to be outside.

"You can clean the parlor," Rosa said.

"Lucky you," Agnese said. "It takes forever to clean up all the chicken poop."

"I don't like the chickens," Angela added. "It hurts when they peck."

Rosa glared at the girls. "Enough with the coarse talk while others are still eating." Then she turned her attention back to Nina. "Start by dusting everything, and don't forget the picture frames. The girls always forget."

"I won't forget."

"You can wipe down the upholstery with a damp cloth, but make sure it's almost dry or it will mark the fabric. Then you can scrub the floor."

"No one has set a single toe in the parlor since last Saturday," Niccolò observed. "Wouldn't it be enough for Nina to wipe down the floor?"

"I suppose that's fine."

The parlor was absolutely crammed with furniture, all of it old but shining with polish and in pristine condition. In the middle of the room was a large oval table, an intricate doily at its center. An ornately carved settee stood before the single lace-curtained window, its upholstery a lowering but practical shade of dark brown. Half a dozen high-backed chairs ringed the room's perimeter, and upon the walls were a similar number of religious prints and photographs of frowning people with weathered features and serious eyes. There was a crucifix, too, and, on a tall pillar in the corner, a statue of a woman in blue robes. The Virgin Mary, she supposed.

It took her three hours to dust the room, every square centimeter of it, and then a further hour to wipe away a week's worth of dust from the terra-cotta-tiled floor, though much of that time was spent in moving around pieces of furniture and then in ensuring she'd restored them to the exact position they'd occupied before.

And then, just as she was stumbling to her feet, Niccolò appeared at the door.

"Finished? It looks perfect. Rosa will be pleased."

"Good." She didn't have the energy to say more than that.

"We'll have supper in a few minutes—just some soup and bread. Then baths for everyone."

Nina told herself she'd feel better after a bath, but then the manner and nature of how she'd take her bath became horribly clear.

There was a wooden tub, only just big enough for a single adult if they didn't mind pulling their knees right to their chest, and it was rolled out from under the sink and set in front of the hearth, and then—she had a feeling this was for her benefit, as there was a good deal of fussing over where exactly it should go—Niccolò and his father set a wooden clothes dryer draped with towels around the tub.

The boys set to filling the tub with buckets of cold water from the tap at the sink, Rosa added a kettle's worth of boiling water, and then the bath was ready.

"You go first," Aldo told his son. "I'm covered in dust from the stables. I'll only muddy the water."

So Niccolò went behind the screen and began to undress, right there in the kitchen, even though she and his sisters were still there. She could see his bare, freckled shoulders from where she sat, and she could hear him splashing and scrubbing himself with the bar of soap Rosa handed him. In a few short minutes he was out and dressing himself, fortunately still behind the screen, and then Aldo did the same, without anyone bothering to change the water.

As soon as their father was finished and dressed again, the boys dragged the tub outside; she could hear it being emptied into the vegetable garden. Back in it came, to be painstakingly filled a second time. Then Rosa disappeared behind the screen.

It was Nina's turn after that, and though Niccolò, his father, and the older boys had left the kitchen, there were still four other people in the room. She undressed hurriedly, almost furtively, and stepped into the tub. The water wasn't very warm, and it was rather unpleasant to think of it having been used once already, but the soap smelled of lemons and it was wonderful to wash away the sweat and grime of the past three days.

"Don't take too long," Rosa said. "The children are waiting for their turn."

"Sorry. I'll just wash my hair quickly." Nina ducked her

head, scrubbed her scalp with the soap until it stung, and ducked again under the water.

"Would you like me to rinse your hair?"

"Yes, please."

Rosa came to stand behind her, and Nina dutifully bent her head and wondered, just at the last second, if the water would be cold, but it was warm, or close to warm, and it felt heavenly as it sluiced over her head and back.

The boys returned to empty and refill the tub as soon as she'd dried herself and got dressed, and then it was the girls' turn, with Rosa helping them with their hair, and it was emptied and refilled once more so the boys might wash. The water they'd used, when it was emptied after Carlo had finished, was so gray that Rosa exclaimed it would kill every plant in the garden.

Niccolò and Aldo returned then, having settled the animals for the night, but rather than go straight upstairs they listened to music on the radio, Rosa set her sisters' hair in rag curlers, and Nina, despite her tiredness, wished she had something to keep her hands occupied. Tomorrow she would ask Rosa if there was any darning or mending she might do. Tomorrow, when she wasn't quite so tired, and the peace in the kitchen wasn't quite so fragile, and she had a better sense of where in this family she belonged.

Chapter 9

Again she woke at dawn.

"Nico?"

"I'm here. You should go back to sleep. We don't go to Mass for hours yet."

Mass. Her stomach churned just to think of it. Last night he had offered to explain it to her—what to expect and how she ought to behave—but she had fallen asleep before he had so much as unbuttoned his shirt.

"What time do we leave?"

"Mass begins at half-past eight, but the bells start chiming at eight o'clock. We'll leave then."

"What shall I wear?"

The bed groaned as he sat to lace up his boots. "What sort of clothes would you typically wear to Sabbath services?"

"The best of my everyday clothes. I didn't dress up too much. Mamma used to say we weren't meant to look like we were going to a party."

"My mother would have agreed with her."

"Should I bring a scarf to cover my hair?"

"Only the older women here do that, and the younger ones don't really bother with hats. That's something for city girls," he said with a grin.

She fell back asleep after he left to care for the animals, but woke as soon as she heard the children's voices in the kitchen. Breakfast was polenta and milk, again, and Rosa refused her offer to help with the dishes, again, so Nina retreated to her room and set about getting dressed for church. She wasn't sure what Rosa would wear, nor did she feel she could ask, so she chose the dress she'd worn for her twenty-first birthday two years before, its pretty blue fabric still crisp and bright.

She was brushing her hair when Nico knocked at the door.

"Come in," she answered. "I'm done now—I'll go downstairs."

"No need. I'll tell you about Mass while I dress. The others are in the kitchen or outside."

She sat on the bed and turned her back, and as he changed out of his work clothes he told her what to expect.

"To start, the service is in Latin, not Italian, so hardly anyone there truly understands what Father Bernardi is saying. It's all memory—we just say the words in the order we learned them when we were little."

"That's a little bit like services at home. I only understand a bit of the . . . well. You know. Where will I be sitting?"

"With me. Men and women sit together in Catholic churches. So it will be easy for you to watch what I'm doing and parrot it as best you can. When it's time for Holy Communion, you'll follow me to the front and we'll kneel at the altar rail, and when

Father Bernardi comes near you'll open your mouth so he can put the host on your tongue. Then you'll make the sign of the cross—forehead to navel, left shoulder to right shoulder—and we'll go back to our pew."

"Won't I get in trouble?" she asked, her apprehension growing anew.

"From who? Father Bernardi? He's the one who said you must come to Mass. If it were for any other reason I would discourage you. But in asking you to do this, Father and I are the ones committing a sin, not you."

She was trying to be brave, but so much had been taken from her already—her family, her home, even her true name. And now her faith was going to become another casualty. Never mind that she had never been very certain in her beliefs; they were precious to her, and she could not, would not, give them up for anything or anyone.

"Maybe I should stay behind," she suggested. "You could say that I'm feeling unwell."

"For every Sunday that you live here? That won't work. You need to go to Mass, and you need to take Communion, because if you don't people will notice, and they'll gossip about it, and that will put your life at risk. If I'm to keep the promise I made to your father, you need to do this. Tell me you understand."

"I do," she admitted, for she, too, had made promises to her father. "I'm sorry for fussing."

"You don't have to be sorry about anything. I only wish I didn't have to ask it of you."

The bells in the campanile began to ring; it was time to leave.

"Are you dressed?" she asked.

"Yes. What do you think?"

He was wearing a dark suit and tie, and though the shoulders were a little tight on his jacket, and the collar of his shirt was beginning to fray, he still looked very handsome and respectable.

"You look very well."

"As do you, Signora Gerardi. Now let's introduce you to Mezzo Ciel."

It was only a few hundred meters back up the road to the church, not long enough to run into more than a few of their neighbors, but as soon as they entered the piazza she felt the force of dozens of eyes upon her, all wondering and judging and possibly finding her wanting. This was more than usual curiosity, it seemed, for there was an avidity to those first assessing stares, and it only grew more noticeable when they entered the church.

The interior of Santa Lucia was far plainer than the Scola Spagnola her family had attended for generations, and there was no women's gallery, only a central aisle with flanking pews where men and women and children all gathered together.

She ought not to have been surprised, for Nico had said she would be sitting with him, but it was a shock all the same. In the *scola* at home, the women sat in a gallery high above the sanctuary; the stairs were a daunting obstacle to all but the fittest and youngest among them, and there were some who complained. Never her mother, though. Mamma had always insisted they were lucky to have such a view of their magnificent *scola*. "Only birds on the wing could hope to see as well as we do up here."

Nico led them to one of the left-hand pews about halfway down the aisle and gestured for her to go in first. "Signora Rossi behind us is deaf," he whispered in her ear, "and the pew in front is broken, so no one ever sits there. Just remember to copy what I do."

He took a cushion from its hook on the pew in front and knelt upon it, so she did the same, and then, as everyone else bent their heads in prayer, she looked around discreetly and tried to make sense of the church's strange interior. She would remember every detail, and one day, when she was again at home with her parents, she would be able to tell them all about it.

There was no decoration to speak of, apart from a series of wall plaques in high relief, their paint badly faded, and several oil paintings so black with age that their subjects were impossible to discern. At the front was an elevated area, separated from the rest of the church by a low wooden rail; at its center was a table draped in an embroidered cloth. Candles in tall brass holders flanked the table, and to the side, in a sort of alcove, was a rather alarming statue of a dying Christ on the cross, larger than life size and naked apart from a small cloth around his midsection, his painted blood flowing from an abundance of wounds. Directly ahead was another elevated statue, this one almost exactly the same as the one in the parlor at the house, only here the woman had a golden crown, and there were rows of candles in a tiered metal frame at her feet.

Bowing her head, Nina tried to arrange her thoughts into something resembling prayer, but she couldn't find it in herself to concentrate. It was silent in the church, but only superficially so, for around them a constant chorus of whispers and shuffling rose and fell, the counterpoint an occasional deafening sneeze from an older man standing on the opposite side of the aisle.

"That's my zio Beppe," Nico whispered. "His hay fever starts in March and doesn't let up until November."

Nico had just bent his head again, likely to whisper another diverting comment in Nina's ear, when a pair of sharply hissing voices pierced the imperfect silence.

"That's the one. No, over there. The one who persuaded him to abandon the priesthood."

"She's not much to look at. What was he thinking?"

"I *know*. All those years of work and study just *gone,* and for what?"

"Poor thing. Of course, Rosa will carve her into little pieces."

"That she will. Oh, to be a fly on their wall!"

That's when Nico turned around. He didn't say a word, but Nina could feel the weight of his pinioning stare.

Facing forward once again, he bent his head to whisper in Nina's ear. "I'm sorry."

"I'm fine. I'm impressed at how quickly you quieted them."

"It's one of the first things we learn in the seminary. How to scowl at people who whisper during Mass." And then he nudged her shoulder, just a little, to show he was joking. Or only *mostly* joking.

It ought not to hurt. Nico wasn't really her husband, and he hadn't truly abandoned anything for her. When the war was over, and she was safely home, they would be free to tell the truth about the fiction they'd concocted, and Nico would continue with his life, seminary or no seminary, on his own.

What hurt rather more was the gossips' belief that she was incapable of doing her fair share of work on the farm. She'd completed every task Rosa had given her yesterday and she hadn't complained, not once. She was smart, and strong, and she would fit in.

She would make those gossips eat their words.

"Nina," Nico whispered. "The bells have stopped. Mass is starting."

Everyone stood and began to sing, but without a cantor to lead them the resulting chorus wasn't particularly tuneful. Father Bernardi passed by, followed by a troop of little boys about the same age as Carlo, and the following hour was an unnerving blur of standing and kneeling and sitting and kneeling and moving her lips like a ghost.

When it was time for the Communion part of things she followed Nico to the front and knelt at the altar rail, her heart pounding like mad because surely the other churchgoers would see that she didn't belong. She did remember to open her mouth, just in time, and Father Bernardi placed a dry little cracker on her tongue, and after she'd swallowed it and traced a cross with her hand she followed Nico back to their pew and knelt until it was time to sit again, the taste of the Communion wafer still bitter on her tongue.

At last the Mass was done. As they waited for their turn to file outside, Nico touched her arm and bent to whisper in her ear. "We'll stop to say hello to Father. I know he'll make a show of welcoming you. That will go a long way to quieting the village gossips."

The church was full, so it was a few minutes before they

reached Father Bernardi, who stood at the steps and greeted everyone who passed by name.

"Good morning, Niccolò. And good morning to you, Signora Gerardi. My sincere felicitations on your marriage. We are so happy to have you here in Mezzo Ciel."

"Thank you, Father Bernardi."

"You are settling in well?"

"Yes, Father. Everyone has been very kind to me."

"Good, good. Niccolò has been singing your praises for months now. Needless to say, I am delighted that he has chosen such a lovely young woman to be his wife."

And that was that. Father Bernardi had announced his approval in front of the entire village. And Nina had survived her first Catholic Mass.

They went home to lunch, which Rosa prepared with the help of the girls, steadfastly ignoring Nina's offers to help, and then Nico took her on another walk, this one leading them up into the fields above the farmhouse.

"I'm sorry again for those women in church. You will tell me if anyone else is unkind to you?"

"I will," she promised, although she had no intention of doing any such thing. "Doesn't it bother you, though? Having people gossip about you that way? As if you've broken some kind of law?"

They'd come to the banks of a stream, and he now sat down, his long legs spread out straight before him, and beckoned her to join him.

"Why should it bother me?" he now asked. "They can't see inside my heart."

"But they said you'd wasted all those years of work and study—"

"What do they know of it? It wasn't a waste." And then, grinning, "I've only forgotten the boring bits."

"I'm trying to be serious," she protested, though she was tempted to answer his smile with one of her own. "By helping me, have you closed a door you might wish to open again one day?"

"Not in the least. If anything, it's set me free. I was so young when I left here." He paused, and it seemed as if he were considering how best to explain. "When Father Bernardi first asked my parents if they'd let me go away to school, it felt like I'd been given this wonderful chance for a life beyond Mezzo Ciel. But the longer I studied, the less sure of myself I became. And the longer I was away, the more I wished to come home."

"And what if you change your mind?" she pressed.

"About you? The best wife I've ever had?" They both smiled at this, but she couldn't ignore what he hadn't said.

"Had you hoped to marry one day?"

He nodded, his smile more tentative now. "I had."

"But my being here—"

"Is good. It is. You may not be my wife, but you are becoming my friend. And for that, Signora Gerardi, I am truly thankful."

Chapter 10

27 October 1943

How was it possible that she'd spent the first twenty-three years of her life with no real notion of where the food she ate was grown? Of the labor that went into its cultivation and harvest? It had simply appeared in shop windows and on market stalls, sorted and washed and neatly displayed, and she had handed over a few coins and never once stopped to think of the true cost of bringing it to her doorstep.

She understood now.

She'd been in Mezzo Ciel for barely more than a month. So little time set against the span of her life; but now, thinking back, she found it hard to remember how she had once filled her days.

She hadn't been idle, not exactly, for she had helped her father, she had studied, she had done the marketing each day and had helped Marta with some of the chores—though not, she could now admit, any of the really difficult or disagreeable ones. Certainly she had never scrubbed a floor until her knees and back were aching, or stripped the feathers from a still-warm and very freshly dead chicken, or picked the pebbles from a pan of dried lentils until her eyes burned.

And she did so little work compared to Rosa, who never seemed to sit, who went to bed after the rest of them and was up again before sunrise, who kept them fed and did the laundry and cleaned the kitchen after every meal and, in her idle moments, baked bread, canned vegetables, made soap, and mended their clothes.

Dominating everything was the harvest, which wasn't so much a finite period as a steadily swelling tide of work that soon consumed every waking hour. First was the haying, with Nico and Aldo swinging the scythes and everyone except Rosa, who was kept busy in the kitchen, raking the felled grasses down the hillside until they lay in great golden drifts to dry in the sun. Nina had done her best, but the wooden rake had blistered her fingers and she'd been so much slower than the others that Carlo had been bidden to help her.

Next they'd all worked to cut and bundle the drying stalks from the cornfield, then they'd lifted the potatoes, then they'd gathered the last of the carrots and onions, turnips and cabbages, apples and pears and pumpkins, all to be stored in the *cantina* beneath the house. And still there were vineyards to be weeded and bare fields to be turned and sown. Nor was there any respite from their everyday chores, with Nico and Aldo rising at four o'clock every morning to milk the cows, feed the animals, and muck out the stalls and pens. When they and the older boys came home after sunset each night, all four were silent and hollow-eyed with exhaustion.

Each day brought new lessons for Nina and new mistakes, too, some of them costly: dropping a pan of shelled beans in the mud, tripping on the stairs while carrying down the chamber pot from the boys' room, letting the milk scorch when Rosa had asked her to mind it.

She wasn't usually so clumsy or forgetful. Before, she had taken pride in how quickly she learned, how easily she managed tasks that others found difficult. Hadn't Papà told her that she was as bright as any of his students? Hadn't his patients complimented her again and again on how kind and helpful she was during her father's visits?

Niccolò and the others made allowances, and they explained away her mistakes by telling her the beans could be rinsed, the stairs could be scrubbed clean, the ruined milk could still feed the animals. But with every new failure she grew more nervous, and less certain of herself, and Rosa's silent disapproval grew ever more glacial.

AFTER LUNCH NINA told the girls she would gather the plates and scrape the scraps into the pail for the chickens. There wasn't much, only some stalks of escarole that Carlo could not be induced to eat. She'd gone to the shelf by the sink where Rosa kept the pail, and was about to push Carlo's leavings in, when the plate was abruptly snatched from her hands.

"You're not wasting that on the chickens—how many times have I told you already? Give it to me."

Rosa went to scrape the scraps into the pot of soup already simmering away, but in turning she bumped against Nina and dropped the plate on the tiled floor.

"That was one of my mother's good plates," she fumed, dropping to her knees and scrabbling for the scattered pieces. "How *could* you?"

"I'm sorry—"

"Did you ever do a decent day's work before coming here? Didn't your mother teach you *anything*? And now we have to feed you, and clean up your messes, and—"

"Enough!" It was too much to bear. Too much, and she was far too tired, and lonely, and achingly sad, and more than anything weighed down by grief for her lost home, her life, and her beloved parents, to bear another word of Rosa's unthinking vitriol. "How *dare* you judge me? You know nothing about me. Nothing of what I've lost—and it's more than a plate. Far more."

They stared at one another for a moment, so shocked they had forgotten to breathe, and then Nina sank into a nearby chair, her legs too wobbly to hold her any longer. What had she done?

Rosa stood, leaving the shattered plate where it was, and sat next to Nina. "I'm—"

"Please. Not now."

"I was going to say that I'm sorry. It wasn't right, what I said."

"The thing is . . . you aren't wrong," Nina admitted. "I haven't ever worked this hard before. And I know I'm clumsy and I never seem to get things right. But I *am* trying."

Rosa sighed, but there was no anger or bitterness in it. Only exhaustion. If ever there were time for a peace offering, this was it.

"You're tired," Nina said. "Let me finish the dishes—I promise I'll be careful. And you can sit down for a minute."

"If I do, I'll never get up again. But if you do the washing up I can get started on soaking the boys' trousers. Caked in mud up to the knees, and their socks are just as bad. Nico's are more hole than sock, too. Lord only knows what he does to them."

"I can darn them. I used to— I mean, I know how to darn and do the mending." She'd almost said that she used to mend her papà's socks and clothing, but she was meant to be an orphan. There never would have been a father's socks to darn.

She took over from Rosa, trying not to flinch when she dipped her hands in the scalding-hot water. There were only a few plates left, and once they were clean and dry and put away, she collected up the dishpan, using the edges of her apron so it wouldn't slip from her hands, and carried it outside to water the rows of winter chicory and kale.

Rosa was back in the kitchen, her attention fixed on a pair of mud-laden socks, when Nina returned. "What should I do now?"

"The table needs scrubbing, then you can sweep the floor in here. After that's done you can help me start the bread for tomorrow, and there's a mountain of mending, too. You might as well get to it while there's still daylight."

That night when Nina fell into bed she was worn out, and her fingers were so raw they throbbed, but her heart didn't feel quite so heavy. It didn't seem likely that she and Rosa would ever be friends, for they were too different, had no shared interests, had yet to have a single conversation that didn't re-volve around the work they had done and the work they had yet to do. But it was a start, all the same, and simply thinking of it helped to unravel some of the loneliness that pinched at her heart.

She woke briefly when Nico came to bed; he and Aldo had still been in the fields when she and the others had eaten their supper. It was a comfort to feel him beside her, and she meant to tell him she was doing better and that Rosa had been happy with her work, but the moment his weight settled next to her, and she felt the comforting cadence of his slowing and deep-ening breaths against her back, she, too, was dragged back into slumber.

THE NEXT DAY, just after breakfast, Nina and the girls were given the task of helping Nico haul the corn down from the granary. It was the first time she'd been to the top floor of the house, which was long and low-ceilinged and dim behind its shuttered windows, and when her eyes finally adjusted to the light she had to stifle a scream at the sight of mice, dozens upon dozens of them, scurrying in every direction. And was that a rat slinking away?

"Your barn cats aren't doing much to earn their keep," she exclaimed, embarrassed at how nervous those darting shadows made her feel.

"There's a limit to their appetites, unfortunately. And the mice won't hurt you. They're barely as big as your smallest toe."

The baskets were large and heavy, so it was a good thing they had Nico's help. He was able to carry two at a time, but Nina and the girls could manage only one between them. It took all morning to get the baskets outside and lined up in the court-yard.

After lunch, with Carlo returned from school, they got started on the shelling. Nico had already set out the machine they would use, fixing it to the edge of a big wooden tub, and now he showed Nina—and reminded the children—how it worked.

"It's simple. Put the cob in the hole here at the top, with the stalk end pointing up, and turn the crank. As the cob goes through, the kernels are stripped off, like so, and the cob pops out the top."

"That doesn't look so hard."

"The cobs are good and dry, so the kernels should come off easily. It's hard on the arms, though—you'll want to take turns."

"And when the tub is full?"

"Transfer the kernels to these sacks, and I'll take them along to the miller."

At this Carlo sighed. "More polenta. Ugh. I hate polenta."

"Rosa says we are lucky to have it," Agnese insisted, ever the serious one. "There are starving children who have far less than we do."

"Agnese is right," said Nico, "but I get tired of polenta, too. What if we ask Rosa to put a little cheese on top of yours? How does that sound?"

Carlo was unconvinced. "I'd much rather have a big slice

of fresh bread, right out of the oven, with so much jam on top that it drips off the edges and makes all the wasps come flying over."

"Enough of that," his brother protested, "or you'll have Nina and the girls daydreaming of jam and not paying attention to the shelling machine, and then I'll come back from the fields to discover the girls have accidentally stuffed *you* through the sheller. There will be kernels of Carlo everywhere, and then we'll really be in trouble with Rosa. You know how much she hates a mess."

Nico stood, dusting the dirt from his knees, and then bent to kiss his brother's head. "I'll be off. Do watch out for the children's fingers," he said, this time to Nina, "and have them collect the scattered kernels. Otherwise the hens will gobble everything up."

They worked for hours to shell the corn and tidy the cobs, which would be used to fuel the range come winter, into the bins where they would dry out even more. By the time they finished, Nina's arms were so sore she could barely hold her spoon at supper. The children were worn out, too, Carlo most of all, and it took far longer than usual for him to eat his soup and bread.

When Rosa moved to clear away his bowl, he sighed gustily and looked longingly at the basket where the bread was kept. It hung from a nail in the ceiling beam, far out of the children's reach—even Nina had to stand on her tiptoes to reach it.

"I'm still hungry."

Rosa was unmoved. "You had plenty. Have a drink of water if you need to fill your belly."

"But Paolo and Matteo—"

"Your brothers get more because they do more work than you. Off you go to bed, and no more whining."

"I'm not complaining," Nina whispered to Nico that night as they lay, carefully spaced, side by side on their narrow bed. "I'm not. But you work so hard and you have so little to show for it. And I could hear Carlo crying in bed just now, and—"

"He was tired."

"I don't see why he and the girls can't have a little more to eat if they say they're hungry. Especially when the *cantina* is full of food."

"That food needs to last us until the summer. If we feast now we'll starve later."

"But—"

"It was even worse when I was a boy. On the mornings when the bread was baked, the smell was enough to drive me mad. All that fresh bread, loaves and loaves of it, but Mamma could only give us a little slice each. It was never enough to take away the hunger."

"But you grow the wheat yourselves, and you have your own bread oven—"

"We can't afford to fire the oven more than once a week. And most of the wheat goes to pay the *ammassi*."

"Can't we just buy bread? There's a bakery in the village." She shouldn't be nagging at him like this, but it made so little sense to her.

"We could, but we also have to buy things like fresh seed and tools, fabric for Rosa to make our clothes, shoes when ours are too worn for the cobbler to repair—and for most of those things, we barter what we do have. Eggs, the cheese Rosa makes, the ham and *sopressa* from the pig. There are taxes to pay, too—even the meat from the pig is taxed. And there's the electricity to pay for, and the tithe for the church, and we try to have some set aside for the doctor, or for a funeral if the worst should happen. And still there is never enough."

"I thought the *ammassi* was a way for everyone to get their fair share." That's what it had said in the newspapers.

"No. It means only that we're forced to sell most of our wheat and potato crop to the government so they can turn around and sell it to the rest of the country for double the price. That's what the government calls fair shares." He covered his eyes with his hands, even though the room was near to pitch-dark.

"You must let me help. I have some jewelry with me. We could—"

"We can't. For us to suddenly appear with money, with gold—it would attract the sort of attention we must avoid. But I thank you all the same."

"My being here has made things harder. I know it has."

At this he sighed. "My sister and her sharp tongue."

"She apologized. And it *is* true."

"It isn't. You are helping. Your being here does make life easier for all of us."

Now he turned to her, his body shifting slowly, carefully, on the noisy and too-narrow bed. A beam of moonlight, creeping through a crack in the shutters, fell across his face.

"I have to leave. Not for good. Only for a few weeks." He had said something of the sort before, but she had hoped . . .

"I'll be helping Father Bernardi," he added. "And I do so with my father's blessing."

"Helping in what way?"

"It's better if I don't explain. Safer. One day, perhaps."

"You will come back?"

"Yes. I promise I will. I . . ."

His voice drifted away, along with the moonlight, and the room was dark again, and cold, but his body was warm, and so welcome, and as long as he was next to her she wasn't alone.

She tried not to think of how lonely she would be when he was gone. She would keep herself busy, and she would work harder than ever, so hard that she would fall asleep the moment she doused the lamp each night. And she would count the days until he returned.

Chapter 11

15 November 1943

*I*t was Monday, laundry day, the day of the week they all disliked the most. It began at eight o'clock, as soon as Carlo had left for school and the water in the big kettles had reached a rolling boil. The wooden laundry tub was already in place, set on a stool so Rosa didn't have to stoop quite so low, and once the hot water was mixed with just enough cold to stop it from stripping the skin from their hands, and Rosa had whisked in scoops of washing soda and her homemade soap, the business of laundering their clothes and linens began.

Rosa trusted no one else to get things truly clean, so she was the one who labored the hardest and longest, her hands constantly scrubbing. Only once she was satisfied did she give each item to Nina and the girls. It was their job to wring everything out, then layer it all in an array of wicker baskets that went on the back of Bello's cart for the journey uphill to the stream.

That took all morning, and by the time they stopped for lunch—always leftover soup, for there was no time for anything else—their hands and forearms were red and raw from the scalding water and harsh lye soap. On Mondays the men stayed well away from the house at midday.

Nina had just finished eating when some instinct had her glance at the calendar, which was tacked to the wall just below a framed photograph of the pope. November. It was November already, and that meant she had missed the High Holy days.

Rosh Hashanah had been less than a week after her arrival in Mezzo Ciel, Yom Kippur ten days after that, and they had passed by without her even noticing. Her parents would have been thinking of her, praying for her, but the days had swept by, governed only by the rhythm of the farm and her work and her self-pity, and she had forgotten.

It was enough to bring her to her knees, this longing for home, for all that was familiar, for all that she loved and had been forced to abandon. All its rituals and rhythms, sounds and tastes, faces and places and voices—all of it had been taken from her, and she was alone now, far from her parents, a world away from everyone and everything she had once known and loved.

"Is anything wrong?" came Agnese's soft voice. "You were making such a face just now."

"No. I have a . . . a sore tooth. That's all."

"Rosa has some oil of cloves," Angela said. "That's what she uses when we get a toothache. That might help."

Carlo wrinkled his nose. "It makes my tongue burn."

"I'm fine. Now go and help Rosa load up the cart while I take care of the dishes."

The others went on ahead while Nina did the washing up and swept the floor, and then she went to follow them, her thoughts turned resolutely away from the calendar and its depressing reminders. The sun was bright, the sky was clear and endlessly blue, and the journey to the stream was exactly what she needed to clear her head.

She walked past the vegetable garden to the bottom of the big fields, empty now and waiting for their seeding of winter wheat, then east along the rutted path, then north again, the land growing ever steeper, until she could hear running water and the sound of the girls' chatter. Up and over a hillock she climbed, her boots slipping a little on the pebbles, and down to the grassy bank where Rosa and the girls were rinsing the morning's laundry in the stream.

"I'm here," she called out cheerily. "Do you want me to bring you another basket?"

"Yes," Rosa answered. "The one with the sheets."

Nina heaved the basket down from the cart and lugged it to the edge of the stream, where a border of wide, flat stones was set into the ground. Although the stones made it a tidier spot for the women to work, they were also awfully hard on their knees. It would be Wednesday or Thursday, Nina knew, before hers would stop aching.

The stream was pretty but its water was breathtakingly cold, and before she'd finished rinsing even a single pillowcase her hands were numb. Dunking, shaking, squeezing, again and again, and still there was more water to wring out. She paused a few times, rubbing her hands on her skirt, trying to restore some feeling, but as soon as she'd warmed them it was time for another shirt, another bedsheet, until her entire body was chilled through despite the golden sun and bluest of blue skies.

Back into the baskets everything went, then down the hill again, Bello refusing to be rushed, and while Rosa made supper she and the girls pegged out everything on the lines that ran from the house to the first of the grapevines, all the while hoping the sun would hold for a little while longer.

She was almost too tired to eat her supper—they all were—but she dutifully helped to bring in and fold the still-damp laundry so it might be hung out again in the morning. Then Aldo switched on the radio, Rosa brought out her homemade salve of beeswax and olive oil for their aching hands, and the girls sang along to their favorite songs.

When the news came on at nine o'clock, Nina wasn't listening, not properly. She'd been turning the heel on a sock she was knitting, always the trickiest part, and just keeping track of the stitches occupied all her attention. At first it hadn't even seemed like something important. There was a congress in Verona, a meeting of the new fascist party, and they'd adopted a manifesto.

"The following constitutes a summary of the principal points that were agreed upon today. In regard to constitutional and internal—"

"The same rubbish as always," Aldo grumbled, and the newsreader droned on, and Nina knitted stitch after careful stitch, her thoughts pleasantly vague.

"Point number six. The religion of the republic is the Roman Catholic Apostolic faith. Any other religion that does not conflict with the law is respected. Point number seven. The members of the Jewish race are foreigners. During this war they belong to an enemy nationality. In regard to foreign policy . . ."

Foreigner. *Enemy.*

She pushed back from the table, the chair legs skittering across the terra-cotta tiles. She stood, not caring when her knitting dropped to the floor and a row of stitches popped free.

"Excuse me. I'm not . . . I'm tired. Good night."

"Is it your tooth again?" Agnese asked.

"I think she misses Nico," Carlo chimed in.

It was true, for Nico would know how to make her feel better. He would know, better than anyone, what to say to take away her fear. But she couldn't admit any of that to the children.

"No, dears. Only that I'm tired. That's all."

She hurried upstairs to bed, to the cocooning shelter of the covers, to the blessed anonymity of dark and silence and solitude. She couldn't stop shivering.

She missed Nico so much. He'd left . . . she couldn't remember how long it had been. Five days ago? Six? He'd warned her he was going away, as he'd done the time before, and he'd said he expected to be gone for at least ten days.

Another five days to wait—that was all. He'd return soon, and he would have answers for her then. Not long at all.

A HAND WAS at her shoulder, pulling her from the comfort of sleep.

"Nina. I need your help."

"Papà?" It had been so long since he had woken her in the night.

"No, darling. It's Nico. I'm sorry to wake you, but I need your help."

"What's wrong? Is it one of the children?"

"No, no. They're fine. I have some people with me. They need food, a safe place to sleep, and—"

"I only need a moment to change."

"Thank you. I'll leave the lamp behind."

She dressed quickly, slipping on a pair of Nico's socks in lieu of stockings, and tiptoed downstairs.

A family, a very tired and frightened family, was huddled around the kitchen table, and Rosa, from the smell of things, was heating up some soup. Two children, hardly more than toddlers, clung to their mother, and the father held a young baby tight to his chest.

She'd taken care to be quiet, but all the same they were startled when she came into the kitchen, their eyes widening in alarm.

"It's all right," Nico said, his voice low and soothing. "This is my wife. She will help." And then, turning to Nina, "The little boy here has a sprained ankle. Took a tumble in the dark. And they all have cuts and scrapes."

"Do you want me to see to them now?"

"They should eat first."

"Where will we put them?"

"I'll show you."

She followed him upstairs and into their bedroom. "Shall

we make up pallets on the floor for the children? I'm not sure the bed will hold all—"

She watched, astonished, as he took the chair from its usual spot by the window and carried it to the far corner of the room. Standing on it, his head just brushing against the crossed beams, he reached up and pushed at the ceiling. Something heavy moved back with a faint groan—a trapdoor. In one fluid motion, he pulled himself up and through, vanishing into the dark.

She edged forward but could see nothing in the space above. "Nico?"

The lower rungs of a slender wooden ladder appeared, followed by his face, gaunt and unfamiliar in the shadows.

"Help me set it down—there. Yes. And I need the lamp. Just to make sure the bedding isn't full of mice."

She heard him walking about, then the familiar sound of cornhusk mattresses being shaken, and then his returning steps. He handed her the lamp and climbed down the ladder.

"But I've been in the granary. There's nothing—"

"A partition wall."

"You never told me."

"I had planned on telling you when I came home this time. In case you ever need a place to hide."

"Will the Germans come looking for them?"

"I don't think so, not tonight. But they could, which is why I'm cautious."

In the kitchen, Rosa had set out the first-aid box, a large basin of warm water, and some clean cloths. After binding the little boy's ankle, Nina tended to the others' cuts and scrapes with soap and water and gentle swipes of iodine.

She led them up the stairs and stood aside as Nico and the father of the little family helped everyone up the ladder.

"Here is the lamp, but keep the flame low," Nico cautioned. "There is a chamber pot, and I'll bring food and more water in the morning. Try to sleep as much as you can. We'll be on our way again as soon as night falls."

The ladder was pulled up, the trapdoor fell shut, and soon there was silence.

"I'll go down and fetch in my father," Nico whispered. "I won't be long."

Nina changed back into her nightgown and returned to bed, her mind brimming with questions, her heart tight with fear. She didn't need to be told who the refugees were fleeing. She didn't need to be told what would happen if they were found.

She was afraid for Nico, too, and his family, and not only because of the people who now hid in the granary. They would be gone in a day, but she would stay on. The mere fact of her presence was enough to doom every last one of them, and never mind that they were unaware she was a Jew, and very nearly a stranger to Nico, and not truly part of their family. The Germans certainly wouldn't care when they executed Nico as a bandit, consigned his father and brothers to labor camps, and stripped the farm of every animal, tool, and scrap of food. They wouldn't think twice about leaving Rosa and the children to starve.

Nico came back into their room, his footsteps soft and

measured, and doused the light straightaway. He unlaced his boots, toed them off, and then got into bed, his movements slow and deliberate, his body facing her.

"I don't dare undress," he whispered.

"Who are they?"

"Best I don't tell you."

"They're running from—"

"Yes."

"Is that what you do when you go away?"

"Yes. And the reason I'm not telling you everything isn't because I don't trust you. I do. But it's safer if you know as little as possible."

"Is it a usual thing to bring people here?"

"No—this is only the second time I've done it. I know it's dangerous. I know I'm risking the lives of the people I love the most. Tonight, though, and the time before . . . it was the only way. I had nowhere else to go. There were too many of them to take to the rectory, and I needed someone to see to their injuries."

"There's a doctor in Mezzo Ciel, isn't there?"

"Dr. Pivetti is a dyed-in-the-wool fascist. He'd turn us in and sleep all the more soundly for it."

"What does your father think? Rosa?"

"Do you think my sister would let me do this if she didn't agree?"

It was almost enough to make her laugh. "True enough. Though I can't help worrying that my being here puts all of you in danger. I think we should find somewhere else for me to go."

"Don't say that."

"It's true. You shouldn't have to risk so much for me. What have I done to deserve such kindness?"

"It isn't something you're expected to earn, Nina. You have the right to be safe here. This is your country as much as it is mine."

"I wouldn't blame you for looking away," she insisted. "I would understand."

A whisper of movement, then his fingertips brushed across her forehead. So gentle. So kind.

"You might forgive me, but I could never forgive myself. If I were to stand aside, I'd be no better than those who persecute you."

"I heard it on the radio tonight. The manifesto."

"Yes. And even worse . . ."

"Tell me," she implored.

"There have been roundups. Not in Venice, not yet. But elsewhere they've been arresting all the Jews they can find. Last month in Milan, Turin, Rome. Last week it was Florence. The people they arrest are put on trains. Some they send to the camp in Fossoli. The others . . . I don't know. We don't know where they are sent."

"Mamma and Papà—"

"Are where you saw them last. Can you hold on to that? If only for tonight? You need to sleep—we both do. And in the morning we'll talk more."

In seconds the peace of sleep overtook him, and she was left alone with her thoughts. He wasn't her husband. He wasn't her lover. He was, instead, her beloved friend. A man who ought not to exist in a time such as this. And what had she done to deserve the kindness he had shown her? Why had she been rescued when others were pursued, captured, imprisoned?

There was no reason for it. Pure chance had led her to Mezzo Ciel, to this farm, to this man. A stroke of fortune alone had saved her—and the same fortune might just as easily consign her to oblivion.

How was she to sleep, to rest, with the weight of such knowledge pressing down upon her? And how might she learn to live with it?

Chapter 12

30 November 1943

"I've the last of the ironing to do this morning," Rosa said to Nina after breakfast. "While I'm busy with that, you and the girls can go to the store for me. We've two dozen eggs. That should be enough to pay for everything."

"With eggs?"

"How else would we pay? With gold? Don't worry—Signor Favaro will be fair with you. He'd better, or I'll have something to say about it. Here's my list."

Nina hadn't yet gone to the store; that task usually fell to Rosa or Aldo, who tended to be late returning because he liked to stop at the osteria for a glass of wine with his friends. Only on Sundays did Nina ever leave the farm, and that was only for Mass.

The day was gray and cool, but the girls skipped along as if the weather was perfectly fine, and in a matter of minutes they were crossing the piazza. Compared to a Sunday morning, it was almost deserted, with only a handful of people coming in and out of the shops, and the osteria still shuttered.

Nina and the girls had just passed the fountain at the piazza's center when a car drove past them, circled the square, and parked in front of the *carabinieri* station. It was big and dark, as sleek and predatory as a panther, and the sense of unease it awoke in her was only bolstered by the black pennant of the SS that was affixed to its fender.

"That's a German car," Agnese said fearfully. "Why do you think they've come here?"

It was the first automobile Nina had seen in weeks, apart from the occasional delivery lorry trundling past the farm. And she couldn't think of a single good reason for a Nazi officer to be paying a visit to Mezzo Ciel.

"I expect they're lost," she fibbed, not wishing for the girls to worry. "That's probably why they've stopped. To ask for directions."

Agnese was unconvinced. "But Papà always says Officer Dagosta can't even figure out how to find his own nose, so how—"

"Hush!" Nina insisted. "You know better than to talk like that in public. Besides, we need to hurry. We don't want Rosa to be cross with us for taking too long."

The sign for Fratelli Favaro was inconspicuous, a small painted plaque above the door, but the shop itself was impossible to miss, its exterior flanked by garlands of baskets on ropes, sheaves of brooms and mops, and neat towers of stoneware crocks. Inside, the shop's walls were tiled with shelves that rose to the ceiling, each packed tight with wares for sale. Food and grocery goods were at the front on the left, where a white-aproned Signor Favaro stood behind a shining walnut counter, while household items and hardware were to the right, and fabric and ready-made garments were at the very back. That was Signora Favaro's domain, and if there was a second Favaro brother, as promised by the sign, he was absent.

The shopkeeper offered a broad smile as they entered. "Good morning, Signora Gerardi. My felicitations on your recent marriage. How may I serve you this morning?"

"Good morning, Signor Favaro. I have a list of items that my sister-in-law prepared." She handed him the list and, in response to Agnese's nudge, set the basket of eggs on the counter.

"Good, good. Let me see," he said, setting a pair of spectacles on his nose. "*'Eight eggs of lamp oil, six eggs of washing soda, four eggs of cheesecloth, a spool of black thread and another of white if six eggs is enough. Otherwise only the black thread.'* Yes, that is quite in order."

He busied himself gathering the requested items without any further comment, as if paying with eggs rather than lire was entirely to be expected. The girls stood quietly beside her—their manners really were faultless—and together they waited, watching Signor Favaro as he bustled about. All the while, though it was almost impossible not to look out the window and see what was happening with the German car, Nina forced herself to remain still and silent and in so doing set a good example for the girls.

The door opened and closed, a flurry of footsteps sweeping past so quickly that she didn't have time to turn and see who had entered. The newcomers' voices carried, however, and it was impossible not to hear what they were saying. Especially since they were talking about *her*.

"What do you think of her? That Venetian girl Niccolò went and married?"

"Such a timid thing. Have you seen the way she clings to his arm on the way in and out of Mass?"

"Imagine what Rosa has been saying. I mean, you can just *tell* from looking at her that she hasn't the first idea of how to do *anything*."

"What was he thinking?"

"He wasn't using his brain—that's for certain. Typical man. They see a pretty face and *pfft*—they're done for."

"That's Papà's awful cousin and her friend," Agnese whispered. "Don't listen to them. If Rosa were here she'd tell them off."

"It is true, you know," Nina whispered back, and she added a smile so they wouldn't worry. "I didn't know a thing about cleaning and cooking and all the things you already understand so well."

"Maybe at first," Angela admitted, "but you've learned a lot already."

"And I think they call you the Venetian girl because they're jealous," Agnese added. "None of them have ever been to the city. None of them have ever seen the sea."

"Have you?"

"Not yet, but Nico says he'll take us to the seaside after the war. To the Lido."

"That's a wonderful idea, Agnese. We'll all go. We'll sit on the beach and go swimming and we'll eat gelato in every flavor there is."

"I've never had gelato. Is it nice?" Angela asked.

"It is very nice. Of course you don't want to eat it too quickly or it will make your teeth ache, and too much of it will upset your tummy. But on a hot day there is nothing better."

She hadn't been to the Lido for years. Not since the racial laws had come into effect and Jews had been banned from the beach there.

Signor Favaro came hurrying back with their things, and if he'd overheard the conversation between his other customers he gave no sign of it. "Here you are, signora. Mind you don't let the bottle of lamp oil tip over."

"Thank you, Signor Favaro," she said, and she made sure her voice was loud enough to carry all the way to the back. "Good day to you."

The car was gone from the piazza when they emerged from the store, and as she and the girls walked home Nina resolved to let the exchange in the store fade from her mind. The important thing, of course, was that they knew nothing of Antonina Mazin. They only knew of Nina the Venetian girl, the hopelessly citified featherbrain who had turned Niccolò Gerardi's head and was a burden to his entire family. That was the story people would remember, and it was an interesting and believable one as stories went.

The basket was heavy on her arm, but if she carried it Agnese and Angela could skip and run and enjoy themselves for the few hundred meters that stretched between them and a day of chores. They were bright girls, both of them, and ought to have still been in school.

And to know they had never seen the sea. If only she could gather them up and fly through the air to the seaside and buy them gelato and show them how to paddle in the water. If only, indeed. It was almost December, for a start, and the sea was ice-cold, and she had not a single lire in her pocket. Nor did she possess wings.

"Nina! Nina!"

The girls came pelting back along the road, their faces ashen with fear.

"What is it? What is the matter?"

The girls dragged her along, the basket bouncing painfully against her hip, and then they came around the curve and all three stopped short at the unwelcome sight of the car from the piazza, the Nazi officer's car, which was parked in the very middle of the farm's courtyard. Of its occupants Nina saw no sign, but Rosa was standing just outside the kitchen door, Selva a tightly restrained presence at her side.

Every instinct she had told her to flee—to drop the basket and run into the fields, as far as her shaking legs would take her, before it was too late. Yet to do so would be to abandon the girls and Rosa.

"What is happening?" she asked, her voice pitched low, as soon as she reached the other woman.

"I'll tell you in a moment. Girls—inside."

A German officer had emerged from the gloom of the stables and was striding toward them. If she'd met him under different circumstances, she'd have judged him an average sort of man, with an ordinary build and a pleasantly boyish face, his hair a medium shade of brown, his eyes an irresolute blue. One of those harmless types who never quite managed to work up the courage to talk to the prettiest girls at parties.

She could not separate him from his Nazi officer's uniform, however, nor could she forget the pistol that was holstered at his hip, nor the two soldiers who now stood a few paces behind him. There was nothing harmless about any of them.

"Good afternoon, Obersturmführer Zwerger," Rosa said evenly. "I'm sorry I was inside when you arrived. How may I help you?"

"You know very well that I'm here to see your brother, signorina. He and I are old friends, after all."

Only with the greatest difficulty did Nina resist the urge to turn her head and goggle at Rosa. Nico was—had been—friends with this man?

"My brother is away."

"Away? On what business?"

"Helping our cousins slaughter the pigs," Rosa lied. "He should be back in a day or two."

A faint look of distaste crossed the man's features. "I see. Yet it was my understanding that he left the seminary in order to help your father with the farm here."

"He did."

"For a man whose presence is so essential to the operation of this establishment"—here his face contorted into another wincing sort of frown—"I am surprised he is so often away. This is, as you know, the third time I have come to call and found him absent."

"Our uncle died last year. Our cousins need Niccolò's help. Shall I tell my brother you were asking after him?"

"Certainly," he said, and then his attention turned to Nina. "Who is this?" he asked idly. "Yet another cousin?"

"No. This is my sister-in-law. Niccolò's wife."

"You're his wife." He looked her over, his gaze assessing and openly contemptuous. "His wife," he repeated, and still he did not look away.

"Yes," she managed, though her throat was tight enough to choke her.

"Congratulations on your marriage, Signora Gerardi. Your very recent marriage, I presume?"

"Yes."

"May I ask how you met?"

"It was by chance. In Venice."

"You are from Venice, then?"

She only had to stick to the story. Add nothing. Merely answer the question he asked. "Not originally, no. I grew up in Padua. I was only there for my schooling."

"Schooling?"

"I was training to become a nurse."

"And your family? Was it not difficult to move farther away from them?"

"My parents are dead." Awful to say such words, but far safer. "I had no one left back home."

"You have known Niccolò for some time?"

What had they agreed upon? Had they ever discussed that part of things? What ought she to say?

"It was a whirlwind romance," Rosa broke in. "Not an unusual thing in these times."

"Indeed. It must have come as a shock to you all."

"A surprise, yes, but a welcome one. We are very happy to have Nina with us. She is a great help to me."

"Very well. Do pass on my felicitations to your husband, signora." He spun around, his polished boots kicking up a flurry of dust, and made to enter his monstrous car. But then he paused suddenly, almost theatrically, and turned to face them once more. "Apart from your father and brother, Signorina Gerardi, there are how many men living here?"

"There are no other men. Only my younger brothers."

"And their ages?"

"Why do you—"

"They are how old, signorina?"

"The older boys are seventeen and fifteen," Rosa admitted. "And the youngest is nine. A child."

"You keep them here in spite of the pressing need for labor elsewhere? Surely you cannot be ignorant of it."

"We need the boys here on the farm. And it is our duty to grow what we can for the war effort, is it not?"

"A farm this size hardly requires the labor of four men."

"And you know this how? Have you ever worked on a farm?"

"Certainly not, but I am perfectly able to judge when others are indolent and work-shy. Watch yourself, Signorina Gerardi. Your viper's tongue does you no favors. In any event, I have wasted enough time here today."

He got into his car and was driven away, and even after

the sound of its engine had faded and her heart had stopped racing—even then Nina was still afraid.

This Nazi was not a man who would give up. He had come in search of Nico three times, and he would undoubtedly return again, and in the meantime he had taken note of her and seen her face and learned she had once lived in Venice. What was she to do?

NICO RETURNED A few days later, tired and dusty from his long walk home in the late afternoon sun, and though she longed to take him aside and tell him everything, the children were hanging off him and it wasn't fair, she knew, to burden him immediately with the story of Zwerger and how he had frightened her. It would have to wait.

That evening, after the children were in bed and Aldo had uncorked a bottle of wine, Rosa and Nina told Nico of Zwerger's most recent visit. He listened, one thumb digging into the crease between his brows, offering no comment until they had finished.

"Can you describe Zwerger's uniform? Did you notice any unusual badges? Think of his collar—did you see the insignia of the SS on the right side? Like you saw on the car's pennant?"

Nina closed her eyes, trying to remember. "I don't think so, no. It was solid black. And on the other side there were some diamonds."

"There was a patch on his sleeve," Rosa added. "His left sleeve. It had the letters *SD* sewn on it."

Nico nodded, but said nothing more, only drank down the rest of his wine.

"I still can't believe you were friends with him," Rosa muttered.

"He wasn't my friend. We were in the same class at seminary, but only for a few years. He left in '38. I assumed he'd returned home to Austria."

"Do you know why?"

"He'd been bullying some of the other students. Poor boys, like me, who were cowed by his boasts of wealth and a powerful family. He stole from them, made them do his work, and I'm almost certain that he hurt at least one of them. Beat the boy up and then made him say it had been an accident."

"What happened?" Nina asked.

"I went to Father Superior, expecting that he'd dismiss me out of hand, but he actually listened. Zwerger was sent packing the next day."

"He must have known it was you," Rosa said flatly. "And that's why he's come back."

"I doubt it. I can't imagine that Father Superior would have told him. And I wasn't stupid enough to tell anyone else what I'd done. I just couldn't stand the thought of his becoming a priest and having power over others."

"So much for *that*," Aldo muttered. "What if he returns and you're absent again?"

"I'll stay at home for a while. You and the boys are planning on helping Zio Beppe when he butchers the pigs next week, aren't you? I have to stay put while you're gone, and if he hasn't made an appearance by then I'll go looking for him."

"If he suspects anything, learns anything, we're as good as dead," Aldo warned.

"How could he? He came here because he wanted to impress me with his exalted position. You heard what I said about his boasting when we were at school. Always wanting the rest of us to know about his family's wealth back in Austria. Always making sure we knew he was better than the rest of us."

"What does the *SD* on his sleeve mean?" Nina asked.

"Sicherheitsdienst. It translates as 'security service.'"

Aldo paled. "Then he does suspect something."

"No, Papà. On my life he doesn't, otherwise he'd have arrested all of us. We do have to be careful, but that's always been the case."

"No one is safe while the Germans are here," Rosa said, and the thread of urgency in her voice made the hair on Nina's nape stand on end. "All the more reason for us to bring their occupation to an end. Zwerger changes nothing."

Chapter 13

10 December 1943

They were clearing up after lunch when they heard the crunch of gravel under car tires. Zwerger had returned.

Nico was outside; now he came to stand at the door. "Get the children upstairs, Rosa. And you, too, Nina. Best if I speak to him alone."

The children were curious, of course, and Carlo was desperate to get a better look at the car outside, but one hard look from Rosa stopped their chatter and had them hurrying to their rooms.

Nico had said to go upstairs, but from that distance it would be impossible to hear what he and Zwerger were saying. Her curiosity outweighing her fear, Nina sat on the bottom step and forced herself into stillness. Rosa did the same.

"—offer you a glass of wine? Or perhaps some *caffè d'orzo*?"

"No, thank you."

She heard the scrape of chairs being pulled back. Felt the weight of the air in the kitchen. Wondered who would be the first to break the silence.

Zwerger gave in first. "It is strange to see you after so long."

"It has only been five years, Karl."

"Still. A lifetime ago. I wonder if you know how much I looked up to you then. You were so immersed in your studies. So devout. So ignorant of the greater world."

"I was a boy."

"We were all boys, but some of us could see what was coming. Some of us could see what was happening to the world—and that we might help to change it for the better."

"You left without saying farewell," Nico said, as if he were just then remembering. "We never knew what happened to you, and no one there would tell us."

"Father Superior never said?"

"No. Why should he?"

"I was called home, back to Austria. My country needed me."

"I see," Nico said, and there was another long pause. "I can tell you are an officer, but my knowledge of Reich uniforms is lacking. Can you enlighten me?"

"I am an Obersturmführer in the Schutzstaffel of the Third Reich. Presently I am based in Verona with the office of the Sicherheitsdienst. You may have heard of my esteemed commander, Hauptsturmführer Theodor Dannecker."

"I have not, but then we are very isolated in Mezzo Ciel. If you're stationed in Verona, why did you come all the way here?"

"A courtesy visit, no more. My work brings me to this corner of the Veneto quite often. I will say I am glad to have found you at home. You are often away."

"We have fields to work elsewhere, and relatives to help, even as they in turn help us. I'm sorry for having wasted your time on your previous visits. Had I known you were coming I would have tried to stay closer to home." More silence, broken only by the hiss of the fire in the hearth. "My sister told me that you'd asked about my brothers."

"I did. I cannot help but notice that on this small farm alone you have four men of working age, yet none of you have seen fit to offer your service to the greater good."

"This is part of your duties with the SD?" Nico asked, and Nina had to wonder if Zwerger could discern the anger simmering beneath the question.

"Of course not. I have nothing to do with such pedestrian concerns. But you leave yourself open—"

"I'll remind you that I am here because my elder brother was killed in North Africa."

"Your sister took the same insolent tone with me, Niccolò. Surely you are not so stupid as to do the same."

"I'm not being insolent. And I'm not saying the republic cannot take the boys for their work details. You have the upper hand here and we both know it. I'm asking only that you consider the circumstances. Look around you. You know we'll struggle if you take Matteo or Paolo. We are barely surviving as it is."

"What of your wife?" Zwerger asked.

Nina couldn't help herself. She got to her feet, ignoring Rosa's restraining hand, and inched forward until she was standing in the shadows, mere centimeters from the door to the kitchen.

"What of her? She's a great help to my sister, but she can't be expected to work in the fields."

"Other women do. No better than animals."

"I don't know about that," Nico said easily. "I'd rather spend a day with my mule than with any number of men I've met."

"Then why is your young wife not out in the fields? Too much the city girl to dirty her hands?"

"She's a city girl, yes. But she's not afraid of hard work."

"She was training to be a nurse—isn't that what you said, Signora Gerardi? I can see you hovering there. You might as well come in."

If only she had stayed put on the stairs. Nina came forward, though it was a real effort to convince her legs to take even a few steps, and stood behind Nico.

"How far advanced was your training?" Zwerger asked.

"I had only completed a year." That was close enough to the truth.

"I see. Forgive me for persisting, but would you know what to do when confronted with an infected wound? Or one that needed stitching?"

"Yes, providing the wound is not too deep, or the infection acute."

Zwerger nodded and then, turning his head, he called for one of his men. "*Komm mal her,* Meier!"

A young soldier, hardly more than a boy, appeared at the kitchen door.

"Meier has a wound that needs attending. He failed to listen to the medic and the stitches have split. Is there anything you can do?"

She waited for Nico to intervene, but he said nothing. "May we go outside where the light is better? Have him sit on one of the stools while I wash my hands."

She washed and dried her hands and, taking up a clean dish-cloth, went to sit on the unoccupied stool. Spreading the cloth upon her lap, she took the soldier's hand and bent to inspect it. There was a deep, jagged cut in the webbing between his thumb and forefinger, and though it had been stitched, the job had been hurried and careless. Several of the stitches had torn loose, and the edges of the wound were angry and inflamed.

"It isn't so very bad. To begin with, the infection is local to the wound. You'll need to have someone remove the remaining stitches, clean the wound, and restitch it. The dressing will have to be kept clean and dry, and as soon as the wound has scabbed over, the sutures will have to come out. Anyone can do that with a clean pair of scissors and tweezers, though. Simply boil them or cover them with iodine."

"Are you able to attend to him now?" Zwerger asked.

"I can, but I have no way of numbing the area. It will be quite painful. Won't you consider taking him to Dr. Pivetti in the village?"

Zwerger spoke to the soldier, and though her knowledge of German was imperfect, she was fairly certain he told Meier to "sit still and act like a man." The soldier was already looking a little green, but he nodded and set his chin.

"Let me gather my things," she said, resigned to the task ahead, and returned to the kitchen.

"I'll need two bowls, one empty and one filled with the water you boiled earlier," she told Rosa, "and can you fetch me the iodine, tweezers, scissors, needle, and thread from the first-aid box? Nico—can you spare a razor blade? A fresh one?"

Outside the soldier was swallowing a great gulp of something from a silver flask. "Not too much, please," she said mildly as she set the tray she and Rosa had assembled on a chair Nico had brought outside. "I can't have him falling over while I'm working."

"Of course, signora." Zwerger cleaned the mouth of the flask with his handkerchief and slipped it into a pocket in his jodhpur trousers.

"Does he speak Italian?"

"After a fashion. Enough to understand basic commands."

"Very well. I'll start by cutting the remaining sutures and drawing them out. I'll try to work quickly." Snip, snip, snip went her scissors, and though the boy flinched when she pulled out the old stitches, he managed to stay still.

Next she cleaned the wound, relying upon Nico to flood it with iodine and Rosa to rinse it with cool water from the kettle. "Can you see where the tissue has died back along the edge of the wound? I need to remove it. It shouldn't be terribly painful, but it will likely turn your stomach if you watch. Can you look away?"

She waited until Meier had turned his head and then she used the razor blade to trim away the necrotic flesh. "Almost there," she promised. Now all that remained was to stitch the wound properly. "I know this is painful, but I am a good seamstress and you'll barely have a scar." It was true. Papà had

made her practice on a ripe tomato, and if she could sew perfect stitches in its uncooperative flesh, she could set sutures in
anything or anyone. "I'm almost done," she promised. "The
worst is very nearly over . . . almost there . . . done."

She finished with a final wash of iodine, then bandaged
Meier's hand so the thumb was well clear of his fingers. "There.
Time for more of whatever was in that flask."

"Good German schnapps," Zwerger said.

"Ah. Well, not too much. I don't want him to have a headache in the morning on top of everything else. You will remember what I said about keeping the wound clean and dry?
And that he must avoid using the hand at all until the cut is
well scabbed over?"

Zwerger translated, and when he was done Meier looked up,
a little woozily, and tried to smile at her. "Thank you, signora."

"We're glad we were able to help," Nico answered, saving her
from a reply. "And I don't mean to be inhospitable, Karl, but
I've hours of work ahead of me still. Was there anything else
you wanted?"

"Not today, no." Perhaps it was only wishful thinking, but
had some of the bluster drained out of Zwerger's manner?

"Can you see a way to letting the boys stay here with us? My
father is getting older, and we do need the help."

Zwerger nodded slowly, his eyes still fixed on the tray in
Nina's hands. "For the time being, yes. I can help you with
that."

"Thank you. And thank you for visiting. It was good to see
you again."

It was a credit to Rosa's patience that she waited at least five minutes after Zwerger's departure before she turned on her brother.

"You honestly thought it was good to see him again? A *Nazi*?"

"Of course not. But I had just got the man to agree to leave the boys here with us. Being rude to him would have achieved nothing."

"I suppose you're right. You just didn't have to sound so . . . so fine about it."

"Nothing about what just happened was fine. Beginning with his forcing Nina to stitch that soldier's wound."

"Do you think he'll leave us alone now?"

"Let's pray that he does."

"Do you think he was here because of the people you've been helping?" she asked Nico in bed that night.

Their room was achingly cold, and the hot bricks at their feet had long ago lost their warmth, and that, she told herself, was the only reason they now lay so close together, her face tucked close to his chest, his arm a welcome weight across her back.

"No. If he'd suspected me of anything, he'd have brought enough men to reduce the farm to rubble. I honestly think he wanted to see what had become of me—and to have me see what had become of him."

"Truly? That's all?"

"Yes. Even so, he is with the SD, and they're as depraved and vicious a group of men as you'll ever find. Dannecker in particular. If Zwerger comes back and I'm not home, and especially if he's with other men from the SD, I want you to go to the hiding place. Don't hesitate—just go. I'll leave the ladder under the bed so you can get up there by yourself. Promise me?"

"I promise."

"I know we ought to be getting to sleep, but seeing him again . . . it threw me," Nico admitted. "It's been so long since I thought of those days."

"How did you end up being chosen for the priesthood? Or was it something you asked to do?"

"If I'm honest, I was too young to know what I wanted. I'd done well in school, well enough for Father Bernardi to insist that I stay on for a few extra years. And then it just . . . happened. He asked my parents if they'd allow me to become a priest, and if they could manage if I went away to school, and of course they said yes. It was an honor beyond imagining for them."

"Did anyone ask you if *you* wanted it?"

"Not in so many words. At least, not that I recall. I do re- member being excited when they told me, especially since I knew it would take me away from the farm and what I saw as a lifetime of endless work. In that I wasn't wrong."

"How long did you have to go to school for it?"

"First I went to the college in Asolo. When I finished at eighteen, I went to the seminary in Padua. I was twenty-three when I came home."

"So you are twenty-six now? I thought you were older."

"I hope that's a compliment."

"It is, silly."

"I was still about a year away from being ordained, but I'd been having doubts long before I left."

"Did you tell anyone?"

"Only Father Bernardi. And for all that he'd been the one to put me forward for a place in the seminary, he was also the first to understand why I was happy to leave."

They lay in silence for some time, and then Nico's arm tightened around her. "I have more news. There's been a further edict."

"And?"

"All Jews are to be arrested and interned in camps, and all their property is to be confiscated."

"When was it announced?" she asked, a spiral of dread slithering down her spine.

"The day after Zwerger's last visit. December first. When you said nothing about it I thought you might not have heard. I didn't want you to worry."

"We didn't have the radio on for a few nights. The electricity wasn't working. Have there been more arrests?"

"Yes. In every part of the country that's under German control."

"What of Venice?"

"I don't know. I'm waiting to hear, but I have to be careful. If the wrong people learn that I'm asking questions we're all done for. You know that."

"I know. I know, and I try not to bother you, but there are days I feel I'll drown in it. All the worry and fear."

"If there is news I will find out eventually. And I promise to tell you."

"Even if it breaks my heart?" she whispered, her eyes hot with tears.

"Even then, my Nina. Even then."

Chapter 14

22 December 1943

*S*he wasn't surprised when Nico woke her. The instant he touched her shoulder, she opened her eyes, fully alert, and dressed so quickly she was still a little breathless when she reached the kitchen.

The strangers gathered at the table might have stepped from a centuries-old painting, the lamplight flickering like chiaroscuro upon their exhausted faces. They were huddled together, their backs against the wall, their chairs drawn close. There was a man and woman about Nina's age, a toddler in the mother's arms, and flanking them was an older couple, their faces so like the younger man's that they had to be his parents.

"I am sure you have come very far and are very tired," she said soothingly. The young man nodded; perhaps he understood her.

She turned to see what had become of Nico, but he had vanished. She would have to explain, then. "We have a place for you to hide and rest. We have food for you. We will help you."

The younger man whispered to the others, presumably translating her message of comfort, and though his words were almost impossible to discern, they felt familiar. For a moment she thought he had spoken in Spanish, but then the syllables untangled themselves and became clear.

It was Ladino. Her father had spoken it very occasionally with elderly patients, and, more recently, with younger ones who had come from Greece. Centuries ago, before her people had been expelled from Spain, it had been her own family's language.

Nico had counseled her more than once to say as little as possible to the people they sheltered, not only for her sake but for theirs as well. She knew he was right, and she knew he would be upset with her for disobeying, but she couldn't stop herself now.

They were fellow Jews. They had to be—and she had to let them know they were not alone. "Shalom," she whispered. "Me yamo Nina. Te ayudaremos." Welcome. My name is Nina. We will help you.

They stared, their eyes widening, but then the older man nodded, and a fraction of the fear that bound them seemed to drain away.

Rosa came to stand behind her. "Can you tell them we have some soup? And can you ask if they want any milk for—"

"Komm her! Hier! Sie wohnt hier!"

Nico was at the door before Nina could even blink. "Hide them."

"Who's out there?"

"A pair of German soldiers, both of them so drunk they can hardly walk. But that only makes them more dangerous. Get everyone upstairs, Nina—*now.*"

"Come with me," she implored, gesturing frantically to the refugees.

They ran with her up the stairs and to the end of the hall, to the bedroom and the promise of safety—but only if she could get them hidden in time. She grabbed the chair and all but threw it across the room, then stood on top and reached high for the trapdoor, but she was too short and her fingertips scrabbled at thin air.

"Come here," she hissed at the younger of the men, her few words of Ladino forgotten. "You need to push back the door there. Do you see it? Yes? And can you pull yourself up?"

He was shorter and slighter than Nico, but desperation lent him strength, and in seconds he had pulled himself through the open trapdoor. "There is a ladder," she told him, still whispering although there were no sounds, as yet, coming from downstairs. What was the word . . . ? *"Eskalara,"* she remembered. "Lower it so the others can climb up. Yes—the *eskalara.*"

Someone began to hammer on the front door, and not the polite knock of expected visitors, but the ruthless pounding of invaders.

"Open up! Open this door!" The voice was accented. German.

Where was Nico? Surely he would refuse to open the door.

"Who is it?" came Rosa's voice. "You know there are thieves and bandits about."

"Not thieves," the German shouted. "Just honest soldiers. And we're hungry."

"Why should we feed you? Go away!"

"If you don't open this door we'll kick it in!"

Nina ought to be telling the refugees to get up the ladder and into the hiding place, but any movement now, even a creaking floorboard, would betray them. Instead they waited, paralyzed, as Rosa unlatched the door and their enemy entered the house.

"Who was here just before?" one of the soldiers demanded.

"No one. I was setting the table for breakfast."

"It's the middle of the night." The soldier was drunk, but he wasn't entirely witless.

If Rosa was frightened she gave no sign of it. "What of it? We rise before sunrise every day. Will you not tell me why you are here?"

"I told you already. We're hungry, and the food at our barracks is no good. Me and Meier here want something to eat."

"How is that my concern?" Rosa snapped, and Nina braced herself for the moment when the German would lose all patience with her.

"We're lonely, too, and you're *much* prettier than the fellow who cooks for us."

"Get away from me!"

"I'm just trying to be friendly," the soldier protested, and it sounded, to Nina, as if he was pushing a chair out of the way.

"Leave me alone! My father will be back soon. My brothers, too."

Where, oh where, was Nico?

The man laughed, a slow and sinister noise entirely devoid

of humor. "If they were home they'd be here already. You're on your own, aren't you? And those men of yours are off in the hills. Setting traps for good German soldiers—that's my guess."

He didn't sound the slightest bit drunk anymore. Only angry, and vicious, and mean.

"They're in the stables," Rosa insisted. "They'll be back any minute."

"Liar."

A clash of pans. A shriek. Rosa's voice rising in pain. "Leave me alone!"

"Signora—" came an urgent whisper from above.

"What is it?" she asked, not even looking round.

"No ladder. No ladder here!"

She turned, and only then did she realize that none of the refugees, save the man who'd pulled himself up earlier, was in the hiding place. Instead they were huddled beneath the trapdoor, staring at her, too frightened to move.

The ladder was under the bed—Nico had moved it there after Zwerger's last visit. She hurried across the room and pulled it free, wincing as it scraped against the floor. "Here—take it. Get them up it as quickly as you can, and pull it up after you."

She had to help Rosa. She had to stop those men from hurting her. Nina ran into the corridor, her lamp in hand, and shut the bedroom door behind her. If only there were a way of locking it from the inside.

She froze at the sound of rough, stumbling footsteps on the stairs.

"Where is he going?" Rosa shouted.

"He's lonely, too, and I know you have sisters up there. Pretty ones, too."

Rosa gasped in horror. "What kind of pervert are you? They're *children*."

"The one with the curly hair isn't a child. She'll do."

"My sister-in-law? Are you insane? My brother is just outside."

"So? What's he going to do? I'll tell you—nothing. If he even puts a finger on me or Meier he's a dead man, and you know it. So shut up and stop fighting me."

Nina stood in the dark, waiting, willing her hand to stop shaking and her roiling stomach to settle so she might think. Just *think,* and somehow find a way to keep both of the intruders at bay.

The man was almost at the top of the stairs, his footsteps growing ever louder, and if a giant were to have jumped from the shadows she wouldn't have been surprised. She waited, her pulse thundering in her ears, but the soldier who finally appeared was no figure of terror. Instead it was the boy whose hand she had stitched not quite two weeks before.

"What is the matter? Why are you here? We've done nothing wrong."

"You are very pretty," he said carefully, his Italian so heavily accented she had trouble understanding him. "I want only to talk. Maybe to kiss you. Maybe more."

"My husband is outside—"

"Stop talking," he warned. "Stop *now*."

"But the children—you'll wake the children."

"Then be quiet."

Something moved in the shadows behind him, and some nameless instinct told her to keep talking. Keep him occupied.

"All right," she said. "But I need a minute. Just a minute to . . . to get ready. Is that all right?"

He flushed, and she wondered if he might be ashamed. If she might be able to urge him to reconsider what he was about to do.

"I'm begging you," she whispered. "Please go. Please leave us alone."

He opened his mouth, about to answer.

Would have answered if not for the blur of movement in the darkness, the hand that wrenched his head back so roughly, the startling gleam of metal. The awful choking, struggling sounds of a dying animal that followed.

A hot spray of liquid hit her face. Still not understanding, Nina wiped at her eyes and was surprised when her hand came away dark with blood. Was it her blood? Had he stabbed her?

But no, for Meier was sliding to the floor, his legs still jerking, and Nico was behind him, Rosa's good knife in his hand.

She would not scream. Could not, or the other German would hear. She covered her mouth with her hands and was surprised by the coppery taste on her tongue. She forgot to scream.

Nico was gone, lost in the shadows again, but the other soldier was still in the kitchen. He was only meters away, and when he came upstairs and saw the blood all over the floor he would know. He would know what they had done.

"Meier?" the man called up, and he was saying something in

German to his friend, and she was too panicked to even try to make out his words. "Meier?" he called again, his voice rising. Still no answer.

"You bitch," he spat out. "What have you done with him?"

Overturning furniture. The piteous sound of Rosa's cries. The bang of a door being flung open. Footsteps on the—

A grunt. A wheezing gasp. And then silence once more.

She rushed to the landing and looked down. Nico was crouched at the bottom of the stairs, and he was pulling his knife from the ragged remains of the other soldier's throat. There was so much blood. More blood than she had ever seen.

She dropped her lamp. The glass shade shattered.

Nico looked up at her, his face a mask of horror. "Forgive me."

She nodded. "What do we do?" she whispered. It seemed important to be quiet, even now. Even though the men were dead.

"Go back into our bedroom and check that everyone is hidden. Make sure they know to be quiet. I'll get my father and the boys. It'll be light in a few hours."

"Should I—"

"Just listen to me. We have to move quickly or we're fucked. Do you understand?"

Shocked by his coarse language, she nodded and returned to her bedroom. Everyone had made it up the ladder, but the trapdoor was still open. The younger man's face appeared at it now.

"What was that?" he asked, his eyes wide.

"Do not worry. I will bring you food very soon. For now, try to sleep. And you must keep the baby quiet."

Back in the hall, Nico had taken hold of Meier under the

arms and was dragging him to the stairs. Without a word, she grasped the dead man's boots, trying hard not to look at his face. Her hands were slippery with blood and sweat, and she kept dropping his legs, but Nico made no complaint.

They were almost at the landing when Matteo pushed past and took over. She followed behind them, unsure of what to do, certain only that there was nothing she could say that would help.

Aldo had brought out Bello, and now he helped his sons to heave the dead men onto the mule's back. Without a word of farewell they set off across the fields, heading up into the hills, Bello's bridle clutched tight in Aldo's hand.

"Nina," Rosa said, and her voice was careful. Hesitant. "The blood. You need to wash it off."

Nina went to the sink, for there was no time to fill the bath, and opened the faucet. She let the water run over her hands, waiting as it grew ever colder, ever more numbing. Her hands were shaking, but she managed to scoop some soft soap from the jar and rub it over her forearms, her face, and her hair. She found a rag and began to scrub, dipping and rinsing, again and again, running her fingers through her hair until her ringlets lay flat against her scalp and the terrible metallic taste in her nose and throat had been washed away.

"That's enough," came Rosa's gentle voice. "Now go change."

"What did you say to the children?"

"That you dropped the lamp and cut yourself on the broken shade. I don't think they could see how bad it was in the hall. And I couldn't think of a better explanation."

"How will we clean it up?"

"We can soak up the worst of it with sand. Papà keeps a pail of it with his tools. Just spread it out and scrape it back into the pail. Then we'll empty it into the stream. Soap and hot water should be enough to clean up what's left. I'll deal with the mess down here, and you can clean upstairs."

Nina changed into a fresh dress and apron, balling up her bloodstained garments and hiding them under her bed, and then she set to work. It wasn't long before the door to the children's room creaked open a few centimeters. Without looking up she knew it was Carlo.

"There's so much blood on the floor. Will you be all right? Rosa said you cut your finger."

She sat back on her heels and tried to smile for him. "I'll be fine. It wasn't a bad cut at all. It looks much worse than it is."

"What was that noise? It sounded like someone fell on the stairs."

"It was Nico," she said, the lies flowing from her mouth like honey. "He heard me drop the lamp and he tripped coming upstairs."

"Did he hurt himself?"

"No, not one bit. Now please go back to bed, or you'll be too tired to pay attention at school tomorrow."

She scrubbed and scrubbed, and after a while she began to hope she'd got out the worst of the stains. But there was still the matter of the droplets of blood on the walls. Likely they would have to sand them down and then give everything a fresh coat of whitewash.

The sky had begun to lighten by the time she emptied her bucket for the last time, but she still had to carry the pail of sand, now revoltingly black, uphill to the stream. She knelt at the water's edge and dumped it out in one disgusting, claggy splash. The water flared red for an instant and then flowed bright and clear. If only it were so easy to wash away memories.

The look on Meier's face. The sound as the knife came searing forward through his throat. The terrible knowledge in his eyes. He had known he was about to die. He had known, and he had been frightened, and she had stood by and let it happen.

Rosa was sitting alone in the kitchen when Nina returned. Her knife, washed clean, was on the table.

"It was my best knife," she said as Nina came in. "I don't know how I'll ever use it again."

Nina wasn't sure how to answer. "The sand is gone," she said instead.

"Good."

"Did he hurt you?" she thought to ask.

"Not badly. Only my knees where I fell. They're a bit bruised. And there's a cut on my lip. Just in the one spot. From . . . well. You know."

"Is it safe to take them something to eat?" Nina asked, remembering the family upstairs.

"Not yet. Not until the men return."

She would wait for Nico outside, under the olive tree. It was strange to be idle—she ought to have been knitting or doing the mending—but her hands were still shaking, and her skin was raw from the hours of scrubbing, and all she could bear to do, in that moment, was wait for him to come home to her.

She sat there for at least an hour, so exhausted it was hard work just to remain upright. Simply sat and watched the stars vanish from the brightening sky. And then, when she had almost lost hope, the four of them came around the side of the house, and Aldo took Bello straight to the stables, and the boys went into the kitchen. She heard, as if from a distance, Rosa's words of concern as she fussed over them and insisted they change and wash and eat some soup.

Nina was aware of the others, but her attention was entirely focused on Nico. He sank down on the stool next to hers and let his head loll back against the rough brick.

"We took them into the hills. There's a cave there, far from the road, and we dug a hole at the very back of it and buried them. If we'd had more time we'd have filled in the entrance, too."

"Won't the Germans wonder what happened to them?"

"They will. But I'm hoping they'll assume it's a case of straightforward desertion. Judging by their accents, both of them were from Austria. And the border isn't so very far. A determined man can walk there in a few days."

"You're sure?"

"No. But it was the best I could do." His eyes still closed, he reached out and grasped hold of her near hand. "Forgive me."

"There's nothing to forgive. If not for you, Rosa and I would both have been raped. And what if Meier had opened the door to our room? He'd have seen everything."

"I know. That's why I did it." Now he turned to look her in the eyes. "I need to help Papà with the animals, and I need to wash, too. Go back to bed. I'll be up as soon as I can."

She waited for him, shivering and alone, and though it could only have been a scant hour before he returned, it felt like far longer. He undressed as quietly as he ever did, and then he went to the window and knelt before it, and she heard him murmuring in prayer. Just as she was falling asleep he slipped in beside her, his hair still damp and smelling of Rosa's home-made soap.

"Are you all right?" she whispered. In that moment, she'd have gladly surrendered every object she owned, every dream she'd ever had, just to take away his pain. He was good and gentle and kind, and he'd suffer for the rest of his life because of those two wicked men.

"No." The despair in his voice tore at her heart. "My family tease me, you know. I'm the one who can't bear to see the pig slaughtered. I'm the one who used to faint at the sight of blood. And yet . . . it was so easy to kill those men. Just like he'd told me it would be."

"Who?"

"An Englishman. A prisoner of war I met. He showed us some of the ways he'd been trained to fight. To kill. I've no idea why. Maybe he was bored." Nico held her even closer, his arms tightening around her back, one big hand cradling her head to his chest. "You take a knife, and you come up behind the man you are going to kill. You pull back his head and stab him in the neck, in the side, just under his ear. Then you punch your arm forward, before you can think twice, and rip out his throat. Just like I did tonight."

"You mustn't dwell on—"

"The Englishman warned me that it would be easy. So easy

to kill a man like that. But he also told me it would be the hardest thing I would ever do."

"Was he right?"

"He was. Oh, God, he was right. All that blood, Nina. How will I ever wash it away?"

Chapter 15

5 January 1944

*G*rowing up in the heart of Venice, hemmed in at every side by Gentiles, Nina had been aware of her neighbors' traditions, but only in the most general way. She'd known of Christmas and Easter and their lesser holidays, but she'd never taken part in the celebrations, nor had she ever needed to pretend she was familiar with them.

She had thought she might hang back from the preparations for Epiphany. Remain at the margin of things, and so avoid drawing attention to her otherness. But it was hard to stay aloof when the children were so excited they could talk of nothing but the great bonfire in the piazza, the once-a-year treat of Rosa's *pinza* cake, and the possibility of sweets and even a toy in the stockings they would leave out for *la Befana* that night.

Carlo was still young enough to believe in the old woman

who'd been too busy with her chores to help the wise men search for the Christ child, and who now left out gifts for children on the night before Epiphany. "But only if you are good," he earnestly explained to anyone who would listen. "Did she ever give you lumps of coal?" he now asked Nina.

"No," she answered honestly enough. "I was always a good girl."

"How big was your stocking? Ours are so small," he grumbled. "We should pin up Nico's socks instead."

Nina pretended to consider the suggestion. "I suppose we could, but what if *la Befana* were to see your brother's big socks and decide you were too greedy? Then it would be nothing but coal for you."

"I promise there will be nothing but coal if you don't get out of my way," Rosa warned him. "How am I supposed to make the *pinza della Befana* with you underfoot? Off you go—and you girls, too. I don't want to see you inside again until suppertime."

Nina had seen similar cakes for sale in bakeries and markets, but had never thought to wonder how they were made. Rosa's version began with a pot of cooked polenta, to which she added flour and sugar and an eye-watering amount of grappa. This she turned out onto the table before kneading in raisins, currants, dried figs, chopped apples, and fennel seeds.

"How do you remember how much to add of everything?" Nina asked.

"Practice, I suppose. I started helping Mamma to make it when I was even younger than Carlo is now. After she died, I worried I wouldn't get it right. But I just got to work and it turned out. Even Papà said it was as good as hers."

While they were talking, Rosa had shaped the dough into a low, round loaf. Rather than put it in a baking dish or tin, she instead set about wrapping it in layer upon layer of fresh cabbage leaves. Once it was covered to her satisfaction, she carried it to the hearth, where she'd been tending a low fire since the morning, and pushed the embers one way and another until she'd cleared a small space on the brick-lined floor. Then she set down the wrapped dough and covered it with the embers she'd displaced.

"There. That's one thing out of the way."

They fetched the children in for supper not long after, but Carlo was too excited to eat anything, and twice he came close to spilling his soup because of his fidgeting, and finally Nico picked up his brother and carried him outside until the *pinza* cake was ready.

When Rosa brought it to the table at last, the cake didn't seem terribly appetizing, for the cabbage leaves were charred and dry and smelled terribly sulfurous, but then she whisked away the last of the wrapping to reveal an appetizingly golden exterior.

Everyone was given a thin slice, with seconds for Carlo, and then Rosa set an even smaller piece aside for *la Befana,* along with a glass of *vin brulè.*

"Not too much," she told Carlo, "since she gets something at every house she visits. She won't have much of an appetite by the time she comes to us."

Soon Rosa declared it bedtime for all the children, even Matteo and Paolo, and though Carlo once again protested and cast longing looks at his empty stocking, his sister was unmovable. They waited until the children had settled upstairs, Aldo and Nico each sipping at a second glass of *vin brulè*, and then the work of filling the stockings began.

Making the gifts over the preceding weeks had involved no small amount of deception. Nina had knitted socks for the older boys and men, working in tufts of roving to make them especially cozy, while Rosa had crocheted lace collars for the girls. For Carlo there was also a finely carved wooden airplane, hardly bigger than Nina's outstretched hand, that she'd seen Aldo working on in spare moments for more than a month.

As showily as a magician, Nico produced bars of cellophane-wrapped nougat, one for each child, followed by three gifts wrapped in plain paper.

"You might as well open them now," he said, smiling shyly. There was a comb for his father, a bar of fine soap for Rosa, and a little jar of jasmine-scented hand cream for Nina.

"I was in Bassano last month, and the pharmacy on the Piazza Libertà was like Aladdin's cave. I didn't have any eggs with me," he added, "but they agreed to accept a few lire."

The next morning the children were up at dawn, and their delight as they emptied their stockings and discovered their modest gifts would, Nina decided, long remain one of her happiest memories. Carlo was less enthusiastic when he was told to put down his toy airplane and ready himself for Mass, but Nico calmed him with promises of Pippo bomber chases in the courtyard afterward.

That evening they lingered over the table after supper was done, too full to even think about sampling the *pinza* cake again, and the girls took turns singing for everyone, and Nico entertained Carlo with a lengthy and dramatic account of *la Befana*'s visit from the Magi so long ago.

And then it was time to walk into the village for the lighting of the *riel,* the enormous bonfire that would act as a beacon for *la Befana* when she returned. They arrived just as everyone was gathering in the piazza, and though the pile of brush and firewood was indeed impressive, it was not, as Carlo had insisted earlier, quite as tall as the campanile.

He now ran off with his schoolmates, promising yet again to be good, and of course he would stay well away from the bonfire, and yes, yes, he would stay in the piazza and come willingly when he was called. Aldo, too, went to join his friends, though only to stand outside the osteria.

To begin the festivities, Father Bernardi offered a blessing, but his voice was swallowed up by the noise of the crowd. A trio of men came forward, torches in hand, and everyone in the piazza held their breath until the flames caught, flickering weakly at first, then growing in strength before they swept to the top of the bonfire.

Around them people were laughing and cheering, and Rosa and the girls were singing about the arrival of *la Befana,* but Nico was unmoved, unsmiling, his manner as alert and restless as Selva when she was set to guard the house.

"What is it?" Nina asked.

"I'm looking for Carlo. I don't want to lose him in the crowd."

But it was more than that, for Carlo was easy to find—he had only just run past them, and the bonfire itself was well contained.

Only then did she notice them. Four German soldiers at

the corner of the piazza, just outside the *carabinieri* station. They were laughing, at ease, their rifles slung over their shoulders. They didn't seem to care that everyone in the village was breaking the curfew.

She took Nico's arm in hers, pulling him closer, and then stood on tiptoe to whisper in his ear. "There is nothing to fear tonight. They're only watching and trying to forget about the war. Just as we are doing."

"I know. I know. Father Bernardi told me not long ago that he'd been speaking with the local head of the Guardia. The man's like a sieve. If the Germans had any idea how much he gossips they'd never tell him a thing."

"And?" she prompted.

"The men who disappeared have been recorded as deserters. That's what Father found out."

"See? Now we really don't have to worry."

He nodded, but his unease was still palpable. "It's only that . . ."

Carlo came roaring up, his eyes wild with excitement. "Did you see? The wind is sending the smoke to the east! We'll have good luck this year!" Then he was off again, darting through the crowd, and Nico smiled and hugged her a little closer, and Nina tried to remember if the smoke was meant to go to the east or to the west. Perhaps Carlo was mistaken and the year ahead would be a bad one.

Just then the wind picked up, casting a cinder in Agnese's eye, and though it was easily rubbed away, Rosa's patience was at an end. She sent the older boys in search of their father and Carlo, and when the latter was returned, his sooty face streaked with tears, Nico was the one to comfort him.

"The bonfire will be nothing but ashes before you know it. And surely you want a little piece of cake before bed? Maybe some chestnuts, too?"

Soon they were home, and the kitchen was warm and bright, and the delight in the children's faces was infectious, and the *vin brulè* that Rosa now ladled out, together with more slices of *pinza* cake, was the perfect cure for a case of the worries.

"It isn't so very late," Nico pointed out, "and I'm still hungry. Do you think we might roast some chestnuts?"

"As if I can say no with all of you staring at me," Rosa pretended to grumble. Nico scored the chestnuts with his pocketknife, Rosa stirred up the embers in the hearth, and Matteo and Paolo took turns holding and shaking the long-handled pan. When the entire room was filled with the tantalizing scent of roasted chestnuts, the pan was emptied onto the table and the work of peeling began, with everyone exclaiming over burned fingers and the occasional withered surprise. No one was faster at it than Aldo, but then, as he explained, he'd had more than fifty years to practice.

They said good night soon after, and it was a joy to settle in bed, the lamp faintly aglow, the sheets warm from the hot brick Rosa had given them to take upstairs. Nico still turned his back while she changed, and she still shut her eyes while he did the same, but it felt natural to lie close to each other, their feet tangled together, and talk of their day in tender, affectionate whispers.

Earlier, as they'd laughed over the chestnuts, he had seemed happy enough; but now, without the gaze of the others upon him, his mask of contentment fell away.

"Whenever I close my eyes, I see that night," he whispered. She knew without asking which night he meant. "I see the blood on your face. The look in your eyes. How can you ever forgive me? If we had been caught—"

"We weren't. Those men were the enemy. They were set on raping me and Rosa, and that was the least of it. If Meier had opened our bedroom door and found the people hiding there, he and his friend would have killed us all. And what if Zwerger had learned of it?"

"If there had been any other way . . ."

She touched his face, her fingertips tracing the arches of his brows, letting them linger on the lines of worry at the corners of his eyes.

"The day I left Venice was one of the worst days of my life," she whispered. "I had to say goodbye to my mother and father, to my home, to everything that was familiar and comfortable and safe. It was truly awful—and yet one part of it was good. The part when I met you."

"If only—"

"Hush. This is the life we have. This is *all* we have, and I don't want to waste a single moment on doubts. No more 'if onlys.' I am glad I met you. I am glad to be here. And if my life were to end tomorrow, I would still think myself the most fortunate of women."

He pressed a soft kiss to her brow. "You honor me."

"I only speak the truth. I never thought I would meet a man as kind and decent as my father, but you are. I know it, and I think my father knew it, too. And that is why he sent me away with you."

Chapter 16

22 January 1944

*I*t was Saturday, cleaning day, but with Carlo and the girls in bed with bad colds it had fallen to Nina and Rosa to deal with the house. Nico had come up to help with the mattresses, but the rest of the upstairs cleaning—sweeping, scrubbing, dusting, and changing the bedsheets—Nina had done on her own.

She hadn't minded, for the children had kept her company while she cleaned their rooms, and after four months of practice she was able to sweep and wash the floors as quickly and neatly as Agnese and Angela. Even the bedsheets took her no time at all to change, excepting the delay as she persuaded Carlo to vacate his bed for a few short minutes.

"It's soooooo cold," he moaned, even though she'd wrapped him in his blanket and put him in his brothers' big bed.

"I'll be done before you know it, and then I'll bring you a hot brick for your feet. That will warm you all over."

"Why can't I sleep in your bed?"

"Because it needs to be changed as well. Now stop complaining and let me finish."

As soon as Carlo was settled again, the promised brick at his toes and his precious toy airplane in his hands, she went down the hall to finish her and Nico's room. She'd washed the floors earlier but, contrary to Rosa's advice, had neglected to first do the dusting. Not that it mattered, for the room looked just as clean as it had the Saturday before.

The only surface that needed attention was the top of the dresser. She wiped down the case that held Nico's shaving things, the wooden back of his hairbrush, and their shared collection of books. His selection, she decided, perfectly embodied his character. There was a Bible; a gilt-edged book of devotions; a guide to modern farming and animal husbandry, its pages dog-eared and marked with penciled annotations; and a beautiful edition of the *Divine Comedy,* with scraps of paper peeking out where he had marked his favorite passages.

"I have more," Nico said from the doorway. "Books, that is. The rest are packed away."

"Why only these four?"

He now came to stand behind her. "When I returned home, I thought I would build a bookshelf. I couldn't imagine living without all my books near me. But I'm so tired at night, I hardly ever read."

She nodded. "I know what you mean. I used to be such a bookworm, but now . . ." She arranged the books neatly on the dresser, his shaving case propping them up at one end and Pietro, the toy rabbit she had brought from home, at the other.

"Perhaps we might read to one another in the evening," he suggested. "Instead of listening to the radio."

"I would love that."

"My father and Rosa would, too. She's the one who ought to have gone away to school. More brains than the rest of us put together." Nico reached past Nina to stroke the worn velvet of Pietro's ear. "Where did he come from?"

"My rucksack. I'd pulled it out from under the bed, so I might sweep the floor there, and Angela peeked inside and found Pietro. She was worried he might be lonely, hidden away under the bed, so I put him out on the dresser. You don't mind, do you?"

"Of course not. He looks well loved."

"Mamma made him for me when I was little. He was always my favorite."

"Why is he called Pietro?"

"That's the name of the rabbit in the book by Signorina Potter. We had it, too. The book, I mean. It was in English, so Mamma would translate as she read. I remember being very afraid of the farmer."

"The farmer?"

"Yes. He wanted to catch little Pietro and bake him into a pie."

"Not this farmer. You know I'm too softhearted for that."

Hearing the smile in his voice, she turned to face him. Her eyes were at the same level as the base of his throat, and she was close enough to see his leaping pulse as it danced under his skin. She looked up, and he looked down, and there was a moment when neither of them remembered to breathe. He tilted his head, as if he were about to ask her a question.

She nodded.

He kissed her. His mouth was gentle, his touch a whisper, no more. She stretched toward him, her shoes creaking as she rose on her tiptoes, her hands curving over his shoulders. He pulled her closer still, one arm wrapped around her back, the other reaching up to cradle her head.

"Nina," he whispered against her lips. "We need to stop."

"Why? I don't ever want to stop."

"Neither do I, but the children are just down the hall, and it's the middle of the day. Later, when everyone is asleep, then we can . . ." He was blushing, the color rising under his day-old beard.

"Later," she agreed, her face equally crimson. "When it's time for bed."

NICO WENT TO join his father in the barn, and it started to rain soon after, so there was nothing else to do but sit in the kitchen, under the feeble light of the oil lamps, for once again the electricity wasn't working, and attend to the mending. Nina darned sock after sock, found ways to patch Carlo's trousers that were already nothing but patches, and stopped only when her eyes watered and burned and she could no longer see the needle in her hand.

At last it was time for supper, a meager meal of soup and stale bread, and with the youngest three children still in bed it was far too quiet around the table. They ate in near silence, the rush of pouring rain a numbing melody, and when Rosa pushed back her chair and told the boys to bring out the bathing tub, Nina's heart missed a beat. They would have their baths, and then it would be time for bed, and then . . .

Rosa was kind enough to share some of her good soap, and after everyone had bathed and washed their hair and had dressed again, she combed through Nina's curls, working through the tangles and twisting her hair into two neat plaits, her touch soft and certain and wonderfully soothing. When she was finished Nina did the same in return, braiding Rosa's hair into one thick plait that fell all the way to the small of her back.

Nico had brought down the *Divine Comedy,* and he now began to read the final cantos from *Paradiso.* The poetry was so beautiful, and his voice was so beguiling, that she didn't even bother to pick up her knitting as she usually did. Only listened, enchanted, as he read of the poet and his Beatrice and their search for happiness. Finally Nico shut the book and told the others he was off to bed, and she followed him upstairs without remembering to say good night. She closed the door to their room, checking to make sure it had latched properly. And then she turned to face him.

"We should get ready for bed," Nico said. "I'll just turn my back?"

She nodded, her mouth too dry for words, and changed into her nightgown as quickly as her fumbling fingers would allow. She crossed the room to where he stood, still facing away from her. "I'm here," she said.

"Will you let me hold you?" He turned slowly, letting her decide. She stepped into the circle of his arms and took a deep breath. At last.

"I've wanted to kiss you for a very long time," he said, his lips soft against her brow.

"How long?"

"Almost since the beginning," he admitted.

"Why did you wait until now?"

"I've never felt this way before. Ever. I needed to be certain of my feelings."

"And?" she prompted, her heart racing.

"I love you, Antonina, but not as a sister, and not as a friend. As a wife. My wife. And I hope you share those feelings. If not, I'll—"

She kissed him before he could say another word, and into that kiss she instilled her regard, her admiration, her delight, her joy, and her love for him. For this man who had so unexpectedly become the hero of her story.

She pulled away, just a little, for she had to see his face. Had to let him see how she felt, too, for words were not enough. "I do, Nico. With all my heart I do."

"My darling," he whispered, and then he kissed her, and he didn't break away until they both were breathless and trembling.

"I wish we were truly married," he said. "I know that makes me sound old-fashioned."

"You're an honorable man. It's one of the reasons I love you."

"Then you understand why we ought to stop. Only . . ."

"What is it?"

"If we were to make promises to one another, exchange vows, would that be enough for you? Only until the war is over, though, and the laws are changed. And if they don't change the laws here, we'll go somewhere, anywhere, and—"

"Yes," she said. "Yes."

"Is that something you do in a Jewish wedding? Exchange vows? Forgive me for my ignorance."

"We do. There's a betrothal blessing at the start, and the groom gives the bride a ring. He puts it on her finger and says, 'ani l'dodi, ve dodi li.' It's from the Song of Solomon and it means 'I am my beloved's and my beloved is mine.' Then there are more blessings. And there are other parts, but nothing, I think, that involves vows. Apart from the marriage contract, I suppose, but the bride and groom sign that before the ceremony."

"Christian weddings aren't so very different. There are prayers and blessings, too, both before and after the vows."

"Do you know the words to the vows?"

"Of course I do. Remember all those cousins? That makes for a lot of weddings."

"I would like to say them."

He nodded, his expression serious again. "Shall we kneel?"

They sank to their knees, facing one another, barely a hand's width apart. Nico slipped the ring from her finger and set it carefully on the floor. Then he took her hands in his.

"I, Niccolò, take you, Antonina, for my wife, to have and to hold, from this day forward, for better, for worse, for richer, for poorer, in sickness and in health, until death us do part."

"I, Antonina, take you, Niccolò, for my husband, to have and to hold, from this day forward, for better, for worse, for . . ."

"For richer—"

"For richer, for poorer, in sickness and in health, until death us do part."

Nico picked up the ring and slipped it back on her finger. "I am my beloved's and my beloved is mine."

She had no ring to give him, but still she repeated the words. "I am my beloved's and my beloved is mine."

He embraced her, so tightly she couldn't tell where his arms stopped and her body began, and then there were more kisses, slow and tender and enchanting. They were both shivering, but she didn't feel cold at all.

"We need to stop for a moment," Nico murmured, his breath fanning sweetly against her lips.

He got to his feet, went to the bed, and reached across it to grasp the woolen pad that sat atop the mattress. He then dragged the pad, along with the pillows, sheets, and blankets, to the middle of the room. Turning, he caught her eye. "I've no wish to waken the entire house, or to answer awkward questions from Carlo tomorrow."

He then crouched to unlace his boots, but once he'd toed them off he made no further move to undress. Instead he sat on the makeshift bed and beckoned her over.

She knelt in front of him, tucking her legs under the skirt of her nightgown, and took his hands in hers.

He met her questioning gaze directly, though for some reason he was blushing, the color rising high on his cheekbones. "I also need to make a confession."

"What is it?"

"I've never done this before."

"Nor have I."

"I worry I will disappoint you."

"You won't."

"Then yes?" he asked, his voice aglow with love and hope.

"Yes, my Nico. Yes, my beloved one."

THE FLOOR WAS very hard beneath the thin wool pad, and the blankets weren't quite heavy enough to keep out the drafts whistling through the window and under the door, but she was in the arms of the man who loved her, and she had never felt safer or more content. To lie so close to him, to listen to the soothing beat of his heart, to set aside her fears until the new day, was to welcome her first true, undiluted moment of happiness since the day her father had taken her aside at the *casa*.

"Are you asleep?" she asked.

"No. I'm too happy to fall asleep. I want these hours to last forever."

"If only they would. If only we could wake up tomorrow and learn that the war is over. Wouldn't that be wonderful?"

"It won't last forever. It can't."

"And when it does end?" she asked. "If you could do anything, what would it be?"

"If anything were possible? I suppose I would like to go to university."

"What would you study?"

"I think . . . I suppose it would be agricultural science. I know it doesn't sound very exciting, but there's so much to learn. How to improve the soil, increase crop yields, guard against disease. That sort of thing. I know so little—that one book on the dresser is as far as I've got—but I want to learn more."

"I don't think it sounds boring at all," she said, and she hugged him a little tighter, just to underscore her words. They'd turned down the lamp a while ago, but she wished, now, that she could see his face properly.

"What would you choose to do?" he asked after a moment.

"I want to study medicine. To be a doctor like my father." It was the first time she'd said it aloud to anyone other than her papà. It was the first time she'd allowed herself to think of it since she'd left Venice.

"You would make a wonderful doctor. You have that way about you. Patient and kind, but strong when you need to be. What sort of medicine, do you think?"

"I'm not sure. My father's specialty was nephrology."

"I know. Father Bernardi told me they met when he went for help with his kidney stones."

"People used to come from all over Europe to see my father, but he had to close his clinic when the racial laws were passed. When he did see patients after that it was in secret, in their homes. Most of them were poor. I don't really remember him being paid."

"How did you live?"

"He had some savings. A Gentile friend kept the money for him, otherwise it would have been taken. And we learned to do without. All we wanted was to live in peace. To stay in the city where I was born, and my parents before me, and all our ancestors for as far back as we could remember. For hundreds of years it was our home, and now . . ."

So much for her moment of happiness.

"It will be your home again. As soon as the war is over."

"By then it will be too late. My parents . . ."

"Deserve none of this. Nor do you," he insisted.

"I used to pray. I used to ask God to protect my family. To keep them safe."

"And now?"

"I haven't prayed for years. Not since Mamma's stroke. Not since the laws that turned my family into outcasts. I hope you don't think that makes me a bad person."

"Never," he whispered, his lips brushing so softly against her brow. "Not least because I have the same doubts and fears."

"Don't you believe in God?"

"I want to believe. I do. But the things I've seen and done have changed me. Marked me. And now I can't imagine how this war will end. Or where I will be when it is over."

"You will be here with me. We will be together," she promised. "Tell me you can believe in that, if nothing else."

"Then I will. For you, Nina, I will believe."

Chapter 17

2 April 1944

It was Palm Sunday, which meant, to Nina's secret dismay, that Mass lasted far longer than usual. Normally she tried to appear attentive, if only to avoid hurting Father Bernardi's feelings, but simply remaining upright and awake had been near to impossible in the crowded and too-warm church. Not that anyone would notice if her attention wandered, for she was in her usual place, right against the wall, and all around her heads were bobbing as people nodded off, startled themselves awake, and drifted again into somnolence.

Nico had been gone for several weeks, and in his absence she'd found it increasingly difficult to sleep. Last night she'd lain awake for hours, wondering and worrying, and no matter how often she'd told herself to be sensible, to be rational, her mind had refused to obey. She had fallen asleep not far short of dawn, her face pressed against Nico's pillow, her body bereft of his comforting warmth and weight.

Instead of listening to the endless and unintelligible Latin of the service, she tried to stay awake by working out, from memory alone, the likely date for the start of Passover. Last year it had begun toward the end of April, but she'd never thought much of how and why the date varied. It might already have passed, for all she knew; there were years, after all, when it had fallen at the end of March.

Her family hadn't done much to mark the holy days in recent years, for her mother had always been the one among them who insisted on doing things properly, and after she had been moved to the *casa* it had felt strange, and a little depressing, to observe the seder without her. But Nina had washed and polished their best china and silver, and she'd ironed the tablecloth and napkins Mamma had always kept for Passover alone, and then she had helped Marta clean the house from top to bottom. Marta had also prepared a simple menu of chicken *brodo* with *polpette di matza,* baked mullet with fried artichokes, and a hazelnut *torta.* Not the abundant feast that was proper, but her father hadn't complained. They had said the prayers together, and she had answered the four questions Papà had put to her, as if she were still a little girl, and together they had recited the *L'Shana Haba'ah B'Yerushalayim.* Next year in Jerusalem. And then, even though it was late already, they had walked over to the *casa* with a slice of the *torta,* which was soft enough that Mamma was able to eat a bit of it, and before they had left, Nina had sung her mother to sleep.

Her wandering gaze swept across the front of the church

before it landed on Father Bernardi. Perhaps he might be able to find out when Passover began. She resolved to take him aside, under some pretext or other, and ask; but not on the church steps, where everyone was hovering and listening. It would have to wait until she could contrive an excuse to visit him at the rectory during the week.

When Mass ended she joined the queue to greet Father Bernardi on the steps of the church, waiting long minutes as he shook hands and kissed the children's heads and patiently listened to everyone with worries or concerns to share. When it was the Gerardi family's turn at last, she was surprised when the priest shook her hand before everyone else, his greeting even more voluble than usual.

"My dear Nina—you're just the person who can help me."

"With what, Father?"

"Nothing of consequence," he answered, and then, leaning a little closer, his whisper strangely loud, "it's my bunions, you see, and I wonder if you might, ah, use your expertise as a nurse . . ."

His expression was strained, but then he was probably feeling a little embarrassed to be discussing the state of his feet in front of so many witnesses.

"Of course, Father. I'll just fetch my things from home, and—"

"No need, no need. I've a well-stocked first-aid kit in the rectory."

"You go ahead," Rosa encouraged, "and I'll set aside your dinner for later."

And that settled the matter. Father Bernardi grasped her

elbow and steered her back through the sanctuary, pausing only to shake hands with a few stray departing churchgoers. They continued on through a sort of antechamber between the church and the rectory, but as soon as they were in his modest residence, and the door was closed behind them, he turned to her with a sheepish smile.

"I apologize for whisking you away like that, but it couldn't be helped."

Understanding dawned, along with a new appreciation for the priest's skill as an actor. "You don't have any problems with your bunions," she stated.

"I do, but they can wait. It's something else. Something more serious."

"Nico?" She couldn't breathe for her fear.

"He is well, but we need your help. One of his, ah, friends has been injured."

"How? When?"

"Nico himself will tell you. They're just upstairs."

Nina flew up the dark, narrow staircase two steps at a time. "Nico? Where are you?"

"Here."

He stood at the end of the hall, the room behind him lost in gloom. He opened his arms wide and she ran to him, forgetting all else but the joy and comfort of his embrace.

It had been several weeks since he'd left, his first long absence since that terrible night in December, and there had been moments, over the past few days, when she'd wondered if her memories were playing tricks on her. If it truly had been so blissful to stand in the shelter of his arms.

She ought not to have doubted. Her body had remembered rightly, for her head still fit just so under his chin, and his heartbeat still soothed her when she pressed her ear to his chest. If there was any more comforting sound in the world she could not imagine it.

Far sooner than she'd have liked, she made herself pull away, for now was not the time for self-indulgence. Not when Nico's friend lay injured and needed her help.

"What happened?"

He caught her hands in his, clasping them tight to his chest, and pressed his lips to her hair. "My darling. How I've missed you."

"And I you. Now tell me."

"We'd caught a ride down from Costalunga with some of the local partisans. It was stupid of us, but we were tired and they insisted the way was clear. So we climbed onto the flatbed of their truck and let them carry us down the mountain. And then, barely a quarter hour later, we came to a checkpoint. Instead of bluffing his way through, the driver swung around and went back up the road—and that's when the Germans started firing."

"Was your friend"—she knew not to ask for the other man's name—"shot?"

"No, but in the panic to get away the truck went into the ditch. We managed to jump clear, but he hurt his ankle on the way down. He's some cuts and scratches, too. I don't think any of them are very deep."

"Did you have to walk the rest of the way home? How far is that?"

"It was only ten kilometers as the crow flies. Maybe a little more."

"How did you manage it? Your friend—was he able to walk at all?"

"Nico carried him," Father Bernardi called from the end of the hall.

At this, Nico sighed heavily. "I didn't mind, and we're here, aren't we? The way of it makes no difference."

"Were *you* injured?" Nina remembered to ask.

"Not so much as a scratch."

"Good," she said, though the single word scarcely captured the depth of her relief. Now she turned to Father Bernardi. "I'll need your first-aid kit."

"Do you still keep it in the kitchen?" Nico asked. "Yes? In that case I'll fetch it. I've already had you running up and down the stairs all night."

Nina went into the bedroom, switched on a nearby lamp rather than open the shutters, and sat on the chair next to the bed. Nico's friend, who looked to be sleeping, was stretched out on top of the counterpane, his boots still in place, his clothes stiff with mud and dried blood. His beard had grown in, and his hair, long enough to touch his collar, was shot through with silver. He was older than Nico, though not by much. Somewhere, perhaps not far, there were people waiting for him. There were people who loved him.

She blinked hard, struggling to keep her tears at bay. She would not—could not—cry. She had to compose herself. Above all, she had to bury her fear.

The warm weight of Father Bernardi's hand settled on her

shoulder. "I know," he said softly. "I know. Few things are harder than fearing for someone you love."

She nodded, for it was true—not only of Nico, but also of her parents. "If only I could help them. But there isn't a thing I can do."

"Not directly, no, but your actions today will make a difference. To this man, and also to his family. To all the people he will go on to help in the months to come. And it's by such actions that you tip the scales in our favor. A few grams today, a few more tomorrow. That is how we will prevail."

She nodded, absorbing his words of comfort, wishing she were stronger. Wishing she wasn't so consumed by fear.

"I never used to be like this," she confessed. "Jumping at my own shadow, my heart pounding at every creak on the stairs, always wondering and worrying if today is the day I'll learn that my parents are lost. If someone will come to tell me Nico has been captured, or hurt, or . . ." She could not give voice to the last, and most terrifying, possibility.

"There's no shame in being afraid, my dear. Even the bravest men are frightened at times."

"So how do I bear it?"

"Simply by bearing it. You already know what it is to send him away with your blessing. You already know how painful it is to wait for his return."

"I do, and I know I mustn't stop him from going. I know that others will suffer without his help. But . . ."

"Go on."

"I can't help wishing he would stay," she admitted. "It's wrong of me, I know."

"It isn't. Who among us doesn't long to keep our loved ones close by? But only think—what sort of man would he be if he *did* stay? If Nico sat by and did nothing, if he told himself the injustices he witnessed weren't his concern, would you love him as you do now?"

"No," she whispered. "I wouldn't recognize that Nico."

She loved him because he had chosen to do what was right. She was alive, and safe, because he had refused to look the other way. Father Bernardi was right, and it was past time for her to stow away her worries and get to work.

"Thank you, Father. I had better see if Nico needs my help."

"No need," he said from the doorway. "Sorry I took so long—I had to rummage around a bit. Does this look all right?"

Nico set down the tray on the bedside table and stepped away so she might inspect its contents. She saw at a glance that he'd thought of everything: bandages, gauze, lint, scissors, tweezers, bottles of iodine and rubbing alcohol, and a basin of steaming water.

"Well done, Nurse Gerardi," she praised him. "I'll wash my hands now."

She hurried downstairs to the rectory's modest little kitchen, and though there was a bar of soap in a dish by the sink, there were no clean towels in sight. Instead she shook off the excess water and hurried upstairs before she could forget her next question for Father Bernardi.

"Do you have any clean towels or napkins I might use? Not your good things, though. Nothing you mind getting stained."

"Of course," he promised, and returned a few minutes later

with a stack of pristine linen towels, each one starched and ironed to a glossy sheen.

"Are you certain?"

"Quite certain. There are mountains in the cupboard down the hall. Only . . . would you mind taking them home to launder? I don't want my housekeeper to fret over the bloodstains."

"Not at all. Rosa will know exactly what to do."

She returned her attention to the man on the bed. He had woken while she was washing her hands, and was now struggling to sit up.

"No, please—not yet. Not until I've had a better look at you."

"Are you Nico's wife?" he asked hoarsely.

"I am."

"You're just as pretty as he says."

"Thank you. How are you feeling?"

"My leg hurts like hell. My arm, too."

"Does your head pain you at all? Do you have any difficulty in moving your limbs? Do you feel nauseous? No? Good. I'm going to begin by looking at your leg, but first I'll have to cut off your trousers."

The man grinned, and was about to say something, but his gaze flickered to a point behind Nina's shoulder and his smile faded. "I, uh . . . I guess that's all right."

"I'll do it," Nico stated, the scissors already in his hand.

"All right," Nina said, "but stay close to the seams. That way there's a chance the trousers can be repaired after. And watch his ankle and knee when you take off his boots."

Nina turned away, privately glad to be freed of the task, and was even more relieved when she saw that Nico had laid a towel over his friend's midsection, though the man's undershorts were still in place. She began by washing the affected limb, sponging away the dirt and blood, and when she had patted the skin dry she looked over his entire leg, manipulating the ankle and knee slowly and carefully, letting her fingertips discern what her eyes could not see.

"Does it hurt when I press here? Or here?" she asked as she pushed against the bones in his ankle and foot, and was pleased when the man shook his head. His skin color was good, his circulation appeared to be unaffected, and there didn't seem to be any mechanical issues with his ankle, though it was badly swollen.

"We can't be entirely certain without an X-ray, but I don't think you've broken anything. I'll wrap it in a cold compress while I look at your arm." And then, to Nico, "Could you take one of these towels and dampen it for me? Let the tap run until the water is good and freezing.

"Now for that arm of yours." With Father Bernardi's help, she raised her patient to a sitting position and, working carefully, eased him out of his shirt and undershirt. Angry abrasions marked his skin where he'd fallen from the truck, and after washing the injured areas and using the tweezers to pry out stray bits of gravel, she swabbed his cuts with iodine and wrapped his arm in a layer of gauze.

"No stitches required—just a good clean," she pronounced.

Nico had returned with the towel while she was still busy with her patient's arm, and without any further direction had wrapped it around his friend's ankle. Now she pulled it back, just to check that it had helped to reduce the swelling, and was pleased by what she found.

It took only a few minutes more to wrap the ankle, but the poor man was shaky and pale by the time she was done. If only she had some way of dulling his pain.

"Perhaps a few sips of grappa?" Father Bernardi offered, as if reading her mind.

"What a good idea. But some water first, please. You too, Nico."

"Very well." Crouching beside the bed, he grinned at his friend. "You bore up well."

"Easy enough with your wife as nurse."

"I'm going to help Nina tidy all of this away, and I'll bring the grappa with me when I come back."

"Thank you, signora," his friend whispered, his smile wan.

"You're very welcome. I'll be back tomorrow to check on you."

In the kitchen she busied herself with disinfecting the basin, tweezers, and scissors while Nico sorted out the rectory's first-aid box. He was finished before the kettle had boiled, so occupied himself by standing behind her and depositing kisses on her temples and the tips of her ears.

"We have to move on tonight," he whispered, his breath tickling pleasantly against her ear.

She nodded, swallowing back her disappointment, and it was a minute or more before she found her voice again. "He won't be able to walk. Not without crutches."

"He'll have help. Don't worry."

"You're going with him?"

"Yes." He took hold of her shoulders and turned her to face him. "What is it?"

She looked up, her eyes fixed on the scattered freckles that adorned his nose, and tried to smile. "I know you have to go."

"I overheard a little of what you and Father Bernardi were saying. I don't want you to worry."

At last she met his searching gaze. "How can I not? I love you, and that means I fear for you. But I also trust you, and I know you won't take foolish risks." She stepped into his arms and pressed her ear to his chest, memorizing the steady rumble of his heartbeat. "How long . . . ?"

"Until I'm home? A week, maybe a little longer. But I will come back to you. I promise I will. And then you will worry no more."

Chapter 18

The promised week passed, and still Nico did not return, and it was hard, at times, to remember his promise. To remember how certain he'd been that he would come home to her.

To make things even worse, she'd begun to feel poorly, her stomach roiling at the sight of nearly every meal that Rosa set before her. After a few days it settled, but she decided to keep up the pretense of feeling unwell a little longer.

Just before leaving the rectory on Palm Sunday, she'd remembered to ask Father Bernardi when Passover began; the following day he had sent her a note—he must have felt very clever when composing it—that read, simply,

> The verse in Scripture that I wished to tell you about is the eighth chapter of the fourth book of Exodus.

Unless she had entirely misinterpreted his message, she took it to mean that Passover began on the eighth of April;

and though she wasn't able to observe the holiday as she'd have wished, she was at least able to refuse bread for the week that followed.

"You'll fade away," Rosa insisted.

"I won't. I'm fine with *brodo* and some vegetables. Anything more is too much."

Though her nausea had abated, a few days later she began to feel faint while they were weeding the vegetable garden. Rosa sent her inside for a glass of water and told her to get started on the mending, and Nina knew better than to protest. So she fetched the basket of mending and settled herself in the shade of the olive tree, and in no time at all she felt much better.

She was almost finished with the mending when she came across the nightgown she'd been wearing when she and Nico had whispered their vows to one another. It needed only a simple repair where the hem had come unstitched, but looking at the garment made her remember, and remembering made her heart grow tight with longing.

She was wiping her tears away, using the gown as a handkerchief, when Rosa returned from the garden and sat next to her.

"I came to see how you were feeling, but I didn't expect to find you crying over the mending. I thought you liked doing it."

"I do. I was having a weak moment. That's all."

"Fair enough. Thinking of Nico, were you?"

"Yes. It's so hard when he's gone. I try not to dwell on it, but everything reminds me of him."

Rosa nodded, her features soft with understanding. "I know. I've lost count of the nights I've lain awake with nothing but my worries for company."

"You must miss him," Nina dared to say.

"Nico? Of course I do."

"I meant Luca."

There was an awful pause, and Nina feared she had pushed the other woman too far. Rosa had never spoken of her lost love with the rest of her family; why would she choose to confide in Nina now?

But then Rosa nodded. "Every day," she whispered.

"What was he like?"

"He was . . . he was a good man. Always so kind to me. Forever coming by the farm to help me with my work, even though he had his own chores to do at his parents'. I was so angry at him afterward."

"After he left for Africa?" Nina asked, remembering a little of the story.

"After he was killed. I wanted to scream in his face—why did he listen to Marco? Why didn't he stay here where he was safe? Silly of me, I know. None of us can change the past."

"No, Rosa. It wasn't silly at all. Are you still angry?"

"Not anymore. And I still have my memories."

"You don't think you'll ever find anyone else? You're young still—you could have children of your own."

"I could," Rosa conceded, "but I'm happy here. And if I can't have Luca, why should I settle for some man who'll always be a stranger to me? I knew my Luca as well as I knew myself. Turning to someone else . . . I can't bear the thought of it."

"Of course. I didn't mean to—"

"I don't mind your asking. I mean, I've asked myself the same question more than a few times. I know my life with him wouldn't have been perfect. We'd have had our share of bad days, same as anyone. But I think—I *know*—we'd have been happy together."

"Are you happy now?"

"You and your questions! I don't know, not really. For certain I've been happier than I am now." She laughed, and there was even a little humor in the sound. "One day life will be better. Perhaps it will even be easier once this war is done."

"When I first came here, you were upset with me. With Nico, too. And I've meant to tell you this for ages, but I'm sorry for it. I'm sorry we hurt you."

"You didn't hurt me. Not really. It's only that I was disappointed to see him give up his fine education. And, well . . . it was hard to find out he'd been keeping secrets."

"Oh," Nina said, and tried not to think of all the other secrets they were still keeping.

"Nico and I had always been close," Rosa went on. "Even after he went away to school, he wrote to me all the time. He used to tell me everything, you see, and when I realized he'd known you for months and months, but hadn't said one thing to me about you, I was so hurt. But I shouldn't have taken it out on you."

"I don't blame you at all. I never did."

"You should. There was no call for me to be so awful to you, and I do regret it. At any rate, it's done and over, and we still have supper to make. Do you think you can face something more than *brodo* tonight?"

"Not quite yet. Do you need me to help you?"

"Just so you can faint again? No, thanks. Finish off the

mending instead, and make the most of this last hour of sunshine."

It was good advice, so Nina threaded her needle and set to repairing the hem of her nightgown. She would do as Rosa said, and make the most of the fading day. She would drink it in, now, and when the nightmares came, as they so often did when she was alone in her bed, she would turn her dreaming face to the remembered warmth of the sun, and she would think of the comfort of Nico's arms, and she would listen hard for the blessed sound of his beating heart.

WHEN NICO DID return some two weeks later, Rosa wasted no time in telling him that Nina had been poorly, and though Nina protested that she barely remembered being ill, and couldn't imagine why Rosa would bother him with such things, Nico fussed over her for the entire afternoon and evening.

Only when they were safely alone in bed, and it was at last safe to talk freely, was she able to tell him the truth.

"I wasn't ill. Not really. It was Passover, and since I couldn't do anything much to celebrate it properly, I made excuses so I wouldn't have to eat anything leavened. But only for the week."

He hugged her close, arranging her head just so under his chin. "I'm sorry I was away. One day we'll celebrate it together. You can teach me about Passover and the rest of the holy days." He sighed contentedly. "So you weren't sick at all?"

"There were a few days, just after I saw you last, when I did feel a bit queasy. I think I must have eaten something that didn't agree with me. And then, even though I felt better, I realized it would be easier to explain to Rosa than inventing some farfetched reason for not eating bread for a week. Apart from the truth, that is."

"You had me worried. I can't bear the thought of your being ill while I'm away."

"But you're home now."

"Yes, although I do have to help my zio Beppe next week. At his fields in Liedolo. We'll stay with Zia Nora—it's too far to come back every night."

"For how long?"

"A few days. No more."

Nico was home for all of Saturday and Sunday, but on Monday he left at dawn, and as soon as he'd vanished down the road the women got to work on the week's laundry. It was midday before Nina was able to spare a thought for anything beyond the baskets of steaming linens, the effort to get them loaded onto Bello's cart, and the numbing work of rinsing every last sheet, tablecloth, and garment in the arctic waters of the stream.

By the early afternoon they were finished at the stream and ready to return to the house with Bello and his cart. Rosa let the girls run on ahead while she and Nina caught their breath and took a short rest.

"Only a few minutes, mind you, or we'll miss the best of the sun," Rosa cautioned, but Nina barely heard. She was so very tired, and the sun was so scorching, and she would give almost anything for the chance to lie down and rest. Five minutes only. That was all she needed.

"Here," Rosa said, and handed Nina a clean and wonderfully cool washcloth from the nearest basket. "Wipe your face and neck. That will help."

"Thank you. I don't know why I'm so tired. I slept well enough last night."

"Have you told him yet?" Rosa asked softly.

"Told him what? That I was ill? You were the one who told him. Don't you remember?"

"No, you goose," Rosa huffed, and it was the same reaction she always had when one of the children, usually Carlo, was being willfully obtuse. "I understand if you don't want to tell him yet, but you don't have to hide it from me."

Nina stripped away the washcloth and opened her eyes. "Hide *what*?"

"You really don't know what I'm talking about, do you? What did they teach you at that nursing college?"

Nina stared at Rosa, who for some strange reason was smiling—and were those tears in her eyes?

"When was the last time we washed the cloths from your monthlies?"

And still Nina stared, her thoughts in the most hopeless tangle. Could it be . . . ? And if so, how had she missed the signs?

"Don't you keep track of such things?"

"I, uh . . ."

"I know you're still feeling off in the mornings, and don't tell me it's something you ate—you went all green when you had to bandage the cut on Matteo's leg the other day. Nina?"

"I have to sit. Just let me . . . let me sit for a moment."

Suddenly her bottom was on the ground. She had never fainted in her life, but this was too much to take in. Too much to believe or even quite understand.

Rosa took the cloth before Nina could drop it and crouched at her side. "Bend your head between your knees. And let me put the cloth against your neck. There. Doesn't it feel good?"

"I'm having a baby. I can't believe it."

"How is it that you didn't realize?"

"I've never been pregnant before. I mean . . . it never occurred to me. What do we do?"

"Nothing much. Babies take care of themselves for the most part."

"What about Dr. Pivetti?"

Rosa laughed disdainfully. "That quack? I wouldn't trust him to help with a calving. No. We'll call Romilda when the time comes. She helps with all the births in Mezzo Ciel. She was attending another birth when Carlo was born, otherwise my mother would probably still be alive. She'll take good care of you and the baby."

"I'm having a baby," Nina repeated, still trying to absorb the revelation.

"What did you think would happen?" Rosa teased. "You two are like lovebirds, you know. Forever cooing away at one another. I'm only surprised it took this long." She stood, then helped Nina to her feet. "Are you all right? Are you ready to walk back?"

Nina nodded, and together they returned to the house, Bello ambling along behind them, and as they walked she did one sum after another in her head, and they all led her to the same conclusion: she was a little more than three months pregnant. Four months, and yet she'd missed all the signs. She had been putting on weight, but she'd assumed it was due to her healthy appetite from all the hard work she'd been doing. Never mind that she'd had to move the buttons on her skirts twice already. How could she have been blind to it?

They were almost at the house when Rosa stopped and gave her a quick hug. "I know it's for you to tell my brother, so I swear I won't breathe a word. But will you promise me one thing? Make sure he's sitting down when you tell him. I don't want him fainting, too."

WHEN NICO RETURNED, very late on Wednesday night, only Nina and Rosa were still awake, for the electricity had held up all evening and they'd managed, between them, to finish nearly all of the mending.

He was bone-tired from the long walk home and his days in Zio Beppe's fields, and without his asking Nina knew what he wanted most was a hot bath. So she and Rosa rolled out the tub and filled the big kettle, and only when the water was ready did Rosa excuse herself with a soft good night and knowing smile.

Though his eyes were half-shut, Nico still noticed. "What's got my sister looking so pleased with herself?"

Not wishing to share her secret until they were safely in their bedroom, Nina shrugged in what she hoped was a believably carefree fashion. "She's allowed to be in a good mood, isn't she? And it was a nice day. That's all."

"I suppose," he said, and then he stood and began to strip off his dusty clothes. Rosa had switched off the overhead light earlier, leaving only the soft glow of the single oil lamp on the table, and even though they were alone, and unlikely to be disturbed, Nina's face grew warm at the sight of his broad back and muscled limbs.

He groaned softly as he lowered himself into the steaming water. "Thank you. I can't imagine a better homecoming than your lovely face and this bath."

"Do you want to shave? I can fetch your things from our room."

"Not tonight. I'm so tired I'd only cut myself." Now he glanced over his shoulder and smiled. "I would rather be in bed with my beautiful wife."

"Would you, ah, like me to wash your hair?" she stammered, her heart racing.

"Yes, please," he answered, and she was ever so relieved. Now she had something to do, apart from ogling him and blushing at his compliments.

She sat on the stool next to the tub, first making sure the sliver of Rosa's good soap was near to hand, along with the pitcher for rinsing. "Will you wet your hair first?" she asked, and he obligingly leaned forward and used his cupped hands to sluice water over his bent head. Straightening, he leaned back, his head almost in her lap, and she began to wash his hair.

Her heart growing ever lighter, she watched, mesmerized, as he relaxed into her soothing touch, the lines of worry and exhaustion gradually fading from his face. But the water was getting cool, and he needed to sleep, so she reluctantly dipped the pitcher into the bathwater and rinsed the soap from his hair.

And then, before she could stop herself, the words slipped from her mouth. "Nico? I have something to tell you." She had told herself she would wait until they were upstairs and alone, but now, with her heart so achingly full, she could wait no longer.

"All right," he murmured, already half-asleep. "What is it?" When she didn't answer straightaway, he opened his eyes and squinted up at her. "Is something wrong? Is it Zwerger?"

He turned in the bath, his abrupt movement splashing water all over the floor, and rose to his knees, his expression troubled.

"It's a good thing," she rushed to reassure him. "A wonderful thing."

Her eyes met his. It was wrong to be shy, she realized, so she steadied herself and, taking his hands in hers, set them on her still-flat stomach. "You're going to be a father," she whispered, and she watched as joy eclipsed the worry in his gaze.

"Oh, my darling. My beloved one. Nothing could make me happier." He bent low to kiss their joined hands. "Do you know when?"

"The autumn, I think. In October."

"Have you told anyone?"

"Only Rosa. She figured it out before I did."

"I've told you before that my sister is one of the smartest people I've ever known. You haven't said anything to Father Bernardi?"

"No. I was waiting for you to come home. What do you think he'll say?"

"He'll want to be sure of my intentions. That's for certain. And he may well feel the need to lecture me. The man is a priest, after all—but he's also a romantic at heart."

"Will he disapprove?"

"Because we aren't legally married? Or because you're a Jew?"

"Both?" she quavered, her elation fading.

Nico smiled. "He may be a little grouchy on the first point. On the second, I think you can set aside any fears. Many would disapprove, but not Giulio Bernardi. Of that I have no doubt."

Standing, he drew Nina to her feet, but frowned when he saw how much water was on the floor. "I've got the front of your dress all wet. We'd better dry ourselves off and see what we can do to clean up this mess. But only if it doesn't take too long. I can't wait to fall asleep with you in my arms."

THEY SHARED THEIR news with everyone the next morning, and then, rather than settle into a long day of chores, they all set off for church. It was the Feast of the Ascension, the significance of which Nico had explained to Nina at dawn, but which still eluded her. The Mass didn't seem to differ in any noticeable way, and after they'd returned home and had their usual midday meal the men went out to the fields, the children were sent to weed the vegetable garden, and Rosa and Nina got started on preparation for a modest party in honor of the holy day and the news of the coming baby.

"Usually there's a big to-do in the piazza," Rosa explained, "but of course it's been banned. Have to wonder why they let the *riel* go ahead at Epiphany but said no to this. So I told Papà we should have our own *festa* here."

"What if someone finds out?"

"Paolo hates dancing, so I told him he could go fishing with his friends on Saturday if he keeps watch tonight. Besides, we're only going to have our supper outside and dance to what-ever music they're playing on the radio. It's not as if we've a shed full of fireworks ready to shoot off."

She'd never danced with Nico before. There were so many things they hadn't yet had the chance to do. One day, once the war was done, they would go to the pictures, and they would eat in a restaurant, and they would dance for hours under the stars. One day.

But first she had to help Rosa get ready for their little party. "So the table's to come outside?" she asked.

"Yes, but we'll get the boys to do that for us. Why don't you bring out the chairs for now? And then we'll get started on the dough for the *crostoli*. Nico loves them."

They ate their supper outside at the big table, and when the sky began to darken they set lanterns in the windows, and hung one in the olive tree, and Matteo moved the radio to a stool by the kitchen door and, after much adjusting of dials, found a program playing American-style dance music.

"Not too loud," Aldo cautioned. "We don't want any unin-vited guests coming to join us."

And then they danced: Aldo and Nina, Nico and Rosa, and Matteo even agreed to partner Agnese and then Angela. Not to be left out, Carlo begged for a dance with Nina, and they shuffled in a slow circle as he stood on her shoes, his sweet little face alight with happiness.

A new song came on, and as soon as its melody became clear Nico reached for Nina, promising his brother they both would dance with him again. "I love this song," he explained, "and I want to dance to it with my wife."

He took Nina in his arms and led her a little ways away, to the edge of their makeshift ballroom, and the music rose and swirled around them.

"Do you recognize it?" he asked.

"'Polvere di Stelle'?" she guessed.

"Yes. It's nicer in English, though."

"You speak English?"

"Only a little. This version of the song, the Italian one, tells of a sweet dream of love. A golden star of a girl with blue eyes. But everyone knows the most beautiful girls have dark hair that curls just so, and hazel eyes, not blue."

She smiled up at him, enchanted by his romantic words and his effortless dancing and the delightful knowledge that he was hers.

"The English lyrics are far better," he continued. "Like poetry, even," and he began to sing to her, first in English, and then, so she might understand, in Italian.

"'The stars are bright, and you are in my arms,'" he sang softly and so sweetly. And then, in a whisper for her alone, "No matter where I am, my Nina, near or far, you are the one who brightens my dreams. You are the one who paints the sky with stardust."

"Is all of that from the song?" she asked, for surely the English lyrics hadn't included her name.

"Only the beginning. The rest is from my heart. For you to remember me by when I am gone."

Chapter 19

7 August 1944

*I*f only she hadn't let herself fall asleep under the olive tree.

Her back had been bothering her, and her feet were swollen, and though she'd insisted she was well enough to help Rosa and the children in the vegetable garden, she'd been overruled. "Better you stay here and work through the mending," Rosa had insisted in her no-nonsense voice that made argument impossible.

She'd felt guilty at first, for she was comfortable in her spot under the tree's silvery shade, sitting on a kitchen chair the girls had dragged out for her, a cushion at her back, her feet propped up on a round of firewood that Carlo had unearthed. She had a glass of cool water at her elbow, and the light was fine and bright, and now and again a cool breeze tickled the curls at her nape.

She was comfortable, and happy, and counting the hours until Nico returned, for yesterday she had felt the baby moving for the first time. A real movement, a proper kick that got her attention, although as the kicks and bumps and little hiccups continued over the hours that followed, Nina realized that he or she had been trying to get her notice for some time.

Today the baby was sleepy, likely because it was warm, and likely because Nina was sleepy, too. It would be heavenly to simply close her eyes and rest. A few minutes, no longer, otherwise she'd never finish up the mending.

The horribly familiar sound of car tires on gravel woke her. The unwelcome sight of a German officer's Mercedes, hissing to a stop mere meters from her feet, was the first thing she saw.

Zwerger had returned. After months of silence he had come back, and she was alone, without even Selva at her side. She had promised Nico she would hide, but then she had fallen asleep and it was too late, now, to run inside and shut the door.

She stood, not as gracefully as she'd have liked, and smoothed down her skirt and the long shirt, formerly one of Matteo's, that Rosa had helped her to alter so there'd be room for her expanding waistline. She waited, her shaking hands folded atop the gentle swell of her belly, as the wretched man got out of his car and marched toward her.

"It has been a long time since your last visit, Obersturmführer Zwerger."

"Yes."

"How may I help you?" she asked, silently cursing him for his curiosity—and herself for stupidly falling asleep. "Nico is in the fields with the other men," she lied. Now she had to pray he wouldn't insist on her fetching him. He wasn't far, only in San Zenone for a few days, helping his widowed aunt with the haying on her farm. She ought to have told Zwerger the truth, for what if he—

"Would you believe it is you I've come to see? Only a friendly visit, I swear. Merely to see how you are settling in to life in this rustic place. It must be quite a change for a Venetian like yourself."

"I'm from Padua. I only moved to Venice for my schooling."

"Why Venice? There is a school of nursing in Padua, is there not?"

What should she say? This wasn't a topic she and Nico had ever discussed. "Yes, but I . . . I started late in the year and there were no places left, and in Venice there was a place for me. At the hospital. And I was able to . . . to start right away."

He nodded, his expression blandly agreeable, as if this all made perfect sense to him. "What was the urgency?"

"I . . . I needed to go to work," she stammered. "I had stayed on at the orphanage for too long. I had to . . . to find my own way." Lies piling upon lies—how would she ever keep them straight?"

"I see. That was very enterprising of you. Leaving the only home you had ever known."

"What else was I to do?"

This question he ignored. Instead he examined the immaculate material of his uniform, flicking away imaginary specks of lint, and when that was done he turned in a slow circle, his eyes squinting even beneath the shade of his cap, his mouth pursed tight.

Presently he returned his attention to Nina. "What was your maiden name? I meant to ask the last time I was here."

"Marzoli."

"Not a common name in this part of Italy."

"My parents were from Rome, or near to Rome. At least that's what I was told. I never knew them." Lies upon lies.

"And the name of the orphanage where you grew up?"

"Why do you need to know such a thing?" It was stupid to question him, but the words flew out of her mouth like starlings from the stable loft.

"Idle curiosity, no more. I often come across children whose parents have died or fled. It's worth knowing of a safe haven for such innocents."

"St. Anthony's."

"Of course. Yes. I remember it from my time in Padua." His cold eyes swept over her once more. "You appear well. Am I correct in thinking you are in the family way?"

"Yes."

"My felicitations. Your husband must be delighted."

"He is." When would this torturous conversation come to an end?

"And yet he does not stay close to home for your sake?"

"He does. He is only up in the fields. I can show you the way if you wish to see him. Only . . . it was raining yesterday. Your boots will get muddy." That ought to be a deterrent. He wasn't the sort of man to dirty his feet if he could help it.

"He leaves no one here at the farm to help you? Protect you?"

"Rosa and the children aren't far."

"There's no sign of them now." He took a step closer.

"I stayed behind to work on the mending. The heat of the day . . . I wasn't feeling well."

"So we are alone." Another step.

"Apart from your men." Would he care that the soldiers would witness whatever he meant to do?

He took another step, near enough now that he might reach out and touch her if he chose, but she held her ground. He would not see her cower. She would not beg him to leave her be.

"I mean no disrespect, Signora Gerardi, but I fail to see the attraction."

"I beg your pardon?"

"Why did he cast everything aside for you? It's not as if you're some great beauty. You have no family, hardly any education, certainly no money of your own. What made him turn his face on his future? On his true vocation?"

"Perhaps he decided I was his future."

Zwerger didn't bother to hide his disdain. "Perhaps. Or perhaps it was a more . . . *carnal* sort of attraction."

"You disgrace yourself with such talk."

He was so close that she could see the beads of sweat that clung to his upper lip. Could see the red line where his too-tight collar dug into the soft skin of his neck.

"My family is returning," she said, though she could hear nothing above the roar of her terrorized heart. "Do you have any more questions for me?"

Still he stared and stared, more drops of sweat rolling down his temples to vanish into the wan brown of his manicured sideburns. Only when Rosa and the children came around the corner of the house did he step back.

For an instant no one said anything. The children's happy chatter vanished, as if it had been swept up and bottled, and Rosa simply stared, openmouthed, at Zwerger and his car and the hovering soldiers.

But Selva was all too aware of the danger, and before Rosa could catch hold of her collar she rushed forward, her snarls building like thunder, and pushed herself between Nina and Zwerger.

He staggered back, and Selva lunged at him, her teeth bared, her fury unleashed. Before Nina could reach her, Zwerger pulled his pistol from its holster, aimed it lazily in the dog's general direction, and shot her.

Selva fell, stricken. The children rushed to her, screaming. Rosa dropped her basket of vegetables and knelt at the dog's side, her hands painted red with blood as she moved them over Selva's golden fur.

Nina managed, just, to stay on her feet. "What sort of man are you, to kill a dog in front of the children who love her?"

Zwerger had been staring at the dog, at the children, at Rosa and the blood that covered her arms and dress. Now he turned to face Nina again. There was nothing on his face—no expression of remorse, of horror, of disgust, even.

"Leave here," Nina commanded, and to her surprise he did just that. Simply swung around and got in his car and was driven away.

"Nina," Rosa called out. "She's still breathing!"

"She's alive? From the way she fell, I thought—"

"Can you help her?"

"I don't know. Help me get her into the kitchen."

Selva was heavy, at least twenty-five kilos, but with the two of them sharing her weight, they managed to haul her onto the kitchen table. The electricity, once again, was not working, but Agnese was quick to light two of the lamps, and she and Angela held them over the table while Nina examined the dog. It was difficult to get close to her, though, for Carlo was hugging the animal, his thin arms clutching her tight, his sobs unrelenting.

"Carlo, darling, let me look at her," Nina pleaded. "You need to stand back."

"He killed her. He took out his gun and he killed her, and she only barked at him! She never bites anyone! She's dead and he killed her!"

"She isn't dead, my darling, she's asleep. Only asleep, and I need to make her better. Let me see her, please."

Rosa pulled him aside, gently, and before Nina even had to ask, the other woman handed her a bowl of hot water and a clean cloth.

Nina set to washing the wound, putting pressure on one area that was still bleeding heavily. "I need the scissors," she told Rosa. "Can you cover them in iodine first? I need to cut away some of her fur—see here? The bullet hit her shoulder, but it was only the muscle. I don't think it hit the bone."

Nina snipped at the fur, wiping away blood as she worked, and before long she could see all of the wound. "The bullet didn't go in—thank goodness for that. It skimmed along the top. If I can clean the wound and stitch it she should recover."

"Why won't she wake up?" Angela asked softly.

"When a bullet hits you, it feels like someone has punched

you very hard. It's a good thing she's asleep, because that means she'll stay still while I'm helping her."

Nina had never tended a bullet wound before, but she knew the rules of antisepsis, and she'd stitched cuts, and as long as her patient remained unconscious she was certain she could save the dog. She flooded the wound with iodine, and then, once she was sure the edges were clean and no debris remained, she stitched it shut, quickly but carefully, all the while praying that Selva wouldn't wake up until she was done.

The dog began to stir as she finished, and Rosa had to help hold her down as Nina bandaged the injury, but even once Selva awoke fully she didn't fuss. Did she know they meant to help her? It had to be terribly painful, but she didn't snap or bite, or even try to lick at the wound; fortunately it was far enough back on her shoulder that she couldn't get at the sutures.

Carlo made up a bed for Selva on the floor by the hearth, and he lovingly held a bowl to her mouth so she might drink some water, and then he fed her little scraps of chicken that Rosa fished out of the leftover soup from dinner.

Their chores forgotten, they waited for Aldo and the boys to return from the fields, and for Nico to come home, and all the while Nina's anger grew and grew until she was choking on it. Anger, and hatred, and worst of all the paralyzing sourness of fear. Zwerger had made her afraid, as he'd hoped to do, and he had terrorized the children and Rosa, and for what? To prove something to Nico? Or to her?

It was dark by the time Nico returned, exhausted after a long day of haying in his zia Nora's fields. The children had gone to bed, reluctantly, and only after Nina had promised to stay with Selva all night. She was kneeling next to the animal, feeding her a little broth from a bowl, when the door creaked and Nico slipped in.

"What happened?" he asked. In an instant he was kneeling next to her, his head bent close to the dog's head, letting her lick his face and snuffle at his ears.

"It was Zwerger. He shot her."

"My God."

"The bullet tore a gouge across her shoulder, and knocked her out cold, but I was able to stitch it before she woke up."

"You were very brave, weren't you?" he murmured to the dog, and she wagged her tail, feebly, as if she understood. "You were so brave. Yes, you were."

"It was my fault." Now he was home, home at last, and she had to tell him everything. He'd be upset, but she owed him the truth.

"How could it possibly have been your fault?"

"I was sitting under the olive tree, doing the mending, and I fell asleep. I only woke up when he drove into the courtyard."

"Why didn't you tell him I was in San Zenone? He might have driven down to look for me there."

"He wanted to talk to me. I was alone. Rosa and the children had gone to weed the vegetable garden. I didn't know what else to do. If only I hadn't fallen asleep."

Nico nodded, his gaze still fixed on Selva. "What sort of questions did he ask?"

"They were about before. The orphanage I grew up in. The reason I went to school in Venice rather than Padua." And then, lowering her voice to the merest whisper, "He frightened me. He stood so close. And he said things . . ."

"What did he say?" Nico's voice was hard. Unfamiliar. And still he did not look up at her.

"He wanted to know why you picked me. He said I wasn't pretty enough, and I didn't come from a decent family, and I didn't have any money. So it must have been for . . . other reasons."

Nico nodded, and then he got to his feet and pulled her up, his hands ever so gentle. "Once again I must ask you to forgive me."

"But I'm the one who fell asleep. If I'd been awake there'd have been time for me to hide."

"I won't go far again, not without making sure my father is here with you. I promise I won't."

She smoothed her hands over his back, as much to calm herself as him. "Why do you think he came today? It's been months and months. I'd hoped he would never return."

"As did I. He must be feeling rattled—they all are. Florence was liberated on Friday."

"So the tide is turning at last?"

"It is, and Zwerger's attempts to frighten you are a sure sign that he's panicking." Nico pulled out a chair, sat down, and lifted her onto his lap.

She cuddled close to him, loving the certainty of his embrace. "Do you think the war will be over soon?"

"Not soon, no. Another year, maybe more."

"As long as that?"

"Yes. And it makes me wonder if now might be the time for me to take you to Switzerland."

She sat up, pushing away so she might see his face properly. "No. Absolutely not."

"You wanted your father to take you."

"That was before. Before I had you, and our baby, and our family. If you take me to Switzerland I'll be alone."

"You'll be safer there."

"I couldn't bear it. If Zwerger comes back I promise I'll hide. No more naps in the courtyard. At the first sign of a car on the road, I'll run upstairs. I promise I will."

"It would be better if I stayed here from now on."

"Better for who? Not for the people who need you. I hate it when you're away—I'm selfish enough to admit it—but I won't ask you to stop. Not ever. Not knowing that people might die without your help."

"Very well. Then let's agree to both be careful. With that, and some luck, we'll both live to see the end of this war."

Chapter 20

12 September 1944

The kitchen door was still closed as they ate their breakfast, for it had been a cool and rainy night, and the morning mist still lingered close to the ground. Nina hadn't slept well, for the baby had been wakeful, its heels finding her bladder with unerring accuracy, so when Selva's bark heralded a visitor outside she didn't look up. There had been no crunch of tires on gravel, after all; likely it was a cousin or neighbor come in search of a tool to borrow or an extra pair of hands for the day.

Nico was the closest to the door. Opening it to the youngest of Signora Vendramin's sons, he listened to the boy's hesitant message, thanked him with a smile, and told the child he'd be along in a minute.

"What's that all about?" Rosa asked.

"A message from Father Bernardi. Sent along his house-keeper's boy to ask me to stop by the rectory."

"Did he say why?"

"No, but I can guess. Either he's jammed the keys on his typewriter, or the sink in the rectory kitchen is clogged. I'll deal with it now."

When Nico returned, nearly an hour later, he went straight to the fields. Nina was still in the garden, hanging out linens to dry, so she missed him.

"He didn't say what Father wanted him for?" she asked Rosa.

"No. Just poked his head through the door and said he was off to join Papà and the boys."

There wasn't time to talk with him at midday either, for rain was threatening and they all had to hurry about their meal; and before she could say a single word to him he rose from the table, thanked her and Rosa, and went back to his work.

At supper they were all tired, everyone intent on their soup and bread, the men talking of little more than their plans for the next day. Nina was still drying her hands on her apron, thinking ahead to the comfort of bed and Nico's warm embrace, when he took her hand and led her to the door.

"Nina and I are going into the village. Father Bernardi was complaining that he never sees her. Only a quick hello at the door after church, he said."

"But it's getting late," Nina protested.

"He won't mind. Do you want your shawl?"

When they arrived at the rectory, Nico didn't bother to knock but instead opened the door and ushered her inside.

"We're here, Father."

"I'm in the parlor," came the reply.

Father Bernardi stood as they entered the room, which was a larger version of the parlor at home, and had been decorated in much the same fashion. Never in her life had Nina seen so many miserable saints and smugly satisfied angels.

"Good evening, Father. How are you?" she asked as she sat on the severely upholstered settee.

Only then, looking from a still-silent Father Bernardi to Nico, did she notice how uncomfortable both men had become, their expressions strained and apprehensive. Although they were sitting at some distance from each other, both men wore the same invisible veil of dread and sorrow.

Without a single word, she knew. "Papà and Mamma."

Tears glittered in the old priest's eyes. "Yes. I had word late last night."

"Dead?"

Nico took her near hand in his. "No. At least, we don't believe they are."

"What has happened?" she asked, her voice rising. "Won't you tell me?"

"They were arrested, along with the other remaining residents of the *casa*, on the night of August seventeenth," Father Bernardi explained. "From there, we think they were sent to Trieste. To the camp at San Sabba."

"Are they there still?" Her voice was that of a stranger. Someone else was forming the words for her and pushing them past her teeth and out of her mouth to linger in the icy air of the parlor.

"No." Father Bernardi's voice was soft yet certain. "They were . . . they were put on a train and deported."

"Where?"

"North," Nico said. "Probably to a labor camp in Germany. We don't know for sure."

"A labor camp? My mother can't even walk. It doesn't make any sense. Why not leave them where they were?"

Neither man answered her; they had no answers to give.

"Were they alone?"

"No. There were others on the train," Father Bernardi said. "One was Rabbi Ottolenghi."

The rabbi was her father's friend. He was a kind man, a good man. But not well. Not the sort of man who was capable of hard labor. "He's almost blind," she said. As if that would have made a difference.

"I am so sorry, Antonina. So terribly sorry to bring such news to you."

"I won't let it rest," Nico promised. "I'll find out what I can."

"As will I. In the meantime, promise that you'll try not to despair."

"I promise, Father," she lied, for it was too late. Too late for hope.

Somehow she was able to stay upright for the walk home, one step after another, huddled in the shelter of Nico's embracing arms.

"I'll take you upstairs. Tell the others you're feeling tired. They won't question me."

She sat on their bed and let Nico unlace her shoes and unwind her shawl and take off her dress. He helped her into her nightgown, leading her arms into the sleeves as if he were dressing a child, and he turned back the covers and eased her onto her back. She lay unblinking, unseeing, her heart a cold, dead weight in her chest.

She was still awake when the sun rose again.

"I'm sorry I didn't tell you right away," Nico whispered. "I wanted to, but I couldn't think of how I would explain it to Rosa and my father. Your sadness, I mean. At least this way . . ."

"I had a few hours."

"All we know is that they were sent away. That's all."

"It's enough."

"If I could take this from you I would. If I could bear it all for you I would."

She licked at her dry lips, swallowed, and found, at last, her voice. "It makes no sense. Why send them to a labor camp if they're too frail to work? I can see why they'd imprison young people—I don't think it's right, but I can understand the *why* of it. But my parents are no threat to anyone."

"I know. I know," Nico soothed.

"My father has spent his life caring for others. He's good, every bit of him is good and decent and kind, and my mother is, too. I . . . I don't understand why they hate us so. I never will."

He rose soon after, though he encouraged her to stay in bed awhile longer. "Rest while you can, and I'll fetch you when I come in for breakfast."

But how could she sleep? It had happened. Her fears had come true. Her parents were gone, sent to some far-off place, and not only did she have to live with that knowledge, she also had to carry on as if nothing had changed. In a few minutes she would go downstairs and eat her breakfast and do her chores and no one, apart from Nico and Father Bernardi, could ever know that her heart had been broken.

A WEEK LATER, in the middle of the night, the German siege of Monte Grappa began. It shook the house and made plaster dust fall like snow from the ceiling, and outside the cows were lowing and Selva was howling, but Nico's arms held her close. He was warm against her back, one of his hands covering the curve of her belly, the other curled around her head. He would keep her safe, she knew he would, but the guns were so close, and with every new boom and rumble she grew more and more afraid.

"It sounds far closer than it is," he murmured against her ear.

"When will it stop?"

"Not until the partisans surrender. And to what end? Paris was liberated nearly a month ago. They're in retreat and they know it, but still they fight on. All that's fueling them now is their hatred. Their fear, too."

"Do you know men on the mountain?"

"Too many to count."

"How will they survive?"

"I'm not sure they can. Try to get some sleep. It will be dawn before long."

HE WAS GONE in the morning. He'd stayed long enough to help Aldo with the milking, and to tell his father he'd be back by evening, but of his destination he'd said nothing. So Nina was left to suffer the agonies of waiting, knowing the mountain at her back was crawling with enemy soldiers, all of them savage with fear, all of them poised to assume any man they encountered was a bandit.

He came home in time for supper, just, and he seemed fine to her. A little distracted, and more than a little tired, but that was all. He waited until the children and boys had gone up to bed, until it was only him and Nina, his father and Rosa, at the table, a glass of Aldo's wine before him.

"The partisans on Monte Grappa have surrendered, but the German cordon around the mountain was easy to evade. Many men were taken, or shot on the spot, but many more escaped."

"Thank the Lord for that," Aldo said fervently.

"It's not that simple. The Germans are offering amnesty to any partisan who lays down his arms and surrenders. And men are doing it. They're coming forward and they're being arrested."

Aldo poured his son more wine, and Nico sipped at it, but then, his expression resolute, he set down his glass.

"I know, or at least I suspect, where some of them are hiding. I have to warn them."

"But it's—"

"*Rosa*. There is no way, no way on God's earth, that the Germans plan to pardon them. At the very least they'll end up in prison, or as slave labor somewhere between here and Russia. Far more likely that they'll be killed."

"What can you do on your own?" Aldo asked.

"If I can save even one of them from coming forward it's

worth it. Some of them are boys no older than Matteo. How could I live with myself if I stood by and let them die?"

"You're certain the Germans won't pardon them?" Nina now asked.

He fixed her with an incredulous look. "Zwerger was seen being driven around yesterday. And this morning he stood on the steps of the church in Possagno and swore up and down that any boys or men who surrender will be pardoned. Do you truly believe a man like him intends to keep such a promise?"

"No," she whispered.

"No, he won't. And that's why I have to do what I can. I'll be careful. I promise I will. And I won't go far—just to the villages nearby where I know the men."

"Surely you have time to rest," Nina protested. "You can leave in the morning."

"Better if I travel by night." Now he looked to his sister. "Would you mind packing me something to eat? I want to talk to Nina."

She followed him outside, to the stools under the olive tree, but rather than let her sit next to him he drew her onto his lap, and she forgot to protest that she was too big, too round, because all she wanted was for him to hold her close.

"Please don't worry," he told her.

"I can't help it. Not now. Not after finding out that Papà and Mamma are lost to me. It's too hard."

"Not for someone as brave and strong as you. Not for my Nina."

"What if something happens to you? I couldn't bear it if you were hurt. If they took you away from me."

"I promise to be careful. But I want you to promise me something in return. If the worst should happen, you must remember what I told you just now. You are brave. You are strong. And you can bear anything."

Chapter 21

26 September 1944

He didn't return the next day, or the next, but the news from Monte Grappa, what little they heard, wasn't especially worrying. Men were still surrendering, but the process was peaceful, no one was being shot on the spot, and the big guns had stopped their pounding of the partisan strongholds.

The weekend passed, and no one at church had any terrible news to share; and so on Tuesday morning, when Paolo asked if he might go into Bassano to buy a spare inner tube for his bicycle, Aldo and Rosa barely looked up from their breakfast.

"It's been months since anyone has had them for sale," Paolo explained. "We used our last spare one a while back."

Rosa waited for her father's nod before answering. "Yes, but don't linger. I want you back here by midday."

So Paolo set off on the wreck of an old bicycle he and his brother shared, and they all got to work, and the morning passed by. When midday came and went, Aldo raised an eyebrow at Paolo's absence, but said nothing.

"He ought to have been back by now," Rosa fretted as she served them soup and slices of fried polenta. "What could be taking him so long?"

"He probably ran into some of his friends," said Matteo between mouthfuls. "I don't mind doing his chores. Let him have some fun for a change."

It was late afternoon before Paolo returned. Nina was doing the ironing, and though it was hot work, and tiring, it was soothing and ever so satisfying to pass the big flatiron, its belly full of coals from the hearth, over the crumpled linens and watch them grow glossy and smooth and perfect.

Rosa had killed the oldest of the hens and was busy making a stew from its meat, but her attention was fixed on the open door and the courtyard beyond. They were both listening for the telltale rattle of the boys' old bicycle, and when they did hear it, and the accompanying skirl of its tires over the patches of gravel close to the road, they looked at one another, relieved but unwilling to give voice to their fears.

There was a crash as Paolo flung the bicycle to the ground, and that alone was enough to send Rosa running. The boys were always so careful with their bicycle.

"What is it?" Rosa asked, her voice rising. "What has happened?"

Nina set the iron on the back of the range and hurried to

the door. Paolo was in his sister's arms, crouching so he might bury his face in the crook of her neck, and he was weeping, his lanky frame racked by great, gasping sobs.

"What is it?" Nina asked, for the stoic Paolo never cried about anything. He'd frowned a bit when Selva had been shot, and he'd stayed up late with her night after night, but he wasn't the sort of boy to cry.

"I don't know," Rosa fretted. "I've never seen him so upset."

"Let's get him inside and sitting down."

They propelled Paolo to a chair just inside the kitchen door, the one his father usually occupied. With Nina at his side, rubbing his back, Rosa knelt before him, her hands grasping his. He wept on, his shoulders shaking, and they comforted him as best they could, and waited until the worst of it was past and he could speak again.

"Where is Papà?"

"I'll find him," Nina offered. "I think he's in the stables."

She ran as fast as she could across the courtyard, which wasn't very fast at all given how far back she had to lean to balance the weight of her belly. "Aldo! Aldo!"

He was standing near the back, occupied with the latch on the milk cows' stall. "Yes, Nina? What is it?"

"Something happened to Paolo in Bassano. He needs you."

Aldo dropped the mallet he'd been holding and ran past her. By the time she made it back to the kitchen Paolo was in his father's arms.

"You're home, my boy. Home and safe. Take a deep breath. Yes, that's good. And another. Good. Do you think you can tell us what happened? Are you in trouble?"

Paolo shook his head, still breathless from his tears.

"Nothing happened with the Germans? With the police?"

"Yes—no. I mean, nothing happened to me. It's what I *saw*." He began to sob again, softly, brokenly. "Oh, Papà . . . I wish I hadn't gone there today."

"Tell me what happened."

"It was the partisans. The ones from Monte Grappa."

A hand of ice took hold of Nina's throat and began to squeeze. She pulled out a chair, its legs stuttering against the tile, and fell into it.

"There were thirty of them at least. The partisans. And I . . . I knew two of them. They were the same age as Matteo. They'd been at school with us here." He wiped at his face with his sleeve. "The Germans brought them in on a truck."

"Where were they? Where were you?"

"On the *viale* by the city walls. The Germans were blocking the roads. They wouldn't let any of us leave."

"So they brought the partisans in?" Aldo prompted.

"Yes, and the Germans put hoods over their heads, and signs around their necks that said 'bandit,' and then they . . . they *hanged* them, one after the other, from the trees along the road. But the trees are hardly taller than me, and their feet were dragging on the ground. It took them so long to die. And one of them, his mother was there, and she screamed and screamed, and she wouldn't stop. One of the German soldiers came over and said he would slit her throat if she didn't shut up. I don't think her boy was even dead, but they had to drag her away. The whole time she fought them, and the look in her eyes was awful. It was . . . it was . . ."

"Oh, my son. My Paolo. I am so sorry you had to see this."

"I didn't want to watch, but the Germans wouldn't let any of us leave. They made us stay there and watch."

"You are safe now," Aldo promised. "Safe with us."

"I'm not, Papà. None of us will be safe until the Germans are gone. As soon as I'm old enough I want to help Nico."

"That's very brave of you, but we had better wait until your brother is home again. We'll talk about it then."

Rosa brought him some grappa, only a scant mouthful, and he drank it down without flinching. He wiped his eyes, handed her the empty glass, and went back outside. The boy he'd been that morning was gone, and in his place was a man.

SHE WOKE TO the gentle touch of a hand at her brow, smoothing back her hair, one soft caress after another. Just as her father had done when she was little.

"I'm home."

She opened her eyes to Nico, his dear face just visible by the light of the moon. Thank goodness she hadn't closed the shutters.

He had to help her to sit up, for the creaking bed made sudden movement all but impossible, and then she was in his arms, and it was hard not to cry even though he was there, with her, alive and unharmed.

"I'm so glad, Nico. So relieved. If only you knew—"

"Papà was still awake when I got back. I think he was waiting up for me."

"He told you what happened."

"Yes. It was exactly as I feared. The men—the boys—they

murdered in Bassano aren't the only ones. They shot another fifteen or more at the barracks, and dozens more have vanished. Likely dead already."

"Were you able to stop anyone from surrendering?"

"A few. Not enough."

"Come to bed. You must be tired."

At this he pulled away, just enough that he could look in her eyes. "I can't. They're looking for me. They're accusing me of being a partisan."

Panic swept over her, and for a moment she thought she might be sick. "But you aren't. You aren't part of them at all." Or was he? She knew so little of what he did when he was away. Perhaps he hadn't always been helping refugees across the mountains. Perhaps . . .

"I'm not. We relied on help from the partisans—we had to, or risk being shot if they came across us in the mountains. But I never fought alongside them. I never carried a gun. Never killed a man, apart from the two who came to the house."

"So why are the Germans looking for you? They can't have figured out—"

"After all this time? No. And does it matter why they want me? Everything I do when I'm away is enough to earn me a death sentence. In their minds, anyone who defies them is a bandit, and deserving of only one end."

"Was Zwerger involved in this? That you know of? Paolo didn't mention him."

"I don't think Paolo's ever laid eyes on him. And I don't know if Zwerger was there in Bassano. I'm not even sure that he's the one looking for me. If he is, why hasn't he come here?

Why not wait for me to show myself? There's no one outside—I was careful to check before I came near the house. No one in the village either, or on the roads."

"Then stay," she urged.

"I can't. Not until I know who's behind this. If it's Zwerger . . . I'd hoped he would leave us alone. Just leave us be. But he couldn't get past my desire to remain here and embrace this life, in all its simplicity, and all that comes with it. He couldn't overlook my having married you. It bothers him. Disturbs him—and I've no idea why."

"He's jealous. He wants what you have."

"I doubt that. He all but held his nose when he sat in the kitchen with me."

"He does envy you. You're happy, and you are loved, and you're part of a family for whom you would do anything. You have everything that matters."

"I never thought to ask him if he had married."

"So what if he is married? He may even have children, but what sort of father could he be? He shot Selva in front of Carlo and the girls, and for all the care he used when aiming he might have killed one of them. A man like that cannot be much of a father. Certainly he isn't fit for comparison with my father or yours."

Simply mentioning her father sent a surge of fresh grief crashing over her, but she forced it back; her own sadness would have to keep. Instead she held Nico close, her head tucked just beneath his chin, and together they listened to the silence, the wonderful silence, for a few minutes more.

"Will you stay for a while? Just until I'm asleep again?"

"Let me take off my boots."

He helped her to lie down, and when she was comfortable he stretched out in front of her, their faces almost touching. With one hand he played with her hair, gently tugging on her ringlets and letting them bounce back. The other hand he placed on her belly, and together they felt their baby kicking and hiccuping.

"He or she is running out of room in there," Nina whispered.

"I know it's still more than a month, but I can't wait to meet this child of ours. I'm as fidgety as Carlo on the night before Epiphany."

"Rosa warned me that first babies are never in a hurry to be born. We might have to wait a little longer."

"Have you thought of names?" he asked.

She had, but she wanted to hear his suggestions first. "What was your mother's name?"

"Anna Maria. But my favorite name is Lucia. A reminder, I suppose, that we must look for light in the darkness. If the baby is a boy, though . . . do you have any thoughts?"

"My mother's father was called Daniele. What do you think of that?"

"I like it. I do."

She didn't want to fall asleep. Wanted, instead, to watch his beautiful face all night. "When will you come home to me?"

"I don't know. As soon as I can. Their interest in me will fade. I'm sure it will."

"And if it doesn't?"

"Even then it won't be long. The Allies are moving north every day. Once they're here we'll be safe."

"Won't you go to Switzerland?" she pleaded, even though she knew how he would answer. "You must know people there. People who would shelter you."

"And miss the arrival of our child? Never."

She was almost asleep when he spoke again, his voice the softest of whispers. "I stopped believing in miracles a long time ago. They didn't seem possible in such a world. But then I met your mother. This war brought me to her, and if that isn't a miracle I don't know what is. Sleep well, my darling. Take care of your mamma. And know that I love you both."

Chapter 22

1 October 1944

Nico had been gone for almost a week, and Nina had grown used to his absence. He would be gone for a long time, she told herself in her rare moments of rest. Only then, when her hands were still, did she worry. Only when she was falling asleep, or waking at dawn, or alone with her thoughts did she worry, but reason always followed, along with the memory of his promises. He would be gone for a long while, he had said, but the war would be over soon, and he would come home to her, and they would both be safe. That he had promised her.

It was Sunday morning, Mass had just ended, and since the day was fine and the sun was shining, nearly everyone was lingering in the piazza to catch up on a week's worth of news and gossip. Nina had found it difficult to stay awake during the service, for the church had been warm and she hadn't slept much the night before.

She confessed as much to the other women, most of them Nico's cousins and second cousins, and all of them mothers several times over.

"It's practice for when the baby comes," one now assured her.

"You'll be up at all hours nursing him," another agreed.

"Why do you say 'him'? From the way she's carrying it's sure to be a girl." This was from an aunt, or was she one of the older cousins?

Rosa had vanished, likely gone in search of Carlo, and Nina felt a little lost without her. She knew nothing of the art of discerning a child's gender from the appearance of the mother's belly, though she imagined her father would have dismissed such speculation out of hand. She knew nothing of babies either, but Rosa had promised to help, and the girls were eager to care for their new niece or nephew, and Nina was confident she would learn.

She was happy, standing there in the autumn sunshine, surrounded by Nico's family, until the moment a convoy of vehicles rolled into the piazza along the via Santa Lucia. German *kübelwagens,* four of them, and in their wake was Zwerger's Mercedes and its sinister SS pennant.

Nina held her breath as the cars circled the perimeter of the piazza, passed by the *carabinieri* station, and drew to a halt a bare meter from the edge of the gathered crowd. The door of the Mercedes opened and Zwerger, flanked by his soldiers, marched toward the church. The crowd parted, as it might for a plague of scorpions, and he ascended to the top of the church steps.

But Father Bernardi was there already, still in his vestments, and was holding up his hands in protest. "What is this? You cannot use my church as your pulpit."

"How do you plan to stop me?"

Zwerger gestured at one of his soldiers, an odd sort of whisking motion with his hand, and the man leaped forward, took hold of Father Bernardi by the back of his robes, and dragged him down the steps.

"Stay," Zwerger ordered, and the assembled congregation gasped at the shock of their own priest being treated like a dog.

Nina was trapped in the middle of the crowd, at least five meters away from the steps, with Aldo to her right and Matteo to her left. She couldn't see the children anywhere, nor Rosa. Surely they knew to keep their distance from Zwerger and the soldiers. Surely they would hide within the crowd.

Zwerger stood at the center of the steps, the church's open doors yawning wide behind him. He waited until the crowd had fallen silent, or something close to it, before he spoke again.

"Can any of you guess why I am here today? No? In that case I shall enlighten you. I am here because I have learned that you, the people of Mezzo Ciel, are harboring a criminal." He paused, waited again, and then raised one hand. In it he now held his pistol. "That criminal is the bandit Niccolò Gerardi."

Nina's knees buckled, but Aldo caught her just in time. "Our Nico is far from here," he assured her. "That swine is posturing. No more."

"For years," Zwerger continued, "the bandit Gerardi has helped fugitive criminals to cross the border into Switzerland, every one of them an enemy of your republic and my

Reich. Escaped prisoners of war. Communist agitators. Enemy aliens. *Jews.* And he did so in collusion with the same lawless brigands who continue to terrorize this region. That is why—"

Rosa burst from the crowd and ran up the steps. "My brother is innocent! Everyone here knows it—including you!" Emboldened by her fury, oblivious to the danger she faced, she spat in Zwerger's face.

He didn't react at first. Simply let the spittle run down his cheek. Calmly took out a folded handkerchief from a pocket in his uniform tunic, wiped his face, and tucked it away.

And then, smiling coolly, he backhanded Rosa as casually as he might bat away a fly. She fell backward, into the arms of onlookers, but he leveled his pistol at them. "Down," he ordered, and they laid her on the ground and backed away.

He descended the steps. Another terrible gasp swept through the crowd, a wave of horror that engulfed them all. Nina could see nothing. "What is he doing?" she cried.

Matteo was taller than them all. "He's kicking her! Papà—"

His father grabbed at his sleeve. "Stay. *Stay.*"

Zwerger had returned to the top of the steps, his anger palpable, seething, rabid. "I know you're here, Gerardi!" he shouted. "I can *feel* it—and I'm never wrong about such things. I know you are here, and you are watching me, and so I have but one question: Can you watch as I kill your family? Can you bear it?"

He scanned the crowd, his gaze narrowing on one spot only a few meters from Nina. He pointed at it with his pistol and the crowd, so many panicked fish in his net, dove out of the way. More words, unintelligible, and one of the soldiers darted forward. He emerged seconds later, his gloved hand clenched around the shoulder of a small, struggling figure. A child—a boy—*Carlo*.

Nina opened her mouth to scream, but Aldo's hand smothered it, his arms banding her chest and arms.

"I've got your brat of a brother!" Zwerger exclaimed, his malice masquerading as delight. "He cries like a baby when he's scared—don't you?" He took hold of poor Carlo's hair, and with every scream of pain from the child, Zwerger pulled ever more savagely. "Shall I shoot you now? Just as I shot that dog of yours? A single bullet would do it."

The crowd began to scream, their chants of "Pig! Pig!" interspersed with pleas to release the child, and a little of the fury faded from Zwerger's eyes.

He kicked Carlo away, the child forgotten. His gaze returned to the crowd, searching once more. "I have a better idea! Let's find your whore of a wife—if she even is your wife. You told me you married her in Venice, but not a single priest in the city knows of it. What—you think I didn't check? And I won't stop there. I won't stop until I uncover the truth. I'll dig up your secrets—yours and hers. You know I will!"

A murmur rushed through the crowd. Eyes turned toward her. She was lost, lost—

And then, at the far fringes of the crowd, a blur of movement. She could barely see, held fast as she was by Aldo, but she had to know. Had the soldiers found one of the girls? Paolo?

"Holy Mother of God," Aldo gasped, and the tumult around them rose, and a voice emerged from the horror of it all. A familiar voice, strong and beautiful and beloved.

"You don't want them."

Nico had been there all along. The crowd parted and he walked forward, straightening to his full height, pulling off the hat he'd been wearing. "They're innocent. I'm the one who has been a thorn in your side. And here I am. Unarmed. Alone."

A gleeful smile split Zwerger's face. "Let them go," he ordered, waving his arm, and there was a further commotion as Rosa and Carlo were pushed into the crowd. "But not you," he shouted, pointing a shaking hand at Nico. "You stay where you are."

Another volley of German, too fast for her to understand, erupted from Zwerger's mouth. One of the soldiers now tied Nico's hands behind his back and pushed him away from the steps and toward the stone wall that flanked the church.

Trapped in Aldo's arms as she was, Nina could only watch, unable to look away, unable to hide. She was frozen, a pillar of ice.

The other soldiers shoved the crowd back and away, and when they were done Zwerger started shouting again, his voice raw and rising. "I declare you, Niccolò Gerardi, guilty of aiding enemy aliens, banditry, and a host of other crimes I can't be bothered to enumerate now. Any one of them is enough to see you hanged"—and here he looked around the piazza, as dramatic in his posturing as Mussolini himself—"but we appear to lack a decent tree. Ah, well. I suppose we'll have to make do."

More words in German, barked at an indecipherable speed. The soldiers rushed to obey, their faces pale beneath their helmets. One, the same who had bound Nico's hands, now pushed him back against the stone wall, then returned to take his place with the others. The soldiers stood in a row.

And she knew.

She *knew*. She fought to free herself, run to him, but Aldo was far stronger. He tried to turn her head, to make her look away.

"No," she implored. "Let me see."

Nico stood alone against the wall. How many times had they walked past it together, arm in arm, content in their lives and their love? He stood alone now, tall and resolute, and surely he had to be frightened. He had to know what was to come.

His eyes searched the crowd, as if he cared nothing of the soldiers and their guns and Zwerger's toxic presence nearby. He was looking for someone—for her.

"Nico!" she screamed.

He heard her. Their eyes met. He did not look away.

The soldiers shouldered their guns. The crowd fell silent.

"Stop this madness!"

It was Father Bernardi, bursting from the crowd so he might place himself in front of Nico.

"Get out of the way!" Zwerger snarled. "He is a bandit—a criminal!"

"You've conducted no trial. You've presented no evidence. If you kill him now, you'll make a martyr of him! And every one of us here will bear witness to your infamy!"

The crowd in the piazza, afire with rage, was growing by the minute. There had to be at least two hundred people gathered, more than enough to overrun Zwerger and his men.

But Father Bernardi wasn't finished. "If you murder him,

you will have to kill me as well, and likely scores of others in this piazza. Our deaths will stain your souls and consign you to eternal damnation. Is that a price you are willing to pay?"

A sweating, shaking Zwerger wiped his brow with his sleeve, and then he smirked, as if he'd just thought of something terribly clever. "Very well, Bernardi. Have it your way!"

He then turned to his soldiers, and whatever he said was impossible to make out above the rising protests of the crowd.

The soldiers began to advance on Nico and Father Bernardi, their guns at the ready. They pushed Father Bernardi away. And then they reversed their rifles and began to hammer at Nico with the guns' wooden stocks, blow upon blow upon blow to his stomach, his back, his shoulders, his arms, and finally his head.

He fell, his blood pooling grotesquely on the ground.

He lay still, so piteously still. If Aldo had not been holding her, Nina would have fallen as well.

Zwerger waved his arm in the direction of the *kübelwagens*. Two of the soldiers grabbed Nico by his boots and dragged him to the back of one of the vehicles, and then, struggling to manage his dead weight, they tossed him inside.

"Where are you taking him?" It was Father Bernardi again, heedless of his own safety. "I demand that you tell me!"

Zwerger leaped down from the church steps and advanced on the priest. "Are you really *that* stupid? Do you honestly believe you have any control over what happens to your precious Nico now?"

"The archbishop will hear of this outrage—"

"The archbishop can go to hell!"

"But what will you do with him?"

"Whatever I like. And there's nothing you, or anyone here, or anyone in your precious church can do to stop me."

With that Zwerger strode back to his car, and in seconds the entire convoy drove off, taking Nico, bleeding and broken, away with them.

Away forever, for Zwerger had spoken the truth. He could do anything he liked to Nico and there was nothing they could do to stop him. *Nothing.*

Someone was speaking to her. "Nina? Nina! Listen to me." It was Aldo. "We need to hide you. What if Zwerger comes back for you, too?" And he put her in the arms of another man.

It was Matteo, his face wet with tears. "Don't fight me," he begged. "Please don't fight me."

He carried her, running now, and Aldo was beside him, a bruised and battered Rosa in his arms, and Paolo had the girls. But Carlo—where was Carlo?

He had fallen, but Paolo stopped and gathered him up, and they ran on.

She caught sight of Carlo's dear little face, maddened by the horrors he had just witnessed, and she recognized the look in his eyes. She had seen it on her father's face more than a year ago, and she knew it was written across her own features now.

The death of hope.

She opened her mouth to scream again, but she couldn't find her breath, not so much as a whisper. Deeper she fell, ever deeper, and then all was night and she knew no more.

Chapter 23

It was almost dark when she awoke. She was on the bed in her and Nico's room, and someone had covered her with a blanket. She was cold, and her head felt fuzzy, and there was a moment, as she floundered back to awareness, when she felt certain it must have been a dream. Only a dream, and when she sat up and went downstairs all would be well.

Then she heard the children weeping.

Not a dream. A nightmare, and she was trapped in it, and there was nowhere to hide from the pain. Such all-consuming pain. She lay on her side, stricken, watching the last of the sun fade to nothing, and she waited for the stars to bloom.

The door opened. A weight pressed down near her feet, and a cool hand pushed the tangled curls back from her eyes.

"Rosa?"

"I'm here."

"It's not a dream. It really happened."

"It did."

"He's dead," she said dully. "Dead."

"We don't know that. Father Bernardi has been trying to find out all day. And I know what Zwerger said about not being able to stop him, but Father says the archbishop will go to one of Zwerger's superiors. Will plead for mercy. They'll probably just put him in prison. Or they might send him to a labor camp in Germany. That's where a lot of the other partisans have been sent."

"Zwerger hates Nico. Hates him for reasons beyond any of this. And he will do what he promised. I know he will. He'll kill Nico, and we'll never find out how, or when, or even where. And I don't think I can bear it. I really don't."

Rosa now took hold of Nina's hands, her grip strong and certain and very nearly reassuring. "You can. You must. For the sake of your baby, and the other children, too, we must all be strong."

"And lie to them?"

"No. I don't think it's fair to tell them that Nico will come back. Not when we know so little. But we can tell them that Zwerger hasn't broken us. We can tell them that we still have hope."

And in the absence of hope? What then?

"You should come downstairs and eat something," Rosa now suggested.

"I'm not hungry."

"The baby is, though. Come."

Rosa was right; it would do the baby no good if Nina starved herself. "Can you help me on the stairs? I don't want to fall."

"Of course."

Rosa leaned forward, setting down the lamp she carried on the stool by the bed, and the light fell upon her face for the first time. Her right cheekbone was badly bruised, and above it her eye was blackened and swollen almost shut. There were bruises on her arms, too, where Zwerger had kicked her.

"Your poor eye," Nina whispered, her heart seized anew by horror.

"It will heal. But that swine Zwerger will never forget the moment I spat in his face. That alone was worth every bruise."

Nina's limbs had stiffened, but with Rosa's support she made it along the hall and down the first flight of steps. She had to stop and catch her breath when they reached the landing, but the second flight was easier, and soon they were in the kitchen.

Nothing about it had changed since breakfast that morning. The room was warm and familiar and comforting, filled with good smells and happy memories. It was still her favorite room at home.

Rosa set down a bowl of soup, and Nina started to eat, though her hand was shaking so much it was difficult to wield the spoon without making a mess.

"It's shock," Rosa said, noticing. "Take your time. It will get easier."

It did, and before long the bowl was empty, and Nina began to feel a little stronger. In a few minutes she would ask to go back to bed, and then she would press her face into the pillow and cry. Once she was alone in her and Nico's room, she wouldn't have to pretend to be strong.

Aldo came into the kitchen, followed by a second man.

Father Bernardi. For the first time ever, in all the years she had known him, he didn't offer her a smile along with his greeting.

"Nina, my dear. How are you?"

"A little better."

"Do you have news?" asked Rosa.

"I do. They've taken him to Verona. To the headquarters of their secret police. The SD."

"That's it?" Aldo asked. "That's all you were able to find out?"

"For the moment. The archbishop thinks we may be able to persuade the Germans that a prison sentence is appropriate. Particularly since the evidence Zwerger cited was pure speculation. And now, if you and Rosa don't mind, I wonder if I might have a few moments of privacy with Nina. So we may speak of, ah, spiritual matters."

Father Bernardi waited until he and Nina were alone, and then he sat on the chair next to her and lowered his voice so only she might hear. "I am not giving up on Nico," he said. "I will move heaven and earth to bring him home to you. I promise you I will."

She nodded, blinking back scalding tears.

"I also have an admission to make. I hope you will hear me out."

"Go on."

"I want you to know that I was a little concerned about your coming to stay with Nico and his family. In the beginning, that is."

"Why? I thought it was your idea."

"Would you believe it was Nico who suggested it? I told him

of my friendship with your father. Of your father's conviction that you were no longer safe in Venice. I told him that I was thinking of having you come to stay with me. I'd pass you off as a cousin of mine. An orphan in need of a home."

"Why didn't you?"

"Nico didn't think it would work. And he didn't think it would be fair to make a young woman hide away in a near-empty house with only an elderly priest for company. So he suggested you come and live with him, which of course would mean you'd have to masquerade as his wife. And that is why I was concerned."

"I'm sorry, Father, but I still don't understand."

"I knew you to be an intelligent, brave, and affectionate girl. I was convinced—rightly, as it turned out—that he would need little encouragement to fall in love with you. And that would mean my selfish hopes for him to one day become a priest, and perhaps even take over from me here in Mezzo Ciel, would never be realized."

"If you're trying to make me admit that it was wrong for us to fall in love, I won't," she said, her voice rising.

"Nina, my dear. I'm trying to tell you that *I* was wrong. More than that, I'm trying to tell you that your love for Nico, and his for you, was meant to be. Some might call it fate. I prefer to think of it as an instance of grace."

"Why are you telling me this?"

"So you won't forget to hope. So you'll remember that your love for him, and the strength you gain from that bond, will continue to exist—no matter how long you are separated, and no matter how distant you are from one another. Your love lives on. Can you remember that for me? Can you find a way to hope?"

"Yes, Father," she whispered.

"I wonder, then, if you might wish to pray with me for a while. Perhaps we might choose one of the psalms?"

Memories assailed her. Nico's face as he'd knelt before her, taken her hand in his, and vowed to love and honor her for the rest of his life. "There is a passage in the Song of Songs. It begins with 'Let me be a seal upon your heart' . . ."

"I know it well." Without opening his prayer book, Father Bernardi began to recite the blessed words. "'Let me be a seal upon your heart, like the seal upon your hand. For love is fierce as death, passion is mighty as Sheol; its darts are darts of fire, a blazing flame.'"

"'Vast floods cannot quench love,'" Nina whispered, "'nor rivers drown it.'" And then, her eyes closed, her memories fixed on the night she and Nico had said their vows, "'I am my beloved's and my beloved is mine.'"

Despair and grief crashed over her, wave upon wave, and she was defenseless, drowning, *alone*. She was so alone.

"Father Bernardi? Are you there?"

"I am, but—oh, my heavens!" He jumped to his feet, his chair overturning, and hurried from the kitchen.

Everyone had left her. Her only companion was the pain, rising and fading and rising again. Only her pain remained.

"Nina? Nina? You need to listen to me." Rosa took hold of her shoulders, her touch gentle but firm. "The baby is coming."

She looked up, and was alarmed by the expression of panic on Rosa's face. Rosa, who always knew what to do.

"I don't understand," she said, and then, following Rosa's gaze, she looked down and saw the dark and spreading stain on her skirt.

"Your waters have broken. The baby is coming, and we must get you upstairs again."

"I didn't notice . . ."

"Well, poor Father Bernardi did. You've given him the fright of his life. Can you get up?"

"I think so," Nina said, but when she tried to stand her legs crumpled under her weight.

"Papà!" Rosa called. "We need you!"

Aldo came running, and between him and Rosa they were able to get Nina to her feet and up the first flight of stairs. As they reached the landing, though, she was felled again by the pain, and only once it had passed was she able to breathe, let alone move.

"Do you remember anything from school?" Rosa asked as they lumbered up the second run of steps.

"From what?"

"Nursing school."

"Oh, ah . . . yes. A little," she stammered, for the only birth she'd ever witnessed had been one of the farm cats having kittens in the spring. "A very little," she amended.

"We'd better call for Romilda," Aldo said, his face white with fear.

"The midwife? But what if she says—"

"We can trust her," Rosa insisted, "and she knows what she's doing. It will be safer for you and the baby if she's here."

At last they reached her room. While Aldo rushed off to fetch the midwife, Rosa helped Nina sit on the bed.

"Let's get you out of that dress," said the ever-practical Rosa. "Where's your nightgown?"

"I only have the one. I'll soil it," Nina protested.

"You can't mean to go through your labor stark naked. I'll get one of mine."

"No. Just a sheet is enough. Just—"

More pain, so consuming she could scarcely breathe, let alone speak.

Hours seemed to pass, though it might have been only minutes. It was so hard to think of anything beyond the pain. Romilda arrived at last, coming into the bedroom just as Nina kicked off the covering sheet that Rosa had insisted upon for modesty.

"No, Rosa," she begged. "I can't bear it. Don't put it back."

"Better that way," Romilda said cheerily. "Will save on washing afterward."

The midwife set about unpacking her bag and washing her hands in the bowl of near-boiling water Rosa provided. And then she took a good look at Nina and informed her that the baby would not be born for hours yet.

"I'm glad," Nina panted, caught up in a contraction. "The baby can't be born today. Not after . . ."

"No fear of that," Romilda said briskly. "First babies like to take their time."

Hour after hour crept past, the pain building higher and higher, the pauses between contractions growing ever briefer.

Romilda examined her from time to time, and just as the sky began to brighten into day she announced that it was time for Nina to push.

"Your baby is ready to be born."

"What do I do? What do I do?"

"Look at me," Romilda ordered, her tone firm but not unkind. "You know what to do. When your body tells you that you need to push, you'll take a big breath in, and then you'll hold it. You'll hold it, and you'll push until I tell you to stop. Rosa will help you sit up a little—that will make it easier for the baby."

She was so tired, and she wasn't sure she would find the strength to carry on, but she did as they told her, one searing push after another, and just as she was coming to the last of her strength Romilda had her reach down so she might feel the top of her baby's head.

"One more should do it, Nina—*now*," Romilda urged.

It was too much, too much, but Rosa was chanting in her ear, reminding her of how strong she was, and she held her breath and pushed until she was dizzy. The pain grew and grew and then, in the space between one gasp and the next, it was gone and a baby began to cry. Her baby.

"It's a girl," Rosa wept, and for a moment Nina was certain that something was wrong. But Rosa was smiling beneath her tears, and her voice was joyful.

"She's healthy and strong," Romilda said. "I'll weigh her in a bit but she looks to be a good size. Here she is, and while you're busy admiring her I'll help you pass the afterbirth."

Romilda set the baby on Nina's chest and covered them both with the neglected sheet, and in that moment, seeing her daughter's face for the first time, Nina was transported. She was in love.

"See if you can get her to suckle," the midwife suggested. "She'll want to sleep soon—you both will—but it'll do you both good if she can get some early milk from you."

It was a challenge to get the baby to latch on, but with a little help from Romilda, and some frustration on the part of both mother and child, the baby began to nurse. Her greedy mouth was surprisingly painful, but it was nothing compared to what had gone before. No amount of pain mattered, not when she could hold Nico's daughter in her arms.

"He wanted to call her Lucia," she now told Rosa. "And I thought we could add Anna as a second name. For your mother."

"What do you think?" she asked the baby. "Do you want to be called Lucia?"

But Lucia had fallen asleep, her mouth slack against Nina's nipple, and Romilda now took her and washed her and wrapped her up in the same soft blanket that, Rosa now explained, had been used for all the Gerardi children. "There," she said, returning Lucia to Nina's waiting arms. "Now you both need to sleep."

"Won't the children wish to see her?"

Rosa was doubtful. "Aren't you too tired?"

"I don't mind staying awake a little longer. Especially if it will give them a happy memory to set against yesterday."

Rosa nodded and slipped from the room, only to return moments later with Carlo, Angela, and Agnese. Their faces were wan and fearful and still stained with tears, but each of them managed a smile for Nina and the baby.

"I hope I didn't frighten you," Nina said as they gathered around her. "Did I make a lot of noise?"

"Hardly any," Agnese said. "Papà told us you were being very brave."

"I'm not so sure about that. I only did what Romilda and Rosa told me to do."

"Can we see her?" Carlo asked.

"Of course." She tilted the baby's face toward them. "What do you think?"

"Hmm," said Carlo. "She's very small."

"New babies usually are, but she'll get bigger."

"What are you going to call her?"

"Nico wants her name to be Lucia. What do you think?"

He nodded vigorously. "I like it."

"That's enough for now," Rosa said. "Nina and baby Lucia both need their sleep." Turning to Nina, she added, "I'll be back once they're settled."

Romilda had finished packing up her bag. "I'll return tomorrow to see how you're doing. Nurse her whenever she wakes, and if you have any trouble getting her to latch, have Rosa fetch me."

"Thank you," Nina said. Suddenly she was so tired it was an effort to even say that much.

"You're a brave girl, Nina. You faced down that labor with as much courage as any woman I've ever known, and I've delivered more babies than I can count. I only hope you'll remember that in the days to come."

Chapter 24

9 October 1944

As soon as Nina was able to climb the ladder, Aldo and Rosa had insisted she and Lucia move to the hiding place. They had made it comfortable for her, even homey, with a freshly filled mattress of corn husks, the same woolen pad from her bed below, and a warmly lined basket for the baby. The children visited her, too, sworn to secrecy.

"No one can know," Aldo had explained. "Not your teacher, Carlo, nor any of your friends."

Rosa was up and down the ladder many times over the course of each day, and Aldo, too, for he loved to hold his granddaughter and sing to her softly, soothe her when she was fussy, and tell her stories about Nico when he'd been a little boy.

"How do you manage it?" she asked, wondering at how he was able to smile and laugh so easily. "I want to laugh. I want to be happy again. But I've no idea how to do it. How am I meant to survive?"

"It's no great secret. We rise at dawn and we do our work and we live our lives. That's all. And we never forget that Nico only wants happiness for those he loves."

"I know, but how am I to shut out the memory of what was done to him? The knowledge of what he is suffering now?"

"You can't. I wish you could, but you can't. Not when you love him as you do. And I do understand, Nina. I do. When my Anna Maria died, I thought I would die, too. Seeing her struggle to give birth to Carlo, watching her in pain, knowing how much she suffered . . . even now I can't bear to think of it. But I survived. I survived, too, when Marco was killed. And I will survive this latest horror, and pray every day that my son will come home to me."

"And what if he doesn't? What then?"

"Then we endure, and we remind ourselves to hope, and one day we wake and the weight of it is a little less."

"I wish I could believe you."

"You will. One day, my dearest daughter, I promise you will."

Lucia was only a week old when Rosa gently introduced the subject of the baby's baptism. "We do need to get it done quickly, if only so she still fits in the gown my mother made. Father Bernardi can do it here, at the house."

Nina nodded, and smiled, and asked if they might talk about it again when she wasn't quite so tired, and Rosa abandoned the subject.

But only until the next day. "I know you don't want to have

the baptism when Nico isn't here. I understand. But we must get it done."

And Nina knew the only way out of it was to tell Rosa and Aldo the truth. Every last bit of it. So she asked if Father Bernardi might come for a visit, as he hadn't yet seen the baby. In deference to his bad knees Nina brought the baby downstairs and they all gathered around the table in the kitchen. Only the adults, for they'd prudently waited to bring her downstairs until it was dark, which meant the little ones were in bed; Matteo and Paolo were outside keeping watch.

Father Bernardi took the chair next to Nina, and he admired the baby, and then his usual merry expression vanished and he put on his serious face, and both Rosa and Aldo noticed right away.

"Is something wrong, Father?" Rosa asked worriedly.

"Have you had news of Nico?"

"No, Aldo. Nothing like that. I'm here because Nina and I have a confession to make." And then, looking to Nina, "Would you like me to begin?"

She nodded, her throat closing in, and listened as he began to tell her story.

"For many years I have been friends with a physician in Venice. His name is Gabriele Mazin. At first I was a patient of his, and then, over the decades—I think it must be close to thirty years now—we became ever closer, and now I count him among my dearest friends." He paused, waiting for Rosa and Aldo to digest that first, seemingly inconsequential, piece of information.

"Dr. Mazin and his wife are Italian. Their parents were

Italian. Their families have lived here for hundreds of years. And still they have been persecuted in this, their only home, simply for the fact that they are Jewish. They are Jewish, and so is their daughter, Antonina. Though Nina is the name she uses now."

The silence that followed, as both Aldo and Rosa tried to make sense of what he had just told them, was achingly painful.

"You are their daughter?" Aldo asked at last. "You are Jewish?" Yet he didn't seem angry or affronted. Only surprised. "Why did you and Nico tell us you were an orphan? Why didn't you tell us the truth?"

"I wanted to," Nina said, blinking back tears. "But Nico thought it best that we keep it a secret."

"We wouldn't have cared," Rosa said. "I was awful when you first got here, but that's because I was upset with Nico. I couldn't believe he'd fallen in love and spent all that time with a woman and never so much as told me her name. All those months and he'd never thought to tell me about you."

"And therein lies the second part of our confession," Father Bernardi said, his expression ever more serious. "Last year Dr. Mazin became convinced that it was no longer safe for Antonina to remain in Venice. He and I had talked of it before— the notion that I would find a place for her to hide until the war was done. I told Nico of it, in the course of some other conversations we were having, and he offered to take Nina in. Sight unseen."

Rosa had been standing, but now she grasped hold of the tabletop and collapsed into the nearest chair. "You weren't in love," she whispered. "That was all a lie?"

"At first it was," Nina pleaded. "I liked him straightaway—how could I not? And then, not so long after, we became friends. And then . . . then it was impossible not to love him. And I do, Rosa. I love him with my whole heart."

"If you weren't married when you first came here, then when?" Rosa asked, flushing a little.

"We're not married," Nina admitted. "And I wish, now, that we'd gone to Father Bernardi. But I didn't want to have a Christian wedding."

"Oh," Rosa said, and she began to dab at her eyes with the corner of her apron.

"The rest, Nina," Father Bernardi prompted. "Don't forget the rest."

"I don't want Lucia to be baptized. I don't want to offend you, or hurt you in any way, but she's my daughter. She is my daughter, and that means she, too, is Jewish. And so that's why . . . well. That's why I asked Father Bernardi to come."

"Did you think we would reject you?" Aldo asked.

"At first I didn't know you well enough to worry. Later, though, I did worry. I still do. How can I not? You hold my fate in your hands. One word from you to the police and I'll be on the next train north."

"Never," Rosa said, and now she was weeping openly. "Never, *never* would we hurt you. Never will we allow anyone to take you from us. You belong to us, Nina. You and Lucia both. Nothing will ever change that."

"We will keep you and Lucia safe," Aldo promised. "I swear it."

"And you aren't upset that we lied to you?"

"Maybe a little?" Rosa allowed. "But only because I wish you had trusted us with the truth."

"I still think it best that the children aren't told," Father Bernardi said. "One day, but not yet. Not while men like Zwerger still hold the power of life or death over us."

Aldo nodded, and then he went to the high shelf above the hearth, to the spot where he kept his best bottle of grappa, and he fetched it back to the table, along with four glasses. He poured a scant measure into each glass, handed one each to Rosa, Nina, and Father Bernardi, and took the last for himself.

"In lieu of a baptism, let us drink to the health and happiness of my first grandchild. To Lucia Anna Gerardi. May she forever know the love of her family and the peace of our hearth. And may her father return to her before she is old enough to remember his absence."

"To Lucia," Nina echoed. "And to her father's safe return."

IT WAS LATE afternoon, and the hiding place was uncomfortably warm, and the baby had fallen asleep at her breast. Nina had slept, too, but only fitfully, and so she was more than half-awake when the shouting and barking began.

She put Lucia down in her little basket, making sure she was securely swaddled, and crawled toward the shuttered window. It would be folly to open it, but if she tilted her head just so, she could see into the courtyard below.

Zwerger was back, and this time he had at least a dozen men with him.

"What more do you want from us?" Aldo cried. "You took my son, and now you come to take away my daughter?"

"Daughter? Is that what you're calling that whore? No—don't even think it. Or do you wish for your other children to witness your death? It's easily done."

"Leave my father alone." Matteo's voice was nearly as deep and steady as Nico's had been.

"Get back—all of you," Zwerger screamed. "Against the wall by the road. Stay where you are. And you there—if you let go of that dog I'll empty my gun into her. That's a promise."

There were noises below, in her bedroom. Nina turned her head just as Rosa's face emerged from the trapdoor. "He's back! You need to pull up the ladder and keep the baby quiet. They're sure to search the house."

"Come here."

"There isn't time!"

"There is. Come here—I'm begging you."

Rosa climbed the ladder, grumbling all the while, and came to crouch next to Nina.

"He's gone mad, Rosa. Just listen to how he is carrying on. And the children—he has all of them lined up against the wall. I can't bear it. I can't."

"That's why you must hide. They'll look, and they won't find you, and they'll go away."

"That man is not going to leave here without me. He'll tear this house apart, beam by beam, brick by brick, and when he finds me he'll find Lucia, too."

"What do we do?"

"Hide here with the baby. Make sure she doesn't cry. She just finished nursing, so she should sleep for a while."

Rosa frowned, not understanding. "Why me? You're the one who needs to hide."

"No. I'm the one who needs to surrender. Listen to me. He will not give up. He will not leave us be. And there's no way for me to escape, not now. He has men surrounding the house, and soon they'll come up the stairs, and they'll find her."

"I can't let you go, Nina. You're my sister—you're part of my *family*. How can I send you away with that man?"

"If we're to save my baby and the rest of our family, you must let me go. Let me do this for you all." Now Nina wrenched off her wedding ring. "This is for Lucia. And my other things, too. My jewelry, and my books, and the photographs of my parents. Tell her their names—Gabriele and Devora Mazin. She is the last of my family. The very last."

Nina crawled to the basket and picked up Lucia. Held her close. Breathed in her milky sweetness. Kissed her perfect face. And then she gave her to Rosa.

"Will you tell her about me?" she asked. "If I don't return?"

"But you—"

"Promise me you will."

"I promise."

Rosa was sobbing now, one hand pressed to her mouth to muffle her cries, and Nina longed to let her own tears fall. But not yet—not until she had faced down her enemies.

"Tell her how much I love her. How much Nico and I both love her. And when he returns," she added, her voice faltering, "tell him that he is forever my beloved."

Zwerger's voice continued to rise and rise, and the children's cries were growing ever more frantic, and there was only one thing left, now, for Nina to do.

She climbed down the ladder and helped Rosa to pull it back up. She waited until the trapdoor was closed and she could see her friend—her sister—no more. She walked downstairs, past the parlor, through the kitchen, and into the afternoon sun.

"I surrender," she called out.

Zwerger whirled around, triumphant, and closed the distance between them.

"It took you long enough."

"I was asleep when you arrived. I had to dress."

He stepped back, looking her over, and his expression curdled into disgust. "What is *that*?"

She looked down and saw the two dark stains against the pale blue fabric of her bodice.

"Where is the child?" Zwerger demanded.

"Dead. Born dead because of you."

"I don't believe it."

"Why? Because my breasts are leaking? Don't you know that a mother still produces milk for her dead child? Yet another horror you have laid at my door."

Zwerger whirled around, his gaze settling on the children. A few paces led him to Angela

"Does she tell the truth? Was the child born dead?"

Angela looked to her father, her entire body quaking with fear, and then to Nina. "Yes," she said carefully. "The baby was dead. Rosa said it was because of the shock."

"Very well. And yet I think a search of this house is still worthwhile."

Zwerger barked out his orders; all but two of the soldiers rushed inside the house. The sound of crashing furniture soon followed.

They were making such a racket. Surely it would wake the baby. Surely they would hear her wails and learn the truth of the hiding place. Nina held her breath, not daring to hope, but eventually the soldiers filed out and made their report to Zwerger.

"But that is impossible!" he raged. "That sister of his—the one who spat in my face. What about her? Where has she got to?" He spun around and advanced on Nina again. "You are hiding something—I know it!"

"I am not."

"But you *are*," he insisted, and he took hold of her arm and dragged her across the courtyard until she stood before Aldo and his children. "Look at her—a Jew! All along she's been hiding here, a cuckoo in your cozy nest, and she is the reason your Niccolò is lost to you. She brought this to your door—can you not see the truth of it?"

"You lie!" Aldo shouted, and only the threat of the soldiers' guns kept him pressed against the wall.

"But I can prove it," Zwerger insisted.

"That she's a Jew? What of it? She is my son's wife. And that makes her my daughter. Nothing can change that. As for your other accusation, we both know that *you* are the reason my son is not here today. You alone are responsible for taking him from us."

Zwerger's face was almost purple with rage. "What is wrong with you people? Are you simpletons? Is that it? She is your enemy!"

Nina pulled at Zwerger's sleeve until he spun round to face her. "You have me now. Why torture them further?"

"I do have you, and I'll see you dead, here and now! You know I'll do it!"

The children were wailing again, and Aldo had broken down, too, the tears streaming from his face. For their sakes she had to stop it.

"Stop!" she screamed. "Enough! It's me you want—only me. Why torment them now? Haven't you sinned enough?"

Zwerger pulled his arm from her grasp. "I am not the sinner here," he snarled. "You brought this on yourself."

One of the soldiers came forward to bind her, but Aldo surged forward and slapped his hands away. "Leave her—just leave her!"

In an instant, Zwerger's pistol was at Aldo's temple. "Stand back and shut up, old man."

"Papà, no!" Nina cried out. It was the first time she had called him by that name. "You must let me go. The children need you. Rosa needs you."

"How can I bear it?"

"You can—you will. Now let me go, and I pray I will see your kind face again one day."

Her vision blurred by tears, she couldn't see him or the children as the soldiers dragged her into the back of their truck. She could no longer see, but she could still hear, and their cries rang in her ears long after the truck had rumbled onto the road and away from Mezzo Ciel.

Chapter 25

The soldiers made her lie on the bottom of the truck, and they laughed whenever there was a bump in the road that jostled her about, and by the time it finally screeched to a halt she couldn't think beyond or around the pain.

They were at the rear of an enormous building, though in which city she had no idea. She was hauled from the truck, her body pawed by one bruising set of hands after another, and it was those same brutal hands that half carried, half dragged her inside and along a snaking corridor to a large interior courtyard.

At its center was a gallows. A man had been left hanging there, his body swaying gently in the late afternoon sunshine, the sky above him achingly blue. The man's head was covered by a black hood, but she recognized him still.

It was by his clothes she knew him, for she had mended the trousers herself, many times, and the dark blue coat he wore was familiar, too, with its faded hem and the bottom button that didn't match. She recognized those trousers and that coat.

They belonged to Nico.

She fell to her knees, and she tried to stop herself from looking again, but she had to do it. Had to know, truly and finally, that it was him.

She stared at the body of the man she loved, her eyes dry, her scream trapped in her throat, and she ignored the men who kicked her and told her to *get up, get up, dumb bitch, just get up.*

Only when one of them took a great fistful of her hair and dragged her to her feet did she let them pull her away from that place of death and the lonely, hanging body of her beloved. They took her along another corridor and down a flight of stairs, and then they pushed her into a room that was painted a horrible dark red, the exact color of dried blood, and locked her in.

They left her prostrate on the floor, unable to rise, her hands still bound. Her breasts became engorged, the pain startling and fierce, and before long her bodice and brassiere and the pads Romilda had given her were all soaked through with milk, its scent inescapable and heartrending.

The guard returned after a few hours, though it might have been far longer, and took her to another room, and there she was made to sit at a table, her arms still bound behind her, and the lights had been left on to stop her from falling asleep.

She sat and waited, and she wondered if she was prepared to die. If she would find the strength to face it as courageously as Nico had surely done.

Hours passed, and she rested her head on the table, hoping

to sleep, but her thoughts were such a tangle, and the lights were so shockingly bright. She would never sleep again. That was one way to die, wasn't it? To be kept awake until madness beckoned.

The door crashed open and Zwerger entered. He sat across from her, and for the next minute or two he occupied himself with opening a file folder and arranging its contents as neatly as chess pieces on a board. There were letters and forms and photographs, and a small booklet that he set to one side, and a single identity card. Her identity card.

Then he adjusted his chair, smoothed back his hair, and steepled his hands on the table that separated them.

"A little more than a year ago, Niccolò Gerardi astonished his family and neighbors by bringing a wife home with him to Mezzo Ciel. They'd always assumed he would return to his true vocation once his brothers were grown and able to take over the farm, but instead he did something very different. He brought home a girl he'd met in Venice, a complete stranger who—and here I quote one of his neighbors—'couldn't tell one end of a bull from the other.' Does any of this sound familiar?"

Unwilling to look upon Zwerger's loathsome face, Nina fixed her attention on the tabletop that separated them. She would not respond. She would not give in.

"Very well. I doubt you will be surprised to learn that not a single church in Venice has a record of his marriage to Nina Marzoli—that is the name you gave me, is it not? Nor is there a Nina Marzoli registered at the nursing school attached to the ospedale. Nor has the director of St. Anthony's orphanage in Padua ever heard of a girl named Nina Marzoli.

"You can see where this has led me, of course. To you. To the whore who wormed her way into Niccolò's confidence, his bed, and his heart. And it does make me curious. How were *you* able to turn him away from his vocation? Away from God?" He waited, his fingers tapping an arrhythmic beat against the tabletop. "You truly have nothing to say?"

"What would a man like you know of God? You were jealous, and so you sought to destroy what you could not have—what you had no hope of ever becoming. A good man. An honorable man. A man who was loved."

"Silence!"

"Nico told me about you. About the reason you were sent away from the seminary. It had nothing to do with your wanting to return to Austria, did it? You were asked to leave because you'd been bullying the other boys. Stealing from them, hurting them, making their lives a misery. Nico stood up to you, and he went to Father Superior and told him everything, and that was *it* for you and your dreams of becoming a priest."

"Shut your filthy mouth!"

It was reckless to goad him so, but she could not bring herself to stop. "When you are on your knees and alone with God, what do you pray for? It can't be forgiveness, for you are blind to your sins. What do you pray for when you are alone in the dark?"

"Victory," he hissed through gritted teeth. "Victory over you and your kind."

"You will never have it. Don't you know the war is all but lost?"

She waited for him to strike her, to scream in her face, to

kill her with the same pistol he'd already used to terrorize her family. Instead he began to laugh.

"You stupid, *stupid* woman. Do you know nothing of what is taking place at this very moment? I've seen it with my own eyes, and I know what awaits you. Go on—sneer away. I have all the proof I need. And all it took was this little card."

Her identity card. Zwerger now tore it in two, then tore it again, and again, until the pieces lay like confetti on the table.

"Last month we arrested a notary in Padua. The wretch blocked his door and tried to burn his files, but he wasn't fast enough. We recovered almost everything, including this little ledger. A list of every man, woman, and child for whom he'd made up false papers. It was locked in his safe, but few men will keep secrets with a gun to their head."

She would not look. She would say nothing more.

"I have it here, and if I open it to just the right page . . . yes, here you are. Nina Gerardi, née Marzoli, along with the fee that was paid for your papers. Five hundred lire—a bargain for the price. And can you see, just here, at the end of the notation?"

He pushed it under her nose, but she closed her eyes. She would not look.

"A set of initials. *NG.* You really should look, because—and this really is very interesting—those same initials appear next to nearly fifty other names. Not their true names, mind you. The names that went along with their false papers. And one of those names was familiar to me, for it was the known alias of an escaped prisoner of war. An Englishman."

He paused, letting it all sink in. "Now do you see? I had enough to draw a line between Niccolò, the false papers, and scores of enemies of the state—your traitorous self included. That much I knew when I put him to death, but I was sure there was more. I knew *you* were guilty of more."

Why would he not stop talking? It would be so much easier if he'd just take out that pistol and shoot her.

"It took only a few days of diligent research on the part of one of my men. He was following a hunch of mine, for I knew you had to have come from somewhere. And I had another hunch—really this was so easy. Too easy, if I'm honest. I told him to begin with the census of Jews. You do remember it, don't you?"

Zwerger set his fists on the table between them, his knuckles popping, and rose to loom over her. She sat ever straighter, refusing to cower, and still she did not look up at him.

"In that census, in the records for Venice, he found a young woman by the name of Antonina Mazin. Her parents, Gabriele and Devora Mazin, were deported in August—but she was not among those who were rounded up. She had vanished, and no one in Venice could say what had become of her."

Zwerger sidled round the table to stand behind Nina, and though he didn't touch her, his hot breath still fanned repulsively against her ear.

"You might as well admit it, Antonina. Else I'll be forced to bring in the rest of the Gerardi fam—"

"They didn't know. To them I was Nina Marzoli. Nina Gerardi."

"That I doubt. Signor Gerardi didn't even flinch when I told him you were a Jew, nor the others. That tells me they *did* know."

"You can't—"

"I certainly *can*. I've already furnished the brothers' names to the authorities, and I promise we will make good use of them in Germany. Even that father of theirs looks strong enough. We might be able to wring out a few years of hard labor from him as well."

"His sister will never be able to manage on her own."

"So?" he spat. "What are her worries to me?"

It was a mistake to listen to his threats. Rosa was strong and tough and fierce. She would never let anything happen to the children. Father Bernardi would help, and the village would rally round, and there were so many cousins. Surely they would—

"Antonina? Are you still listening? Good, because I haven't touched upon the best part. Do you want to hear what it is?" He edged ever closer, his mouth now grazing her ear, and it took the last of her strength not to flinch.

"It really was your fault," he hissed. "I first came to Mezzo Ciel because I wanted to know what had become of my old friend. Nothing more. I was prideful—I'll admit it—and I wanted him to see how I'd risen in the world. Not least because I'd always suspected he'd been the one to rat me out to that old fool in charge of the seminary. But can you guess what happened next? It's really quite delicious. I saw you and I knew something wasn't right. You were the reason I grew curious. You were the reason I returned. And so *you* are the one who led him to his death. Tell me you see it."

She would not believe it. She would not.

"Nothing to say? What if I told you the promise I made to your beloved Niccolò as the noose was placed around his neck?"

No. *No.*

"I told him I would find you, and the mongrel you carried, and I would send both of you to the place where every Jew belongs. A place from which there is no escape and no end but death. A charnel house for those who have earned oblivion. My words were the last he heard."

Traitorous tears flooded her eyes, spilling down her face, but she ignored them. With her hands still bound there was little to be done.

"Oh, come now. Where are your insults? Your demands? Your pleas for mercy?"

She would not think of Zwerger. She would remember, instead, one of her last evenings with Nico. It had been a week or so before the attack on Monte Grappa had started, and they'd all squeezed around the kitchen table after dinner. The electricity had fizzled out at dusk, but they'd lighted enough lamps to brighten the room, and Nico had read from the *Divine Comedy,* and the poetry had been so beautiful. So lovely, and made lovelier still by his narration. They had all been so happy. Before she could stop herself the words slipped from her mouth.

"'The soul unto its star returns,'" she said, remembering.

"What? That doesn't mean anything."

"It does, but a man like you wouldn't recognize it."

"Shut *up*—"

She would not shut up, for she had found her voice again, and with it her courage. She would not be quiet. "You are caught up in a nightmare of your own making, and the evil you do will bury you, as it is sure to bury every man who stands at your side. The poet knew that, but do you?"

"I don't need to listen to some corrupt Jew text—"

"It was from the *Divine Comedy*. The fourth canto of *Paradiso*. But what would a man like you know of Dante?"

Zwerger overturned the table and dragged her from the chair. He shoved her against the wall, his hands encircling her throat, and his breath was so rancid against her face she wanted to vomit. Yet still she found her voice.

"What more can you take from me? You murdered the man I love, my baby, and my parents. They're gone, and with them any power you have over me. You have made martyrs of us all— can you not see it? History will remember men like Niccolò and my father, but darkness is all that awaits you and your kind."

His hands tightened around her throat, choking the life from her, and it was almost amusing, in that moment, to see how enraged he had become. She had maddened him and there was nothing he could do to stop her. What was death in the face of such truths?

She heard, dimly, the crash of the door. Advancing footsteps. Zwerger's hands were wrenched from her neck. She fell to the floor, her throat on fire, but no one came to help her.

"Zuerst der Partisan, dann die Jüdin? Wann lernst du es endlich?" First that partisan and now this Jew. When will you learn?

"Sie hat mich provoziert—" She provoked me—

"Schick sie nach Norden. Läßt jemand anderen deine Probleme wegräumen. Das ist ein Befehl!" Send her north. Have someone else clean up your mess. That's an order!

Retreating footsteps. A muttered curse. A boot prodding her side.

"Get up," said the officer who had argued with Zwerger, and

he kicked her just hard enough to propel her to her knees, and from there, somehow, she managed to get to her feet. He drew a knife from his belt, and she held her breath, waiting for him to strike, but he only cut the rope that had bound her wrists.

He grabbed her arm and dragged her from the room, along a hall, and outside. Into the night.

A truck was waiting, idling, and he pushed her forward until grasping hands pulled her into the truck. It was filled with other prisoners, nearly all of them men, and they stared at her, their jaws agape, their expressions a mix of horror and pity and disgust.

She looked down, wondering, and remembered that the bodice of her dress was soaked through with milk. She glanced lower still, to her skirt that was stained with blood. The blood that came after a baby was born.

They found a place for her, one act of kindness to lighten her pain, and the truck lurched forward. She sat, rubbing the life back into her arms, and tried to look outside. But the only light came from above, where a wide rent in the truck's canvas top lay open to the starry dome of the night sky.

She and Nico had danced under such a sky. They'd sung of love and stardust and the promise of brightening dreams, and she'd been so stupidly certain their happiness would endure. Yet how could goodness endure, let alone flower, in a world that emboldened and embraced men such as Karl Zwerger? And how was she meant to survive when her Nico was no longer a part of it?

Chapter 26

12 October 1944

The stars faded as the night bled into dawn, and still the truck rumbled along, never stopping, relentlessly bearing her away from home and hope. Hour by hour, Nina's thirst and hunger and grief carved steadily away at the last of her courage, and even the milk in her breasts, so painful in the hours after her arrest, soon shrank to a bittersweet memory.

Nico was dead. He was gone, lost to her forever, and though she tried to still her mind, to close her eyes to the memory of his body hanging from the gallows in that unspeakable place, she couldn't stop herself from imagining his last moments.

When they'd placed the hood over his head and set the noose around his neck. When Zwerger's pitiless words had rung in his ears. When Nico had known that death was seconds away, and he'd been frightened, alone, and tormented by fear for her and their baby.

It hurt to breathe, to think, to *be*. Grief roiled through her, and she was defenseless, drowning, desolate.

Yet her daughter lived. Lucia was safe with Rosa. She was safe, and happy, and Nina would return to her. She had only to survive this one day, and the next, and the next day to come. It was that simple—and that terrifying.

It was growing dark again when the truck slowed, made a series of lurching turns, and then finally, mercifully, stopped. Unseen hands wrenched open its tailgate, followed by a flare of dazzling light. Harsh voices shouted unfamiliar words—but was she meant to stay where she was? Or come forward?

It seemed to be the latter, for the men around her jumped from the truck one by one, some of them so weak they struggled to keep their balance. She was supposed to get down, too, but terror numbed her limbs and froze her in place.

"*Bitte*," she begged. Please.

One man, faceless in the dizzying glare of the light, seized her wrist and pulled her out of the truck. She landed heavily, pitching forward onto her knees, but he dragged her up and through a narrow gate, past high fences garlanded with barbed wire, and across a patchily graveled courtyard to a low brick building. Wrenching open the nearest of its doors, he pushed her inside.

They were in an office. It was bright and clean and the air smelled of beeswax and lemon. It held filing cabinets and desks and typewriters, and there were neat stacks of stationery and pots of sharpened pencils on its desks. It belonged to another world.

A high counter separated Nina and the guard from the rest of the space; behind it stood another man in uniform, his attention focused on an open ledger. He looked up as they entered, his face a stolid blank, and rattled off a string of words in German. When she failed to respond he repeated them, and then, his expression hardening, switched to Italian.

"Name. Place of birth. Age. Occupation."

"Antonina Mazin," she answered. They were imprisoning her because she was a Jew. Why not give them her true name?

"And?" the clerk snapped. "The rest of it?"

"I was born in Venice. I am twenty-four years old. I am . . ." And here she hesitated again. If she was here to work, they'd want her to be strong. Tough. Used to hard labor. "I am a farmworker."

The clerk wrote it all down in his ledger, as serenely as if he'd recorded the delivery of a piece of furniture, and then he nodded, his attention still fixed on the page before him, and the guard dragged her along the corridor to another office, this one a stockroom of sorts.

"*Nummer?*" The clerk here was a woman no older than Nina. The guard shook his head. "*Keine. Jüdin.*" No number. Jew.

The woman reached for the topmost of a stack of folded uniforms at her hip. She shook it out, nodded in satisfaction, and flung it at Nina. A moment later the guard grasped her arm, his fingers bruisingly tight, and led her back out to the courtyard.

"Where are you taking me?" she pleaded, and when the

guard didn't slow his pace, let alone respond, she tried again in German, fumbling for the half-forgotten words.

"Wo bringst—" Where are you taking—

"Halt die Fresse!" Shut up.

"Bitte, mein Herr, möchte ich . . ." Please, sir. I want—

He stopped short, pushed roughly at her shoulder until she faced him, and then he punched her in the face, his closed fist landing like a hammer just below her left eye. The pain was stunning, an explosion of agony that sent her to her knees, but before she could catch her breath he'd hauled her up and they were off again.

"Blöde Kuh! Halt deine blöde Fresse!" Stupid cow! Shut the fuck up!

They reached another building, its door open wide despite the chill of the late afternoon. He shoved her through, but her toes caught on the raised sill at its threshold and she fell once more. He marched off, his heavy boots crunching over the muddy gravel, and a little of her fear bled away.

It was a few minutes before she was able to stand, and even then it was an effort to stay upright, for she was so dizzy she might have been balancing on the deck of a gale-bound ship. Instead she stood at the door of what was obviously a cellblock, its gloomy interior taken up by two long rows of three-tiered bunks.

"You're new."

A girl was sitting on one of the top bunks. She was young, no more than fourteen or fifteen, with fair hair bound in two stringy plaits and a sweetly heart-shaped face.

"Yes," Nina said. "I'm not sure what to do."

"Take the bottom bunk over there. By the broken window."

Nina inched along the central aisle until she spied the broken window. At least it would let in some fresh air.

"Are there others here?" she asked.

"They're lining up for the latrines. I went before, when we were out in the fields. Stupid to wait. And no one saw, besides."

"Oh," Nina said, taken aback by the girl's candor. "Where am I?" she asked.

"They bring you in by truck?"

"Yes."

"The locals call it via Resia. The Germans call it the *Durchgangslager*. Either way it's awful, so don't get your hopes up."

"So we're still in Italy?"

"Just. Bolzano."

She'd been to Bolzano with her parents, years ago, on their way to a walking trip in the mountains. It had been a pretty place, almost comically quaint, with a backdrop of towering mountains that kept their snowy tops even in the summer. She'd thought, then, that it belonged in a fairy tale.

Now Nina sat on the bunk closest to the broken window, too tired to think of more questions, and unfolded her uniform. It was a plain sacklike dress, quite large enough to go around her twice, and made of a rough blue fabric that would undoubtedly feel dreadful against her skin. A yellow triangle was sewn to its left breast, and a large red X was painted across its back.

Resigned to wearing the awful thing, she started to unbutton her own dress, by now little more than a fetid rag, but the girl interrupted her.

"Don't. Keep your clothes on underneath. You're lucky they didn't take them away."

"But they smell awful," Nina protested.

The girl shook her head. "Everything smells here. It doesn't matter. Better to be warm." Her voice was atonal, as if she were a robot rather than a person. As if the work of speaking was enough to exhaust her.

"Thank you."

Of course the girl was right, not only about staying warm but also about the stench in the bunkhouse. The stables at home were a rose garden in comparison. Before long, she was sure, the odor of her soiled dress would be unnoticeable to her beleaguered senses.

"Get some rest while you can," the girl added. "And don't take them off."

"What? My boots?" Nina asked, pausing in the act of unlacing them.

"If you do, they won't be here when you wake up. Trust me."

"All right. Thanks."

It was strange to crawl into bed, even one as spartan as the straw-matted wooden bunk, while still fully dressed. She lay back, remembering her thin mattress at home with a bitter-sweet fondness, and pulled the filthy blanket atop her.

She was exhausted, cold, hungry, and achingly sad, but she was alive. She was strong and healthy, and for Lucia's sake, as well as Nico's memory, she would endure. She would survive.

SHE HAD ONLY just fallen asleep when the others returned from the latrine. No one said anything to her at first, but as they lined up in two rows along the central aisle another woman took pity on her.

"You'd better get up before the guard comes. It's time for *appell,* and she'll have a fit if she finds you lying down."

Nina nodded, though it made her blackened eye throb unbearably, and somehow managed to drag herself from her bunk. The others made room for her in the line, and then they marched outside together.

Once in the courtyard, which was fenced off from the rest of the camp, they assembled themselves in neat banks of five women per row, and once they were in place they simply stood where they were. No one talked or even whispered. No one so much as sneezed.

The female guards counted them twice, and marked down their observations on sheets of paper affixed to clipboards, and then, rather than allow their captives to return to the meager warmth and comfort of the cellblock, they simply watched them shiver and shake in the deepening cold.

After about an hour, though it might well have been longer, the guards nodded, and then the women formed another queue, this time for supper: a few mouthfuls of undercooked polenta and a scant cup of watery vegetable soup. The polenta was rancid, and the vegetables in the soup were little more than peelings, but it was enough to ease the worst of Nina's hunger, if not her misery.

And then to bed. Two other women shared the bunk with her, which meant she was pressed against the suppurating damp of the brick wall. At her feet, frigid night air drifted in from the broken windowpane. The nearest of her bunkmates didn't even look at her before falling dead asleep, but the woman was as warm as a furnace and would keep Nina from freezing through before morning.

The shrill screech of a whistle woke them when it was still dark. She barely had time to eat the slice of cold polenta she was handed, and then get through the line for the stinking latrines, before it was time to queue up again for *appell*.

Instead of counting them and making everyone stand for ages, the guard began to call out numbers in German. Dozens of women came forward and were marched away by pairs of guards. After a few minutes only Nina and about thirty others remained.

"Nur Nullen bleiben," the female guard said to no one in particular, and then she laughed as if she had made a fantastically entertaining joke. Only zeros are left, she had said. But it made no sense.

Nina stared, forgetting to look away, and the woman's smile sharpened into a menacing scowl. She had an incongruous halo of bright blond hair pinned in thick plaits atop her head, a face that might once have been pretty, and a voice steeped in purest venom.

"You Jews. Nothing," the woman spat out in halting Italian. "No numbers. All zeros."

And then, her rancorous gaze sweeping over the rest of the group, the guard switched back to German, barking out a series of orders so quickly that Nina couldn't decipher a single word. The prisoners formed a queue, with the nasty female guard at its head and a male guard, his rifle held at readiness, at the rear, and they set off across the open ground, back in the direction of the gate Nina had passed through the day before.

No one was panicking; no one seemed particularly fretful or frightened. Perhaps it really was nothing more sinister than a work detail. The girl from the bunkhouse was there, not far ahead, walking calmly enough. She'd mentioned working in the fields. That was something Nina knew how to do.

They walked on and on, kilometer after kilometer, nearly the entire way uphill, and if there were other living souls about they remained hidden behind closed doors and impenetrable hedgerows. At last they turned onto a private drive, its gravel pockmarked with puddles and dead weeds. At its terminus was a fine old palazzo, its many windows shuttered tight, though men in uniform were coming and going from its main entrance.

The guards led them inside, into an echoing ballroom where the least movement cast up flurries of dust, and pointed at a jumble of buckets. A few of the women seemed to know what to do, for they gathered up their buckets, plucked a few rags from a pile on the floor, and filed through a door at its far end. Nina collected her own bucket and rag and followed them along a gloomy corridor to a scullery, where they each filled their buckets from a single cold-water tap. Back to the ballroom they went, and one by one they dropped to their knees, a meter or so apart, and began to scrub the floor.

It was thankless work, not least because they'd been given no soap, but Nina, thanks to Rosa, did know how to scrub a floor properly. A few of the women had no notion of what to do, or worked so slowly that they angered the guards. One poor old lady's hair was pulled savagely by the female guard for failing to wring out her rag with sufficient vigor.

It was torture to hear and witness such things and be too afraid to intervene. Nina's heart bled for those who were being treated so awfully, but she knew she would be beaten if she tried to stop any of it. And she didn't think she could bear for anyone to hit her again.

Instead she worked. She stopped her ears and averted her eyes and thought only of each single square of parquet before her. She worked and worked, and when they were told to empty their buckets and queue up again for the journey home, she reminded herself the way back to camp was downhill. It would be an easy walk, and there would be something to eat after *appell,* and when she was at last in bed she wouldn't fall asleep straightaway. Instead she would think of her baby.

She would remember how delicious it felt to hold Lucia in her arms. How her whispery lashes curved upon her cheeks as she slept. How her rosebud mouth trembled when she was hungry. She would remember that her baby was safe and loved, and that alone would be enough to carry Nina through another cold night and another wretched day.

She and the other Jewish women—not zeros; never zeros— worked for a few more days at the hotel, and then they were sent to a nearby apple orchard. At first she was elated, for the walk there was far shorter and the smell of the apples in the late autumn sunshine was ever so pleasant. As one of the strongest in her group, she was given the work of collecting the baskets of fruit once they were full. The baskets were heavy and awkward to carry, though, and after only a few hours she was faint with hunger and fatigue.

She was ravenous, but she knew better than to sample even the most flyblown piece of fruit. One woman took a bite of half-rotten windfall, one single bite, and she was beaten almost to death for it. The sound of her piteous cries, together with the sickly-sweet smell of the overripe apples they labored to harvest, were enough to turn Nina's stomach—and yet she wolfed down her supper of gritty polenta and moldy vegetable scraps that evening without a moment's hesitation.

THE WHISPERS STARTED a few days later. In the queues for the latrines, in the fleeting moments as they assembled for *appell,* in the coldly blanketing night when the guards had retreated to their comfortable quarters, the women spoke of one thing only: the threat of another transport.

"The guards were talking about it. They say it'll happen any day now," Nina overheard in the queue for supper.

"What do you mean by 'transport'?" she asked.

"What do you think?" came the answer. "People are transported away from here. They line up and they march away and they never come back."

"Where?"

"North, across the Brenner Pass. And from there no one knows. No one's ever returned."

Her last day in camp began no differently from the rest.

She and the other Jewish women waited as the others, the ones with numbers, were organized into work *kommandos* for the day. She waited patiently, hoping they would not have to walk too far. Hoping the blister on her heel wouldn't burst.

Their guard, the same awful woman who persisted in calling them zeros, was in a good mood; that was enough to set Nina's nerves on edge.

"Today you go to via Pacinotti," the woman said, and her smile was feral in its intensity.

Nina chanced a glance at the other prisoners surrounding her, but no one seemed to know what the guard meant. Perhaps it was a road they were going to repair? Or the address of a building they were meant to clean?

She joined the queue that was forming. It was far larger today, at least a hundred strong, and it included dozens of women she'd never seen before. Some were still dressed in civilian clothes; some were elderly and had been absent from the work *kommandos*.

None of the women had numbers.

They marched out of the camp and along a bridge, and after they'd been under way for ten minutes or so they came around a corner, to the edge of an open swath of scrubland, and though they weren't anywhere close to the Bolzano station, a train was waiting.

It was made up of boxcars, their doors drawn wide, and the men guarding it, the same men who were now coming forward to surround the women, wore the black-and-gray uniforms of the SS.

It was too late to run. Too late to hide.

The women at the front of the queue began to protest, to shy away, and to scream. She did, too, but it was no use. A heartbeat later she was at the foot of the ramp that led to the last of the boxcars. It was full already, but still she was pushed up and along by cruel, mauling hands, and with one last shove she was inside. The door swept shut behind her with a stomach-turning clang.

There were dozens of women in the boxcar, so many that it was impossible to lie down or even to sit. The train lurched forward, startling her. An older woman, her back bent by age, clutched at Nina's arm, and together they managed to keep their balance.

"I beg your pardon," Nina said, amazed at how she could remember her manners in the midst of such horror.

"It's not your fault, my dear." The woman smiled tremulously and then, her touch ever so gentle, patted Nina's arm. "Do you think you might be able to see outside?"

"I'll try."

It was hard to turn, not without elbowing the others around her, but by slow increments she managed to press her face to the side of the car, where narrow gaps between the planks let in the barest wisps of fresh air. The wood was rough and unfinished, and smelled of the warm earthiness of a barn. Of its animals.

She would not think of what became of those animals when their journeys in such cars came to an end.

"I can't see much," she said, and it was true. Only fleeting impressions of trees and rocky slopes and little more. "From the sun I think we're going north."

She lost her place by the door when she needed to empty her bladder and had to make her way to the end of the car, only to discover that the toilet was simply an open barrel a little less than a meter high. The women nearby averted their eyes as she used it, and some even smiled encouragingly once she was finished.

They had not lost their humanity. They knew how important it was to restore a fraction of the dignity that had been stolen from them.

She managed to shuffle a little distance away from the stinking barrel, but the elderly woman had taken her spot at the side of the car and she couldn't begrudge her the relief of a solid surface to rest against, nor the chance for a few breaths of fresh air.

"Do you know where they're sending us?"

Nina didn't recognize the speaker, who was young and very pretty. Perhaps she had been kept in another bunkhouse with the older women? She hadn't been part of Nina's work *kommandos*.

Nina shook her head, wondering if she ought to introduce herself. Would it be helpful to cling to such pleasantries? Or would it be salt in an ever-deepening wound?

"No," she said, leaving the question of names for another time. "I think they're sending us to a labor camp. At least that's what I've heard."

"Me too. There were men in my neighborhood in Vicenza, soldiers who were captured last year. Their families got postcards saying they were in labor camps."

"There you go," Nina said, but she wasn't able to put much conviction behind her words.

"They weren't Jews, though."

"No," Nina agreed. "But the Germans need workers. And we're both young and strong."

"We are. Only . . ." And the woman looked down, and Nina noticed—how could she have missed it before?—that she was pregnant. So pregnant there was no way of hiding it. Despair pinched at her lovely face, and Nina, try as she might, could not think of a single word of comfort.

So she took the other woman's hand, and she held it tight, the way you might hold on to a beloved child when crossing a busy road. And she tried to remember what it was to pray.

Chapter 27

The train traveled on, never stopping, through an entire day and night and another day, and as the sun set once more Nina could think of nothing save the maddening thirst that consumed her. The intervening hours had seen her migrate back to the side of the car, a pebble caught up in a turning glacier, and at some point—an hour ago? a day?—she'd noticed a few trembling beads of water on the bolts in the door. Condensation from the women's exhalations over the past days.

Fear distilled.

She'd licked the metal dry, but it had done nothing save stoke the fire of her thirst. Soon they'd all be dead. To starve a person took weeks; to deprive them of water required only a matter of days.

The oldest and sickest of the women, no longer able to stand, sat huddled together in the middle of the car, and at first they'd talked and wept and prayed together, their voices rising and falling in an achingly beautiful lament. "Lead us in peace and direct our steps in peace," they sang. "Guide us in peace, and support us in peace, and cause us to reach our destination in life, joy, and peace."

But now they were silent, their prayers silenced by exhaustion and thirst. It had been hours since anyone in the boxcar had spoken.

The train stopped on the morning of the third day. The door was hauled open.

Around them, an empty plain of fallow fields and skeletal trees stretched to the horizon. A few meters distant, close enough for passing trains to rattle the glass in its windows, stood a house. It was abandoned now, its gardens overgrown, but the fountain in its forecourt was still pumping water. The merry sound it made was so incongruous, so obscene, that a croaking laugh erupted from her mouth.

One of the guards pointed at Nina and beckoned for her to jump down. *"Wasser,"* he said. Could it be possible their captors were allowing them to have some water?

Two more women, chosen from other cars on the train, had also been ordered to descend. She scrambled down and called out to the women still inside.

"Give me your cups—give me anything that will hold water. I'll fill them for you!"

They handed her tin cups, an old canteen, even a little saucepan, the sort one used for heating milk, and she ran to the fountain and let the water fill them. And she drank, ducking her head low to the corroded spout, but after only a few gulps she was pulled away and shoved back toward the train.

She handed up the brimming vessels, but more were thrust

at her, and the others' faces were so desperate that she approached the guard, her head bowed submissively.

"*Noch mehr, bitte,*" she begged. More, please. He nodded, so she rushed to the fountain, gulping what water she could as the cups filled up, then ran back to the car and handed them over.

But when she turned, hopeful of a third chance at the fountain, a different guard was standing between her and the beckoning water. He shook his head, and when she looked past him she saw how the other guards had advanced, their guns pointing at her and the other women who had been fetching water. Their reprieve was over.

She scrambled back into the car, scraping her shins on the rough threshold. The door slammed shut, the train began to move, the wind began to whistle through the cracks in the wood siding, and Nina realized she was cold, far colder than she'd been before.

Looking down, she saw that the front of her smock and its long sleeves were sopping wet.

"Give me a cup," she asked the women surrounding her, and right away they understood what she meant to do. She wrung the water from her dress, careful not to spill so much as a single precious drop, and when its bodice and skirt were all but dry she shrugged her arms from her sleeves and let others mine them for even more water. Not until the last drop had been chased from the dirty fabric did the other women retreat, their whispered words of thanks a balm to Nina's despairing ears.

She'd had more water than the others, but it had made no difference. Her thirst still consumed her. Emptied her. Hollowed her out.

Left her thin and fragile, a scrap of paper crumpled in an indifferent fist, discarded, and left to dissolve underfoot.

ANOTHER DAY CRAWLED by before the train stopped again.

It was dark, and she was on her feet only because there was no room to fall. Outside, beyond, somewhere in the night, Nina heard metal scraping upon metal, the muffled shouts of angry men, and the gruff, staccato barks of agitated dogs.

But the door did not open.

The train heaved itself forward, then stopped.

Forward, stop.

Forward, stop.

There was a moment of silence, stretching thin and taut, and then a terrifying eruption of noise: barking dogs, men shouting in unfamiliar languages, and all around her the startled screams of the women in the boxcar.

The door was slammed back and the darkness was abruptly obliterated by disorienting beams of light. Nina shielded her eyes, wary of falling from the train. She looked down, blinking, just as a heavy plank was dropped into place between the edge of the boxcar and the back of a large, canvas-topped truck that had pulled up about two meters away.

"Raus! Raus! Schnell!" Get out! Quick!

They wanted her to cross the beam and go into the truck, but she couldn't see beyond the lights. Couldn't see where her feet were meant to go, and she dared not imagine what would happen if she fell.

But the other women were crowding forward, unaccountably eager to leave the boxcar, so she stepped into the abyss and lurched across the makeshift bridge. By some miracle she did not fall.

Trucks took them to a huge, echoing shed. One after the other, the vehicles disgorged their passengers and departed, and when the last group of people had been harried inside, the shed doors were slammed shut and bolted.

And still no one came with water.

The concrete beneath her feet was cold and filthy, but Nina could stand no more. She crumpled to the floor, drew up her knees, huddled in on herself, and willed away her dread of what was to come.

This was tolerable. This was something she could survive.

If only someone would give them water.

The first pale glimmerings of dawn crept in through the high, barred windows, painting the people around her with faint stripes of gold. The minutes passed, measured in heartbeats.

She was dozing, dreaming of the fountain at the house on the empty plain, when the doors opened again. Six men entered, each carrying a large bucket, and they were dressed in striped uniforms that looked like something out of a comedy short.

Then one of the men came closer and the sight of him drove any memories of laughter from her mind. He was desperately thin, closer to a corpse than a living man, and he moved as if every step and gesture was infinitely painful.

"*Toilette*," he said softly. "Toilet."

At last someone who spoke Italian. Others gathered around the man, whispering their questions, rightly wary of the guards who still flanked the shed's open doors. The scant answers they received rippled through the crowd like a tidal wave.

They were in Poland. At a place called Birkenau. Food and water would come later. Later.

"After what?" someone asked.

A selection. People would be chosen for work. To be chosen you had to be strong. Fit. Young.

Her parents had not been young, or fit, or strong.

"What happens to those who cannot work?"

It was the girl who had greeted Nina on her first day in Bolzano, her carapace of toughness peeled back to reveal a solitary and bewildered child.

"They are eliminated," the man now said, his eyes averted.

Eliminated. Erased. *Extinguished.*

"Sent elsewhere?" the girl asked, her voice halting.

The man shook his head. And he drew his finger across his throat.

Nina caught the girl before she could fall. Calmed her as best she could. Swallowed down her own pain and fear with a silent promise: *Later you will mourn. Later you will rage. Tonight you must remember how to live.*

"I'm Nina. What is your name?"

"Ste . . . Ste . . . Stella Donati."

"I remember you from my first day in Bolzano. I'd have lost my boots if not for you."

"I wasn't very nice. S . . . sorry."

"You were wary. Of course you were."

"They took my parents before me. I hid in our flat, but I had to go out to buy food, and that's wh . . . when . . ."

"I know. I know."

"I just wish I knew where they took my mamma and papà," Stella wept.

And what could Nina say? How to answer such a question when the truth was more than she herself could bear?

Instead she made Stella a promise. "I'm alone, too. I'll be your friend."

Stella nodded, and her thin arms tightened around Nina. "There were dead people in my boxcar. One of them was standing next to me almost the entire way. She cried and cried, and I remember wishing that she would stop. Just stop making so much noise. And then she did stop, and I looked at her, and she was dead. Her eyes were open but she was *dead*."

"Hush," Nina told her, and held the child even closer, and she rubbed her back. Just as she'd once soothed Carlo when he'd been frightened or upset.

The men in the striped uniforms left.

The sun rose.

The doors of the shed burst open once more.

Soldiers came in, hard-eyed men armed with rifles and clubs and vicious dogs, and they quickly moved to encircle the desperate crowd. Among them were three officers. The soldiers began to nudge people forward, using their rifles as prods.

One by one they came forward to stand before the officers and be judged.

A nod, a barely discernible gesture, and the person was sent to join one of three groups. Young men, young women, and everyone else. The third group was by far the largest, and among it were children, elderly people, the infirm, and the sick. Nina knew that she did not want to be put in that last group.

But Stella—if she didn't act quickly the girl would be sent to join them. She was nearly as tall as Nina, but her schoolgirl plaits made her look terribly young.

"You need to look older," she hissed in her ear. "*Be* older. If they ask, tell them you're sixteen. What's your birth date?"

"May sixteenth."

"Yes, but what year?"

"Nineteen thirty."

"From now on, it's 1928. We've only changed the year. Can you remember? You were born in 1928."

"Yes," the girl whispered.

As they spoke, Nina unraveled Stella's plaits, combing through the lank strands with her fingers, her hands steady in spite of her fear. She twisted it back off the girl's face and used a ribbon from her plaits to secure it.

"Look at me? Yes—that's better." She pinched Stella's cheeks, just enough to add color, and did the same to her own. "We need to look healthy. Bite your lips, too."

"How do you know what to do?" Stella asked.

"We've a better chance of surviving if they believe we can work for them," she explained. "We don't want to end up with the old and sick, or the children."

The look on Stella's face made Nina regret her honesty. "Not now," she cautioned. "Don't let yourself feel anything now. You need to be strong. Just stand tall and do whatever they tell you to do. Don't look them in the eye—they won't like that. And remember that you're sixteen. You were born in 1928."

They held hands until they were at the very front, and when Stella passed the selection Nina forced herself not to respond in any way, for these were the sort of men who would send a woman to her death for the sin of a smile.

And then it was her turn. She came forward and stood in front of the officers in their black-and-gray uniforms. She did not look up, for if she did they would surely see the hate in her eyes. So she focused instead on the shining buttons on their uniform jackets.

One of the officers beckoned her with a single, lazy curl of his gloved hand. She tottered forward, breathless with fear. He grasped at her upper arm, feeling for the muscles there. Then he took hold of her right hand and turned it over. Rubbed his thumb over her calloused palm.

He nodded in approval. *"Dieser Transport hat starke Tiele."*

She was still puzzling out what he'd said as she was pushed toward the group of young women. Something about the pieces being strong?

Of course. She was one of the pieces. An insensate object to be assessed, inventoried—and discarded if found lacking.

When everyone had been sorted there were fewer than two dozen women in her group, about the same in the group of young men, and hundreds of people in the third group. Among them were the old lady who had steadied Nina on the train and the pregnant woman whose name she'd not dared to learn.

She would never learn it now.

NINA AND THE other young women were driven outside and across a barren plain, mud sticking like glue to their boots.

The air was thick with fog and a throat-clogging sort of smoke that, breath by ragged breath, grew ever more intolerable.

A building rose from the mist. They were led inside and made to queue.

They did so dutifully, quietly. Nina did the same, all thoughts of protest evaporating. She only wanted some water and a chance to sleep. She would save her resistance for another day.

If she behaved they might give her some water.

Soon she was at the front of the queue. Before her was a table, and behind it sat a clerk. He was dressed in a striped prisoner's uniform, just like the men they'd seen in the shed, though he was less gaunt than they had been.

He barely looked at her before posing the same questions she'd been asked in Bolzano.

"*Name. Alter. Geburtsort. Beruf.*"

She had to dig deep to remember enough German to answer. "Antonina Mazin. *Vier und . . . vierundzwanzig? Venedig.* And, ah, *Landwirtin?*"

Another room. Another queue.

The women were searched by men with rough, grasping hands. Nina had nothing but her clothes, no money or jewelry or any other belongings, and she was glad of it. Glad beyond measure that she'd left her wedding ring with Rosa.

The woman next to her cried out when her earrings were snatched from her pierced lobes, leaving them torn and bleeding. The man who'd hurt her was a prisoner, too, but shrugged away the woman's shock and pain. What sort of man had he been, Nina wondered, before he had come to this place?

They joined the end of another snaking queue.

Nina reached the front. Her arm was pulled forward.

Her name was replaced with a number.

She could only stare, astonished, at the blank-faced man with his needle and pot of ink. At the marks he was driving into her skin. The pain was nothing compared to the sight of those indelible digits.

She had been reduced to a number. A line in a ledger. A piece on an assembly line, only here, in this place of death, she was being taken apart, layer by layer, until nothing but her soul remained.

The soul unto its star returns.

Onward they were driven, and those who stumbled or fell were harried to their feet with threats and kicks. "Sauna," someone said.

The guards were shouting, and around her women were undressing, removing even their underwear, and those who balked or moved too slowly were punched or kicked or forcibly stripped.

So Nina shed her clothes, and when she tried to shelter herself from the guards' leering eyes her hands were slapped away by a dead-eyed man who first shaved her head and then every part of her body.

And the worst of it wasn't her nudity in front of rabidly staring men, awful though it was. It was the loss of her beautiful hair. The glossy ringlets that Nico had so loved had been shorn away, *stolen,* and her stubbled skull felt cold and unfamiliar beneath her questioning fingers.

Again they were propelled forward. Naked, shivering, she stood in a tiled room and waited. Stella was at her side once more, the smallest of consolations, and they held hands as they waited . . . for what?

A blast of cold water came streaming from the ceiling. Nina looked up, squinting, and for the first time noticed the shower heads set into the ceiling. The water grew warm, then scalding, and in an instant was frigid again.

She didn't care. She didn't think of washing herself, begrimed as she was. All that mattered was the water. She tilted back her head and opened her mouth wide and was grateful for every drop she swallowed. Nothing would ever again taste as good as that water.

Long before she was able to drink her fill, though, the water ceased and they were hustled onward once more.

Now they were given uniforms. Hers was a striped tentlike dress, even dirtier and rougher than the one she'd had in Bolzano. By sheer chance she was handed a proper pair of shoes. The soles were nearly worn through and they were a size too large, but most of the women had been given *zoccoli* to wear. Any sort of shoe, no matter how worn-out, was better than those rough wooden clogs.

Then food, the first meal she'd had since leaving Italy, and it was dreadful: a few mouthfuls of thin and bitter soup and a slice of hard black bread that only scraped against the void of her hunger.

Just as she was reaching the last of her strength they were led to a hut. It was many times more wretched than the cellblock in Bolzano had been. It was colder and dirtier and packed with twice as many women, and the stench inside was insufferable even to her benumbed nostrils.

She and Stella hadn't even found places among the bunks when a bell began to clang.

"*Appell! Appell!*"

"That's the *blockowa*," someone muttered. "Get yourselves moving, or we'll all catch it from that bitch."

"What's a *blockowa*?" Nina asked, exhaustion clinging to her like a shroud.

"She runs the block here—hurry!"

So they rushed outside to a muddy yard and arranged themselves in neat rows, hundreds of women, all of them shorn and pale and trembling from the cold, and anyone who was so much as a millimeter out of line was pushed into place by the *blockowa*, who didn't hesitate to use slaps and pinches to punish anyone who moved too slowly for her liking.

When everyone was arranged just so, a young woman in a smartly tailored uniform came to stand before them. She was slight and rather small, with delicate features, smooth and shining dark hair, and staring eyes that missed nothing.

Her gaze swept over the assembled formation, her nostrils flaring for an instant, and then she looked down at the clipboard in her hands and began to call out numbers at a ferocious clip. It took Nina a moment to realize that she was calling out their numbers, the ones they bore on their arms, and she was still staring at her own number, vainly trying to remember its translation, when the *blockowa* grabbed her arm and hoisted it in the air.

"*Hier, aufseherin,*" she shouted, and then she slapped Nina across the face. "*Blöde Sau.*"

One after the other they were counted, dozens upon dozens,

and nearly everyone earned a blow or worse for failing to respond as promptly as their captors required. And then, when the last number on her list had been found and checked off, the dark-eyed woman in the smart uniform—the *aufseherin*?—nodded at the *blockowa*, and then . . . nothing.

They stood in place and waited, and the moon rose, and still they waited, and those few who were unwise enough to shuffle or scratch at a louse bite or rub their frozen hands against the fabric of their uniforms were rewarded with more slaps, more pinches, and even, once, the sharp crack of the *blockowa*'s club against defenseless shoulders. That was the punishment for a woman who had fallen to her knees.

The moon rose ever higher, but its light was dimmed by spiraling drifts of smoke from the looming chimneys.

"Ovens," came a whisper.

The guards were only meters away. What if they heard?

"Where the bodies are burned," the same voice added.

"Alive?" Stella asked, and her clear child's voice carried across the yard.

The *aufseherin* looked up from her clipboard, her sharp eyes moving over them, judging and assessing, much as a crow might look at carrion when considering how best to pluck out its eyes.

When she spoke, it was in Italian overlaid with a heavy Austrian accent.

"No. Not alive when they burn." A pause, another birdlike tilt of her head. "They gas them first. Those who fail selection. Lazy ones. Sick. The troublemakers. They all go to the gas."

Nina's world shrank to the *aufseherin*'s mouth and the poison she spoke and the calamitous truth embedded in her words. *They all go to the gas.*

Her parents were dead.

Since the day Nico and Father Bernardi had told her of their deportation she had known, but she hadn't been brave enough to face it. And now she could shut her mind to it no longer.

She *knew*.

The guards would have separated them. Mamma would have been alone. Defenseless, unable even to stand. Would she even have survived the journey?

But Papà would have been alive when they had torn him from his beloved's arms. When they had pushed him onto the train. When they had led him to the gas.

He had known what was being done to him and the woman he loved.

Nina looked up, hoping for a glimpse of the sky beyond the swirling plumes of smoke. It was a clear night, the moon a delicate, gleaming crescent, and the stars hung low and bright and almost close enough to touch.

Mamma and Papà were waiting for her. Nico, too. They had already made this journey; they knew what it was to die. And they were with her, still, in the starry dome of the heavens. They were with her.

She would not be alone at the end.

Chapter 28

30 October 1944

Another day ground by, endless and enervating, its every hour made rancid by fear.

Apart from the few survivors from their train, no one else in their block spoke Italian. The languages all blurred into one homogenous and frightening mystery to Nina, but Stella recognized some of them and was even able to converse, after a fashion, with a handful of the others.

"Most of the women here are from Hungary," she told Nina after evening *appell*, "and I only know enough Hungarian to say 'hello' and 'how are you.' So that's not much help. But there are women here from all over Europe. Poland, France, Belgium, the Netherlands, even Denmark."

"How do you know so many languages?"

"I don't. I mean, not really. My parents had a company that published guidebooks for tourists, and they included little phrase books with each guide. I used to read them, just for fun." There was a hitch in Stella's voice at the memory of fun.

"Were you able to learn anything else from the others?" Nina pressed. "Apart from where they're all from, I mean."

"A little. I was able to understand quite a lot of what the Frenchwoman told me."

"And?"

"She said that most newcomers aren't here for very long. A few days, maybe a week or so, and then their numbers are called and they leave. She's been here since September."

Nina had to force her next question past her lips. "Does she know what happens to them?"

"No. But she did say no one is sent out to work in this part of the camp. We just have the two *appells* each day and that's it."

Because Stella seemed cheered by her discoveries, and because Nina didn't think either of them could face the stark truth of what happened to those who were called away, she nodded and climbed onto her bunk.

Women were being called away—but why, if there were no *kommandos*? Simply thinking of it made her stomach churn.

"It will be lights-out soon," she said, and patted the narrow strip of bare bunk next to her. "Climb on up while you can still see."

The lights went out, the dark closed in, and Stella first began to shiver and then to cry, her shoulders heaving silently, her scrap of cheer vanquished by the bleak and bitter night.

Nina held her close, and rubbed her hand gently over the girl's naked scalp, and she tried to think of something to say that wasn't a lie.

But the words stuck in her throat. She had no comfort to give.

"Sleep," she whispered. "Go to sleep."

"And tomorrow?"

"Will be here before you know it. So sleep while you can."

APPELL! APPELL!

It was the middle of the night, the moon still bright in the sky. There was no reason at all, save malice, for them to have been woken so early.

As they had the night before, and the morning before that, the women assembled themselves and were counted, and by the time the *aufseherin* was satisfied, the sun had begun to rise. Yet she made no move to dismiss them.

Nina was very nearly asleep on her feet when the *aufseherin* began to call out numbers for a second time. Not everyone was being summoned, she realized—only about one in three. As their names were called, the *blockowa* pulled them from the formation and had them stand in a queue to one side. But why?

Stella was hauled to the side, and then the snarling *blockowa* came stomping over and Nina realized that her number, too, had been called, and before she had wrapped her mind around the truth of it, her feet had carried her across the yard to the end of the waiting queue.

It was for a *kommando,* she told herself. The Frenchwoman had been wrong. They were being sent out for work and they would be back in their bunks by nightfall.

So why did the *aufseherin* seem so pleased? Why did her eyes spark with malice? Why had her mouth curled into a knowing smirk?

Their route as they left the yard took them very near to the *aufseherin*, and as Nina passed she turned her head, just for an instant, so she might look the woman in the eye.

"*Störenfriedin*," the *aufseherin* spat out, and her smirk broadened into a noxious smile, and Nina took another half-dozen steps before she realized what the woman had said. *Troublemaker*.

Troublemakers were not sent out for work. Troublemakers were sent—

No.

She could protest. She could resist. She could run back to the *aufseherin* and scratch out her eyes and show her what it was like to be hurt. To be afraid.

It was tempting, but they would shoot her like a dog, as Zwerger had once shot Selva, and that would leave Stella alone at the end. Her friend did not deserve to die alone.

So Nina kept walking, though her legs had turned to water and she had forgotten how to breathe. Stella was just in front of her, no more than an arm's length away, and Nina was desperate for the touch of her hand, the warmth of her skin, the knowledge that she was not alone.

How long? How many minutes were left to them?

She shut her eyes to the leaden sky above and the mud beneath her feet and the stench of suffering that enveloped her. She remembered, instead, the sound of birdsong, the scent of flowers in bloom, and the delicious heat of a sun-drenched day. She inhaled every sweet and vanishing moment of life, her one precious life, even as she swallowed down her howls of despair.

Suddenly she could bear her memories of loveliness no longer. There was so much she had yet to see and feel and do, and it was being stolen from her, and she could do nothing—*nothing*—to save herself.

"Nina."

It was Stella, risking a goodbye while the guards were near enough to notice.

"No," Nina whispered, shaking her head, her eyes clenched shut. "Not yet."

"*Nina*. Look where we are," Stella persisted. Her voice was trembling, but not with fear.

With hope.

Nina opened her eyes. They were back at the railhead, and the scores of women ahead of them were climbing steep wooden ramps into one boxcar after another, and then she and Stella and the remaining women were urged inside and Nina waited for something awful to happen.

Instead the door closed behind them. The train began to move.

"I listened to the guards as we were walking," Stella said. "They're sending us to Germany. One of them was angry that we're going there while he has to stay in this 'shithole to end all shitholes.'"

"How would you know a word like that?" Nina asked, and in spite of everything she had to suppress a laugh.

"From one of the other prisoners in Bolzano. She was Austrian."

"What else did the guards say? Why are we being sent to Germany?"

"I think we're meant to work for them. They said we're going to an '*arbeitslager.*' A work camp."

"Doing what?"

Stella shrugged, and then she hugged Nina tight. "Who cares? Anything has to be better than this place."

THEY WERE ON the train for three days, and this time they were supplied with water and the latrine bucket was emptied twice a day. They weren't given any food, but Nina had been hungry for so long she hardly noticed. The car wasn't too horribly crowded, and it was possible to sit at times and even catch glimpses of the passing landscape from a gap at the edge of the door.

As the train carried them west, the weather grew steadily more damp, if not objectively colder, and the plains were replaced by hills and then foothills. Surely they would be in Germany before long.

The train halted at dusk on the third day, its doors opening onto a forested valley. On the opposite side of the train was a fast-flowing river; before them was a small camp, its scattered buildings surrounded by high fences.

The women scrambled down from the boxcars, their clogs and ill-fitting shoes slipping on the snowy ground, and the guards led them through the gates and across a stretch of open ground to a long and low wooden building, its few windows crisscrossed with iron bars. It smelled of diesel fumes and machine oil, as if it had once been used as a drive shed, and its concrete floors were cracked and buckling. The walls were in even worse condition, with wide cracks between their rough-hewn wooden planks. Just looking at them made Nina shiver in anticipation of the arctic nights ahead, for it was a barracks, filled end to end with tiered wooden bunks.

But the bunks were made of new wood that still smelled of the lumberyard, and they were lined with straw mats that had yet to grow foul, and at the foot of every bunk was a blanket, an actual wool blanket. Nina went over to the nearest of the bunks, and she touched one of the blankets, and it was clean, or something close to it, and that alone was enough to bring sudden, stinging tears to her eyes.

The male guards from the train had vanished, presumably along with the train itself, and now a pair of female guards brought in pails of rough black bread that had been torn into chunks and adorned with dabs of watery jam. They ordered the prisoners to form a queue, and one by one the women received their supper, and one by one they wolfed it down in mere seconds.

There was just enough time for everyone to visit the latrines, newly dug and as fresh as a field of daisies compared to the stinking pits at Birkenau, before the call came for *appell*.

At the direction of the guards, the women arranged themselves in formation on a stretch of flat ground between the barracks and other camp buildings. The last of the sun was fading, and everyone quieted and waited to be counted.

A woman came to stand before them. Her face was pink and round, her figure just well fed enough to pull at the seams of her crisply tailored uniform. She looked almost pleasant. Someone who might, in another life, have masqueraded as a decent person.

The woman cleared her throat and waited until the only sound to be heard was the wind in the trees, and then she began to talk, her voice high and weirdly atonal, and she spoke so quickly that Nina couldn't manage to unravel one single syllable from the next.

Nor, from the look on their faces, could most of the other prisoners, and the *aufseherin,* or whatever she was, just kept droning on, a slowly deflating balloon, oblivious to the bafflement on the faces of those she was addressing.

At last she finished, and whatever she said next seemed to be some kind of dismissal, for the guards who had carried in their supper earlier now shooed the women back to the barracks, returning minutes later with a bucket of lukewarm tea and a stack of tin cups. Once again each woman stood in line and gulped down a few unsatisfying mouthfuls of tea and ceded her place to the next woman in the queue. The brew was bitter and tannic, and Stella protested at her first sip, but Nina urged her to drink it down.

"The water in this was probably boiled," she explained quickly, fearing the guards would push Stella aside, "and that means it's clean. Go on."

"But there's a tap in the latrines," Stella protested. "Some of the others were drinking from it."

"Yes, and they're the ones who'll get sick first. I promise they will. So drink that tea. Hold your nose if you have to."

As soon as the tea was gone and the cups were handed back, the guards retreated to the doors, but not before issuing one final round of instructions.

"We've got half an hour before lights-out," Stella translated. "There's a bucket at each end of the barracks for anyone who needs to use the latrines during the night."

"What did that woman say to everyone at *appell*?" Nina asked. "I couldn't keep up."

"She said she is Oberaufseherin Klap. I think that means she's in charge of the others? She said we're here to work, and if we don't work we're useless to her. We need to earn our keep. We need to meet our quotas and behave or we'll be punished."

"Did she say what sort of work we'll be doing?" another woman asked.

Stella shook her head. "Only that *appell* tomorrow morning is at five o'clock and work starts at seven."

They found space on an upper bunk without much trouble, and soon they were settled under the blanket, which smelled of nothing worse than muddy sheep, and when the lights went out it wasn't quite so hard to face the dark.

THE CAMP, THEY soon discovered, was a small armaments factory, set up only weeks before to produce submachine guns. Nina had hoped that she and Stella would be allowed to work together, but instead she was sent to the kitchens and Stella to the foundry. Alarming images of molten metal and blazing furnaces came to mind, but there was nothing she could do without marking herself as a troublemaker; no protest she could raise that would make the slightest difference. She watched her friend march away, across the muddied *appell* ground to a shambling row of brick-built workshops, and turned to follow her own group to the kitchens, which were just next door to their barracks.

She and the other women were forbidden from doing any of the cooking, which was the sole province of local laborers, all of them men, all of them too old for military service. Instead she was set to washing dishes, so many that Sisyphus would have declined to take her place at the sinks, and her only tools for the task were a threadbare rag, a pail of sand, and a jar of caustic lye soap.

By midday her hands were raw from the paste of sand and soap that she used for the dirtiest of the pots and pans. By evening her fingertips were cracking and bleeding and her forearms itched unbearably from the hours of immersion in greasy water.

Stella returned from the foundry even more miserable, her hands and arms marked by countless small burns, like bee stings but a hundred times more painful.

"I was filling molds with metal," she explained. "The men pour the molten metal into these smaller containers that look a bit like pitchers, only without any handles, and we have to pick them up with tongs and fill the molds for the gun parts."

"With your bare hands?" Nina asked, swallowing her own complaints about soap and sand and greasy water.

"The tongs aren't hot. And they gave us leather aprons so our uniforms wouldn't catch on fire. These are from all the sparks." Stella held out her arms, looking them over, tracing her fingers over the myriad burns.

"Can't they find men to do that work?"

Stella shrugged. "There are plenty of men in the foundry, but they're busy with the furnaces. And it's not so bad, you know. We're inside. We're not up to our knees in a muddy field. It could be worse."

She was right, of course. So why could Nina not stop herself from hoping their lives could become just a fraction more bearable?

The guards ate well, their meals hearty and plentiful, and some days the smell of the forbidden dishes was almost enough to make her swoon. Fresh bread, meaty stews, and even fruit-laden dumplings emerged from the kitchens and were borne upstairs to the guards' dining room, and all that ever returned were empty plates, for the scraps were fed to the guards' dogs.

One of the other kitchen workers, a Polish girl not much older than Stella, was caught reaching for a carrot top that had fallen near the patch of floor she'd been scrubbing. She'd only reached for it, hadn't even laid a fingertip upon the forbidden scrap of food, but that had been enough. The *oberaufseherin* had been summoned, and she'd laid the girl's hands raw with a leather crop, and then she'd watched and smiled as the girl had been forced to mop her own blood from the floor.

It was torture to be surrounded by food, day after day, and be given so little to eat. A cup of tea for breakfast and another at bedtime, then a few hundred grams of stale bread for supper, never quite softened by its accompanying scrape of dismal jam.

Their main meal, taken at midday, was nothing more than soup. Nina saw it being prepared each day, and she knew that it was made of water, vegetable peelings, and a rare handful of slimy turnip greens. Whatever scraps the dogs wouldn't touch, and would otherwise be thrown out, went into the soup pot, and not so much as a gram of salt was added, not ever, to season it. Often the peelings were thick with dirt, and on those days the soup tasted of mud.

She and the other women were starving, their cheekbones and noses rising into high relief, their bodies reduced to knobbled elbows and protruding shoulder blades and skeletal hands. Centimeter by centimeter, gram by gram, they were being erased. And each day was harder to endure than the one before.

Yet every day, every hour, Nina forced herself to hope. She made herself believe that she would survive. For herself, for Lucia, and for Stella. And since hope was fragile and needed nourishment to grow and bloom, Nina tended its seedlings the only way she could: with memories of Mezzo Ciel, shared in whispers with Stella before they fell asleep each night.

She described Bello and his moods, Selva and her loyalty, the green gardens and golden fields of the farm, the clear, cold waters of the rushing stream, and the dappled shade of the olive tree by the kitchen door. And she told her friend about Nico and his family, and baby Lucia, too, but only the good parts. Only the sunny days.

Stella, in turn, talked of her childhood in Livorno. Of her parents who had doted upon her, for, like Nina, she had been an only child, and their family had been small. They had lived in a tiny flat above the print works where her parents' guides were made.

"I can still hear the presses sometimes. When I'm half-asleep. Whirring and thumping. And the smell of the ink, too."

"Tell me about your parents. What are their names?" Nina was careful to speak of them in the present tense.

"My father is Andrea Donati. My mother is Caterina del Mare. Her hair is fair like mine. Papà calls her his little star because she shines so brightly. That's why they called me Stella."

"What of your grandparents? Your other family?"

"They died when I was little. My father had a brother, but he moved away a long time ago. To France. I remember visiting him once. He had a house in a place not far from Paris. It was called Colombes, and his house was on the rue des Cerisiers. The street of the cherry trees. Only he didn't have a cherry tree in his garden. I was annoyed when there weren't any cherries to eat, but the grown-ups just laughed and told me I was being silly. 'It's only June,' Mamma said. 'It's too early for cherries.' Funny how I remember that now, but I can't remember her voice."

They were silent for a while, both of them listening for the lost voices of their loved ones.

"We didn't have any cherry trees in Mezzo Ciel," Nina said once she was sure she wouldn't cry. "At least, not at the farm. But there were apricots and peaches and apples and pears. Far more than we could eat at once, so Rosa bottled them and dried them and we ate them all winter long."

"Was it nice there? On the farm?"

"It was. I . . . I think you should come home with me. After the war. You're of an age with Agnese." And then, when Stella didn't answer, she rushed to reassure her. "Everyone will love you. I know they will. And when the summer comes we'll go to the seaside and eat gelato and let the freckles sprout on our noses. I promised the girls I would take them to the seaside after the war."

"We used to go to Sottomarina on holiday," Stella whispered. "Did you ever have holidays there?"

"A few times, but my parents liked the Lido best. It was closer to home. And the water was always so warm."

"I don't remember what it's like to swim in the sea. Not really. I was eight when the laws were changed."

"After the war we'll be able to go wherever we want," Nina promised.

"We will. We'll go to Paris and I'll teach you how to speak French, and we'll use every one of the phrases from my parents' guidebook. 'Can you recommend a good dentist? Does this hotel have a laundry service? What time is the next train to Biarritz?'"

"That sounds wonderful."

"I won't use any of the words I've learned here, though. I'll never say them again. I won't even think them. No *oberaufseherin* or *appell*. No *schnell* or *steh auf* or *blöde sau*. And no strings of numbers instead of my name. None of those words. Never again, not ever, after this war is done."

Chapter 29

The gray days blurred together, and winter settled deep upon the valley, and Nina could no longer remember what it was like to feel the sun on her face. November—gone. December— gone. A new year begun, and still the war raged on.

Her days were long and lonely, for the women in the kitchens were forbidden to talk to one another, and when the men gave her an order she was allowed only to nod or say *"ja."* She worked in silence, her mind occupied by memories of happy days and comfortable nights and the smiling ghosts of those she had lost, and if there were moments when she could bear the loneliness no more, and she wept silently over her work, there was no one to notice or care.

It was some weeks before she realized that one of the local workers, despite every order to the contrary, was trying to help her and the other women. He was careful about it, and only intervened when the guards were distracted or absent, but he was watchful and persistent and was never far away when

Nina needed to lift the heaviest of the pots from the sink to the draining boards. He even saved her from a beating when she splashed water on the floor, claiming that he had jostled her first.

She never spoke with the man, was too cowed by the guards to even whisper her thanks, and had he ever walked past her in the yard she wouldn't have recognized his face, for she was careful never to look him in the eye.

She knew his first name was Georg, for that's what the other men called him. She knew he suffered from pains in his hands, just as she did, for she noticed how he rubbed at his arthritic knuckles and sometimes stopped to massage them with a salve he scooped from a little tin.

He knew she was a Jew, for her uniform still bore its yellow symbol, and she had to wonder if it mattered to him. If he, like so many others, had been taught to hate her for it. Or if he had decided to embrace kindness instead.

He must have seen how raw her hands had become, working as she did at the sink each day, and one morning, when the guards were still milling about in the yard, he pressed his tin of salve into her hand. It was small enough for her to slip inside her shoe, and she was able to rub a little of it into her hands at lunch, and the relief was immediate and lasting.

The salve helped with Stella's burns, too, and though Nina was fairly certain it was a simple concoction of beeswax and rosemary-scented oil, with no special healing properties or analgesic ingredients, it soothed her hands, and it comforted her soul, and it let her believe, if only fleetingly, that her tomorrow might be better than her yesterday.

THE SALVE LASTED a month. When it ran out, the pain in Nina's hands was so unbearable that she was driven, within days, to the unthinkable. Thievery.

The cooks kept an empty can on the floor by the range, and when they had drippings that were too burned or rancid to use again, they poured them into the can and let the fat solidify. When it was full they sent it over to the foundry, where it was used, Stella told her, for greasing machinery.

The empty salve tin held so little, barely an ounce. It would make no difference to anyone. It was only an ounce of inedible fat.

She was able to scoop out what she needed without anyone noticing, but then, before she could put the tin back in her shoe, one of the guards walked past, and she must have noticed the glint of metal in Nina's hand. Perhaps she thought that Nina was trying to steal a knife.

The woman snatched the tin from Nina. Opened it and frowned at the contents. And then she dropped it in her pocket and hurried off, and Nina counted herself lucky that her punishment had amounted to nothing more than the loss of her little tin.

Her reprieve lasted only minutes.

"*Sie will dich in ihrem oben Zimmer sehen,*" the woman said when she returned, and Nina knew, even before she'd finished deciphering the words, that she was being taken to see Oberaufseherin Klap.

Her stomach heaving at the prospect of the punishment to come, Nina followed the guard upstairs and along a darkened corridor to the *oberaufseherin's* sitting room.

Klap was dozing in an easy chair, her right leg propped up on a footstool, and when they came to stand at the open door she startled, her mouth thinning, her eyes glassy with pain. Likely she'd been self-medicating with whatever liquor was provided to the guards.

How long had it been since Nina had set foot in such a homey place? Apart from the upholstered chair and footstool, the room held a desk and chair, a small stove pumping out so much heat that her fingers began to tingle, and an oil lamp with a frilly glass shade. The rosy glow it cast belonged to another world entirely.

"Come forward," Klap ordered. "Why did you think you could steal?"

Nina didn't answer straightaway; she was too surprised. The *oberaufseherin* had spoken to her in Italian, not German.

"Out with it!" the woman barked.

"I took the grease to make a salve for my hands. To heal them. To heal the burns on my friend's arms."

"You lie."

"Her burns will become infected if they aren't treated. We all have burns. We all have chilblains and sores that are making us sick."

"What do I care if you fall sick?"

"Then care about what your superiors will say. If none of us can work, who will make your guns? And it takes so little to keep us well." The words were out of her mouth before Nina could stop herself. She held her breath, waiting for the inevitable outburst. Waiting for Klap to scream for the guard.

But Klap only frowned and fussed with a loose thread on

the upholstered arm of her chair. And then she surprised Nina again. "What do you know of healing? Are you a doctor?"

"No. Only a student of medicine." That was close enough to the truth.

"The doctor in Zschopau is an idiot. I want you to look at my leg. Help me with my boot." And then, when Nina didn't leap forward immediately, "Are you an idiot? Didn't you hear me?"

"I did. I wasn't certain that I understood properly."

"I want you to look at my leg. Is that simple enough?"

"Yes. Yes, of course."

Nina approached the footstool and took hold of the woman's heel. Slowly, carefully, she pulled off the boot, revealing a leg that was bandaged from shin to knee.

"I didn't realize it was bothering you. I never saw you limping."

"As if I would ever let the others know that I'm afflicted. I'm not stupid. Go on—look at it."

"May I have more light? By the window, perhaps?"

It took a while for the *oberaufseherin* to rise so that Nina might push her chair and footstool a scant meter closer to the window, and then the curtains needed to be drawn back and the window heaved open to admit some fresh air.

Crouching by the footstool, Nina unwound the smelly and none-too-clean bandage on Klap's outstretched leg. Nearly all the exposed skin, from her lower shin up to her knee, was covered in a bright red rash that radiated heat when Nina let her hand hover a centimeter or so above it.

Nina chanced a look at the woman: her eyes were squeezed shut, and her hands had curled into fists on her lap.

"I'm just going to pick up the lamp. I need some extra light."

Holding the oil lamp in her left hand, Nina bent low to examine the rash. She now saw that the rash was slightly raised and, tellingly, had a defined edge that set it apart from the surrounding skin. She sat back on her heels and considered what to say next.

"What did the doctor in Zschopau tell you?"

"I am not sure of the word. In German it is *Ausschlag*. I think, perhaps, that 'rash' is the correct term."

"Yes. Well, I can see how he was mistaken. It's not a simple rash, though. I think you have erysipelas."

"*Erysipel*," Klap said. It was fortunate that the German term was so similar.

"Yes. It's a bacterial infection in the skin. It must be treated or the infection will spread."

Klap nodded again, seeming to understand. "How will you heal it?"

It had been years since Nina had discussed the new sulfa drugs with her father, and she couldn't be sure the doctor in Zschopau would have any version of them at hand. But she had to offer Klap something.

"There isn't much I can do, but there is a medicine that might help. Sulfanilamide. It's German. Made by Bayer."

Klap reached into the breast pocket of her uniform tunic and pulled out a little notebook, the sort that came with its own pencil clipped to the side. "Write it down," she said, and handed it to Nina.

Erysipel, Nina wrote, hoping she had spelled the German name of the disease correctly. *Rss: Sulfanilamide*, she added.

With a gesture, the woman indicated that Nina should re-wrap her leg.

"I was a teacher before the war," Klap said, her voice hardly more than a whisper. "I taught literature at a school in Berlin. One of the best schools. The very best. And now . . ."

Now she fixed Nina with an implacable stare. "I will provide salve and bandages for those who are burned. You will care for them."

Nina nodded.

"If you steal again I will have you shot. Now get out."

Nina spent the rest of the day in a lather of anxiety. What if the doctor in Zschopau disagreed with her diagnosis? What if he objected to a prisoner second-guessing his judgment? What if Klap was allergic to the drug? Nina hadn't even thought to mention that possibility.

The *oberaufseherin* was present for evening *appell,* and her expression seemed a little less pinched than it had been that morning. She didn't acknowledge Nina, not even with a nod, but neither did she order that Nina be punished. That was what passed for mercy in the camp.

That night, tired and sore and miserable though she was, Nina couldn't manage to fall asleep. She lay where she was, not wishing to disturb anyone else, and tried in vain to think of good things. Happier times.

For so long she had told Stella that the war would be over soon. That they only had to stay strong a little longer. A few more weeks, perhaps only days, and it would be over and they would be free.

She began to cry, silent tears that she was too tired to swipe away, and after a moment she felt a gentle hand on her shoulder. It moved to her brow, stroking back over her cap of still-short hair, and the touch was wonderfully familiar and welcome. Stella must have woken and noticed her crying.

"Antonina," came a voice. Her father's voice.

She opened her eyes. He was there, standing by the end of her bunk, his back stooped a little so he might set a kiss upon her cheek. He was exactly as she remembered him.

"Oh, Papà," she whispered. "It's so good to see your face. Even if it is just a dream."

"Why must it be a dream?" he asked, and his accompanying smile was gentle and so wonderfully familiar. "Why doubt what you see?"

"I don't want to doubt, but you can't be real. You died there . . . at that place." She couldn't think of the name. It didn't matter, though. Not when her Papà had returned to her.

"Why can't you sleep?" he asked.

"I don't know. Worries. Just like when I was little, only now they're worse. Now the monsters under my bed are real." She closed her eyes, and then she remembered something important. "Is Mamma with you?"

"She is, my darling. We were never parted. Now I want you to listen. Are you listening, my Nina?"

"Yes, Papà."

"You will survive. You will live to see the end of this war. I promise you will."

"I miss you and Mamma so much. And Nico, too. Even thinking about him, remembering . . . it hurts so much. It makes me so sad."

"I know, my darling."

"I wish you could have known him, Papà." And then, even though she knew it was silly to ask, "Can you see him where you are now? Can you tell him that I miss him? That I love him?"

She tried to stay awake, for her father hadn't yet answered her question, but she was so very tired, and her sadness was such a weight upon her. When she opened her eyes again he was gone, and all she could recall was the lingering memory that once, not so long ago, not so very far away, she had been loved.

Chapter 30

9 April 1945

Winter gave way to spring, even in the mountains. The snow was melting, the days were growing longer, and one morning, during *appell,* Nina was captivated by the sound of birdsong, joyful and exultant, in the nearby trees.

Later that day, while wiping a pan dry, she flipped it over to ensure she'd polished away every speck of grease. The pan's bottom caught the light just so, and she froze as she glimpsed a face in its reflection.

The face was pale and wan, and was framed by a nimbus of frizzy ringlets. It had wary, searching, deep-set eyes. Lips that were cracked and dry. Cheekbones so angular they'd be better suited to a caricature. It was the face of a woman who was dying.

Closing her eyes, she forced herself to turn the pan away, finish with it, set it down, move *on.*

"Nina."

It was Georg, come to stand at her side, his gnarled hands taking the pan before she could drop it.

"*Die Sowjets sind nicht weit entfern.*" The Soviets are not far.

She was afraid to move, even to breathe.

"*Nicht verzagen.*" Don't give up.

Reaching out blindly, she found and grasped his hand. Only for a moment. Just so he would know she was grateful for his kindness. And then she got on with her work.

THE FIRST TO fall ill was a guard. Fever, came the whispers. The woman recovered, but was weak and addled and hardly able to stand.

Then it struck the prisoners. One after the other they sickened, grew ever weaker, and died. They were given no medicine and saw no doctor.

Klap no longer left her rooms; did she fear the contagion, or had she, too, fallen ill? There was no way to prevent it, at least not that Nina could discern. She and Stella kept themselves as clean as they were able, and they drank nothing but water that had been boiled, but others did the same and were still struck down.

The outside workers had stopped coming to the camp; the furnaces had cooled and the workshops were empty. Even Georg had vanished from the kitchens. The end had to be near, but there was no knowing how long it would be. How distant they were from their liberation.

There was no warning when the train arrived to evacuate the prisoners, only a shouted call for *appell* before the sweating, nervous guards pushed the women through the gates and into a string of waiting boxcars. Nina knew a moment of panic when she couldn't find Stella, but the girl appeared after a few minutes, pushing her way through the crowded car, her eyes glittering with excitement.

"This is it! They're sending us home!"

"I don't think—"

"That's what everyone is saying. They're sending us . . . well, we're not sure, not exactly, but it doesn't matter, does it?"

"We're still under their thumb, Stella. They could be sending us to another camp. Back to Birkenau, even. That's probably what they're doing."

"But the war is *over*—"

"No, it isn't. Not yet. The guards on this train are scared and angry, and if we get in their way they'll kill us. They won't even think twice."

"Why can't you believe in something good for a change? Why can't you let yourself hope?"

"I want to. I do, but—"

"But what? What now?"

Suddenly she was too tired to go on. And what was the point, besides? Either the train was taking them straight back to Birkenau, in which case they were doomed, or the train was going somewhere . . . else. Somewhere better, as improbable as it seemed. Wishing or wanting or hoping would change nothing.

Stella believed, though, and it was too cruel to steal that away from her. Not after she had already lost everything else. So Nina smiled, and sat down, and patted the dirty floor beside her.

"You're right. I'm just being grumpy. Come and sit. Aren't we lucky there's enough room this time?"

The rest of the day scraped by with painful slowness. Nina's head began to pound, but she told herself it was only because she was hungry and thirsty. That was all. The train stopped and started, over and over again, and the guards opened the door to give them water and change out the latrine bucket every few hours.

"Where are you taking us?" the others cried, but the guards ignored their question.

On the second day Nina was woken by muscle pains, deep and racking and violent.

On the third day the fever set in. Along with it came roiling waves of nausea, though her stomach was so empty she heaved up nothing more than air.

On the fourth day she saw the rash for the first time, scattered constellations of red, impossible to ignore against the pallor of her skin. And she knew, at last, what the fever meant.

Typhus.

The others in the boxcar kept their distance, and if Nina hadn't been so weak she'd have told them not to worry. The typhus bacterium had been the gift of an infected louse, not another person, and the wretched insect itself was likely still in the barracks back at the camp. If there was any justice in the world, of course, it would have instead found its way to the *oberaufseherin* and bitten her.

She lay on the disgusting boxcar floor, her head in Stella's lap, and wondered what would become of the people who had terrorized them over the past months. Who had tried to reduce them to nothing. To zeros.

Would the *aufseherin* from Birkenau, the one with the cold, dark stare, go back to her old life, as if she'd only been away on some sort of demented holiday? Would Klap's former teaching colleagues ever think to ask where she had been during the war? Would any of them ever be compelled to give an accounting of their crimes?

Already she knew the answer. It was no, for there was no justice, or peace, or mercy left in the world. Simply—*no*.

On the fifth day the train stopped in a little town that might have been in Germany or Poland or any point in between. The expressions of horror on the faces of passersby when she and the other women lurched from the fetid boxcar and staggered through their tidy streets would have made Nina laugh if she'd yet had the strength to do so.

It was Stella who propped her up, who bore her weight, who kept her moving as the guards drove them ever onward. And she wanted so badly to tell the girl to just set her down at the side of the road and keep walking, for the bacteria from the louse bite she hadn't even felt were going to kill her anyway.

Her throat was so dry, and it hurt so awfully to swallow, let alone speak, but she had to make sure Stella knew what to do.

"Promise to go to Mezzo Ciel. You'll find a home there. You won't be alone."

"Of course I won't be alone, because you'll be with me. Now stop talking and keep moving. They'll shoot us if we stop."

"Rosa will take such good care of you. I know she will . . ."

It was so hard to keep going. She was becoming a shadow, closer to wraith than woman, stripped bare of everything save her stubbornly yearning heart.

She tried to sit down. Tried to persuade Stella to stop, just for a moment, just stop and let her rest. They both needed to rest. But Stella would not listen.

"We're almost there, Nina. Only another kilometer or so."

"Promise me you'll tell them I tried. Tell them how much I love them all. Tell Lucia . . ."

"You'll tell them yourself. Come *on*—"

"It's too far."

"But we're here—can't you see? We're here in Terezin. No one can hurt us now, and we never have to see that awful Klap again—and there are doctors, Nina, doctors and nurses from the Red Cross."

Stella was crying, and then she was shouting at someone, and Nina plucked at her sleeve, trying to get her to pay attention.

"It's all right. You go on without me," she told her friend. Her only friend.

"Don't you dare—you can't die on me now. Just let the doctors help you—oh, please, won't someone help her? She's so sick, and I don't know what to do!"

"That's all right," Nina whispered. "I'm all right now."

She was floating. She was rising, flying, soaring high over the wretched road and its caravan of ragged refugees, over the neat little towns and fields, higher, ever higher, until she was across the mountains and rushing down to the familiar hills of Mezzo Ciel.

She was home, and Nico was there, too, standing under the olive tree in the courtyard, his arms open wide. He was waiting for her. All this time, he'd been waiting for her to come home.

WHEN SHE WOKE she was in a bed, a proper bed with a real mattress and clean sheets and an ethereally soft pillow beneath her head. The room was bright with sunshine, and one of its windows was open, and she could hear children playing and laughing outside.

Children.

She blinked hard, and tried to raise her hand to rub at her eyes, but she only had the strength to lift her arm a centimeter or so before it flopped back onto the pristine coverlet.

"You're awake!"

Stella had been sitting in the corner of the room, reading, and now she put down her book—a book, an actual *book*—and came to sit on the side of the bed.

"What happened?" Nina asked fretfully. "We were walking somewhere. You were helping me."

"You don't remember when we arrived?"

"I think . . . maybe? You were saying we were almost there. That there would be doctors. That we never had to see the *ober-aufseherin* again."

"Yes to all of that. We're in Terezin now. Near Prague. They took you straight to the hospital and put you in quarantine, and I was worried they were going to leave you to die, or, well, just finish you off. But the nurses—they have proper nurses here, and doctors, too, from the Red Cross—they promised to take good care of you. And they did."

"How long . . . ?"

"We got here on April twenty-first, but I wasn't allowed to visit until just last week."

"Oh," Nina said, and already she was so tired, so tired. But she still had one more question for Stella. "Is the war over yet?"

WHEN SHE WOKE again Stella was still there, still waiting, and the look of delight on her face was enough to make Nina cry.

"Why are you crying?"

"I don't know. It's just so good to see you smiling. And you've put on some weight."

"Only a little. They're very strict with us—in a good way. If we eat too much we'll get ill, so we have a sort of diet to follow. The nurses say it's safer to put the weight back on slowly."

"Is the—"

"Is the war over? Yes! It's been more than a week now. The Soviets got here on the seventh of May, and then the next day it was over. I asked the nurses to tell you, but I think you were still mostly sleeping then. You don't remember hearing the cheering and shouting and the car horns?"

Nina shook her head. "Not one bit of it. What day is it now?"

"The sixteenth."

"Your birthday," Nina said, remembering. "Happy birthday, my dear. And thank you for staying with me."

"As if I would have left you. Oh—I almost forgot. The Red Cross nurses were handing out postcards, so I sent one for you. I put down that you had been ill but were getting better."

"How did you know where to send it?"

"Well, you said that Mezzo Ciel was a small place. So I just addressed it to your husband. Niccolò Gerardi in Mezzo Ciel. Do you think it will get to him?"

Nina nodded, and she clutched at Stella's hand, and she forced her tears to retreat. "Yes," she lied. "I'm sure it will."

Chapter 31

At the beginning of June they were moved to a hospital in Prague, though Nina tried to persuade her doctors that she was well enough to make the journey home. They were sympathetic but unmoved. Not until her lungs were clear—she'd also developed pleurisy—and she'd put on another ten kilos would she be allowed to travel. Nor could Stella, as a minor, be permitted to leave on her own.

So they waited. Nina wrote to Rosa every week, though she couldn't be certain her letters would ever be delivered; nor was there much she cared to tell her sister-in-law at such a distance. But still she posted her letters every Monday, without fail, and waited for replies that never came.

By some unfathomable stroke of luck, the doctor in charge of the clinic had recognized Nina's maiden name on one of the forms that had crossed his desk.

"Are you any relation to Gabriele Mazin? The nephrologist?"

"He is my father. Was. He was killed at Birkenau."

"I am very sorry to hear it. I met him once. He came to speak at the university, and I was invited to the dinner afterward. Are you . . . do you have any family left?"

"Yes. My husband's family live near Bassano. How soon—"

"Soon. I promise."

Dr. Koller came to visit her nearly every day, taking a marked interest not only in her health but also her plans for the future. He was skeptical, though politely so, that the daughter of Gabriele Mazin would be content to live on a farm for the rest of her life.

"With your husband gone, there's no need for you to return to live with his family in the middle of nowhere, generous though they have been."

"My home is with them. They are my family, too."

"I understand, I do. But did your parents not wish for you to have an education? I know your schooling was interrupted, but you're a bright girl. A spot of private tutoring, a year or so of hard work, and I'm sure you'd pass the entrance exams."

"I don't know. I've my daughter to think of."

"Only consider it. Your father has many friends who would be glad to help."

"What are you suggesting, Dr. Koller?" she asked at last.

"That you go to medical school. I'm certain your father, were he still alive, would encourage you to at least try. And you're more than capable. Our conversations over the past weeks are ample proof of that."

Dr. Koller's belief in her was flattering, and terribly encouraging, but his plans would have to wait. All she wanted, now, was to return to Mezzo Ciel. One day, perhaps, she might go back to school. One day.

By the middle of September she and Stella were judged well enough to travel. There had been no objection to their remaining together, though Dr. Koller had fretted that Nina was too young to take over the care of a teenager.

"It's quite one thing to care for an infant, but you're not much older than Stella yourself. Perhaps it would be better if we tried to find a place for her through one of the orphanages—"

"No. *Never*. She is coming with me. She will have a family with us in Mezzo Ciel."

For their journey home, she and Stella traveled in the unimaginable luxury of a third-class carriage, complete with upholstered seats, windows that opened, a WC at the end of every car, and a tea trolley that passed their compartment once an hour. They had bread and cheese and apples, a gift from one of the nurses, and Dr. Koller had given Nina ten whole American dollars. The steward happily accepted fifty cents in return for eight cups of tea, two each for the days they spent on the train to Munich.

From there she and Stella were put on a bus heading south to the Allied base in Mittenwald, right at the Austrian border, where they and the other passengers, all refugees, were furnished with new identity papers and the nearly unimaginable sum of five hundred lire each. Fearful of being robbed, they retreated to the nearest restroom, opened a seam in the lining of Nina's new coat—yet another parting gift from the hospital staff—and tucked the money inside.

It took another long day, squashed in the back of an enormous

GMC truck, to get to Innsbruck, though the GIs traveling with them were polite and respectful and generous in sharing their sandwiches and chocolate. From there they found a train south to Italy, the Brenner Pass having finally reopened; another day would see them back in Bassano.

"I AM VERY sorry, signora, but there are no more trains this evening."

The ticket agent at the train station in Bolzano was a perfectly pleasant man, and he didn't seem to bear her any ill will, yet all the same he was determined to prevent her from returning home. Or so it felt to Nina, who was utterly weary of trains, train stations, and anywhere in the world that was not Mezzo Ciel.

"But there was supposed to be a train to Bassano del Grappa at half-past seven. We have tickets—look." Their train south from Innsbruck had arrived almost three hours late, but it was only seven o'clock. Surely they hadn't missed it.

"Your tickets are quite in order, yes, but alas there is no train. Not tonight." The ticket clerk shrugged, his expression properly mournful. "There will be one in the morning. That is not so very long to wait."

"No, I suppose not. Is there anywhere we may stay?"

"By that do you mean a hotel? I can recommend—"

"No, thank you. I meant here. I don't want to leave the station."

One day she might visit Bolzano again, but not yet. Not while her memories of via Resia were still vivid enough to haunt her waking dreams.

"Of course. Our waiting room will be open all night, and the guard will be nearby. You and your friend are most welcome to stay."

They found the waiting room without much difficulty, and after installing herself and Stella in a pair of seats in the very far corner of the space, Nina inspected her satchel in the hopes that some of their provisions might linger in its depths. Luck was with her, insofar as food was concerned, for there were two apples remaining, neither of them badly bruised, twenty or thirty grams of cheese wrapped in waxed paper, and a very stale chunk of pumpernickel bread, which she'd been unable to persuade Stella to eat that morning. But they were both hungry, and home was another day away, if not more, so she would give the cheese and apples to Stella and find a way to choke down the dark bread that reminded her so horribly of the refuse that had passed for food in the camps.

She was tired, for she hadn't slept at all well on the train from Prague to Munich, and then she'd had no chance to do more than doze on Stella's shoulder on the shorter train and bus journeys since. She was tired, but she was too fretful to sleep, and it wasn't even half-past seven.

If only she had something to read. She wasn't fussy; even a discarded newspaper would do.

"I'm going to wander around for a bit," she told Stella. "I won't go far."

"That's all right. I'll try to sleep for a bit."

The station's cleaners were efficient, however, and after pacing the length and breadth of the ticket hall two times over, looking under every bench and even peeping in the top of the rubbish bins, Nina wasn't able to unearth so much as a single sheet of printed matter.

Only that wasn't quite true. The ticket hall of the station, like so many others she and Stella had passed through in recent days, featured a large noticeboard that normally would be covered with timetables, announcements, and advertisements. As with those other stations, though, the board in Bolzano's ticket hall was instead shingled with pieces of paper, some faded, some only days old, and on each small notice there was a name, and beneath that name was a plea for help.

She was tired, so tired, and it would be far more sensible for her to simply return to the waiting room and try to sleep. Instead she began to read the notices.

Ricardo Rossi, age 22, last seen on march from Dachau April '45. Information please to his mother, Signora Rossi, via Vittoria, Borgo Vallessina.

Marco Foà Recagni, age 36, sent to Fossoli in August 1944. Last seen in Flossenburg. Any information gratefully received by his wife and children at via San Felice in Maragnole.

Guerrino Salvati, age 18, last seen on Monte Grappa in September '44. If you have news of him please write to his father, Signor Ettore Salvati, presently living at 2 viale Trieste, Castelfranco Veneto.

She read through every last notice on the board, one after the other, and not because she thought there was a chance of her recognizing any of the names. She never had, not once, in any of the stations she and Stella had passed through on their way home. But someone ought to read them. Someone ought to spare a moment to think of those lost lives.

She stepped back, wiping her eyes, and went to turn back to the waiting room and her quiet corner and the meager meal that waited for her there. And then she stopped short, her breath catching, for a man had come into the station, and for some ridiculous reason she thought she might know him.

He was standing in the shadows, his attention focused on a ticket in his hand, and as she watched he shook his head, took a deep breath, and let it out in a huffing sigh.

The man stepped back, only a little, and a beam of light fell upon his face, and her heart seized as she recognized him.

As she discovered that joy could be as painful as grief.

"Nico?" she whispered. And then, finding her voice, she called to him. "Niccolò!"

He turned his head, surprised at hearing his name so far from home. The bag he'd been holding fell from his hand.

"Nina? How on earth . . . how did you know I'd be here?"

Here was far from home, and she was thin and frail, and there was no child in her arms. In an instant, Nico saw all of it, and Nina, in turn, was witness to the moment it broke his heart.

He fell to his knees. She ran and knelt before him, her hands coming up to cradle his anguished face.

"Why are you here? What happened to you?" he demanded,

pushing her away, his hands shaking like wind-borne leaves, his horror so palpable she could taste it.

"Won't you hold me?" she begged him. "I am alive and well. Truly I am."

"Tell me *now*. Tell me the truth!"

"It was Zwerger. He came for me. He threatened your family. And so I went with him—I had no other choice. He took me to the SD headquarters in Verona, and there was a man hanging from the gallows in the courtyard. And . . . and he was dressed in your clothes. Zwerger told me you were dead, and I believed him. I believed you were lost to me."

"Nina. Oh, *Nina*. All this time I believed you and our baby were safe and well. How can I bear it? Do you . . . do you know if it was a boy or a girl? Were you even able to—"

"She was born before they took me away," she rushed to reassure him. "I named her Lucia, as you wanted."

"She is safe? Truly?" he asked, the tears streaming down his face and vanishing into his days-old beard.

"She is," Nina promised, and she prayed that it was true. She hadn't had any news from Rosa, but she would believe that Lucia was well. She would believe enough for her and Nico both. "It's been a long time since I saw her last, but she was a very pretty baby."

"I don't . . . I can hardly wrap my mind around all of this," Nico whispered, and still he wept.

"I know. Let's go into the waiting room," she suggested. "The benches there are much more comfortable than this floor."

They struggled to their feet, both a little shaky, but before they took a single step he enfolded her in his arms, his touch careful, almost tentative, as if he feared she might break. They held each other for long minutes, and it was the first time Nina had felt safe in a long, long time.

Reluctantly she pulled back, just so she might see his face as she shared one more revelation with him. "I have something else to tell you. Something good," she added hastily, seeing how he flinched. "When I was imprisoned I made a friend. Her name is Stella and she's still a girl. Still so young. She saved me, Nico, more than once, and her family are all gone. She has nowhere else to go, and so I thought . . ."

"Of course. Of course she must come with us," he answered, as she'd known he would.

Nina woke Stella carefully, worried that she might take fright at the sight of a strange man standing so close by.

"Do you remember how I told you I'd stopped believing in miracles?"

"Yes," Stella said, her still-sleepy gaze darting uncertainly between Nina and Nico.

"I think I have to take it back. This is Nico."

"Your Nico? He came to fetch us? That's lovely, but I wouldn't call it a miracle."

"But it *is*. I thought he was dead. All this time, I thought he was lost to me, and I never told you because I couldn't bear to talk of it."

Stella frowned, still trying to make sense of what Nina was telling her. "Why did you believe he was dead?"

"I thought he had been killed. I was shown the body of a man, still hanging from a gallows, and he was dressed in Nico's clothes. But I was wrong. Zwerger—he was the Nazi who had me arrested—wanted me to think Nico was dead, likely for no better reason than to torment me. And I believed him."

"I'm very pleased to meet you, Stella," Nico now said, though he came no closer. "Thank you for helping Nina."

"No more than she helped me."

"All the same, I'm very grateful. I want to welcome you into my family. And I want you to know you will always have a home with us. Always."

STELLA WENT BACK to sleep not long after, but Nina and Nico stayed awake for the rest of the night; and though it felt daring to do so in a public waiting room, she sat on his lap and let him cocoon her in his arms. Safe in his embrace, she told him her story. Not all of it; not anything close to the entire, bitter, horrifying truth. But enough.

Bolzano and the zeros. The terrible journey to Birkenau. The selection and the women whose names she never learned. The moment her own name was replaced by a number. The chimneys and the *aufseherin* with her dead-eyed stare. Her horror when she first understood what had become of her parents. Stella. The cold, dark months in the nameless camp near Zschopau. The salve and Georg and the *oberaufseherin*. Typhus and Terezin and sleeping through the end of the war.

He wept once more when she showed him the number on her arm, and then they were quiet together for a while. She pressed her face against his chest and listened to his heartbeat and told herself that she would never forget this night. She would never forget to be grateful for the blessing of his steadfast heart.

"What happened after they arrested you?" she asked after a long while.

"They took me to Verona as well. They stripped me naked and threw me in a cell and left me there. I hardly remember that part. Only how cold I was. After a few days they dragged me out and put me on a truck. I didn't see Zwerger again."

"Did they send you to Bolzano, too?"

"Yes, but I was only there for a few days before I was put on a train for Flossenburg. After I'd healed enough that I was well enough to work, they sent me out to one work camp after another. At one point I was in Chelmnitz. Not far from Zschopau at all."

"Oh, Nico. What I'd have given to have seen you. Just to have caught sight of you and known you were alive."

"When the Americans were no more than a day or two away, the guards forced us to start marching for Dachau. Anyone who faltered was shot or left to die. I still can't believe I survived."

"You're so thin."

"Would you believe I've put on twenty kilos since I was liberated? I was lucky, you know. I was given a bed in the American hospital in Linz, and the medics there knew how to fatten me up without killing me. I was lucky, and yet . . ." He shook his head, as if hoping to rid himself of his memories.

"We both had a bad time of it," she acknowledged.

"I know you've only told me a part of what you endured. The very smallest part. You must promise to tell me all of it."

"One day, yes. Not now. Not until we both can bear the telling."

"I hope you'll be able to forgive me. I was so set on being the hero that I never once considered what might happen to you if I was arrested. I am so very sorry, my darling."

Now she sat up, turning in his lap so she might look him in the eye. "*Nico*. Listen to me. There is nothing to forgive. I survived, as did you. As did the scores of people you saved. And do you know what we're going to do next?"

He smiled, the same crooked smile that she'd missed so much, and her love for him bloomed anew. "No," he said. "Tell me."

"We're going to have supper together. A delicious meal of one wrinkled apple, a very small piece of cheese, and a few mouthfuls of some truly awful bread. We'll wash it all down with water from the drinking fountain. Clean water, no less. After that, we'll wait here until morning, and then we will take the first train south. We'll be home by supper."

Chapter 32

*I*n the end, it took them two more days to finish their journey, for the train they boarded the next morning went no farther than Trento. From there they took to the roads, hitching one ride after another, traveling east around the looming massif of Cima Dodici and then south along the banks of the Brenta.

In Primolano, Nico found them space in the back of an empty van heading past Bassano del Grappa. The driver was apologetic, but couldn't spare the time or the petrol to take them directly to Mezzo Ciel.

"The old bridge was bombed in February. Still standing but you can only cross it on foot. Should be easy enough to find someone on the east bank who'll drive you the rest of the way."

The walk across the once-beautiful bridge in Bassano, its Palladian arches a tangled mess of blackened beams, was disconcerting, and once or twice Nina was convinced they would fall into the rushing waters of the Brenta far below. The streets of the old town were almost impassable, too, filled with rubble as they were, and it took ages to reach the northern outskirts and the familiar view of the rising hills beyond.

"I can see home from here," Nico said, but Nina was looking back at the *viale* above them, the one by the ancient walls. The one with the line of trees, each garlanded with ribbons and medals and wreaths of long-dead flowers.

"That's where they hanged them," she said. "Do you remember? Poor Paolo. The poor child. To see such a thing."

"I remember," Nico said, "but it's a beautiful day, and we're almost home. Will you come with me now?"

So they set off together, the autumn sun at their backs, and hardly more than an hour had passed before Nina spied the shining white tower of the campanile in the piazza, at first a dot in the distance, then growing ever larger, until they were climbing the last hill before home, and though it was even steeper than she remembered, every step she took was welcome and precious to her.

The graveled road gave way to cobbles, the close-set houses along via Mezzo Ciel were replaced by the broad expanse of the piazza, and ahead, unchanged, were Fratelli Favaro, the cobbler, the bakery, and the osteria, its benches still occupied by dozing, white-haired men.

She tried not to think of the last time she had stood in the piazza, cowering at the back of the crowd, watching Zwerger lead the attack on Nico.

"Should we visit Father Bernardi?" she asked.

"Later. Tonight. Come along, the two of you—we're almost there."

They walked past the church, past the flanking stone wall where Nico had so nearly died, the ground beneath still stained, revoltingly, with splashes of dried blood. They came around the bend in the road. Nico held out his right hand to Nina, his left to Stella, and the three of them broke into a run.

SELVA WAS THE first to realize they were home. The dog burst from the stables, barking so loudly that Nina was tempted to plug her ears, and then the rest of the family was crowding about them.

"We've been waiting and waiting," Rosa sobbed. "The post-cards from the Red Cross came so long ago. Did neither of you receive my letters?"

"No, but it doesn't matter now. Hush, Rosa," Nico crooned, gathering his sister in his arms. "Hush. We're home. We're safe."

"Who is this lovely young lady?" Aldo asked, noticing Stella; the girl had halted a few meters from the rest of them, her expression uncertain and a little wistful.

Nina now drew Stella forward, one arm around her shoulders. "This is Stella Donati. She grew up in Livorno, but she's going to live with us now. She saved me time and again when we were . . ."

She couldn't bring herself to talk of where they had been. Not with the children so happy and Rosa and Aldo still so anxious.

"When they were away," Nico said. "But now we're home, and we're desperate to see Lucia. Where is she?"

"Asleep in her crib. It's in your room."

They rushed up the stairs, forgetting to be quiet, and opened the door to their room. Lucia was awake, sitting up in her crib, her eyes widening at the sight of the strangers.

Nico was, predictably, smitten. "Oh, my darling. My darling girl. You are so lovely. And you have your mamma's hair."

"Go on," Nina encouraged him. "Pick her up."

He was nervous, his hands trembling, but he shouldn't have been; it was clear that he knew how to hold a baby. Lucia stared up at him, her eyes round, and after a long moment her little hand reached out to tap his nose.

"I can't believe it," Rosa said from the doorway. "Normally she's shy around strangers. I mean . . . I mean new people. New faces. Of course you aren't strangers to her."

As soon as Lucia saw Rosa, though, the spell was broken. Her little mouth bent into a pout, and then a frown, and Nico, his smile fading, handed his daughter back to Rosa.

"Don't worry. It won't take long for her to recognize you both. And perhaps she already has an idea of who you are? I've been telling her about you every day.

"Do you know who is here, Lucia? Do you? It's your mamma— the pretty lady here with the curly hair. And your papà is here, too. You have your mamma and papà again. They came back to you, just as I said they would."

Now Rosa began to cry. "What you both have gone through . . . I can't even let myself think about it. The stories we've heard. And the photographs in the paper were enough to turn my blood cold."

"We don't have to talk about any of that today," Nina promised her sister-in-law. "Not if it makes you sad. But we're both very hungry, and I've been telling Stella about your soup for months and months."

They were just finishing off their meal when Father Bernardi arrived, Carlo having taken it upon himself to run to the rectory as soon as he'd gobbled down his supper.

Poor Father Bernardi could barely speak for weeping, and Nina resolved, yet again, to save the details of what had happened to her and Nico for another day. Instead they gathered around the table, and Aldo brought out his best bottle of grappa, and all of them save Carlo drank a toast to the miraculous return of Nico and Nina, and the felicitous addition to the family of Stella.

Agnese and Angela then announced they were going to show their new sister around the farm, and when Carlo began to fuss at being left out Stella took his hand and asked him if he would introduce her to Bello, for she had heard all about him from Nina and wanted to see the world's prettiest mule for herself. Paolo and Matteo were already upstairs, set to work by Rosa on rearranging the beds so everyone might have a place to sleep that night, Stella included.

"So you simply happened upon one another in Bolzano?" Father Bernardi asked, his composure restored by the grappa. "At the little station there?"

"We did," Nina confirmed. "It was like something out of a book. I turned around and there he was. The hero of my story, and I didn't have to go looking for him. Instead he came to me."

"Wonderful, wonderful. You are both well? And dear Stella, too?"

"We are. A little too thin, but we're in good health. I'd say it was a miracle if I still believed in such things." Nico softened this last statement with an easy smile.

Father Bernardi nodded, and he opened his mouth to say something, but the words seemed to stick in his throat. It was the first time Nina had ever known him to be at a loss for words.

"Is anything the matter?" she asked. "Is there something else we need to know?"

"I don't want to stain this joyous day in any fashion, nor bring up upsetting memories, but I think you should know that Zwerger is dead. His soldiers deserted him, right at the end, and he thought he might be able to escape back to Austria. Instead the partisans found him, and they brought him back here, to Mezzo Ciel. They'd already beaten him half to death, and likely they would have happily hanged him from the nearest tree, but someone remembered that Zwerger had very nearly killed Nico in the piazza. So they propped him up against the wall and shot him."

"Did you see it happen?" Nina asked, grimly fascinated and yet still, somehow, appalled.

"I was too late to intervene, but I did go to him as he lay dying and offered him the sacrament of extreme unction. One final chance to repent of his sins. But he refused. He turned his head away, and he was dead a few minutes later. Unfortunately I find I cannot regret his having met his end in such a way. It is a failing of mine, and I have prayed upon it, but still. My heart is stubborn."

Nico nodded slowly, his eyes fixed on Nina's face. As if he weren't quite certain of what he saw. "I don't blame you for it,

Father. If ever a man truly deserved to meet such an end, it was Karl Zwerger. The world is well rid of him."

Lucia had been asleep in Nico's arms, but now she stirred, her lacy eyelashes fluttering against her perfectly rosy cheeks, and this time Nina was brave enough to reach for her baby, cuddle her close, and revel in the weight of her sturdy little body, the feathery softness of her wispy curls, and the calming cadence of her steady exhalations.

"Since you're here, Father, Nina and I want to ask if you will grace us with a blessing when we are married. The synagogues are still closed, so we will have to be content with a civil marriage for now."

They had talked of it in the station on the night of their reunion, but she hadn't expected him to bring up the subject so soon.

"I would be honored to do so," Father Bernardi readily agreed. "When were you thinking?"

"As soon as possible. And we'll have a celebration after. A proper *festa* for everyone."

"They'll be shocked if they learn the reason why," Rosa commented with a smile.

"I think that can remain our secret," Nico said. "Let us tell them, instead, that it's to celebrate our homecoming. As indeed it will be."

The others talked of the farm and the village for a while, and though Nina tried at first to listen, it was easier, and far more pleasant, to simply sit and *be*. Everything around her was so ordinary, so familiar, and so wonderfully precious. No place would ever again be so welcome to her as this plain, homey kitchen; no people would ever be so dear to her as those gathered around its table.

The sun had begun to set when Father Bernardi took his leave, extracting only a promise that they set a date for their civil marriage as soon as bureaucratically possible. "Humor an old man, will you? If only so I may know the joy of blessing your marriage all the sooner."

Nico and Nina, still holding Lucia, came outside to say goodbye; and then, rather than retreat to the kitchen, Nico led them in the direction of the stables. With Selva glued to their heels, they enjoyed a brief reunion with a sleepy Bello before moving on, Nico stopping now and again to greet the friendlier among the barn cats, until they had come around the back of the house and were looking out over the fields.

They had returned to the place where, only two years before, he had introduced her to his world. He had shown her the land where he worked; he had told her of the ordinary life he had chosen to embrace. And it was then, in that moment, when she had begun to fall in love with him.

"I was so afraid I'd never see this place again," he said, turning to her. "But that alone wasn't enough to keep me alive. It was you—you and our child. The memory and the hope of you, and the vows we made."

"'I am my beloved's and my beloved is mine,'" she said, remembering.

"There was one night in Flossenburg, early on, when I was close to giving up. And then it came to me—a memory from before. From here, when I was safe with you. It was in August, I think, and I'd come home late from my uncle's farm. I was so tired I could hardly move, but I was too restless to sleep.

And so we lay in bed, and rather than turn down the lamp you fetched my Bible and read to me from the Song of Songs. '*My beloved speaks and says to me: Arise, my love, my fair one, and come away; for now the winter is past, the rain is over and gone. The flowers appear on the earth; the time of singing has come.*' Those were the words that sustained me on those long nights when I couldn't sleep. When I'd forgotten how to hope."

She was still wiping away tears when he spoke again, his voice hesitant, even fearful. "How did you face those nights?"

"Without the hope of you?"

He nodded, and then he gathered her and their daughter into the shelter of his arms.

"Lucia was waiting for me," she answered, not wishing to tell him how deeply she had despaired. How lost she had been to the promise of hope. One day she would share it all with him, but not until they'd both had a chance to heal.

"I would give anything to take that suffering from you. To put myself in your place."

"I know, my darling," she soothed him. "I know. But now the night is over."

He bent his head to kiss her. "The winter is past."

"The winter is past," she echoed. "The rain has gone, and our days of joy? They have only just begun."

Epilogue

3 July 1946

Never had she known a more perfect day.

They had arranged for Nico's cousins to come and take care of the farm, and everyone—she, Nico, Lucia, Aldo, Rosa, and all the children—had piled into Zio Beppe's ancient truck the evening before and made the journey, far shorter than if they'd gone by mule cart, to Cousin Mario's farm in Campalto.

That morning they'd risen at first light, the children more excited than they'd been at Epiphany, and one of Mario's neighbors, whose daily delivery route took him from the mainland farms to the Rialto market, had ferried them to the Fondamente Nove and its hourly *vaporetto* to the Lido. They could only afford two days away from the farm, and as this was their one day at the seaside, they were all determined to make the most of it.

They would never be wealthy people, but the recovery of Nina's parents' savings some months earlier had been an unexpected, and altogether providential, windfall. Of her family's home and its contents she had received nothing: the house had been seized by the fascists and sold to Gentiles; her parents' possessions had vanished, and no accounting had been made of their dispersal. All that remained were the few things she had packed into her rucksack on the day she had said goodbye to her mother and father.

The savings, though modest, would be enough to pay the wages of a farmhand while Nico returned to university; he was set to begin his studies at the University of Padua in September. They had found a little flat that would be just big enough for the three of them and, before long, a fourth; their baby was due in the new year.

When her children were a little older Nina, too, would return to school, for she was determined to fulfill the dream that she and her father had shared. Until then, she would savor every kiss, every laugh, and every sun-drenched day as the gifts they truly were.

They had rented beach chairs and umbrellas on the same stretch of sand where Nina had once spent long, golden afternoons with her parents, and they'd all changed into the bathing suits she and Rosa had sewn and knitted in anticipation of this one glorious day, and then they had tiptoed into the water, Lucia held high in Nico's arms, the girls clutching each other's hands. They'd cringed when the first startling waves had lapped at their ankles, and then, laughing, had plunged forward, heedless of the cold, and welcomed the sea's embrace.

They'd brought baskets of food from home, bread and cheese and hard-boiled eggs, and chunks of *sopressa* for everyone but Nina and Stella, and Mario's wife had surprised them with bottles of tart homemade lemonade. They'd eaten their lunch with sandy fingers, their noses already pinkened by the sun, and with the last crumbs devoured, the children had rushed off to build castles in the sand.

"But not a toe in the water until your lunch has settled," Rosa had ordered, and Stella had run back to give Rosa a quick hug.

"Don't worry, Zia Rosa," she'd promised. "I'll take care of Carlo while you rest."

"Such a good girl," Rosa had said lovingly. "I don't know what I'd do without her. It's hard to remember life without my three girls all together."

"I think she would say the same," Nina had agreed, though it wasn't entirely true. Stella was healthy and happy now, and she seemed to feel secure and content, and she was devoted to everyone, Rosa most of all. Agnese and Angela called her their sister, and the three of them were never apart. But she still had nightmares; she still wept for her parents, who, like Nina's, had vanished into the abyss of Birkenau. All that remained of Stella's life from before the war were a few battered copies of her parents' tourist guides. They were gifts from Nico, who searched for them in every bookstore he passed.

The day was more than half over now, and Nina resolved that for the rest of it she would think only of sunshine and blue skies. It was easy to do with those she loved at her side, the joy of another baby on the way, and the promise of brighter tomorrows to come.

After lunch, Lucia had fallen asleep in her grandfather's arms; now she sat up and began to rub at her eyes.

"Mamma?" she asked, pouting a little.

"Yes, darling?"

"Where my papà?"

"Here I am," Nico answered, plucking her from Aldo's arms. "Do you think it might be time for some gelato?"

"Gelato!" Carlo roared, forgetting his half-constructed castle in his haste to join them. "Gelato, gelato, gelato!"

"Let's find the man who sells gelato, and we'll see if he'll bring his little cart along the beach so we can all choose our favorite flavors. Shall we go? Who's with me? Girls? Paolo and Matteo? Off we go!"

Nina watched the little procession skip along the beach, heading toward the gelato seller with his brightly painted cart, and tried not to think of how much she would miss the children when she and Nico moved to Padua in September. They would return home each summer, of course, and there would be visits as often as they could manage; but it would be four years, if not longer, before they came home to Mezzo Ciel for good.

Tonight they would return to Mario's house in Campalto, and in the morning, at dawn's first light, she and Nico would go back across the water to Venice. Back to the house that had once belonged to her family, but whose door was forever closed to her now.

No one would notice the two small stones, scarcely more than pebbles, smooth and warm in her hand, that she had found under the olive tree at home. She would set them near the green door, tucked close to the crumbling stonework of its lintel; no broom would find them there.

She would close her eyes and say a silent prayer for her parents, for those whose lives had been stolen, and for those who had been left to go on alone. Then she and Nico would return home, but she would not forget. She would always remember.

And one day, once they were old enough to understand, she would beckon her children, hug them close, and tell them of the family she had lost, the family she had been given, and the love story that had brought her to a place called Mezzo Ciel.

Acknowledgments

This book was a labor of love, in both its research and its writing, and though I could not have completed it without the help and advice of the people below, any errors of fact or judgment that remain are my responsibility alone.

I owe an enormous debt of thanks to my husband's family, in both Canada and Italy, for so graciously sharing their memories with me. I would specifically like to acknowledge Lucia Bizzotto, Guerrino Crespi, the Gazzola family (Angela, Mario, Carmen, and Oscar), and Maria Zardo. I am also very grateful to my husband's late uncle, Francesco Crespi, for the memories he shared in his unpublished memoir. My sister-in-law, Michela Jach, helped me with translations and added immeasurably to my knowledge of her grandparents' way of life, and I am so very grateful to her.

In Borso del Grappa I was fortunate enough to interview Domenico Salvalaggio, an Italian survivor of Buchenwald. His recollection of his imprisonment, and his grace and fortitude in describing such difficult memories, were profoundly important to my understanding of the suffering he and others endured. I am sincerely grateful to him, and to Professor Zuglio Gigliotti, who facilitated our meeting.

In Venice, Dr. Chiara Ponchia generously shared with me her unsurpassed knowledge of the Jewish ghetto and its people; she then spent many hours reading and commenting on this novel in manuscript form. I am deeply grateful for her wisdom and guidance.

Edward Trapunski and Dill Werner Brice were both gracious enough to offer their informed and expert opinions on my depiction of Jewish life in Italy in the 1940s, and I thank them sincerely for their patience and understanding.

I would also like to thank Dr. Madison Lyon and Dr. Aaron Orkin for patiently answering my questions relating to medicine; Dr. Julie Downer for checking my description of veterinary emergency medicine; and Natalie and Sean Macdonald for their assistance with German terms and phrases.

In the course of researching *Our Darkest Night*, I relied upon the collections of a number of libraries, archives, and museums. I would particularly like to acknowledge the Associazione Nazionale Ex Deportati Nei Campi Nazisti (ANED), the Auschwitz-Birkenau State Museum, the Bodleian Library, the Bolzano Municipal Archives, the archives of KZ-Gedankstätte Flossenbürg, the Museo Ebraico di Venezia, the Toronto Reference Library, the U.S. Holocaust Memorial Museum, and the World Holocaust Remembrance Center at Vad Vashem.

Once more I am indebted to my editor, Tessa Woodward, for her understanding, sensitivity, patience, and encouragement.

This book would never have been finished—or indeed begun—without her.

I also wish to thank my literary agent, Kevan Lyon, for her wise counsel and warm friendship, as well as her colleagues at the Marsal Lyon Literary Agency, among them Patricia Nelson, for their support.

I am so grateful to Jessica Lyons and Dave Knox, my publicists at HarperCollins, along with my personal publicist, Kathleen Carter, for their untiring efforts on my behalf.

My thanks as well to the wonderful people at William Morrow, in particular Robin Barletta, Carolyn Bodkin, Jennifer Hart, Martin Karlow, Elle Keck, Mumtaz Mustafa, Carla Parker, Shelby Peak, Mary Ann Petyak, Elizabeth Semrai, Alison Smith, Liate Stehlik, Diahann Sturge, and Amelia Wood. The producers at HarperAudio have once again created a beautiful audiobook. I'm also grateful to the HarperCollins sales team in the U.S., Canada, and the international division, as well as everyone at HarperCollins Canada who supports me so ably.

As always, I would be lost without my friends, among them Amutha, Denise, Jane D, Jane E, Jen, Kelly F, Kelly W, Liz, Mary, Michela, and Rena. Nor would I have emerged from the fog of Book 6 without the counsel and group texts from the Coven: Karma Brown, Kerry Clare, Chantel Guertin, Kate Hilton, Elizabeth Renzetti, and Marissa Stapley. My sincere thanks as well to fellow authors and friends Janie Chang, Karen Lord, and Kate Quinn for their unwavering support, advice on conquering Scrivener, and readiness to share virtual cocktails at the drop of a hat.

As with all my books, I end these acknowledgments with thanks to my family.

To my sister, Kate Robson: you are my touchstone; I would be lost without you.

To my children, Matthew and Daniela: you are the reason I wrote this book. You, my darlings, are my moon, my sun, my Mezzo Ciel.

And Claudio, my Claudio. You are my beloved. You are the hero of my story.

Insights,
Interviews
& More . . .

Meet Jennifer Robson

Natalie Brown / Tangerine Pho

JENNIFER ROBSON is the internationally bestselling author of *The Gown: A Novel of the Royal Wedding, Goodnight from London, Moonlight Over Paris, After the War is Over,* and *Somewhere in France.* She holds a doctorate in British economic and social history from Saint Antony's College, University of Oxford, where she was a Commonwealth Scholar and an SSHRC Doctoral Fellow. She lives in Toronto, Canada, with her husband and children. ⌯

Author's Note

The following notes address some points of history and culture that merit further explanation in regard to *Our Darkest Night*.

Antonina and her parents, as I imagine them, were ethnically and culturally Jewish, but in their religious practices they were not especially observant. This reflects the broader experience of many Italian Jews of the time, as well as Dr. Mazin's personal beliefs and philosophy. My portrayal of their practices was inspired by contemporary accounts of other Italian Jews, among them Victoria Ancona-Vincent, Carlo Levi, Liliana Segre, and Piera Sonnino.

Every place I describe in this book is real, with one significant exception: Mezzo Ciel is a fictional amalgam of San Zenone degli Ezzelini and a nearby village, Borso del Grappa, which is located on the lower slopes of Monte Grappa. I must also confess to borrowing the name for my fictional village from an actual place several kilometers north of San Zenone. I apologize to the residents of the real Mezzo Ciel for appropriating its name for my purposes, but how could I ignore the appeal of a name that translates as "halfway to heaven"? On my website you can find a link to a Google map that charts all the places I mention in *Our Darkest Night*, as well as an illustrated map of the fictional Mezzo Ciel and surrounding ▶

area. I have also included photographs of the places and buildings that inspired me in my descriptions of the Gerardi family's farm, the Mazin family's home in Venice, and the beautiful northern Italian countryside where so much of the novel takes place.

Because the dialogue in *Our Darkest Night* is rendered in English (at least in its original writing), anyone familiar with the Italian language will notice that I've made little mention of dialect. In Italy—even more so in the 1940s than today—regional differences in language are marked not by accents (as is the case in England, for example), but rather by highly localized dialects. At first I attempted to describe the differences between formal Italian and dialect, and the confusion such variations might provoke, but I soon realized there was no straightforward way to describe the differences between formal Italian and the dialect that was spoken in Mezzo Ciel. Instead I have confined myself to a few mentions of formal versus informal modes of speech and left it at that. I beg the pardon of native Italian speakers for my consequent failure to capture the beauty and complexity of their language in all its incarnations.

My descriptions of life on the Gerardi farm, and in the village of Mezzo Ciel, are based upon extensive interviews with my husband's relatives, among them Lucia Bizzotto, Guerrino Crespi, Angela Gazzola, Mario Gazzola, Carmen Gazzola, Oscar Gazzola, Michela Jach, and Maria Zardo. Francesco Crespi, my husband's late uncle, wrote a private memoir that describes his horror at being made to witness the Nazi massacre of partisans in Bassano del Grappa, as well as other notable memories of the war; I thank his sister Lucia Bizzotto for sharing it with me. Selva the dog is named after a much-loved family pet; and while one of her forebears was, sadly, shot and killed by a German soldier as she tried to protect my husband's grandfather, the fictional Selva survives for one reason: I promised my children I wouldn't allow her to die.

Anyone seeking to retrace Nina's journeys should begin with the memorials to the millions who were abused and killed by the twin scourges of Nazism and fascism. In Venice you will find a memorial to the city's murdered Jews in the main piazza of the Gheto Nuovo, as well as *stolpersteine* (stumbling stones) near the last known residences of many Venetians who were deported and murdered. In Poland the museum and memorial at Auschwitz-Birkenau, though often crowded, is nonetheless a deeply moving memorial. There is no memorial in Wilischthal, the forced labor camp near Zchopau, unnamed in *Our Darkest Night*, where Nina and Stella spent the last months of the war; its few buildings are now little more than ruins. In Bolzano, memorial friezes mark the perimeter of the now-vanished detention camp. And in Bassano, on what is now known as the viale dei Martiri—the avenue of the martyrs—memorial plaques are affixed to each of the manicured trees where thirty-one young men were hanged by the Nazis on September 26, 1944.

This Stolpersteine, or stumbling stone, is located near the Casa di Riposo in Venice's Gheto Nuovo. It reads: "On 17 August 1944, from this house, 21 elderly residents were deported and murdered in the Nazi death camps."

I have yet to visit the World Holocaust Remembrance Center at Yad Vashem in Israel, though I hope to go there one day. Among the more than twenty-seven thousand individuals named Righteous Among the Nations is the man who was the inspiration for Father Bernardi. Some might say that Giulio Bernardi, so clear-eyed in his goodness, is an improbable figure in the midst of so much intolerance and hate. I might be inclined to agree, if not for the little-known heroism of Father Oddo Stocco, a humble village priest who recognized evil, stared it in the face, and steadfastly refused to look away. ⌒

Defeating the Silence

In late 2018, shortly before the publication of *The Gown*, my son came to me with a question. He'd been studying the Second World War, and with it the Holocaust, in history class at school. As school-related questions go, it was a big one: "Is it true that Daddy's grandparents hid Jewish families during the war?" he asked.

I had to tell him that I wasn't sure. I wanted it to be true, but I couldn't be certain.

My husband, Claudio, and I first heard the stories about his grandparents on a visit to Italy in May 2016. We were staying in his parents' hometown of San Zenone degli Ezzelini, about forty-five minutes to the northwest of Venice, and a few days after our arrival we went to visit one of his aunts. Claudio and Zia Maria were chatting in their local dialect when, in response to his questions, she began to talk about the war. I still remember the moment when I managed to untangle a few words from their conversation. "*Hebrei*," his aunt said. "*To nonno i ga scónti*," she added. Jews. Your grandfather hid them.

We peppered Zia Maria and our other relatives in San Zenone with more questions, and were astonished by their revelations. They told us that Claudio's grandparents, Giovanni and Emma Guarda, had been asked by their parish priest to offer shelter to Jewish families in danger of arrest and deportation. Although Giovanni and Emma were poor—they shared a small farmhouse in San Zenone with their four children and his elderly mother, as well as his brother, sister-in-law, and their two children—they said yes. Between 1943 and 1945 we believe they sheltered at least three different families, though there may have been more; their surviving children's memories are unclear on this point.

My husband's aunts do recall a number of telling details. The roof of the adjoining stable was the place where their guests hid when strangers came to the door; to further conceal them, a large wardrobe was pushed in front of the window that led to the stable roof. His aunts also told us how, at the very end of the war, their father gave away precious food and blankets to retreating German soldiers because he was fearful they would come into the house, take what they needed, and discover the people he was still faithfully hiding. Unfortunately, although they remember many details of the people themselves, his aunts can no longer recall their names. Giovanni died in 1991, and Emma before him in 1978; my husband never had the chance to speak to his grandparents about their lives during the war.

That is where our research would have ended if not for my son's timely question. Could the stories be true? I decided to try to unearth some answers.

I began by consulting the online databases maintained by Yad Vashem to see if there was any quantifiable evidence of Jewish families being sheltered in San Zenone. To my surprise and relief, there was. Father Oddo Stocco, who served as the town's parish priest from 1931 to 1948, was named Righteous Among the Nations in 2010 for his heroism in saving more than fifty Jews by securing hiding places for them among his parishioners.

Some of those parishioners were also accorded the honor of Righteous Among the Nations, though not my husband's grandparents. But did this mean they hadn't been involved in Father Stocco's efforts? Or only that the accounting of those who were involved was incomplete? One sentence in the citation from Yad Vashem gave me hope, for it confirmed what I already suspected: "The entire village helped [Father] Stocco feed the dozens of Jews and many other refugees and political fugitives, despite the heavy burden this entailed, because they respected his leadership and good deeds."

As I write this essay, in the early summer of 2020, I have yet to uncover documentary proof of my husband's grandparents' involvement; it may no longer be possible after such a span of time. The historian in me hesitates, ever cautious, wanting more proof, yet I cannot say that such evidence is truly necessary. And that's because the story of Giovanni and Emma Guarda's humble courage, the story that led me to *Our Darkest Night*, is not the reason I wrote this novel. I wrote it because my son's question made me wonder about the people who were forced into hiding. What were their stories? How did they survive? And might it be possible for me, a Gentile, to write a story from their point of view? ▶

Nina is at the center of this novel because it was her perspective, from the beginning, that resonated most profoundly for me. Every time I sat down to write, it was her eyes that allowed me to see. No other point of view seemed possible, let alone desirable. The actions of many of the Gentiles in *Our Darkest Night*, among them Nico, Father Bernardi, and Rosa, are selfless and heroic, as indeed were those of Father Stocco and the parishioners of San Zenone. They were heroes, to be sure; but the heart and soul of this novel belongs to Nina, and with her the thousands of Italian Jews who were persecuted, terrorized, murdered, and silenced.

In the creation of *Our Darkest Night*, I studiously avoided any alterations to the historical record. I also decided against featuring any known historical figures among my central characters. To fictionalize the story of Piera Sonnino, for instance, whose memoir *This Has Happened* was so central to my understanding of the Shoah in Italy, was unthinkable. In so doing I would be subduing her truth into my fiction. I would be silencing her voice.

Instead I searched for spaces within the historical record where my characters might plausibly reside. To employ but one example: there really was a deportation train that left the detention camp in Bolzano, Italy, on October 24, 1944, and arrived at Birkenau after an indescribably harrowing four-day journey. Rather than remove any single voice from the historical record, and subsume that person's truth into my story, I decided to *add* Nina's voice to the chorus of women on the train. In so doing, I sincerely hope that I have helped to amplify the voices of those who were forced to undergo that journey, as well as the millions more whose lives were cut short by the horrors of the Holocaust.

I was inspired to adopt this approach by Susanne C. Knittel's *The Historical Uncanny: Disability, Ethnicity, and the Politics of Holocaust Memory*, in which she describes the act of "vicarious witnessing." Such an approach, she explains, "does not entail an act of speaking for and thus appropriating the memory and story of someone else but rather an attempt to bridge the silence through narrative means."

Millions were silenced by the Holocaust. More than seventy-five years on, the inexorable passage of time is silencing the last of its survivors and its witnesses. Each year there are fewer among us who can bear direct witness to the horrors they endured; soon they will all be gone. And that is where vicarious witnesses, among them writers and historians like me, can attempt to defeat the silence. With my creation of Nina, her family, her struggles, and her triumphs, I am trying to make a difference. I am trying to act as a vicarious witness so these stories are not lost.

Antonina Mazin is a construct of my imagination, but her story was inspired by those of real people who lived, suffered, and died; people who loved and were loved; people whose lives have ended, but whose existence mattered. Their sacred memory must not be allowed to fade. ᕲ

Glossary of Terms Used in This Book

Ammassi: the compulsory sale of grain and other farm products to state-managed granaries and distribution centers in fascist Italy

Appell: term for roll call in the Nazi camp system

Aufseherin: rank of female guard in the camp system; roughly equivalent to overseer

Blockowa: informal title for female guards in the camp system; of Polish origin

Brodo: broth or a light soup

Caffè d'orzo: a substitute for coffee made of roasted barley

Caffettiera: stovetop coffeemaker in widespread use before the invention of the more familiar moka pot

Calle *(plural:* **calli)**: Venetian term for a narrow street

Campanile: bell tower; typically a separate structure from its adjacent church

Cantina: a storeroom, typically belowground, for food and wine

Carabinieri: Italy's national police

Casa di Riposo: rest home; typically used to describe old-age homes

Crostoli: deep-fried squares or wide ribbons of lightly sweetened dough

Durchgangslager: transit camp

Erysipelas: a bacterial skin infection; commonly known as St. Anthony's fire

Festa: a party; used to describe both family gatherings and larger community celebrations

Fondamente: quay or bank

Gheto: the Venetian spelling of ghetto; the name is derived from the iron foundries that once occupied the islands where the historic Jewish ghetto was first established in Venice

Gondoliere: person who steers a traditional Venetian gondola

Grappa: a grape-based brandy

Guardia: the Guardia Nazionale Repubblicana, or National Republican Guard, which partially replaced the Italian national police between December 1943 and the end of the war

Hauptsturmführer: a Nazi paramilitary rank roughly equivalent to that of captain

Il Duce: the nickname by which Benito Mussolini was known; translates as "the duke" but in his regard meant "the leader"

Kommando: a work detail or detachment in the Nazi camp system

Kübelwagen: a military vehicle similar in purpose though not design to a U.S. jeep; made by Volkswagen

La Befana: in Italian folklore, the figure who brings gifts to children on the eve of Epiphany; the following night she is welcomed home by the light of a large bonfire. In some regions, by contrast, her effigy is burned in the bonfire

Ladino: a form of Judeo-Spanish once widely spoken by Jews of Sephardic descent

Nonno/Nonna: the Italian terms for grandfather and grandmother

Novena: the Catholic custom of devotional prayers that extend most commonly over nine days

Oberaufseherin: a rank of female guard in the Nazi camp system; translates as senior overseer

Obersturmführer: a Nazi paramilitary rank approximating that of first lieutenant

Ospedale: the Italian term for hospital or, less commonly, orphanage

Osteria: a tavern that sells wine and simple food

Pastina: tiny pieces of pasta, typically cooked in broth; often served to children and invalids

Pinza della Befana: a polenta-based cake consumed at the feast of the Epiphany

Pippo bombers: the name given to the unseen airplanes, long thought to be apocryphal, heard at night in northern Italy in the final years of the war; some historians now believe they were De Havilland Mosquitos on Allied reconnaissance missions. (They are also the aircraft that appear on the cover of this book.)

Polpette di matza: the Italian term for matzo balls

"Polvere di Stelle": title of the Italian translation of the classic song "Stardust" ▶

Glossary of Terms Used in This Book *(continued)*

Republic of Salò: informal name for the Italian Social Republic, the Italian puppet state established in September 1943 and controlled by Nazi Germany; its nominal head was Benito Mussolini

Riel: the local dialect term, peculiar to the region near Bassano del Grappa, for the large bonfire held at Epiphany; in other parts of the Veneto it is called a *foghera*

Sanpierota: a traditional fishing boat of the Venetian lagoon

Schutzstaffel (SS): a paramilitary force that eventually assumed responsibility for not only Third Reich security and intelligence but also the planning and direction of the coordinated Nazi effort to exterminate Europe's Jews

Scola: the Judeo-Italian term for synagogue; Nina's family attended the magnificent sixteenth-century Scola Espagnola

Sicherheitsdienst (SD): the intelligence agency for the Nazi party

Sopressa: a cured pork sausage similar to salami

Sottoportego: an alley that passes under the second story of a building

Torta: a flourless Italian cake; often made with ground nuts in place of flour

Vaporetto: a Venetian public waterbus

Viale: an avenue or boulevard

Vin brulè: the Italian term for mulled wine; distinct from the French *vin brûlé*

Zaeti: a Venetian cookie, typically made with cornmeal and raisins and formed in a diamond shape

Zio/Zia: the Italian terms for uncle and aunt

Zoccoli: wooden clogs, usually homemade; often made with a wooden sole and a vamp of leather or canvas ᷿

Suggestions for Further Reading

As a full bibliography would stretch to many pages, I offer instead a brief selection of works for readers who are interested in learning more about the historical backdrop to *Our Darkest Night*. A few titles are now out of print, but they should be accessible via your local public library or any bookshop that specializes in hard-to-find titles. I have included general histories of the period, specialist works, memoirs and personal accounts, works of fiction, several websites, and one documentary film.

General and specialist histories:
The Guns at Last Light: The War in Western Europe, 1944–1945 by Rick Atkinson
The Death Marches: The Final Phase of Nazi Genocide by Daniel Blatman
Auschwitz: A New History by Laurence Rees
The Jews in Mussolini's Italy: From Equality to Persecution by Michele Sarfatti
Benevolence and Betrayal: Five Italian Jewish Families Under Fascism by Alexander Stille
KL: A History of the Nazi Concentration Camps by Nikolaus Wachsmann
Jews in Italy under Fascist and Nazi Rule, 1922–1945 by Joshua D. Zimmerman
The Italians and the Holocaust: Persecution, Rescue and Survival by Susan Zuccotti ▶

Suggestions for Further Reading *(continued)*

Memoirs and first-person accounts:
Beyond Imagination by Victoria Ancona-Vincent
Christ Stopped at Eboli by Carlo Levi
If This Is a Man (also published as *Survival in Auschwitz*)
    by Primo Levi
*La memoria rende liberi: La vita interrotta di una bambina nella
    Shoah* by Liliana Segre and Enrico Mentana
This Has Happened by Piera Sonnino
Night by Elie Wiesel

Fiction:
The Garden of the Finzi-Continis by Giorgio Bassani
The Tuscan Child by Rhys Bowen
From Sand and Ash by Amy Harmon
A Thread of Grace by Maria Doria Russell
Beneath a Scarlet Sky by Mark Sullivan

Websites:
Memoriale della Shoah di Milano: http://www.memorialeshoah.it
Museo Ebraico di Venezia: http://www.museoebraico.it
USC Shoah Foundation: https://sfi.usc.edu
The World Holocaust Remembrance Center at Yad Vashem:
    https://www.yadvashem.org
The documentary film *Memoria*, which features ninety
    interviews with Italian survivors of the Holocaust, among
    them Liliana Segre, is posted to the Fondazione CDEC's
    YouTube channel. The film is in Italian with English subtitles:
    https://www.youtube.com/watch?v=j_RBlqfvGlk ∿

Discover great authors,
exclusive offers, and more
at hc.com.